# ARAKNID

**Other Works by Christopher Andrews**

TRIUMVIRATE SERIES

*Pandora's Game*
*The Darkness Within*
(collection)
*Of Wolf and Man*
(Bronze IPPY winner for Horror)

PARANORMALS SERIES

*Paranormals*
*Paranormals: We Are Not Alone*

NOVELIZATIONS

*Dream Parlor*
*Hamlet: Prince of Denmark*
*Night of the Living Dead*
*Macbeth*

SCREENPLAYS

*Thirst*
*Dream Parlor*
(written with Jonathan Lawrence)
*Mistake*
*Vale Todo/Anything Goes*
(written with Roberto Estrella)

WEB SERIES

*Duet*

VIDEO GAMES

*Bankjob*

Praise for Christopher Andrews' *Triumvirate* series

# *PANDORA'S GAME*

"Christopher Andrews is an exceptional writer and a master of storytelling ... his characters have complex and often unexpected traits that give them a strong emotional resonance ... completely engrossing ... Rarely does a book come along that is so well written that I can't tolerate interruption. A book that's so well written that I can't tolerate it interrupting *itself* is unheard of. To maintain this level of complexity for twenty-one chapters is an incredible storytelling feat."

— Marcus Alexander Hart, Author of *The Oblivion Society*

"Andrews is a brilliant writer and a wonderful storyteller. I started and finished it without putting it down."

— Julianna Smith, Author of the *Dream Catcher* series

"Andrews shows versatility ... as much competence and style as Poppy Z. Brite or Anne Rice ... BOOK OF THE MONTH."

— Lesley Meade, *Booknet*

"... a spellbinding novel ... fascinating, riveting ... hard to put down ... a talented writer ... would convert wonderfully to the screen ..."

— Grabbermcgrew, *Sharp Writer Reviews*

"*Pandora's Game* is written in a unique way ... Christopher Andrews writes like an author with much more experience ... fantastic ..."
— Pat McGreal, *Horror Novels Online*

"An interesting story ... I couldn't wait to see what happened next ... the characters are appealing and the concept is absorbing ..."

— Conan Tigard, *Book Browser*

"... incredible ... sharp ... creative ... original and interesting ideas driving the plot and drama ... an ending like a kick in the gut."

— Alex Zawacki, *Class-B*

## "CONNEXION"
### (collected in *The Darkness Within*)

" 'Connexion' was ... completely worth the five bucks on [its] own ... Very highly recommended ..."

— Grimlock, 5-star Amazon review

## *OF WOLF AND MAN*
### (Bronze IPPY winner for Horror)

"Better than 'New Moon' ... Andrews is amazing with character ... [won] an IPPY award bronze [medal] ... should have won the gold."

— Marcus Alexander Hart, Author of *Caster's Blog*

"Outstanding sequel! ... everything that a sequel should be ... interesting and creepy ... addresses some bold issues, and does so very well."

— John Howard, *Book Reader 222*

# ARAKNID

A *Triumvirate* Novel by
CHRISTOPHER ANDREWS

Rising Star Visionary Press trade paperback edition: May, 2018

**A Rising Star Visionary Press book for extra copies please contact by e-mail at <u>risingstarvisionarypress@earthlink.net</u> or send by regular mail to Rising Star Visionary Press Copies Department P O Box 9226 Fountain Valley, CA 92728-9226**

Thank you, as always, to my wife, editor, and Imzadi,
*Yvonne Isaak-Andrews*,
for her boundless love, feedback, and support.


Thank you to my friend, and now colleague,
*Daniele Serra*,
for the fantastic job he did on the cover art.


And thank you to my daughter,
*Arianna Kristina Andrews*,
for bidding farewell each morning on her way
to school with the words, "Work on your book
as hard as you can!"

The following story takes place approximately
four months after the events depicted in
*Of Wolf and Man*.

*She'll never see it coming,* Mitch congratulated himself as he poured the wine. *They never do.*

Mitchell Gamall — "Mitchell" to his clients; "Mitch" to his friends, and to the women he seduced — made a decent living as a photographer. He was quite proud of this fact, as the Los Angeles area often seemed to have more "photographers" peddling their work than wannabe actresses who begged their services. Not that Mitch was above such proclivities, of course; that's why he was Mitch tonight.

Step One: Get the tasty young ladies into his pad, cater to and/or exploit their insecurities, take a few photos to demonstrate that he really could make them look good. And start the whole process by getting them to take a sip of wine, just a sip or two, so that they would relax. He always bought the good wines, too; the better to cover the taste of his special additive of self-brewed GHB.

Step Two: Once the augmented wine loosens them up, resume taking photos. Said photos become increasingly erotic, but still elegant enough to pass muster as their acting headshots and on their websites. And apply more augmented wine.

Step Three: Once they were completely out of it ... fuck the shit out of them.

Of course, the camera never stopped; that was key. Because when the surprisingly few figured out what had happened to them and started making noise about it, he would reveal the unexpurgated galley of their session — making it clear that if they didn't *stop* making noise, said gallery would find its way online, where anyone and everyone could enjoy it.

The noise stopped then, every time. Such was the beautiful, terrible power of the World Wide Web.

His latest acquisition was due to arrive in a few minutes. She had moved into the apartment building across from his a few months ago, but to be honest, he hadn't really noticed her at first — a bit too homely, too short, too frumpy ... scarcely enough to show up on his radar.

Then, one morning, they bumped into each other at the local coffee shop.

Mitch had been nursing a mild hangover from a private session the night before — he never sampled the augmented wine, of course, but that didn't mean he couldn't have a few drinks as the evening progressed — but a legitimate gig today forced him out of bed. He grabbed a muffin with his espresso and sat down for a quick breakfast while he thumbed through his phone. When a woman approached and mumbled a request to share his table, he barely registered her presence as he gestured for her to help herself.

A minute of silence later, he heard another short mumble, which he belatedly absorbed had been the word, "Hello."

Looking up, he realized it was his new neighbor, and that she wasn't quite as homely as he'd first thought; beneath that long, drab-brunette hair, oversized nose, and dowdy sundress, she might prove fuckable after all. This was enough to curtail his usual perchance of avoiding conversations with people while hungover.

They didn't chat long. She proved so shy, he was

surprised she had initiated the conversation at all. And she was a real space case, mumbling about focusing her qi to build confidence — he bit his tongue against the comment, "Honey, it's not working" — and experimenting with self-hypnosis toward the same goal. The real pay dirt came just as he was excusing himself to leave: She was hoping for some new portraits of herself — to focus her qi upon, you see — and she had heard that he was a photographer ...

*There it is.* He turned his discerning eye upon her once more and, finally, decided that maybe she was worth his time after all.

Besides, sometimes the ugly ones work harder.

So Mitch handed over his business card and told her to shoot him an email.

It later occurred to him that he'd never asked for her name, but that didn't matter; *if* she focused her qi long enough to email, he'd figure it out then. But after a few weeks, he stopped catching glimpses of her as they came and went, and he forgot all about her.

And then, to his surprise, she emailed him after all.

"Summer" turned out to be her name — which prompted a laugh; she was the least "Summer" girl he'd ever decided to bang — and she was due to arrive at his place any minute now.

Finished mixing his augmented wine, Mitch set about tweaking his photography lights. He preferred to start his shoots a bit earlier in the evening, with the setting sun's radiance caressing its way through his oversized windows. That way, he'd have a nice selection of natural and artificial lighting to choose from. Regardless of his ultimate intentions, he always approached his work with a serious eye. More than once, even his more lecherous sessions had provided some solid shots that he, and his subjects, were quite proud of; he doubted that would be the case with Summer, but one never knew.

But, for God only knew what reason, Summer had been strangely adamant about scheduling this gig after sundown, so like it or not ...

A quiet knock at the door brought a smile to his face. Showtime.

"Come on in!" he called, making a deliberate display of adjusting a final light ...

... except she didn't come in. She just knocked again.

"It's open!" he called. "Come on in!"

She knocked yet again.

*What the fuck?* he wondered, then made his way across the studio. *Whatever. Maybe she's plain looking* and *hard of hearing.*

Mitch opened the door ... and his jaw dropped.

Summer stood before him, looking far less "drab" — hell, she was fucking hot. Had he really been indecisive about *this* sweet little number?

Funny thing was, Mitch couldn't articulate exactly what was so different about her. Her nose was still too big for her face, and though this shirt-&-skirt were markedly better than the frumpy thing she'd worn that morning in the coffee shop, she could still use a wardrobe makeover. Maybe it was her hair? She had definitely darkened it, and it suited her ... or, wait. *Had* she darkened it? Or was her skin just paler than he recalled? Yeah, he thought that was it. Either way, she looked better. A lot better.

Summer still wasn't a "summer," but she would've made a perfect *Autumn*.

And then Mitch realized that he had just been staring at her for several long seconds, like a fuckin' amateur.

"Hi," he managed to say, also like a fuckin' amateur.

Summer offered him a closed-lip smile. And Mitch returned it with a grin that he could feel looked dorky as hell.

*C'mon, Mitch! Get your head back in the fuckin'*
*game! Do you wanna bang this bitch or not?*

But it was Summer who spoke next. "I'm still new at
this," she said, and her voice wasn't nearly as reticent as
before; it also struck him as far more melodic. "I'm not
sure if I need you to invite me in or not."

That statement was just odd enough to snap Mitch out
of it. He scraped together enough dominance to respond
with a sarcastic, "That's what most people mean when
they shout 'Come on in' from across the room."

She smiled again, but said nothing and remained
where she was.

"Ooookay. Summer, would you please come inside so
I can close the damn door?"

*Don't overdo it now, Mitch. Get back in the game,*
*take charge, but don't run her off.*

Summer finally got her ass inside, and he led her over
to where his lights were set up, the large, cleared-out
living room that doubled as his studio. "You can set your
purse ..." he started to say, until he realized that she wasn't
carrying one, or anything at all — not even a makeup bag.
This chick clearly was not acclimated to life in Los
Angeles yet. Where had she moved from? He didn't
remember, and didn't really care.

Summer took her place center stage without being
asked. Her shoulders were back and her head was held
high; not at all like their meeting in the coffee shop, and
not exactly conducive to his ultimate goal.

"Just relax," he told her as he made his way around
his two primary lights — he was going to have to make
more adjustments for that pale skin. He gestured toward
her augmented beverage. "Why don't you have a sip of
wine first?"

"No, thank you."

*Doesn't touch up her makeup* and *doesn't drink? She's not gonna last out here.* Out loud, he said, "You should try it — it'll help you unwind, make for more natural, candid shots." When she still didn't pick up the glass, he added with a smile, "It's a very good Cabernet Sauvignon."

Amusement played across Summer's face, and she said, "I never drink ... wine." This made her giggle for some reason. Mitch got the feeling she was quoting something; it sounded familiar.

*Whatever. Maybe I won't need it with this little weirdo.*

"All right then, Summer," he conceded as he stepped behind his camera. "Let's start by having you open up that top button and ... let's have you face this C-stand right here ... good ..."

As soon as he started shooting, Mitch slipped into the zone, forgetting his ulterior intentions — well, at least setting them aside for the moment. He knew some photographers who studied the digital display after every shot, but Mitch preferred to lose himself in the optical viewfinder and do his perusing in segments.

Summer surprised him once again with how tranquil she was; all that self-hypnosis stuff must've actually been working for her. He was forced to admit that, as a model, she was a natural; he liked how well, how easily, she took his direction. Maybe he really wouldn't need the wine after all. To help things along, though, he opened a button on his own shirt — he did pushups every day, so what the hell, right?

The minutes stretched on as the shots stacked up. He reached the point where he would normally ask her to switch into her next clothing choice, but since she hadn't brought a damn thing with her, he didn't bother — he just asked her to undo another button, which she did without hesitation, in spite of the fact that she wasn't wearing a bra. He snapped a handful of chest-favoring closeups, then stepped back to collect his thoughts.

Summer waited, that close-lipped smile looking more and more sultry to Mitch's appreciative eye. Speaking of eyes, hers were glistening in a peculiar way. He couldn't put his finger on what exactly it was, but he snapped another couple of shots, this time focusing more on her face ...

Without prompting, Summer undid yet another shirt button, leaving only the bottom two still connected. Was she trying to pull his lens back down, or just draw him in?

*Yeah, I'm definitely not gonna need the wine.*

And yet, as he met her gaze once more, he felt almost dizzy. What was *with* him tonight, anyway?

"All right," he declared, rallying to take charge. "You just stay right where you are, little lady, while I look over what we've got so far."

She nodded, her eyes still shining with what he thought must be excitement. What else could it be, right? It should've given him a hard-on ... but instead, he felt the faintest shudder of uneasiness.

Turning away from her — and feeling strangely relieved to do so — he stepped over to his laptop and called up tonight's folder. Or he meant to, anyway; instead of getting his first shot of Summer, all that popped up was a blank photo of the backdrop, a test shot he didn't recall doing. Huffing with impatience at himself, he clicked over to the next photo ...

And the next. And the next. What the fuck?

All he kept getting were more empties of the backdrop. Did he accidentally leave it on continuous shooting mode like an idiot? No, that didn't make sense, because the backdrop kept shifting in every shot, as with the minor adjustments he would've made while shooting Summer.

"Everything all right?" she asked, and her tone smacked of teasing. It irritated him.

"Everything's fine," he told her, not quite snapping. "Don't you worry your pretty little head. I'm just ... checkin' the shots, that's all."

"Do we need to take them again?"

He ground his teeth, because he was guessing that maybe they did. Something had to be wrong with the camera; there was no other explanation. And he had been so fixated on tonight's post-curricular activities, he hadn't bothered charging his backup-camera's batteries. What was he supposed to do now, use his phone's camera? He had to do something — he needed his safety net in place if he was going to bone this chick. Or did he? She sure as hell wasn't acting shy at all tonight.

*But wait a minute,* he told himself, sitting down before the computer. *Stop thinkin' with your dick for a second.* Something really weird was going on here, something that didn't make any sense. If his camera had a glitch so bad that Summer wasn't showing up in the photos, then why could he still see the backdrop so clearly? If the edges of the frame were aligned right—

Mitch glanced up and nearly jumped out of his skin. Summer had crossed the room and planted herself just beyond his laptop. How the fuck had he not heard her coming? For that matter, how the fuck had he not *seen* her coming in his peripheral vision?

"I asked if we need to take the pictures again," she stated, staring at him with a light smirk upon her red lips and those rich, green eyes. Had her eyes always been so emerald? Weren't they a mundane hazel-green even when he first opened the door?

"I ..." was all he managed to get out.

Summer reached out and pushed the laptop closed; Mitch jumped again when it shut with a loud *snap*, and hated himself for doing so. What was happening here ...?

"Let's not worry about the pictures," she told him, leaning forward. He could feel a fevered heat coming off her, but her face wasn't flushed. "I think we both know that's not why I'm here tonight."

"B-but ..." he stammered like a moron, "your, uh, your qi portrait ...?"

Summer giggled, flashing pointy little teeth. "Oh, Mitch, I'm impressed! I didn't think you'd bother remembering that." Pushing the laptop aside, she moved around toward his side of the table and parked one ass cheek on the edge, then leaned in to loom over him. "I didn't think you cared about *anything* I said. Not that I blame you. I was such a loser when we first met. I was so intimidated by how good looking you were, I just prattled on and on." She rolled her alluring, unnerving green eyes. "But let me tell you a secret ..."

She leaned further forward, her braless tits practically hanging out. But for the first time since before puberty, Mitch didn't feel any urge to touch breasts so close to him.

"I'm *not* a loser now. Not anymore."

Mitch yearned to run away from her, and he didn't understand why.

"I had a plan for this," Summer told him as she reached out with one finger and probed into the open collar of his shirt. "It was a whole seduction thing. I'd let you feel in charge, then *I'd* take charge, get you in your bedroom and give you a nice surprise." She chuckled at that, her eyes practically luminescing. Her finger stroked upward now, coming to rest underneath his chin. "But you know what ...?"

Mitch grunted something akin to "What?" as he made an impotent effort to pull back.

Summer snagged his chin between her thumb and finger. "I've decided to skip all that and go straight to the surprise." She leaned all the way in, her loose tits brushing against him — her nipples felt, not just erect, but strangely sharp — as she whispered into his ear, "Because I'm hungry."

Mitch couldn't say anything. Hell, he was having trouble breathing. His heartbeat pounded in his ears.

Summer pulled back to reveal glistening eyes that had gone completely solid green, with no white showing at all. And Mitch found his voice.

He started to scream.

Summer shifted the hand that was holding his chin and thumped his throat. That's all she did — thump him with one finger — but it felt like she had karate-chopped his Adam's apple back into his spine. He gagged and struggled for air, thrashing up from his chair on instinct.

Summer snickered and shoved him down hard enough to topple the chair over backward. When he struck the floor, any residual oxygen in his lungs took flight.

Before he could move an inch, Summer was on top of him, sitting on his belly with her knees pinning his shoulders. Mitch had a vague recollection of heat coming off her just seconds ago, but now her flesh radiated cold straight through his shirt.

Summer grumbled with a playful pout, her tone suggesting nothing more than she might have chipped a fingernail, "I wanted to drag this out, I really did. I was going to take you to bed, then turn on you right before you came — to see how long you could keep it up as I sucked the blood right out of you." She sighed, then offered an apologetic shrug and a big smile that showed two rows of nothing but fangs. "But, like I said: I'm new at this. Maybe I'll be able to hold back longer next time."

Mitch caught almost none of her speech. His vision was fading out as he pissed his pants, and he wondered why he'd been such an asshole his whole life.

Summer bent over him, her features distorting further, becoming more bestial. Even her voice was deeper and rougher as she sing-songed, "Bye-bye, Mitchy!"

*Mama* ... he whispered in his mind.

Then a blast of wind swept over Mitch, as though the window had blown open in the middle of a hurricane. Except it was over in an instant, and Summer was no longer on top of him.

A loud crash drew his still-dim vision to the left. Summer was sprawled on the floor against the wall, a large dent concaved right into the drywall above her. She shook her head as though dazed, and it pleased Mitch to see it. But what the fuck just happened?

Summer looked up and past him, and her emerald eyes widened. She looked less human than ever, but he was still able to read shock — and fear? — on her gnarled face.

"No," she growled. Then rage overtook everything else, and she sprang into a crouch so fast it was nothing but a blur. "*No!*"

Mitch managed to draw a tight breath, which triggered strained coughing. Summer ignored him as she leaped toward his apartment door.

She didn't make it. Mitch continued coughing uncontrollably, so he couldn't see exactly what occurred. All he caught was what appeared to be an ivory mist shooting past him, slamming her into the wall once more, and then his spasms turned into retching, and his eyes closed against his will.

When he finished vomiting, Mitch drew a slow, deep, painful breath. Throat abused inside and out, he desperately wanted something to drink, would've drunk almost anything put before him — even the augmented wine. But even more than that, he wanted to know where the fuck Summer was and whether or not he was safe.

Lifting his head, which felt enormous and doughy, he cast about the room. To his surprise, almost everything was in its proper place, and this somehow offended him — after the experience he'd just had, shouldn't his whole apartment be in shambles? That would compliment the disarray that was his current state of mind.

*... Summer's glistening eyes had gone completely green ...*

Mitch shuddered, a pathetic whine escaping his maltreated throat, and looked around more frantically.

He finally located Summer, but what he saw didn't make much sense. She was halfway to the door, pinned to the wall by the ivory mist; she was struggling but could not break free. Her creepy-ass eyes were wild with fear now, her voice muffled by the mist over her mouth. And a man wearing a trench coat stood over her, his back to Mitch.

But now that his vision had cleared, Mitch realized that it was not "mist" covering Summer's body. It was ... well, he wasn't exactly sure *what* it was, but he thought it might be some sort of ... webbing?

The man standing over Summer hunkered down before her; her struggles grew so fierce that the wall around her began to split and crack, but she still could not free herself.

*Serves the freaky bitch right!* Mitch thought, but his

nerves were still on high alert, his skin crawling and his instincts screaming at him to run! The problem was, Summer and this stranger were between him and the door, and he wasn't thrilled with the idea of getting any closer to them than absolutely necessary.

But whoever the stranger was, Summer seemed terrified of him, so that made him one of the good guys, right?

"Hey, man ..." Mitch began, but his voice was so croaky he had to cough more, which hurt like hell. When he could, he spoke louder, "Hey ... thanks, man ... for, uh..."

The stranger had been reaching toward Summer, his fingers wriggling toward her belly — long, skinny fingers, Mitch's photographer's eye noted; *arachnodactyly*, "spider fingers," a term he only knew from his brief foray into shooting hand models. When Mitch spoke up, however, the man paused. His head cocked to one side, as though uncertain as to where the sound had come from; Mitch could only see wiry black hair over the shoulders of his filthy trench coat, the coat of a homeless man.

Mitch wished he had not spoken. Where had this guy come from? Why did he show up when he did? How did he get in here? And, more importantly, how had he *stopped* whatever the fuck Summer was?

Mitch knew he wasn't ready to walk yet, let alone run, so he settled for scooting backward, away from his unwanted guests ...

Moving was a mistake. Whereas his coughing and vomiting had evidently been ignored, and his voice had seemed to only confuse the stranger, the second Mitch started his clumsy retreat, the man leaped back to his feet and spun around. His large, black, unblinking eyes pinned Mitch with their malevolent glare.

That is, the man's two *biggest* eyes did. The six smaller ones, three arcing around the larger one on each side, were too small for Mitch to read. That, plus he was equally distracted by the two gargantuan teeth that dominated the lower half of the man's inhuman face.

Taken as a whole, that face was just too much to process. Not that Mitch tried. He was too busy screaming, and this time shitting his pants.

The stranger apparently did not like the screaming. He held open his dirty coat, exposing a mottled torso covered with thick, spiny hairs and four additional, undersized arms reminiscent of a Tyrannosaurus Rex's. A stream of that ivory webbing shot out from somewhere below where a man's belly button should be, crossing the room and coating Mitch's face.

Mitch kept trying to scream, even as he smothered, because the webbing had missed his left eye, and he saw the spider-thing coming for him ...

# ONE

The dead man lay in the shadows, slumped against the fence behind the hedge and out of sight from the main street.

The cat, a mangy stray that had been lurking about the neighborhood for weeks, crept closer. The animal knew carrion when she smelled it, and it had been a full two days since she had caught her last bird. She was hungry. This was food.

And yet, something about the body set the cat on edge. Not that it took much; cats tended to be skittish by nature, particularly homeless ones. She wanted the food, but the hair along her back rose and would not relax.

The cat looked around, her ears twitching every which way. A big dog dozed on the stoop across the street, a chain around his neck. A little dog yapped from the window of the house next door, but that glorified rat barked incessantly; the cat had learned to ignore him some time ago. Two birds chirped in the tree above — oh, how she would love to bring down those strident fliers! A car drove by, the big metal thing going too fast for concern.

The cat's gaze returned to the dead man. She licked her chops, her whiskers twitching in concert, and took a tentative step closer.

The body did not move, of course. The man was dead. The cat knew this. And yet ...

She played this game for nearly half an hour. One step forward, stop and look around, two steps forward, then arch her back and retreat a step. Over and over. There was a duffel bag lying next to the body; she paused to investigate this for a while.

Finally, she drew close enough to give the body a tentative poke with her forepaw, then retreated again.

The body did not move.

So the cat closed the distance once more, hunched over, looked around one last time, then opened her jaws to take a bite.

And the dead man grabbed the cat by the scruff of her neck.

The zombie lifted the animal to inspect it closer. Modern lore taught that "scruffing" a cat virtually paralyzed them. The zombie had even seen a video on YouTube where a vet put a binder clip on the back of the cat's neck, and it was like turning off a robot.

Not so in this case; the cat went berserk. Hissing, spitting, growling, and scratching at him for all she was worth, the terrified little furball twisted and turned in a desperate attempt to escape the dead man's grasp.

The zombie held the cat away. The last thing he wanted was to have to explain any scratches he might receive. He also wanted to make certain she wasn't wearing a collar or any other indications of ownership. He had been watching this cat since it appeared on their street, but he wanted to be extra sure.

The cat grew noisier, showing no signs of wearing herself down. The large dog on the stoop across the street lifted his head and guffed a few times.

He needed to finish this before the yowling drew unwanted attention.

The zombie lifted his other hand and smacked the cat

atop her head. Just hard enough to stun her, not to kill her.

He needed her alive. For a few more seconds, anyway.

Trey Matthews took the dazed animal's hind legs in his free hand, turned her sideways ... and sank his teeth deep into the cat's belly.

*     *     *

*A web ...*

*Trey, sitting behind a hedge ...?*

*A man hovering before a fire, speaking something like French, but not ...*

"Leve, araknid ..."

*A spider ...*

Alistaire Bachman rarely dreamt.

Months or even years might pass between them; for him, the hours of daylight were more like unconsciousness than sleeping. And when he did dream, he almost never recalled the details upon waking, but would be left with lingering impressions that occupied him for days to come.

These scarce "feelings" almost always proved apropos to events in his very near future, important events. Such an occasion preceded their first meeting with Trey's sister, an encounter which led to their gaining the third member of their Triumvirate. Another dreaming incident helped them locate Trey here in this world, where Alistaire and Sean found themselves drawn into the bodies of college students Neil Carpenter and Mark Hudson.

The latter example was, in fact, the only time Alistaire had dreamt since crossing over to this world ... until now.

The erratic images persisted in more rapid succession, flitting through the darkness of Alistaire's mind:

*Trey, with blood on his face, all around his mouth—*
*The man over the fire again, his dark face hidden except for a malignant smile and piercing, bright blue eyes—*

"Obeyi, araknid ..."

*The face of a very large spider — a tarantula, perhaps—*
*Trey shaking his head—*
*A large spider—*

"Obeyi, sèvitè ..."

*A web—*
*Trey—*
*A spider—*

"Obeyi, esklav!"

*Trey!*
*... and then Alistaire's mind slipped back into oblivion.*

# ... 2 ...

After he finished eating, Trey buried what was left of the poor kitty behind the hedge, making sure the remains were deep enough not to stink too soon and give it away. He dropped the dirty trowel back into his duffel bag and reached out to his other side to turn the garden hose on low. Even the sound of slow-running water might have drawn attention from the homeowners, but Trey had made super, extra sure they were still on vacation before starting this venture.

Once his face and hands were pretty clean, he spent some time swishing his mouth out. He then returned to his duffel and pulled out a Ziploc bag of raw beef. It took his sluggish fingers a moment to open the plastic seal, but he was soon stuffing the bloody cow meat into his mouth, chewing longer than normal to make sure the juices worked their way into every crevice of his teeth and gums.

Since his roommates were a vampire and a werewolf, he knew that hose water alone would not be enough to hide the smell of kitty meat on his breath.

*Poor kitty ...*

Those who knew Trey Matthews only casually (and, to be honest, the only exceptions in this world were Alistaire and Sean) would have been surprised, maybe even shocked by his attention to detail. When he spoke, the words dragged out with a lot of effort, and sometimes he lost focus. These days it was politically incorrect (a term he had learned online) to label someone a "retard," but most of the people he talked to (which mainly meant the people the Triumvirate saved from monsters) probably thought he was one.

They were all wrong. Trey's thoughts came slowly ... but they did come.

Satisfied that he was as cleaned up as he could get, Trey placed the plastic baggy back in his duffel and pulled the leather strap over his shoulder. Crawling on his hands and knees, he peered out through the leaves — given his large size, he would need plenty of leeway to emerge from behind the hedge, so he wanted to make sure the coast was clear.

It was not. A young brown-haired girl was walking along the sidewalk, coming toward him. Trey didn't know why she wasn't in school, but settled in to wait for her to pass him by.

She took her time, scuffing her sneakers along the pavement in some private pattern. She paused frequently to examine everything from a dandelion to a pill bug; once she stopped to poke at something completely invisible to Trey. The brown-haired girl was clearly in no hurry to reach her destination.

Trey doubted that would be the case if she knew a real live zombie watched her from less than twenty yards away.

When she was as close as she would get before passing beyond his line of sight, she stopped yet again, crouching down to watch a little, unremarkable butterfly.

*She's so close*, a deep, dark, *hungry* part of Trey observed. *So close. You can smell her, smell her blood, smell her* flesh. *If she were just a little closer ...*

Trey shook his head. He swallowed hard, the

lingering memory of the kitty not enough to satisfy his craving.

*She's a curious young thing. You could make a sound. Something kind of soft, just enough to spark her interest, draw her near the hedge ...*

His teeth ached to tear into her flesh.

Trey squeezed his eyes shut and fought against his hunger.

He had always been (as Sean put it, with his sometimes potty-mouth) pretty damned lucky with his curse. Since breaking free of the voodoo priest who brought him back from the dead, Trey'd had little difficulty resisting the cannibalistic urges that consumed most masterless zombies. Maybe it was because so much of his living mind came back, or maybe it was just a happy fluke. But so long as he ate raw meat every day, he almost never felt the hunger that should have controlled him.

The biggest, hardest temptation happened when he first came over to this place, this other world with so little of the supernatural in it. His mind entered the recently dead Travis Bekele, and when he first rose from the hospital bed, Trey had been so disoriented that, if it had not been for Alistaire, he probably would have attacked — and eaten! — Travis' grandfather, Lucius. But Trey had always chalked that one up to his difficulty with the passage between the two worlds — as far as he was concerned, that had been *Travis'* hunger overpowering him, not his own. Once he got control of himself, got his brain in charge of the leftover memories from Travis, his hunger abated to its normal, low levels.

But all that started falling apart up in Alaska.

A few months ago, the Triumvirate of Alistaire Bachman, Sean Mallory, and Trey Matthews had gone up to Alaska to deal with a pack of werewolves. Funny enough, the shapeshifters turned out to be shape-shifting *wolves,* instead of shape-shifting people. This, and the cold and those weird "white nights" worked against them, but in the end, the Triumvirate won. As always!

While they were up there, Sean finally dealt with some personal stuff about his sister, which left the Irishman still kind of sad but also somehow more calm and relaxed since their return to California.

Things had turned out less happy for Trey.

Not long after they got to Alaska, the werewolves attacked the Triumvirate in their rented cabin. During the fight ... well, Trey lost control, throwing one of his tantrums that sometimes took over (which always left him so embarrassed afterward!). And in the middle of it, Trey had bitten one of the wolves, chewing deep enough into its belly that he swallowed its meat.

This was not the first time Trey had bitten a bad guy in a fight, but ... for some reason ... *this* taste stayed in his mouth a long time. And he liked it. Like it a *lot*. Liked it so much that, when their mission was coming to its big finish, and Trey was fighting more werewolves ... he did it again.

Except this time, he did not have the excuse of being in a tantrum. And this time, he ate more of the wolf. A lot more. Enough to kill it.

Since then, Trey's hunger had grown bigger and bigger. Cow meat, not even bloody-raw, was no longer good enough. He wanted *more*.

The little brown-haired girl finally got up and went along her way. And Trey, who didn't really need to breathe anymore (unless he wanted to talk), let out a long, grateful sigh.

Putting on sunglasses over his dry, milky eyes, Trey crawled out of the hedge as fast as he could, looked around to be extra sure no one had seen him, then walked out onto the sidewalk. The house where he lived with Alistaire and Sean was a few streets over on his left, but he started walking to his right. It would take longer, making him loop around a whole extra block, but the faster direction would make him follow the little girl. He didn't want to do that.

Trey had been keeping his new problem a secret from Alistaire and Sean. He knew he shouldn't, but he couldn't help it. He wasn't afraid they might kick him out of the Triumvirate — he knew that Alistaire and Sean were better friends than that. It was ... well, it was embarrassing. Forgetting the potty-mouth jokes from Sean, he and Alistaire had always been so proud of Trey, of how strong he was against his hunger, but now Trey felt like he was suddenly the weak link in their Triumvirate. Because Sean only had to be locked up during the three nights of the full moon, and Alistaire kept from taking victims with just will power!

All of that, plus Trey's hunger didn't bother him as much when he had something important to think really hard about. If Alistaire and Sean knew that he was close to giving in to this ... this evil *thing* ... then they would probably not let him help in their missions. And that would leave him with nothing else to do but his daytime "guard duty" while Alistaire got his vampire sleep and Sean got his normal sleep (being a zombie, Trey never needed *any* kind of sleep).

Even now, during the quiet times (and that's all they'd had for a couple of weeks), Trey had to make do by sneaking out of the house as Sean slept and catching and eating any animals he could get his stupid zombie hands on, like that poor, poor kitty back there. Raw beef might not help like it used to, but he found that living animal flesh did — some, at least. He had tried aquarium fish and even a canary from a local pet store, but just like dead fish and chicken meat never helped him before, it turned out the same with the living versions.

It had to be something living, something *mammal*.

Trey was not stupid. He knew that, sooner or later, Sean would catch him away from the house — not to mention regular people might catch him eating poor animals behind hedges. He was just hoping, even praying (which would make Alistaire very happy), that he could beat this demon on his own before it came to that. If Alistaire could beat his—

*Alistaire still drinks blood,* his hungry side nagged at him. *Drinks* human *blood. There's nothing like that for human flesh. What are you going to do — study cloning on your computer and grow your own meat garden?*

Trey had wondered if maybe human blood might help him, but how could he explain needing it? And he couldn't just take it from Alistaire's supply — *that* would be noticed within a day!

Reaching the end of the street, Trey turned right again and started around the block.

As Trey pursued his secret practice of eating live animals, he slowly became aware of other things that might give him away — which was funny-*not*-funny as far as he was concerned, because they should have been *good* things! Yes, he'd still had some trouble opening that Ziploc bag, and yes, he'd taken a long time to get out from behind that hedge ... but as the months went by, Trey noticed he wasn't quite as clumsy as he used to be. He found himself talking without so many pauses, not bumping into walls and furniture so often, typing on the computer a little faster and without so many typos ... and as near as he could tell (it was kind of hard to be sure), his body stank less of decay.

The *biggest* good thing was that the injuries he got up in Alaska had healed faster than ever before! This change pleased him the most, but he also knew it could give him away the easiest — Sean had even commented on it last week, but he had not sounded suspicious ... yet.

That's what made the whole thing funny-*not*-funny to him: Eating living flesh was helping him in almost every way, making him more "normal" ... but to get more normal, he had to act like a *monster*.

Sighing in frustration, Trey continued on his way home.

# THREE

Sean Mallory woke at sunset, prompting him to chuckle through a yawn. He hadn't planned to sleep the whole day away, but he had pulled three all-nighters in a row with Alistaire, and naps could only take a person so far, even if said person was a werewolf.

It hadn't helped matters that the long nights had primarily entailed going over Bachman Foundation business, a subject that never failed to bore Sean to tears. Yes, he understood that the Foundation's success was vital to both their financial security and a steady supply of blood for Alistaire — God knew he would be grateful to avoid any more "necessary evil" blood theft — but still ...

*Please, no more business law,* Sean grumbled inside as he cringed at the mere notion.

Standing, Sean stretched until his joints cracked, slipped into a pair of boxers, and stepped out of their house's only bedroom. A quick glance at the hallway floor told him that Alistaire had not yet arisen, but he knew it wouldn't be long.

Audible keystrokes from the living room told him that Trey was on the computer, as usual. It sometimes seemed that their zombie friend *existed* online these days; gone were the simpler times of his making do with cartoons or children's books, though he still got into his LEGO bricks every once in a while. In fact, Sean considered as he walked down the short hallway, Trey behaved less like a "toddler" with each passing year, as though — mentally — he truly were growing up as time passed.

*More likely his intellect further reasserting itself*, he corrected himself. In the early days, it had been easy to forget that Trey Matthews had been a fully developed adult upon his death. His mental sluggishness had been misleading.

"Evenin', Trey," he greeted as he entered the living room.

Trey glanced over his shoulder, then returned his attention to the monitor. "Evening. You slept late."

On cue, Sean stifled a yawn. "Aye. Sorry 'bout that. Anything interestin' to report?"

Trey shook his head.

That's all he did, answered Sean's simple question with an acceptable head gesture. Perfectly normal and expected.

And yet, something about the set of Trey's shoulders, about his steadfast gaze at the computer screen, tickled at Sean's intuition. It was probably nothing; the dead man was just doing his Internet bit.

But this had been coming up with increasing frequency of late. Trey — whose words were always terse, to avoid the gaps and near-stutters he had to wade through in order to speak — would indicate that nothing of note had occurred over the course of his day, and for some bizarre reason, Sean felt a gentle tug of suspicion, as though Trey were hiding something.

At the same time, this feeling struck Sean as unfair, because the big man hadn't said anything to warrant such misgivings. He should get over himself and just ask Trey point-blank about his day ... except that he had, which prompted this silly merry-go-round.

*For God's sake, Mallory! Ye've got nothin' to go on here, so just drop it, ye dolt!*

Noise from the hallway flowed into Sean's train of thought: Alistaire, emerging from his coffin for the night. Good. He would pull his German friend out of earshot — which meant going outside, in this tiny place — and get his feedback on the matter. If Alistaire told him that he was being foolish, then he could let it go with a clear—

One look at the vampire's face as he entered the living room drove all of that from Sean's mind. Alistaire could be damned stoic most of the time, but Sean had learned to read him pretty well. "Ye've had one o' yer *feelings*, haven't ye?"

"*Yes,*" Alistaire confirmed.

"Anythin' solid to go on?"

Alistaire's pale brow furrowed as he considered this. As always, almost all the details eluded him. "*Allow me to consume some blood while I mull this over. For now, my strongest impression concerns—*"

"Alistaire ...?"

Alistaire and Sean looked toward Trey, who had turned his chair around to face them. The monitor behind him showed a field of small text, with one segment highlighted.

"Sorry to ... interrupt," Trey said, "but does your feeling ... having anything to do ... with spiders?"

\*     \*     \*

Randy McDonnell swatted at a spider that wasn't really crawling up his arm. He knew damn well it wasn't there, that he was suffering from a growing case of "the itchies," but he swatted at it just the same ... then cursed himself under his breath and followed the arm-swat with a mild face-slap, trying to snap himself out of it, if only in gesture.

As a single incident, it wouldn't have bothered him all that much. But it was happening more and more, and in his profession he could not afford — literally — to start getting itchy over phantom bugs.

How the hell could he maintain his career as an exterminator if the pests started freaking him out?

A little tickle ran up the side of his neck ...

*Leave it alone*, he scolded himself even as his muscles tensed. *You know it's nothing, just a bead of sweat or something.*

*It's running* up *my neck, it can't be sweat.*

*Whatever. It's not a spider. You spray and maintain this office like it's an operating theater. Hell, you spray so much of the shit you'll probably get cancer from it. So it's* not *a spider. Ignore it.*

But he couldn't. Hadn't been able to for days now. So he slapped at his neck, and cursed again when his hand inevitably came down on nothing. He had reached the age where he bruised a lot easier, so he could only imagine what he was going to look like by the weekend.

The cause of his little problem started a few weeks ago. Three? Four? He wasn't sure, because it had been gradual. His office got lots of calls, of course, for all the usual complaints of cockroaches, termites, or especially ants — ants were an exterminator's bread-and-butter in Southern California. He always got his fair share of spider calls, too, especially since the Brown Widows had made their presence known some years back.

But nothing like the past few weeks. The spider complaints had started rolling in, eclipsing all others. That was cool, he could always use the money — his kids' college debts weren't paying themselves. First the Brown

Widows went crazy. Then the Black Widows fought back. *Then* the Cross Orbweavers begged for attention, and the Black and Yellow Garden Spiders freaked people out, the Carolina Wolf Spiders exploded like he had never seen before, the Gray Wall Jumpers, the Goldenrod Crab Spiders, the Bold Jumpers ...

All known offenders. It was like they were eating crystal meth or something, with oddly aggressive breeding and behavior, but at least he recognized each breed, knew them from around the proverbial neighborhood.

Then Randy came across the first spiders he didn't recognize.

Even to exterminators, most spiders that fell within certain categories looked a lot alike, so it didn't sink in at first. It wasn't until he was doing a carcass cleanup that they caught his attention. Back in his truck, he had fished a few out of his vacuum's bin and looked at them under his magnifying glass. He sat and stared at them, the engine running, until the client eventually came out to the driveway and knocked on his side window, asking if everything was all right.

Where in the world had these little guys come from?

He convinced himself it was a fluke. Maybe the client had been traveling recently, and the critters piggybacked to the west coast in their luggage. So he let it go.

Then the same thing happened a few days later, and they were a *different* species he had never seen before. Okay, time for a little research.

After having called his wife, Lori, to tell her he might be a little late again, he had spread the latest fellows out flat under plastic and started cross-referencing with his online resources.

An hour later, he was pretty sure he had narrowed it down, though he wouldn't have sworn to it in a court of law. If his pro-am sleuthing was correct, these were a subspecies of silk spiders native to Haiti.

From Haiti to Southern California? A strange trek, sure, but nothing unheard of in his line of work. Bugs might hail from a particular region, but they could turn up anywhere, in an entirely foreign environment.

After his positive ID on the Haitian spiders, Randy felt a little more comfortable, more on top of the situation ... but on a routine call the very next day, he discovered yet *another* foreign species, and that newfound comfort dissipated. That was when "the itchies" flared into full bloom, the constant feeling that something was crawling on him when he knew damn well there wasn't.

Until that point, Randy had refrained from calling any of his fellow exterminators. There weren't as many independent contractors these days, what with the bigger companies either buying up or grinding down their smaller competitors, so the little guys were inclined to network when practical — sharing calls if they were too busy, comparing trends, shooting off heads-up emails when ant or termite nests were on the move, stuff like that. But for some stupid reason, Randy felt that if he called about this new spider "invasion," his comrades would either ask what in the world he was talking about ... or worse, they would confirm his findings, making the situation all the more real, and his itchies would get completely out of control.

But tonight, sitting here in his office, looking back and forth between his laptop screen and the tarantula he had caught this afternoon, he didn't think he could put it off any longer.

Southern California had its share of tarantulas, and they did show up a lot more in the fall, when the males were out looking for mates. People tended to freak out because of their sheer size, and especially when they popped up in unexpected places — like swimming pool filters — but this big guy ended up inside someone's car, where the dozens of nooks and crannies made him a real pain in the ass to capture alive. And Randy wanted him alive, had begun keeping living specimens of each newcomer. Why? He wasn't sure, couldn't articulate it, but his gut told him he might have found one more for his growing collection.

And sure enough, if his real-life-to-source-images comparison was right, he had yet another arachnid that did not normally hail from this part of the world. This guy was usually found in Cuba, Jamaica, the Dominican Republic, and Haiti. Always Haiti. Each of these damned things might turn up from Florida to Ecuador, but Haiti was always somewhere on the list. Did that mean anything special? Hell if he knew.

Sighing, Randy pulled out his phone. Scratching at a suspicious itch — this time he was wholly unconscious of it, and therefore did not shame himself — he swiped over into his Contacts list:

His first call went to voicemail. No surprise, given the hour.

His second call was picked up by the exterminator's wife, who said her husband couldn't come to the phone because he was sick. Randy offered his best wishes for improved health and a good night's sleep, and hung up. It was only afterward that he wondered what kind of "sick" that might be, but he would feel absurd calling back to ask, especially if it turned out to be a simple flu, so he let it go.

His third call got through, but she was in the middle of a job — which was unusual after nightfall. She promised to get in touch tomorrow, but she sounded distracted, and he wouldn't be surprised if he had to make a followup call to her.

His fourth call was also a bust ... yet it was also very telling, giving him chills as he finished listening to the answering message:

*"Hello! You've reached* Simon's L. A. Pest Control*! I'm afraid I can't come to the phone right now, but if you leave your name, telephone number, and the reason for your call, I will get back to you as soon as possible. Thanks!"*

All benign enough, and Randy was on the verge of hanging up, but then the background tone shifted, and Simon's voice returned in what was clearly an addendum added to the original message:

*"And if your reason for calling involves* spiders*, please press One. Thanks!"*

Without their having spoken, Simon had answered half of his questions: He was clearly dealing with the same aggressive spider behavior that started this whole mess.

Randy left a message, asking Simon to call him back at his convenience.

What the hell was going on?

Once again, Randy felt a tickle along the side of his neck, this time running sideways toward his jaw. He didn't bother with the inner debate, he just slapped at it, hard. Maybe he should start knocking the shit out of himself, turning the whole thing into a sort of negative association so that his subconscious would lay off ...

A second later, he felt his neck burning in a way that went beyond his slap. And he felt the lumpy texture beneath his fingers.

*No. No fucking way. I spray this office all - the - time! It's just my mind playing stupid, silly tricks on me again.*

Randy brought his hand around in front of him. The spider was mostly squashed, its juices smeared across his skin, but he would recognize it anywhere. He was, after all, an exterminator.

It was a Southern Black Widow.

*     *     *

Sean exited the freeway and parked along the curb a ways down the street from the medical examiner's office. They could just see the front of the building ahead of them, an easy walk but not too close.

"Okay, Alistaire," Sean said, "what next?"

The German vampire was quiet for a moment. Trey leaned forward from the backseat of their four-door sedan, his massive body filling Sean's entire rearview mirror.

Sean waited, his nerves showing as he tapped his fingers on the steering wheel. Whenever possible, the Triumvirate tried to avoid entanglements with the law. *They* might not be known in this world, but the bodies he and Alistaire occupied were still "persons of interest" from the string of corpses Alistaire's old enemy, Bishop, had left back in Oklahoma. As time passed, they found themselves looking less like Neil and Mark and more like their old selves, but the transformation was by no means complete, if it ever would be. And while Trey, too, had gradually swollen, his musculature reshaping to match his previous build, he was still inhabiting a native dead man, Travis Bekele. All complications for which they would not be able to offer any explanations — none that would be accepted, anyway.

This situation, however, was different. Most of their missions involved scenarios that had been misinterpreted, disregarded, or simply ignored by the authorities. No one in this world accepted that vampires, werewolves, or zombies were real; indeed, until recently, they weren't.

Only the crossover, the thinning of the barrier between the two realities — this one, and the Triumvirate's — had changed matters, and the people here had a lot of catching up to do. More often than not, the Triumvirate answered desperate cries for help when no one else could.

Part of Trey's current duties involved monitoring the Internet for hints of all the above, and he did it well; more evidence of the greater intelligence that lurked beneath his child-like demeanor. And tonight he had gotten an unusual hit — "unusual" even by their standards.

"*We have discussed,*" Alistaire spoke at last, shaking Sean from his musing, "*the possibilities that might derive from your facial contortion. Have you been practicing?*"

"Some," Sean admitted with a smirk. "It's not the most comfortable thing to do — not like changin' just my hand or arm. But aye, I've practiced it a time or two."

"*And?*"

Sean breathed heavily through his nose, then stated, "Yeah, I can do it."

"*Please do so now, so that Trey and I may offer our opinions.*"

Sean nodded, then reached up, angling the rearview mirror so he could see his own face, and concentrated.

The muscles and bones of Sean's face stretched and distorted in ways his partners were not used to seeing. His face flowed like soft clay, as though molded by an invisible potter's careful hands — his nose elongated, but the nostrils remained mostly the same; his brow sloped back in stages, even as the ridges around his eye sockets thickened; his chin pinched smaller and more pointed; and his ever-present sideburns expanded, the hair becoming more lush as it spread along his jaw.

Releasing his held breath, Sean considered his handicraft in the mirror, then clucked his tongue. He felt both his companions stiffen as he muttered, "Well, that sure makes me one ugly motherfucker." But he didn't apologize for his language this time, merely turned his head and asked, "What do ye think? Would ye recognize me as me? Or as Mark Hudson, for that matter?" Even his speech sounded a little different, thicker than usual.

Alistaire took in his new appearance, then shook his head. *"Not with any conviction, no."*

Sean nodded. "Good. Trey? Yer thoughts?"

Trey looked him over for several long seconds, then looked embarrassed as he agreed, "You're right. That ... does make you ... um ... very, very ugly."

Sean chuckled, "Yes, well, the things we do for duty, right?" He looked back to Alistaire. "Next?"

*"You and I shall enter the facility alone. Trey, if you witness anything—"*

"I have to stay ... in the car?"

This brought both Alistaire and Sean up short. Trey often had to remain in the background, given his having the least normal day-to-day appearance. And he was not typically given to questioning Alistaire's imperatives — not while sounding so petulant about it, anyway.

Alistaire turned in his seat to face him. *"Sean has proven able to alter his facial appearance. I, likewise, cannot be recorded by any security devices that will surely be in place, and can use my powers of persuasion when absolutely necessary. You, unfortunately, between your necrotic appearance and large physique, would prove more problematic for this clandestine sort of operation."* He paused, then asked, *"You do understand all this? This is not the—"*

"I understand," Trey stated, though he still sounded like he was sulking.

Alistaire noted the tone, but chose to ignore it. *"Good.*

*As I was saying, if you witness anything untoward —
alarms, people exiting the building in haste, additional
authorities rushing in — then please, by all means, make
your way to the facility. We may need you."*

Trey nodded, but said nothing.

Alistaire exchanged a brief look with Sean, then they
got out of the car.

Once they were a good distance on their way to the
medical examiner's office, Sean commented, trying to
sound casual, "Trey's in a bit of a tiff today, wouldn't ye
say?"

Alistaire nodded. *"Yes. I feared for a moment that we
might be facing one of his tantrums. But the circumstances
felt wrong for that."*

Sean grunted his agreement, and it was on the tip of
his tongue to voice his concerns from earlier that evening,
that something more might be going on with their ward ...
but he decided that maybe now wasn't the time for it.

One of Trey's many online connections, a few of
whom were "associated" with local law enforcement
agencies, had submitted a blog post for him late this
afternoon. A photographer had been murdered in Los
Angeles the night before, and the crime was just strange
enough to snag the attention of Trey's fellow "Watchdogs
of the Weird & Unusual" (whose website shocked
absolutely no one when the Home page played the theme
to *The X-Files*).

The body of Mitchell Gamall — or what was left of
it — had been discovered after a downstairs neighbor
spotted blood soaking through their ceiling. Police arrived
to find the masticated remains in the middle of his living
room floor, his blood-splattered photography equipment
still set up for a photo shoot. A second body, a woman
later tentatively identified as one Summer Levin, was not

so molested, with her likely cause of death attributed to two large punctures in her abdomen — in fact, paramedics were surprised by the lack of blood shed by Levin. Her identity was listed as "tentative" because the authorities found no ID on her, and digital photos had to be shown around the neighborhood. And there were "unusual alterations to her face and teeth" which caused said neighbors to hedge their statements with uncertainty.

But Gamall's bewildering manner of demise and Levin's facial and dental "alterations" were not the only reasons the crime had garnered the attention of Trey's fellows: Gamall's apartment, and in particular Gamall's and Levin's bodies, had been covered with what officers on the scene labeled as "enormous spider webs." Indeed, the web-like substance, which was described as "too copious and resilient" to be of literal arachnid origin, was particularly problematic for the removal of Levin's body, as she was pinned against the apartment wall by the stuff. They eventually had to use bolt-cutters in order to remove her from the scene.

An autopsy performed on Gamall's remains this afternoon suggested that a large animal had eaten much of the soft tissues throughout his body — possibly beginning while he was still alive — but the medical examiner in charge of the case had thus far refrained from identifying what *kind* of animal had done so, stating that she would need to consult with veterinary specialists before drawing any conclusions. Rumors claimed that she had also contacted a prominent arachnologist, but she denied this.

The autopsy for Levin was scheduled for first thing tomorrow morning. And there had been no further progress on the final labeling of the web-like substance.

A savage death, a second victim whose face and teeth had changed enough to have her neighbors second-guessing her identity, and webs from the world's biggest spiders? No question as to how the tale had found its way to Trey's group.

Together, Alistaire and Sean climbed the steps and entered the building.

*    *    *

James Eisenberg looked up from his book, annoyed that the lobby's front door had opened in the middle of a particularly good fight scene. He had taken this security job, not only to augment his regular police salary, but also because he had been so sure it would be nice and dull — how many people were going to wander into the coroner's office after hours, right?

Yeah, it hadn't worked out that way.

He could have guessed, of course, that bodies would be brought in around the clock, but those came in through the back. What he had not factored in was the steady flow of loved ones who showed up at all hours, sometimes to provide a positive ID on the deceased — that much he got — but also to harass the poor sap who monitored the front desk, nagging for updates on the statuses of their respective cases. *Come on!* he wanted to shout at so many of them. *Do you really think I'm gonna have any news on the toxicology reports for your dead little addict at two o'clock in the morning?!*

Then he got the totally random cases. Like, take these two guys:

One dressed in a fancy business suit sans tie, looking like a strict conservative except for the long-ish hair; the other wearing just a T-shirt and jeans — probably to show off how ripped he was, 'cause he sure was hurtin' in the face. James couldn't see them being here to view the same body — unless maybe the fancy one was a relative and the other was a low-grade employee? But the way they were looking around the admittedly fancy lobby, he got the "tourist" feeling. And what kind of tourist would want to check out the medical examiner's office?

*Too many*, he groaned inwardly as he slipped his bookmark into place and rose to his feet.

The ugly guy in the T-shirt was gaping at the sign for the gift shop, and James heard him mutter, "A *gift shop* in a coroner's office? Thank ye, no." James had to agree with him on that note; the whole gift shop thing had struck him as ridiculous at first, until he saw how many visitors actually bought something from the damn place. And what accent was that? Ugly Guy sounded sort of like a Leprechaun but with a deeper, slower voice, so he guessed that made him Irish (one *ugly* Irishman, bless his heart).

The other man, Business Suit, barely spared the sign a glance as he made his way to the front desk, and Ugly Guy moved to catch up.

"Gentlemen," James greeted them, his tone polite but firm, "I'm afraid office hours are long over. Unless you're expected, in which case I need to see your I.D. and have you sign in here." He indicated a tablet computer as he placed it on the counter, then glanced over to his left ... and frowned.

Below the counter was a monitor that showed three images, all displaying the lobby, the largest of which dominated the top half of the screen and featured this very desk; that camera was high on the wall over James' right shoulder. James had been following his casual habit of making sure the camera had a good look at the visitors' faces — after all, if they weren't expected, he wasn't going to buzz them in, and they might get upset and make a scene.

But the problem was, he was only seeing *one* visitor on the monitor. He could see himself and Ugly Guy clear as day, but where Business Suit strode up to the desk was nothing at all ... no, wait. On second look, he thought he could maybe see *something*, some kind of wavering ripple, but definitely no businessman approaching him.

James looked up at the two as they reached him, then back down to the monitor, and his glower deepened. He didn't understand what was going on, and he didn't like it, not one bit. His back straightened and his shoulders stiffened, but he managed to plaster a facsimile of a smile on his face as he slid his right hand toward the silent alarm button. He had only used the alarm once since he started here, but he sure as hell wasn't going to play the pride card in a weird situation like—

*"There's no need for that,"* Business Suit stated.

The hackles on James' neck shot straight up — mostly in anger for Business Suit's fucking gall, but partly because the man's voice carried a strong, unnerving quality, a weight that augmented its otherwise normal timbre. Still, he hadn't been a cop this long by rolling over for just anyone with an authoritative tone. His posture tightened further as he raised a pointed finger and got ready to put Business Suit in his place ... until they made eye contact. The instant James looked into those blue eyes, his balls shriveled and a chill ran down his spine.

"Wha ..." James cleared his throat and tried again. "What did you say to me?" Actually, what *had* the man said to him? He suddenly felt dizzy, out of sorts, not at all like himself. And he couldn't seem to look away from those deep, blue eyes. They *were* blue, right? For a moment they almost looked pure white, but that didn't make sense, did it?

*"I merely suggested that you need not bother yourself*

*on our account,"* Business Suit told him, his voice echoing more than the lobby's size justified. *"If you would please see to it that the door into the main building opens for us, you may go back to reading your book."*

"My book ..." James repeated. He did want to get back to his book, that was true. He was in the middle of a good fight scene.

*"Yes,"* Business Suit agreed, as though reading his mind. *"Please open the door and go back to reading your book. You may then forget we were ever here."*

"Forget you were here?"

*"Would that not be easiest for all of us?"*

He had to admit, Business Suit had a point, that would be the easiest thing to do. Hell, it had been an otherwise quiet night for a change. And he really wanted to get back to reading his book.

James Eisenberg reached out with his right hand once more, but he didn't go for the silent alarm this time. He just wanted to buzz them in and forget they were ever here...

\*     \*     \*

"Ye know, oh Jedi Master," Sean smirked as they strode through the Authorized Personnel Only hallway, "my mighty morphin' face and yer Invisible Man trick aside, in an ideal world, ye could've also told him to erase their security videos."

*"An ideal world, yes,"* Alistaire agreed. *"But you know how uncomfortable I am manipulating the minds of innocents. He already wanted to return to his book, he already wanted to avoid the hassle we represented. I merely—"*

"I know, I know, I'm just sayin' that ye could've

added 'and erase the videos' or somethin'."

"*And if the man did not have direct access to said videos? If he had been required to leave his post—*"

Sean cut him off again with a placating hand. "Okay, never ye mind. I get it. I do, really." He drew a deep breath through his nose, scowling as he did. "Damn. Maybe we should've at least asked him for a few directions. The smell of death is so overwhelming, I donna know how we're going to find what we need in here."

"Excuse me?" came a male voice from behind them. "Hey! *Excuse* me? Can I help you gentlemen?"

As they turned to meet the newcomer, an overweight, irritable-looking fellow, Sean commented under his breath, "Right on cue ..."

By the time the man continued on his way to the restroom — a need that was suddenly more urgent than before — he had guided Alistaire and Sean to the proper holding room, and then meeting them slipped his mind altogether.

What they found, unfortunately, did not please either of them.

"Dear God," Sean whispered as he took in the large, chilled, overcrowded chamber. From wall to wall, they could see little more than bodies, bodies resting upon every gurney and, in some cases, literally piled atop one another on metal shelves along the walls. Some of the bodies were covered in white sheets, but most of them were wrapped in translucent plastic, with hastily tied ropes holding the gruesome packages together. Off to their left, Sean noticed one sheet had been opened midway down the torso, but whoever had inspected it had not bothered to close up behind themselves, leaving a yellowed arm in plain view.

"Is ..." Sean began, "... is it always like this?" His

throat clicked as he swallowed. "Ye know, in morgues or whatever?"

Alistaire nodded. *"In major metropolitan areas, I'm afraid so. The apparent neglect you see before you is not intentional. They are overworked and understaffed, and this is the result."* He looked around. *"Fortunately, for our purposes, the higher profile cases, particularly those involving murder or media attention, are given preferential attention. The bodies we seek should not be buried too deep. The names were 'Gamall' and 'Levin,' I believe?"*

"Aye."

*"With the autopsy for Gamall's remains completed, it is possible that his body has already been claimed by surviving family. The girl, however, should definitely be here. We must locate her."*

Sean nodded with vigor. The sooner they found her, the sooner they could get the hell out of there.

Once he got over the initial shock, Sean was able to attune himself to Alistaire's professional, detached mind set. They moved among the many dead, checking less with their eyes than their other senses as they sought the bodies that brought them to this place.

They found Gamall first. His body had not yet been claimed after all; if only "body" were the best word for it — *remains* definitely felt more accurate in this instance. A portion of the damage was a result of the postmortem examinations, but it was quite clear that what was left of Mitchell Gamall had been in sorry shape before his arrival here.

"I've never seen bites like these," Sean commented as he probed with a careful pinky at the torn flesh of Gamall's hip. The tissue collapsed easily beneath his touch.

"*Nor I.*" Alistaire bent close to the wounds, studying them. "*The size of the apparent incisors ... I have never witnessed any vampire achieve these proportions. Note here ...*" He gestured to where a particular bite had broken through the victim's clavicle. "*Even were I to open my mouth as wide as possible ...*"

" ... ye'd never leave a mark like that," Sean finished. "A werewolf coulda done it, but the shape is all wrong. And like yerself, my eyeteeth never get *that* large." He poked around the torn hip again, watching the skin buckle. "It's like he's been hollowed out or somethin'." He stood up and shook his head. "No werewolf did that, either. But could it maybe be another kind of lycanthrope? We've heard stories."

"*That would not necessarily explain the 'hollowed out' effect you observed,*" Alistaire responded as he, too, straightened before the remains. He thought a moment, then said under his breath, "*Eine Spinne.*"

"What?"

"*The officers did speak of 'spider' webs found throughout the man's apartment. Indeed ...*" He pointed to a spare patch of unchewed skin at the shoulder and along the side of Gamall's neck, up to where his face disappeared beneath the mastication. "*A residue remains even now.*"

Sean looked up at him, his eyes widening. "Are ye suggestin'...?"

Alistaire offered a graceful shrug. "*I do not pretend to be any sort of expert on arachnids, but I have been around long enough to pick up much trivia. I am given to understand that spiders do not typically consume their prey whole. They inject digestive enzymes to liquefy their prey, then proceed to feed.*" He nodded toward the areas Sean had examined. "*That might explain the 'hollowed' effect, and the amount of missing flesh."*

"So," Sean said after a few seconds, "ye think it could be, what? A were-*spider*, then?"

*"That would conform to the feeling I experienced upon awakening. But lycanthropy need not be involved. I defer to you in this area."*

Sean considered all of it, bent to take one, long sniff of the many wounds, then stood once more as he shook his head. "No. I donna think it's a were-anything. It doesn't ... well, it doesn't smell right to me, somehow."

*"Then let us assume we are dealing with something else entirely."*

Sean grunted. "What a pleasant thought."

*"Indeed."* Alistaire looked around the cold chamber once more. *"We should locate the woman ..."*

Their next search did not take as long, though they were interrupted by another graveyard shift employee — the young lady left a little confused but mainly focused on her need for another, more leisurely cigarette break.

Like Gamall, Levin's body rested near the front of the chamber, and as reported, no autopsy had yet been performed. Sean freed her of her body wrap as he and Alistaire retook positions on opposite sides of the gurney.

After a brief moment's look-over, taking in Levin's face and teeth, Sean offered, "Definitely a vampire, right?"

Alistaire scowled as he continued to survey the body. Several seconds passed before he replied, *"Likely ... but there are a number of strange discrepancies."*

Sean inspected Levin once more. "Dust," he realized after a moment. "Shouldna she have turned into dust by now?"

Alistaire shook his head, his eyes never leaving the body. *"Not necessarily. If she were a very young vampire — as I sense she probably was — the odds were that enough of her mortal self may have remained. It is the older vampires who rapidly crumble into dust."*

Sean continued to ponder the situation as Alistaire reached out to Levin's mouth; he pulled her lips apart, rotating her head slightly as he scrutinized her teeth. Sean noticed his scowl deepen. "What?"

*"Her teeth,"* Alistaire replied, *"are all sharp."*

Sean peered in and saw that his partner was right. Upon first glance, he had only made note of the enlarged canines before his eyes shifted to the demonic shape of her brow. Now he absorbed that *all* of her teeth, included her bottom incisors and even her back molars, were pointed, giving her an almost shark-like appearance.

"So ..." Sean said, "... not a vampire, then?"

*"If she were, these teeth suggest that we may be seeing some new variant of vampire with which we are not familiar. Perhaps like your wolf-weres we encountered in Alaska."*

" 'Wolf-weres'?" Sean repeated with a slight smile; he was not aware that Alistaire had labeled those cursed animals as such.

Alistaire did not return his smile. His brow furrowed until he was positively glaring at Levin's body ... then he startled Sean by pounding a fist on the metal gurney and growling, *"Was für ein verdammter Narr war ich!"*

"What?" Sean sputtered, not at all used to such outbursts from his pensive friend. "What is it?"

*"Here I stand,"* Alistaire spat, shaking his head in self-disgust, *"talking of her teeth and state of decomposition, when I completely overlooked a glaring contradiction."* He glanced up at Sean. *"It was Gamall's remains and the oversized webs that initially ensnared Trey's friends' attention, but what did they tell us about Levin?"*

"Well, uh ..." Sean gestured helplessly toward Levin's face. "Her neighbors weren't sure if they recognized her because of how she looks now."

"*Yes,*" Alistaire returned with impatience, "*and did they march her neighbors in to look at the corpse?*"

"No, Trey said they showed them some photos of her and ..." His voice trailed off as he finally got it.

"*Correct,*" Alistaire affirmed. "*They showed them photos of Levin. Photos they should not have been able to take in the first place — indeed, I am here with you because we knew the security cameras would not detect me. And did Trey not also mention the police found Gamall's own camera and laptop computer filled with blank photos of his studio?*"

"Aye," Sean answered, still processing it all. "He did. The police had been hopin' to find some pictures of their assailants, but ended up with a whole lot of nothin' at all."

"*Which implies that the photographer may have taken many shots of Levin, with the results we would expect from a vampire subject. And yet, after the assault ...*"

"Aye ..."

They stood silent for a minute, each staring down at Levin's body and thinking it all through.

At last, Sean repeated, "So ... not a vampire, then?"

Alistaire sighed, then replied, "*No, I believe that she probably* was, *despite all evidence to the contrary. She is simply more evidence of something that is occurring outside our realm of considerable experience.*" His expression tightened once more. "*But — for now — it is neither the preserved remains, nor the unusual teeth, nor her post-mortem visibility to photography that begs the most important question yet.*"

Sean could see that Alistaire was gazing upon the large puncture wounds in Levin's abdomen, wounds that would have been quite nasty for a human being, but that should have barely slowed down a vampire.

"*I would like to know how, exactly, she was destroyed.*"

## ... 4 ...

Trey sat in the car and pouted.

He knew he wasn't being fair to Alistaire and Sean. He knew they were right. Even if he kept his sunglasses on over his dead eyes (heck, maybe even *because* he would be wearing sunglasses in the middle of the night!), the people who were still out and about on the streets of this big city were bound to notice him. Not only did his skin always look "sick" and he smelled bad (he used lots of deodorant, but that stuff was meant to cover up people's *sweaty* stink), but he was also pretty tall and had even more muscle than Sean. Put it all together, he would draw more attention to them than they needed when their mission was supposed to go sneaky.

But he didn't like it, now more than ever. He wanted to stay focused, not have too much time to think ... or to feel.

He was surprised that so many people were walking the streets this late. Down where they lived, down in the suburbs, there were stores that stayed open all night, sure, but you didn't see a lot of people just walking around at this hour (driving, maybe, but not walking). It wasn't too cold out, not in California and not for another month or more, but didn't most people—?

A squeaking pulled his attention to the right. The wide alleyway between two buildings didn't have any working lights in it, but the street lamps spilled in there just enough for Trey to see a homeless guy pushing his grocery cart into the alley.

Trey watched the vagrant as he rooted around in the cart, eventually pulling out a large, dirty blanket and wrapping it around himself. He also pulled out a clear bottle and took a drink from it. Trey knew a lot of people would assume it was alcohol, but to him it looked like a water bottle.

The guy continued rooting, his eyes focused on what he was doing. He had no idea that Trey sat so near, watching him.

*Just smell him,* the hunger inside him whispered. *Can't you smell him? His flesh?*

*That's dumb!* Trey snapped at that part of himself, even as the muscles in his jaw flexed. *I can't smell him from inside the car. The windows are all rolled up.*

The hunger didn't answer that, though Trey felt as though it snickered at him, and sounded very mean about it.

Through it all, Trey never took his eyes off the homeless guy, who shuffled around behind his shopping cart and sat down with his back against the wall. Only his feet were left visible.

*No one can see him ...* came the whisper.

*Yeah, but they would see* me*! Any of these people would see me get out of the car, see me walk into that alley.*

*So?* the hunger challenged. *It's not like they would care.*

Trey's mouth began to water (at least, it felt like it). Which in turn made him feel sick to his stomach because of *why* it was watering.

A moment later, he realized his hand was resting upon

the door handle. When had that happened? He knew he should let go, put his hand back in his lap—

Trey nearly cried out when Sean jerked open the driver's door. He yanked his hand back just as the Irishman threw himself in behind the steering wheel. But when Trey realized that Alistaire was not with him, he forgot all about the homeless guy.

"What happened ... to Alistaire?"

"What happened," Sean growled through clenched teeth, "is that Alistaire has lost his fuckin' *mind*!"

Trey sat back, alarmed by Sean's outburst.

Sean started the car with a harsh turn of the key, and cursed when he saw that he couldn't pull out into traffic yet. He drew a deep breath, then blew it out so hard it puffed his cheeks. As he waited for an opening, Trey could see in the rearview mirror that his face was turning back to normal.

"But ... where *is* Alistaire?" Trey tried again as his nerves built.

"Up on the rooftops, I'd guess," Sean answered, his tone still sharp. "We have to move the bloody car off the main street, get away from any soddin' traffic cameras." He slapped the steering wheel in frustration as traffic persisted. "I had to haul arse once I got outta the building, startin' off one direction then zig-zaggin' around so they wouldn't— Oh, for fuck's sake!"

Trey didn't see what had happened to bring that on, but the next thing he knew, Sean was peeling away from the curb with sharp squeals from the tires.

Trey was starting to get mad — Alistaire was gone and Sean wasn't explaining himself and he still felt tense about his hunger for the homeless guy and he didn't like that everything was happening so goshdarn fast!

"What *happened*, Sean?!"

Sean kept most of his attention on the other cars, but Trey saw his shoulders go up and down in a better kind of deep breath, a sigh that said he might finally get some answers. And he was right.

"Somethin's off about the Levin woman," Sean said as he turned onto a smaller street. "And I'm not talkin' about her bein' a bloody vampire. She's not. Or ..." He huffed again in frustration. "She *might* be, or she might be somethin' else now. That's what's off about her. To top the whole thing off, we're not even sure how she was killed — destroyed, whatever — and *that* has got Alistaire in a right snit." He barked an unhappy laugh. "He's bloody well lost it, if ye ask me."

Sean made another turn, away from the buildings and toward regular houses. Given what he had said about the traffic cameras, Trey thought he might be looking for some place dark, away from the lights.

The Irishman continued, "In spite of the hour, we kept runnin' into staff people, and Alistaire didn't like havin' to mess with their minds. So he decides to throw *all* caution to the fuckin' wind and steal Levin's body."

"What?!" Even Trey could see how much trouble *that* could cause. Wasn't that why Sean made his face look different, why Trey had been told to stay in the car? Weren't they trying to *avoid* attention?

Sean seemed to know exactly what he was thinking, and agreed with all of it. "Aye, goes against everything he usually preaches, doesn't it? Ye can see why I'm a bit cheesed off!"

They reached an area to Sean's liking and he guided the car over to the curb. Throwing the gear into Park, he shut off the engine and got out. Trey did the same, scooting over so he could follow him on the driver's side.

"How was Alistaire ... going to get the body *out*?"

Sean scoffed, "Oh, he had a 'plan,' if ye can call it that. More like a vague notion, far as I'm concerned." He crossed his arms over his muscular chest. "He sent me out first ..."

Sean trailed off as he cocked his head to one side, then gazed up and over his right shoulder. Trey followed his look in time to see Alistaire come sailing over the house across the street (Alistaire could move like he weighed hardly anything at all!). He could see that Alistaire was carrying a bundle in his arms, and guessed that it was probably the maybe-vampire's body. Alistaire skipped over the house in just two light footsteps on the rooftop, then landed across the street from them with almost no sound.

"Damn it, Alistaire," Sean sighed as he strode silently toward them, "I was hopin' ye'd change yer bloody mind."

Alistaire, whose vampire ears were almost as good as Sean's werewolf ears, addressed Trey's question, "*I sent Sean out first, for their security cameras to record that he did* not *have Levin's body with him.*" He hefted the sheeted bundle, confirming Trey's guess about what it was. "*I realize this will be far from conclusive, as he was presumably the last civilian recorded entering the building, but any muddying of the waters is welcome.*"

As he continued to speak, Alistaire moved around to the back of their car. Unhappy as he was with the situation, Sean realized what he needed and moved to open the trunk.

"*After he departed, I moved Summer Levin's toe tag to another female — again, simply to confuse the issue — then collected Levin and held her as tightly against myself as I could. I am hopeful that, with my arms wrapped around her and her body against my torso, my 'photographic invisibility' might have obscured her from the security cameras as well, if not totally then at least partially.*" He lowered Levin into the trunk. "*Did it work? I honestly do not know; I have never tried such a maneuver. But as we have discussed before, the exact mechanics behind the vampiric photographic invisibility remain unclear. My clothing, for example ...*"

Trey got the feeling that Alistaire was giving him a chance to guess where the German was going with it. He did. "Your clothes ... are invisible with you. They ... don't show up in mirrors ... when you're wearing them. We don't ... see them walking around ... by themselves."

"*Precisely,*" Alistaire said with approval as he closed the trunk. "*If — a strong 'if,' I grant — this turns out to be the case, if I was successful in masking her, we must remember it for future missions. For now ...*" He turned to Sean, who still had a sour face and was giving little shakes of his head. "*... let us return home by the most roundabout route that time will allow.*"

\* \* \*

Alistaire laid the maybe-vampire's body on the table in their small dining area off the kitchen (with Sean grumbling under his breath that he ate at that table, and if Trey could hear him, then Alistaire could, too), then unwrapped the sheet from her so that she rested exposed. Except for her girl parts. Trey was not surprised that Alistaire kept all her girl parts covered.

As they had told him, she showed no signs of turning to dust. She didn't look very dead, either. And Trey saw that, even though the two holes in her belly were puckered and swollen, very nasty to look at, they were not something that should have brought a real vampire down.

"All right, Alistaire," Sean grumbled in resignation. "Ye got her in private, and ye've got about an hour before ye need to head off to bed. What's next?"

"*I am hoping to conduct my own experiment in forensics, of a sort.*" He glanced at his two partners. "*I do*

*not know how long this will take, and I presume I will be
distracted throughout. If we do approach sunrise, please let
me know; I will, of course, still hear you."*

Trey and Sean exchanged a look of confusion. Trey
began, "Um ... Alistaire ...?"

But Alistaire no longer stood before them, at least not
in his normal body. He broke down into his ivory mist
(which Trey always thought looked pretty), the cloud
spreading forward, stretching out over the table, then slowly
lowering onto Levin's body. The mist enveloped the
woman, hugging her tighter and tighter until it finally
looked like she was coated with thick, moving, white cotton
candy. The mist swirled and whirled back and forth over the
body, and Trey saw that some of it even looked like it was
going into her open mouth.

"What is ... Alistaire doing, Sean?"

"Not sure," Sean admitted, "but I'd guess he's lookin'
her over a lot closer than we could from ... well, just *lookin'*
at her." He pointed to where Alistaire's mist was
penetrating the wounds on her torso. "Sort o' like
performin' an autopsy without ever makin' a cut. And he'll
know a lot more about what to look for than any regular,
human doctor ever could. At least in this world."

"Yeah ..." Trey mumbled as he watched the mist in
fascination, wondering what it was like for Alistaire right
now. He knew that Alistaire could kind of see and hear
when he was mist, but what would it *feel* like to wrap
around a body like that? "So what ... do we do now?"

Sean glanced at the clock on the wall over their small
stove, a little gadget with a dry-erase board for its face and
a little red mark that showed when dawn came this week.
"Now, my friend," he said, "we wait ..."

# FIVE

Francis Morse sat on the floor, hunched forward in a tight ball, his lower back pressed against the wall and his arms wrapped around his legs — not the most comfortable position for a man of his age and corpulence, though he had lost a great deal of weight over the past month. It would help if he leaned back more, but he didn't dare, not since that first spider crawled down the back of his shirt collar when he had slumped in a drowse. He had already shoved all the furniture and other objects away from this wall — no more dresser, no more standing mirror, no more framed poster of his first Oscar-nominated documentary.

Francis had also cut his hair very short, a haphazard buzz-cut that was the best he could do when using the clippers on himself. He rarely wore more than a tight T-shirt, tighter shorts, and sandals; he had first worn skin-covering layers for "protection," until he learned that the fuckers could creep inside without his realizing it. Now he wanted to be able to *see* them when they crawled onto his body — which was inevitable — so he could bat them away.

So here he sat, rocking somewhat and scratching at the slightest hint of any itch or tickle, the result of which was a growing number of scabs. He just waited there in one of his downstairs guestrooms, watching the clock and praying for sunrise. His house was never safe anymore, but it was more tolerable during the hours of daylight. Then he could maybe steal a few winks of sleep, which was the best he could hope for these days — he couldn't remember the last time he had gotten any *real* sleep; hell, he wasn't entirely sure he remembered what real sleep felt like. He had no one to watch out for him if he tried to wind down for more than a catnap — his ex-wife had moved out again before all this started, thank God.

Francis was alone with no one but *Young Bondye* and his damn spiders.

*Vini non isit la,* a voice echoed through the house.

But was it truly echoing everywhere, or was it only in his mind? Francis honestly didn't know.

*Vini non isit la, kounye a,* Bondye's voice came again. Francis didn't speak the language, and the man damn well knew that, but the meaning was evident, especially since he had heard it so often: *Come here, now.*

Releasing a long moan which trailed off to a whimper, he forced his aching muscles to move. He crawled first onto his hands and knees, then pushed up until he was kneeling. He rested there, just for a moment...

*Vini non isit la, kounye a,* Bondye repeated, startling him. Had he actually fallen asleep just now, kneeling like this? And for how long? He wasn't sure, he couldn't remember exactly what time the clock had last shown him, but the voice betrayed a growing impatience, and that was not a good thing.

Francis stumbled to his feet and hurried, as best he could, out of the guestroom.

In the hallway, the spiders were worse, crawling in open sight over the floor, the walls, the ceiling. They varied greatly in size and shape, but he didn't know which were venomous. There were too many to count with any certainty, but if he had to guess, he would say there were over two hundred of them in just this little, twenty-yard stretch of space; that wasn't including the ones he could already see swarming over the winding staircase.

Francis made a token effort to keep an eye on them as he moved about, but after a few weeks he had learned this was ultimately impossible. If he stayed away from the walls and kept his eyes on the floor, he might avoid the worst of them, but they had dropped from the ceiling onto his head more than once — hell, more than a dozen times, probably. His solution was to keep his eye line high, watching for any suspects crawling overhead as he was about to pass, and to walk with a very high-stepping gait, clomping his feet down to squash any of the little assholes underfoot before they could get into his sandals. He knew he probably looked like a fucking idiot, walking this way with his flabby legs, but he didn't give two shits about that. His clumsy little march didn't always work, but what the hell else could he do? Bondye wanted Francis to come upstairs, and the last thing Francis wanted to do was piss off the evil motherfucker.

This was his life now, filled with constant fear and anxiety and exhaustion. And a strong dose of shame and self-loathing, because all of this was his own goddamned fault ...

Francis Morse had been contemplating what topic to explore for his next documentary when he happened to catch the 1988 movie *The Serpent and the Rainbow*, which covered the subject of voodoo. The movie itself was typical Hollywood horror movie tripe — which was fine; unlike many of his fellow "serious" documentarians, he saw no problem in making movies for pure entertainment — but he vaguely recalled that it had been based on a non-fictional book. A little more research showed that there were a number of books and documentaries dealing with

voodoo and the like, but almost all of them used the hook,
"What if it's all real?" They would hem and haw,
examining this and that, superstition versus truth, and so
on and so forth, but in the end they tried to dangle that
lame-ass "What if?" over their viewers' heads — "We
might never know for sure" and all that garbage.

The subject was intriguing, but what if *he*, Francis
Morse, Academy Award-winning pro that he was,
approached it with the end goal of showing that it was all
complete and utter bullshit? He snared his first Oscar
nomination with a documentary short that debunked
UFOs, taking the most treasured, mysterious, and
"unexplainable" reported sightings and tearing them to
pathetic shreds. He hadn't done that sort of aggressive
debunking in years, so why not return to the sub-genre by
going after voodoo?

Francis bounced the idea off his producers, but they
didn't see the point. Most people in the modern world
already believed the old voodoo legends were
superstitions, outdated myths that haunted a legitimate
third-world religion, so what would be the purpose of
showing them what they already knew?

Francis understood where they were coming from, but
they weren't following his particular angle. He wasn't just
planning to say, "See? Voodoo is all in their minds." He
wanted to show that the Haitian voodoo priests were
outright charlatans. They didn't believe their own bullshit
any more than child-touching Catholic priests believed in
Christ, but kept at it for the same reasons: They were
duping their followers for the sole purpose of gaining a
little bit of power. And maybe he could segue the whole
topic over to those more familiar, corrupt Catholics, or
better yet, Muslim extremists?

*That* his producers could chew on. Francis didn't

know if that was really where he wanted to take the whole thing — it was shining a burning light on the voodoo folklore that intrigued him — but the premise had been enough to get them to fund an exploratory trip, for himself and his usual crew, to Haiti ...

Francis reached the winding staircase, and this was where things always got tricky. He couldn't keep looking at the ceiling without stumbling, and he sure as fuck wasn't putting his hand on the wriggling bannister. He would have to take the stairs in stages — look up for potential droppers, look down and take a step or two, pause to look up and again, and so on. If only he hadn't nodded off while kneeling earlier, he could've taken more time here, but if he took long enough to be *Vini-non-isit-la-kounye-a*-ed again, there would be hell to pay. The itch from the bites on the backs of his knees were just now calming down from the last time he made the sonofabitch wait too long — and those didn't hold a candle to the *dozens* he'd received, all over his body, the one and only time he tried to make a run for it over the backyard wall.

No, he couldn't risk making Bondye angry, for any reason.

Moving steadily, but carefully, Francis reached the second floor landing with only one incident, and he managed to kick that fellow off his foot before it crawled more than an inch. The familiar stench — a smoky, gaggy reek that he stopped noticing anymore from downstairs — grew stronger up here as he trod onward toward his old bedroom, the "master" bedroom in the most literal sense of the word, now. This was where Bondye spent every hour of the day, where he ate and slept — *if* he ate or slept — and most of all, where he worked nonstop on whatever the hell it was he was doing. Francis didn't ask, didn't want to know. He knew too much already, and this was coming from a man who had made a career out of learning things ...

The first three weeks Francis and his crew had spent in Haiti were a colossal waste of their time. He knew full well how painstaking research could be, but come on! Over those first twenty-plus days, they met dozens of vodouists, all of whom practiced a religion that mixed classic voodoo with traditional Roman Catholicism — they spoke of the Christian Saints as often as they did loa, the spirits who served the "good God," whom they seemed to also think of as the Christian God? This struck Francis as contradictory, but he knew that was only his outsider's point of view. The religions of the world were full of such contradictions.

The real problem for Francis was that all of these voodoo priests came across as completely sincere, true spiritual guides who wanted nothing more than peace for their flock. Good men, who meant what they said and said what they meant. This, of course, ran against the theme Francis had planned.

He wasn't above bending the truth a little at times, but as they met genuine vodouist after genuine vodouist, Francis knew he was adrift. He had no interest in making just another voodoo documentary — the history had been done, the study of their rituals, of the ingredients of their trade ... all well-trodden material. If he couldn't follow his "crooked schemers" theme, then he sure as hell better find something else to focus on, something new, or he would just call the whole damn thing off.

So, for the final week of their exploratory trip, Francis searched for the really creepy stuff, the old Bokor shit, the core upon which the darker legends were based. Yes, he was well aware that this was the most well-trodden area of all — hell, it was the driving force behind the movie *The*

*Serpent and the Rainbow*, which started him down this path — but what else was he supposed to do with the time he had left? Besides, since he sure as hell didn't believe in the supernatural, this would be his best chance to locate some of those charlatans he was originally gunning for; find a few fakers, report his findings to his producers, then return for some real digging.

They had been two days from leaving when one of his scouts brought back good news. From out in the areas that were most devastated during the big earthquake a few years back, word was circulating about some new Bokor hotshot, a true dark vodouist who was building an underground reputation for himself. This vodouist claimed to have experienced a recent "awakening" during meditation, having gone into his trance a mere pretender and come out a real badass. The whispers claimed the man was not mere *houngan sur pwen*, not even *houngan asogwe*, but a *mèt Bokor* — translation, not a servant, not a high priest, but a *master*.

Francis was interested, sure, but the story didn't demand his full attention until he found out the guy's alleged identity: Young Bondye. With "Bondye" meaning "God," Francis first thought this was being used as an adjective, that this guy was being described as a "young god" by those who were talking about him. But then his scout clarified that this was supposedly the guy's actual *name* — first name "Young," which was uncommon but not unheard of, surname "Bondye."

This vodouist had taken the title "Young God," the most painfully obvious stage-name Francis had ever heard. *This* was the charlatan Francis wanted!

So Francis and his team went looking for Young Bondye. And, Christ help him, they found him ...

Francis reached the master bedroom door. Should he

knock? Did he knock last time? He was so fucking tired he couldn't remember. He decided to split the difference and — after blowing two spiders off the knob first — knocked as he opened the door, and the wall of fumes that greeted him made his eyes water and his throat clench up. He felt a desperate need to sneeze, but it wouldn't come. In spite of its being night out, the shades were all drawn against even the moonlight, leaving the hot room a flickering contrast of light and shadow.

Young Bondye sat before the fire, which blazed from inside a massive bronze kettle that Francis had never seen before and had no idea where Bondye had gotten it. At first Francis thought the man was perched on the edge of a chair, then realized there was no chair — he appeared to be *hovering* as he bent over the blaze, defying gravity as he sat cross-legged and naked as the day he was born. Just a short time ago, Francis would have called bullshit, knowing with certainty that it was an illusion of some sort, a cheap stage magician's trick. Now he knew better.

Bondye ignored Francis as he waved his hands over the fire, the flickering light gleaming off his dark skin while accenting his bright, blue eyes; he muttered under his breath and occasionally tossed in sundries that Francis could not identify in the dark, smoky room. Francis suspected the delay was a power game, making him hurry his fat ass up here only to have him stand and wait as he swayed on his feet. But knowing it was a game didn't change anything, so he clasped his hands in front of him and waited with his mouth shut like a good little boy, trying not to imagine just how many spiders surrounded him ...

As he stood in silence, his mind flittered back to his misfortune of finding Young Bondye on that doomed trip to Haiti, but his eyes were losing focus in exhaustion, and this reflected the state of his thoughts. He relived flashes of wandering through earthquake-ruined streets, of peering into gloomy, collapsed buildings, of trying to pay locals to help them and receiving nothing but harsh silence and turned backs, of Henry Aaron, the youngest member of his crew, nearly dropping the camera when a spider bit him on the neck, of all the crawling things, hundreds of them—

"You will get me more supplies."

Francis jerked back to full awareness with a snorted jolt. "Supplies," he repeated, his voice croaky. "Sure. What do you need?"

"White sage," Bondye stated, his voice clear and very deep, in spite of his average size. His accent was a little heavy, but Francis had learned to understand him. "Cinnamon oil. Sandalwood oil. Powdered jellyfish. Ammonia. Birdlime."

*White sage cinnamon oil sandalwood oil ...* Francis memorized as fast as he could; he had learned not to make Bondye repeat himself. Unfortunately, he had to admit, "I can get all that, sure, but I, uh, I've never heard of 'powdered jellyfish,' and the birdlime—"

"You will get all of these supplies for me."

"I *will*," Francis assured him. "I will, I promise. But for the jellyfish stuff, and maybe the birdlime, I, um, I might have to leave, just for a little—"

The spiders swarmed over him. They crawled up his legs, jumped onto his arms, dropped onto his head.

Francis screamed and thrashed, crying out at the hundreds of tickling legs and numerous painful bites, "I'll get it! I'll get it *all*! I swear! *I swear*! Please, *please*—!"

And just like that, they were gone, fleeing his body as fast as they had attacked. Were it not for the itching pain of their many bites, he might have wondered if the whole thing had been an illusion.

Except Young Bondye did not work in illusions. Sometimes literal smoke, but never mirrors. Francis knew this, knew the spider assault had been very real, knew it well.

He stood very still, whimpering quietly to himself, waiting.

Bondye, who had never turned his attention from the crackling flames, stated, "You have money. You have your Internet and your computer." He said this with some derision. "Make it happen. You will get it all before the sun sets tomorrow night. Go."

Francis nodded and fumbled for the door in his haste to get the hell out of there. Just before leaving, he heard Bondye speak once again, but sniveled in relief when he realized that it was directed toward the fire rather than to him.

*"Leve, araknid ..."* Bondye murmured, meaning God only knew what — Francis certainly didn't want to know. *"Obeyi, araknid ..."*

Francis shut the bedroom door behind him.

## ... 6 ...

*Leve, araknid ...*

Trey looked up from his keyboard. He'd been poking around the Internet to see if the morgue place had discovered the maybe-vampire's body was missing (he knew it was probably too soon, since the sun had not come up yet, but he wanted to look anyway because the whole thing made him nervous). He hadn't found anything important-looking so far, and had been trying to come up with other ways to be helpful when he thought he heard a strange man's voice—

*Obeyi, araknid ...*

There it was again! And he was also pretty sure it wasn't coming from the computer speakers. He didn't know the language ... except that it did sound familiar. It had stopped now, but where had it come from? Maybe he should—

"Trey," Sean spoke up from the doorway to the kitchen. "I think Alistaire's comin' out."

Oh! That was good. He was curious about the maybe-vampire. He would ask Sean about the strange man's voice later.

When he entered the small dining area, Trey saw that Sean was probably right. Alistaire's mist form was smooshing together near the head of the maybe-vampire's body. It condensed, took the cloudy shape of a man, then looked exactly like Alistaire if he were made of fog, then turned back into the real Alistaire (looking tired, which didn't happen a lot).

"Well?" Sean asked, his voice a little impatient. "What did ye find?"

Alistaire kept staring at the maybe-vampire as he answered, *"Not as much as I had hoped, except to confirm some of our existing suspicions: She was a vampire; I recognize all the trace qualities all too well. But she is changing into something else."*

"She's ... wait, ye mean she's *still* changing? Now?"

*"Yes."*

Sean, who had been standing with his arms folded, dropped them to his side and took the smallest step backward as his hands curled into fists. "So she's still alive, then?"

*"Still 'active' might be the most fitting term, but that is difficult to answer. She is certainly inert — I felt not the slightest reaction to my probing, no involuntary withdrawal or attempts to repel me. For all purposes, she seems to be gone ... yet, her cells are doing something, something I have never before encountered."*

"This mission is just gettin' started," Sean commented, "and I'm already uncomfortable with all these things that *you*, of all people, haven't seen before."

*"I feel the same, my friend."*

Trey looked at the changing-vampire's body and asked, "So ... does that mean ... we stole her body for no reason?"

*"I wouldn't say that. I will study her again tomorrow night as soon as I rise, evaluate the change as it occurs. If it is merely an unusual form of deterioration — perhaps a side-effect of whatever brought this vampire down — then so be it. But if this is some sort of metamorphosis—"*

Sean pinched the bridge of his nose and muttered, "Oh. Great."

"—*then I am grateful to have her here, rather than under the observation of mortals who will understand what they are seeing even less than we do.*"

"How long would ye guess this 'metamorphosis' might take?"

"*I have no way—*"

"I'm askin' for yer best guess, Alistaire."

Alistaire considered. "*The sun is rising very soon; I can feel it. Given her initial condition as a vampire, I would* guess *that very little will change during the daylight hours. Whatever happened to her occurred almost two nights ago ...*" His brow furrowed as he further mulled over it. "*I would imagine that we might see the end results, whatever they might be, sometime tonight or the night after.*"

Sean sighed and glanced at the clock over the stove. "Ye need to get to bed, Alistaire."

"*Agreed.*" The German headed for the doorway back to the living room, the Irishman moving to follow him.

But then Trey noticed something. "Wait ..."

The two stopped, looking back.

Trey pointed. "Were those bumps ... on her face before?"

His partners returned to the dining table, staring down at the changing-vampire. After a moment, Alistaire answered, "*No. I do not believe they were.*"

Six bumps formed half a crooked circle around the woman's eyes, three on each side of her face. The first of each was just on the outside tip of her eyebrow, the other sets of two reaching from the sides of her eyes down toward the cheekbones. They looked to Trey like really bad mosquito bites, with the centers a little darker than the rest of the woman's skin.

Sean reached out with a curious finger, but stopped before actually touching any of them. "Hell," he muttered, "I'm not even sure they were there when Alistaire pulled off her."

Trey asked, "This is part of ... her changing, right?"

"*I cannot think of any other explanation.*" Alistaire looked up, first to Sean, then Trey. "*Be vigilant today, my friends. We are most certainly in unchartered waters.*"

Trey might've been slow sometimes, but even he was getting uncomfortable now. Both Alistaire and Sean were confused over everything with this mission, and they knew a lot about all sorts of weird things (most regular people would've said "impossible" things, but Trey was walking proof that the word "impossible" was iffy sometimes).

And on top of that, something about all of this was nagging at Trey, pulling at the back of his brain like a doggy would pull at a piece of beef jerky. He couldn't figure out what it was, *hoped* that it would come to him as so many other things did, eventually. For now, something about it just ... *tasted* familiar. But did that make sense? Could a situation have "taste"? That was the best word he could think of ...

*Maybe*, whispered the hunger inside, *it's because you're wanting a little* taste *of something better than cat meat.*

*Shut up!* Trey snapped as he followed the others out of the kitchen. *I don't have time for you now. We're on a mission, so this is where you leave me alone for a while.*

The hunger did not reply, though he had a sneaking suspicion that it might've sneered at him. Like, to suggest, *Oh, you really think so?*

\*   \*   \*

Once Alistaire was in his coffin for the day, Trey returned to the Internet.

First, he checked again on the morgue place. One of his fellow Watchdogs (who must live right in that area) reported that a lot more cop cars were showing up than would normally be expected so early in the morning. Trey thanked him and asked to be kept updated, then typed up a carefully worded, very friendly scolding about giving away too much about his personal identity or whereabouts.

After that, Trey just stared at the monitor, thinking. Sean paced around behind him for a while, then sat on the couch by the front door, leaned back, closed his eyes, and looked like he dozed off ... but Trey knew better. If Sean wanted to get some real sleep, he would say so and then disappear into the bedroom (those were the times when Trey knew it was safe to sneak out of the house). He might look like he was zonked on the couch, but he could be alert and on his feet at the drop of a hat.

Trey continued to stare at the monitor without really seeing it. With things quiet again, and with his hunger keeping its mouth shut for a change, he returned to wondering why something about this mission "tasted" familiar. And hadn't he thought he'd heard a strange man's voice earlier? Yes, he had. He had forgotten about it while they were talking about the changing-vampire, but he remembered now. That voice, more than anything, struck the familiar chord somewhere in the back of Trey's mind. Not that he recognized the voice itself (he was super sure that he'd never heard it before), but it was the feel of it ... and yes, the *taste* of it. He didn't think it had been aimed at him. He thought maybe he had just caught a piece of it as it passed by, like when he was standing on the sidewalk and a big bus drove by kind of fast and a bunch of steamy, smoggy air blew into his face. Wait, did that mean it was the *smell* of it that was bugging him, instead of the taste after all? Was he getting confused again? It was so frustrating when that happened!

But he knew from experience that, if he focused hard enough, it would come to him sooner rather than later. That was one of the funny-*not*-funny things that had gotten better since he started eating living animals in secret. Things came to him quicker and quicker these days.

Trey stared at the screen. Waited. Breathed in and out slowly, even though he didn't really need to breathe anymore. Sit, quietly. Wait. Let it come ...

His hands reached out, fingers searching for the keyboard. He used to be what Sean called a "two-finger typist," but he had gotten better (again, especially since he started eating things) at using all his fingers. He reached the keys, but he didn't type anything. Not yet. Not until he figured out *what* he wanted to type ...

Trey closed his eyes, his fingers moving, clicking the keys. And it was funny, because he honestly could not say for sure what it was that he was typing.

His fingers stopped. He opened his eyes.

In the search field, he saw the word voodoo.

Trey didn't think about voodoo too much. For one thing, the Triumvirate didn't encounter it very often. Aside from the mission where Alistaire and Sean met him for the first time (back when he was still a slave to the voodoo priest who had turned him into a zombie), they told him they'd only had one other mission together involving voodoo, and Alistaire only encountered it a couple times more in the centuries before that. And that was back in *their* home world, the place they came from that had so much more supernatural stuff in it.

As far as they had seen, voodoo (or "vodou," as the computer auto-suggested) was nothing more here than a religion that some people practiced. Nothing supernatural about it (by the Triumvirate's standards, anyway).

Now Trey wasn't so sure.

*Is that why this tasted-smelled familiar?* he wondered. *Does this changing-vampire have something to do with the same kind of voodoo that made me into a zombie?*

Trey sat forward, his hands perched for more typing. Time for a little research. If he added the words—

A soft *crackle* drifted through the house. Trey paused, his head cocked as he listened, trying to figure out what the sound had been and, more importantly, where it had come from. Had it come from the dining room? He wasn't sure, but if it had ...

Trey looked over to where Sean sat on the couch. Sean hadn't bolted upright or anything, he was still slumped against the back cushion, but his eyes were open and his gaze met Trey's. He had heard it, too.

When a few long seconds passed without repeat, Trey started to relax a little ... and they heard the *crackle* again.

Yeah, it had come from the dining room.

Trey and Sean rose together. Trey reached the doorway to the kitchen first, and didn't bother looking around the room. He knew what had to be the source of the noise.

The woman was sitting up.

From where he stood, Trey could only see the back side of her profile, and he was more curious than afraid. Was she even awake? She wasn't moving or saying anything, so maybe she was still asleep-dead, and this was part of the change Alistaire talked about?

The *crackle* sounded yet again, and Trey saw something twitch under the sheet. Alistaire had covered up her girl-parts, but the sheet had slid down toward her lap when she sat up. It was still kind of wrapped around her belly area, though, and the shift had happened somewhere along her ribs on the side closer to him.

Maybe Alistaire shouldn't have been so worried about her girl-parts.

Trey sneaked a peek back at Sean, who nodded to him, then took a step into the dining area.

The instant Trey's heavy foot creaked onto the floor, the woman twisted around toward the noise. Her eyes were still closed, and those dark bumps were a lot darker, a glossy black in the morning sun that glowed through the drapes covering the east window (morning sun that didn't seem to bother her at all, even though she was a vampire before she was ... whatever the heck she was now). He had stopped moving as soon as she turned, and she was still again. Should he take another step forward? Back up into the carpeted living room? He could ask Sean, but he thought that maybe talking wouldn't be the best idea right now. Maybe he should—?

Before Trey could make up his mind, the woman's eyes snapped open. They, like, really *snapped* — her eyelids cracked into little pieces of dried, flaky skin and crumbled away. Beneath were two large, shiny black orbs, exactly like the bumps on either side but much bigger. Bigger than her original eyes must've been.

Were her eyes gone? Were these her *new* eyes, and she was looking right at him?

Sean placed a gentle hand on Trey's left bicep and tugged, suggesting a retreat—

Faster than Trey could follow, the woman spun around and off the dining table. The sheet fell away at last, and in a blur she jumped onto the wall, then twisted around onto the ceiling, facing them upside-down. He barely had time to duck before she bowed her lower body toward him and something shot out. Sean shoved him forward, and the white, gossamer stream struck the corner of the doorway right where Trey's face had just been.

"Fuck!" Sean cussed, his voice deepening as he grew hairier.

The woman's head tilted almost completely sideways as she studied Sean. She opened her mouth, revealing that her pointy vampire eyeteeth were *really* big now. She made a hissing sound, softer than Trey would've expected but still vicious.

While she was doing that, Trey finally got a better look at her sides. There were four really weird things poking out, two on each side, like she had grown deformed baby arms while they were in the other room. He also realized that her skin, which had been pale and smooth when Alistaire first uncovered her, was now mottled. Ugly, stiff-looking hairs were poking out in some places, too.

Two big eyes and six little bumps that matched. Four new maybe-arms sticking out of her sides, giving her eight limbs. Bigger fangs, freaky body hairs, sticking onto the walls and ceiling, and biggest clue of all, she'd shot what looked a heck of a lot like a string of *webbing* at him.

Even a slow-minded zombie could figure out where this was going.

The vampire-turned-spider-thing twisted her ever-nastier face back around to Trey. Her look toward Sean had been pure malice, but her expression (weird-looking face or not) toward him seemed more curious. Did that mean anything?

"Sunlight's not fazing her," Sean growled, echoing Trey's own thoughts from earlier. "Any ideas on how we—?"

The spider-thing hissed again as she twisted her head around once more, her body shuffling until half of her was back on the wall. Trey thought she was reacting to Sean again, but the angle didn't seem right. She then cocked her head the other way, turning it so far a normal person's would be popping all over the place. Was she listening to something? Smelling something, maybe?

The spider-thing reared back, her huge fangs actually spreading outward ... and then she curled inward and busted straight through the dining room wall into the living room.

"Shite!" Sean roared as a second crash immediately followed from their large bookcase tumbling over in her wake. Sean lunged after her, but before his whole body was through the doorway, the spider-thing slammed into him, carrying them both out of Trey's sight.

"Sean!" Trey called, willing his lumbering legs to move faster as he chased after them.

The spider-thing had Sean pinned to the hallway floor, her new limbs already larger and clutching little handfuls of Sean's T-shirt, her skin even more mottled than it was a few seconds ago. She was hissing and he was growling, and Trey couldn't figure out how to get in there and help him. The walls were just too close for his big body to squeeze in on either side of them, not with how frantically they were struggling.

He settled for grabbing one of her bare feet and yanking, but her foot felt too narrow in his hand, her toes pointier and curling under, and she had a lot of those ugly hairs (and they were a lot stiffer) all over her sole. She kicked back at Trey with her free leg, while her arms and new-arms held onto Sean.

Sean, who was in full wolfman mode, barked as she snapped down at his face, then countered with his own attempt to bite her. In the back of his mind, Trey wondered if all the noise was going to bring the police to their house, but he couldn't focus on that. He had to get this spider-thing off his partner before she—

Too late! She finally zigged when Sean zagged, and she sank those huge teeth of hers into his shoulder.

Sean roared, tucked his legs in until they were under the spider-thing's torso, and shoved so hard that she sailed up and over Trey's head, gouging a line through the plaster on the ceiling as she went. She struck the front wall of the house, but bounced right back onto her hind legs, threw aside the strips of T-shirt that had torn off in her new hands, and surged forward once more.

Trey spread his arms wide, but he was too slow. She skittered up the wall and along the furrowed ceiling, shooting past him faster than he could track. She jumped back to the floor, but this time she knocked Sean aside and began tearing at the hallway tiles.

Wait, she was tearing at the floor? Why would she—?

Alistaire was down there in his coffin, underneath the house! She was trying to get to Alistaire!

Sean must've had the same idea, because he jumped right onto her, locked an arm around her throat, and heaved. Her spine curled backward further than a normal person's could, her main arms flailing even as her new arms kept clawing at the floor, sending bits of broken tile flying everywhere. She hissed again and bucked once, twice, three times, but Sean held on.

Trey lifted his foot high and tried to stomp on one of her legs, but he missed. He raised his foot to try again—

The spider-thing stopped attacking the floor and pushed off with her new limbs, demonstrating how strong they already were. With Sean on her back, she arced up and over, her sticky feet anchoring her to the floor as they both collided with Trey while his leg was still in the air. All three slammed down onto the remains of the fallen bookcase with a tremendous *thud!* that shook the whole house.

Sean released a sound that was either a cough or a curse (hard to tell when he was in wolfman form), then barked in anger and pain as the spider-thing bit into his forearm. She whipped her body forward, doing a sort of tight somersault so that she was still crouched over Sean while getting onto all fours (or all eights). She did a weird hip-thrust, and webbing shot out from somewhere right below her belly button, spraying across Sean's chest and the loose books and carpet around him.

Then she leaped away, and a second later, Trey could hear her tearing at the hallway tile again.

Sean rolled over, getting off Trey even as he tugged at the web that bound him to the floor. When he realized he wasn't going to get free right away (the books were flopping around and the carpet was stretching and tearing, but the webbing was holding strong), he growled, "Get her, Trey! Kill the bitch!"

Trey sat up and tried to scramble forward, but the loose books and shards of bookcase kept shifting around under him. Sean tucked his legs in to place his shins against Trey's back, then shoved to get the big zombie onto his feet faster than he could've on his own. Trey nodded a Thank You before rushing back into the hallway.

In the two seconds it took Trey to close the distance between them, he saw that the spider-thing had gotten through the floor in gouged strips that let him see the top of Alistaire's coffin. She was so fixated on getting to their vampire friend, she didn't seem to notice that he was coming.

*Why do they always focus on getting at Alistaire? The wolves did the same thing in the cabin up in Alaska. Why do they all assume that the* vampire *is this biggest threat?*

Trey was worried about Alistaire, and irritated that this spider-thing was tearing up their house, but this latest thought left him insulted and angry. He could feel one of his tantrums looming closer, like heat trying to press through the walls on a blistering summer day, but he didn't have time for that, so he pushed it away as best he could.

At the last instant, the spider-thing realized Trey was towering over her. He held his left arm out to the side and his right arm up over his head, leaving her no room to get past him in the narrow hallway. If she had thought about it (and just how much *could* she still think anymore?), she would've jumped away from him, toward the bedroom and bathroom, but instead she tried for the ceiling again.

Her mistake.

Trey's big right hand caught her around her thin waist, his thumb hooking around the lower of her new left-sided limbs. He continued moving forward, stepping over the strips she'd torn through the tile, and slammed her down as hard as he could, adding cracks to the damage she had already done to the floor. This affected her, but not enough as she seized his arm and tried to scuttle closer, her mouth open to sink her teeth into—

Trey's left fist connected with her face with such force, one of her newly enlarged fangs broke loose, dangling from its root by the narrowest strip of enamel (or whatever spider-fangs were made of). *This* finally stunned her, but Trey didn't let up.

He punched her again and again, in the face, in the throat, in the chest, and when she tried to pull away, he squeezed her little arm so tight that he heard it crack, and he pulled her in to punch her more. He hit the spider-thing again, and again, and again, barely aware that he was snarling and yelling louder and louder with each hit but he didn't care so he hit her and hit her and hit her—

"Trey ..." Sean said from behind him.

He didn't pay attention at first, because he wanted to hit her one last time. And, okay, maybe one more time after that—

"That's enough, Trey," Sean called a little louder. "I'm pretty sure ye got her."

Trey listened this time, finally considering the carcass he was holding before him. They couldn't be *sure*-sure, because she had been a vampire and then she was some spider-thing that they had never seen before, but Sean was right that he had messed her up pretty good. Both fangs had broken off, her nose was flat, her jaw looked like it was hanging from only one hinge. She had bled some, though not as much as the damage suggested she should have, and it was a weird, clearish-bluish color.

Trey dropped the spider-thing onto the floor, where her body eased inward, curling into herself just like he had seen dead real spiders do.

"Are ye all right?" Sean asked him. There was an odd quality to Sean's voice that made Trey turn around in worry.

Sean didn't look too good. Swaying a bit on his feet, he had reverted back to human form, and his face was very pale and sweaty. One hand was gripping the shoulder that the spider-thing had bitten, and the exposed bite on his forearm looked awful, swollen and an ugly shade of purple. "I'm okay, Sean. But ... are *you* all right?"

Sean shrugged as he tugged half-heartedly at the webbing that still clung to him in places. "I'll be fine, lad. I just think—"

Without warning, Sean vomited on the hallway floor. It started coming out before he could even bend over, so some of it got on the wall and one leg of Trey's pants.

There was a lot of it, too, and it spread out and started dripping through the torn strips onto Alistaire's coffin below.

It was kind of gross, but Trey was too concerned about Sean to care about that part.

When he finished heaving, he spat a couple of times. He stayed bent over, but turned his head so he could offer Trey a weak smile. "Sorry 'bout that, Trey. Kinda caught me—"

He wasn't done vomiting. His eyes bulged and it *really* shot out now, hitting Trey's same pant leg (ew!) again.

Trey wondered if he should try to help him get to the bathroom, so he could throw up in the toilet instead of all over the hallway and Alistaire's coffin. But he thought that might just spread the mess out further.

He was getting more worried by the second. He had never seen Sean get sick like this. He didn't know that werewolves *could* get sick!

Sean collapsed to his hands and knees, all four landing in the growing puddle of barf, but he didn't seem to notice.

When this wave finally stopped, he didn't even look up. "Okay ..." he said toward the floor, his voice sounding croaky. "I think that was dinner from last week, so ..." He heaved one more time, but it was dry.

Trey stepped, very carefully, over the mess and Sean, so that he was on the clean side. He then knelt down next to his friend. "What can ... I do?"

Sean spat some more. "Water'd be nice."

Trey nodded. "Be right back."

He hurried into the kitchen, filled a glass at the sink, then rushed back as fast as he could without spilling it ... except that it didn't matter, because he dropped the whole thing when he returned to the living room.

Sean was convulsing on the floor. His eyes were wide open, but staring at nothing, and there was actual foam coming out of his mouth.

"Sean!" Trey cried as he crouched beside him. He started to roll Sean over onto his back, but then worried he might choke on his own fluids. He settled for gently holding Sean in place so he didn't hurt himself with his thrashing. That's when he realized the Irishman was burning with fever.

Trey looked around the room, seeking ideas for what to do, but finding none. Even if he turned to the Internet, even if he could get his stupid, slow fingers to type fast enough for this emergency, what could he look up? How to treat a werewolf when he's been bitten by a vampire-spider-thing? And he couldn't call 911, because that would hurt more than it would help. How could he explain everything when they arrived to find a dead man standing over a sick human with a curled-up spider-thing behind them and a coffin visible through the hallway floor?

Sean had two or three more really big convulsions ... then his eyes closed and he passed out. His fever spiked worse than ever.

"What ... do I do?" Trey pleaded. "What do I *do*?!"

But there was no one to help him.

# Seven

Francis Morse screamed when the human-sized spider opened the bedroom window and crawled inside.

Only after the fact did he realize it wasn't an actual spider, but it was fucking close enough — eight limbs, coarse body hairs, too many eyes, *huge* fangs! He had been slumped forward in his usual position on the floor against the wall, drifting somewhere between sleep and the waking world, when he saw *that* crawling in. It didn't even drop down to the floor, but continued along the wall until it disappeared out the bedroom door — which Francis didn't even remember leaving open, showing just how out of it he was getting.

So yeah, he screamed. And kept screaming even after it was gone.

Francis had seen plenty of shadowy things, heard strange noises, since Young Bondye had taken up residence in his home. Aside from the freaking spiders that crawled everywhere, he had never gotten a really good look at any of it, since most of the weirdest shit happened at night. But now, a mutant human-spider was crawling along the wall? That was the end of daylight being his "safe" time to try and sneak some sleep. He was lucky it didn't give him a fucking heart attack—

As if summoned by the mere thought, a sharp pain shot through his chest. He gasped, then wheezed as an aching band tightened around his torso. He hunched over, placing one hand on the floor to keep from falling, and paying no attention to the spider he squashed in doing so. His head spun, and he was certain he would pass out, which brought images of his lying there in a stupor while eight-legged brigands roamed over his helpless body ...

Finally, the symptoms eased and eventually retreated, but the process was long and grudging. He felt better physically, but the gloomy shroud under which he had lived these past weeks was bleaker than ever.

Francis did not want to die. Death had been a perpetual threat, sure, but he had been focused on Bondye, assuming that his demise would come from the voodoo bastard if, or when, the time came. He had not considered the possibility that his poor diet, poorer sleep, and constant fear might give him a goddamn heart attack.

He didn't want to die ... but what the hell could he do?

\* \* \*

Young Bondye smiled into his undying fire as the last of his *araknid* arrived; his eyes need not leave the flames — even those who crowded in outside his peripheral vision were beacons to his ethereal senses. That, too, elated him, for his senses were stronger in this world than in his native domain; the extra-normal was so scarce here, thereby removing all the "white noise" of which he had never before been conscious, that what little did exist stood out with a vibrancy he could not have anticipated.

Yes, things were going well. The *araknid* around him were merely the beginning. Though, he was forced to admit, their growing ranks would be for naught if he could not find the means to bridge the gap between the two worlds.

He must learn to convey the *physical* across the barrier between worlds as well as the spiritual.

His improved senses had led to superior focus, which in turn opened new possibilities to him. And the sweetest of all was that his new vodun bewitchments propagated from the very enemy which he sought to—

Bondye had been so euphoric in his growing self-assurance, he almost missed a vital discrepancy. Almost.

One of his new *araknid* was absent.

Focusing his eyes as well as his mystical senses, he counted the *araknid* around him. The latest to arrive — the one which had likely prompted the pathetic screams from the former owner of this over-endowed house — brought the number present to eight. Granted, his creations were forced, for the time being, to avoid detection as they made their way back to their new master, so that not all had arrived as one.

But he sensed no further *araknid* approaching. And since, over the course of the last several days, he had felt their numbers swell to nine, that meant something had destroyed one of his precious *kreyasyon*.

Bondye was not pleased.

Closing his eyes, he murmured the necessary words, subvocalizing them in a rumbling hum that the *araknid* around him — were they capable of reflecting upon such things — would have felt rather than heard. The flames before him flared bright yellow once, then compressed into a bluish simmer. The kettle thrummed, and his senses expanded out into this foreign world.

His probe was not as distinct as it would have been at night; this place lent refined precision to his arcane perceptions, yes, but the punishing sun, with its so-called "cleansing rays," ever sought to dampen those things from beyond the veil. As such, it took Bondye some minutes to locate and track the residue of his absent *araknid*.

Ah, there it was. First, she had been at the abode of her initiation — her progenitor stood across the flames on Bondye's left — where she had lain dormant until the mortals moved her.

From there, she had rested among the dead, her initial metamorphosis building momentum. And there he would have expected her to remain until the transfiguration was complete. Clearly, someone had interfered. But who? And why? He must know ...

From the bone house she had been taken south, out of the metropolis proper, down to comparatively less populated environs. It was here that she should have awakened, should have begun her journey back to him, compelled by his command. So what had ...?

Bondye unleashed a hateful, almost bestial growl. His lips curling back, he hissed, "*Vanpir*," then spat into the flames.

Another vampire had evidently interfered; the despised creature slept now, but its presence could be no coincidence. *It* must be responsible for moving Bondye's vassal-to-be, and must have had a hand in her apparent destruction. But why had she not simply converted this one as well? This should have been her strongest instinct upon awakening, stronger even than survival — so Bondye had commanded. Another vampire should have made his flock number *ten*, not eight.

Focusing his probe, Bondye stole a closer look at the object of his animus, and a frown deepened on his face ... along with the barest hint of something he had not experienced in some time: Apprehension.

*Old*. Age hung upon this vampire like a fine wine. It had walked the earth for many hundreds of years, longer than any Bondye had personally encountered. He had heard tales of elder ones like this, but this thing was proof. Indeed, in the face of such supernatural maturity, Bondye was uncertain if his *araknid majik* could force the transformation upon it.

And yet ... the creature slept under the light of day. Given the timing of his summons, his *araknid* should have arisen even as the vampire declined. So how could this thing have struck down his *kreyasyon*?

Redoubling his efforts, Bondye focused past the dank stench of the vampire and scrutinized its surroundings. Yes, there lay the remains of his *araknid*, and he detected other beings near it, in the very next room. Not more vampires, he was certain, and yet ...

For the first time in he knew not how long, Young Bondye was startled. The vampire had been unexpected in the moment, but beyond its considerable age, it lay well within the realm of his experience. But this he could not have foreseen.

"*Lougarou*," he whispered aloud as his mind's eye surveyed the werewolf. He had so rarely encountered them, he had half-suspected the vampires were wiping them from existence. This beast would have appeared human to normal sight, but Bondye's senses saw beyond its current pretense. It was truly a werewolf.

Then, this werewolf had destroyed his *araknid*? He looked closer still ...

To be sure, the beast had crossed tooth and claw with his *sèvitè*, as her venom ran through the beast's veins. Yes, he would have to keep an eye on it, to evaluate how the *araknid* venom worked against the alleged healing strength of the werewolf. And yet, when he had probed her remains, her destruction had not appeared to derive from—

Another being entered the room, crossing to kneel next to the sickly werewolf.

Ah, what was this? A *zonbi*?

Not only that, but a zombie under the same roof as a werewolf and a vampire? And more, the zombie appeared to be trying to *help* the beast, rather than attack and eat it as Bondye would have expected. Did this zombie have a master, then? No, Bondye would have sensed that brand of *majik* in an instant.

"*Ki kote ou te soti?*" he again whispered aloud as he stroked his chin. *Where did you come from?*

To Bondye's surprise — this morning seemed full of them — the zombie halted its ministrations and looked around the room. Had it actually *heard* Bondye speak? This had not been his intention; he had not consciously sought to project himself in this manner. But then, he was already watching the creature give aide to the stricken werewolf, wasn't he?

Bondye took stock: No master, indications of irregular intelligence, no overt hunger or drive to violence, and becoming aware of Bondye without his desire for it to do so?

Exactly what manner of *zonbi* was this?

Bondye leaned away from the fire, withdrawing his link down to the thinnest thread but remaining connected to this wondrous abode. He had never encountered such a collective as this strange trio; to discover them *here*, in this bland world with its diminished supernatural assets, was nothing short of astonishing.

But what impact might they have upon his plans? Had they not already interfered by their apparent abduction — and destruction — of his *araknid*, he might have dismissed them out of hand. Perhaps he should focus on their immediate elimination, lest they prove problematic at a time out of his choosing?

Then again ... he could certainly use the vampire, *if* the element of its impressive age could be overpowered. The werewolf he hoped would die, thus removing itself from the equation. But the zombie?

Bondye did not typically dabble with undead thralls, the staple of lesser Bokor. His inherent speciality lay within the *araknid wayòm*, and he had cultivated his expertise in this area. The zombie was masterless, true, but he must also consider its unexpected equipoise of control and evident intelligence.

So strange. This zombie required further thought.

Bondye straightened his posture and stretched his muscles, thus realizing their fatigue. He could push this vessel — which once belonged to a man named Odney Achee, a *houngan sur pwen* of pathetic inability — to great lengths. But if he were to even consider seizing the zombie or facing off with the elder vampire, then he must provide it with some rest and nourishment.

Bondye projected summons to Francis Morse, and was satisfied with the *zouti*'s response time today; perhaps the fool was finally learning his lessons, though Bondye was prepared for further discipline whenever the need arose. Morse stood in his usual place, his eyes wide and his breath rasping in terror as he gaped at the *araknid* assembled around Bondye.

After making the fool wait a minute as he mulled over what might be necessary in dealing with such an old vampire — the base mixture must be strong, strong enough to kill a mortal — he stated, "I need more supplies."

The fool nodded, his eyes never leaving the *araknid*. "Yeah. Okay. The other stuff's already scheduled to arrive, so—"

"I will need," Bondye interrupted; he had no interest in the fool's sniveling, "crushed hemlock. Powdered Jimsonweed. Poisonwood leaves. Sandbox tree sap. Liquid chlordane. More birdlime. And make haste; do not try my patience." Just to make his point clear, he commanded the closest spiders to dance across Morse's feet.

The fool nodded, his face scrunched with concentration, probably in his effort to memorize the list. "Okay. Okay, I'll, uh, I'll get right to work on that." He turned to leave, shuffling sideways so as not to turn his back on the *araknid*.

"Wait," Bondye commanded, and again sent the spiders scurrying.

The fool whimpered. "Y-yeah?"

"Bring me food."

The fool blinked in surprise; this was the first time Bondye had asked for sustenance. "Um, okay. What, uh ... what do you want?"

Bondye considered this. His first impulse had been to demand spiced *legim* stew, but he also recalled Odney Achee's favorite food whenever the man could get it. Why not indulge himself?

"Bring me pizza."

Morse gaped at him as though he had grown a second head; it was almost enough to make Bondye smile. "You ... you want *pizza*?"

"Sausage pizza. With peppers. Spicy sausage, spicy peppers."

The man was so dazed, he merely nodded and left the room. As soon as the door was closed, Bondye allowed quiet laughter to slip free. Such a *moun sòt*.

The moment passed, and Bondye returned his attention to his *araknid*, still standing in silence around him. Enough about the zombie and vampire and sick werewolf.

For now ...

*     *     *

*Pizza!* Francis groused. *He's got me ordering a fucking* pizza. *What kind of evil voodoo villain orders pizza? I always knew he had to be a charlatan in some way. Looks like I finally found my angle.*

This last bit struck him as far more amusing than he knew it really was, and he bit down on his lip until it bled to contain the laughter. Bondye might hear it, and he believed that his survival hinged on staying off the bastard's radar whenever possible.

Blowing the handful of spiders away from his laptop, he batted off a few stubborn slowpokes with more force than necessary. Then, while he waited for the computer to boot up, he jotted down the latest shopping list as quickly as he could before he forgot it.

*Crushed hemlock, powdered Jimsonweed, poisonwood leaves ... Jesus, what the hell* is *this stuff?* He thought he recognized hemlock, and he knew the birdlime by now, but that was pretty much it. The rest sounded like plants, but chlordane?

Once he had the laptop up and running, he ordered the man's goddamn sausage and peppers, requesting "extra spicy" and hoping the store could meet Bondye's standards. He entertained a brief fantasy of somehow getting hold of ghost peppers for it — "Here's your *spicy*, asshole!" he would scream. "Enjoy it!" Wouldn't that feel good? Until one of those giant spiders ate him, that was.

Once that menial task was out of the way, Francis started Googling the stuff he had written down.

In very short order, he realized that the man was ordering a shit-ton of *poison*. Bondye never told Francis what amount of these things to get, so he always ordered as much as he could without rousing any suspicion — the last thing he needed was a visit by the local police, which would only get him, and the cops, killed. But with all this stuff, he was definitely going to have to use one of his alternate IDs and order it through a discreet server. Hell, that chlordane stuff turned out to be a pesticide that hadn't been sold in the United States since 1988. How he was supposed to get his hands on that without raising—

*Pesticide.*

He stopped.

*Chlordane is a pesticide.*

While Bondye would no doubt react violently to an unexpected visit by the police, he *had* to tolerate delivery people bringing stuff to the front door, since Francis had become his personal shopper but wasn't allowed to leave the house. And all this toxic shit was going to require signatures, no matter how much money he spent to grease the wheels.

Okay, so chlordane — assuming he could get it; please, God, let him be able to get it! — and all this other poison would be arriving soon. Could the bastard truly be aware of any additional poisons crossing the threshold? He was betting that Bondye wouldn't deign to notice the details.

For the first time in a while, a vague hope kindled within Francis. Just how connected was Bondye to his normal eight-legged critters? He knew they monitored his movements throughout the house; they swarmed the windows and doors if he got too close. But would Bondye "feel" it if a bunch of them suddenly died?

*Careful, old man. You don't know how this stuff*

*works. And even if it does, what if the bastard* can *feel it when they die? And what if he's got an honest-to-God voodoo doll of you up there?*

The thought made Francis' chest ache, literally. A reminder of his near-coronary earlier.

But what choice did he have?

Francis spent the next two hours — excepting the interruption to accept Bondye's fucking pizza — ordering the items from the list; as expected, it took so long because the stuff was hard to get, and he ended up clicking around some pretty shady websites.

Then he started doing more research on chlordane. It was mostly used for termites, but it could also be used to kill spiders.

*Okay, looks promising ...*

But no, as he read along, he saw that it didn't do what he needed most — to kill spiders *fast*.

*Okay, something else then. There has to be* something, *something newer, something faster!*

Looking further, he found a number of aerosol pesticides that claimed to kill spiders instantly, but a nearly equal number of bad customer reviews stated that it didn't. And Bondye had specifically asked for liquid chlordane, which wouldn't camouflage the arrival of aerosol cans as well as Francis was hoping.

The more he poked around Google, the more confused and frustrated he became. He found tons of information, and just as much conflicting info. This works; this works better; always use this; never use that; on and on it went until his eyes lost focus.

If only he could get some fucking *sleep*, even for just one hour ...

What he needed was feedback from a professional, someone who knew what the hell they were talking about, not a bunch of list-making amateurs or hippies trying to protect Mother Earth.

His first impulse was to pull up the biggest pest control companies in the Los Angeles area. But places like that would probably have a waiting list for an appointment, and who knew if they were willing to talk to a do-it-yourself guy?

He needed a smaller operator, someone very local with an excellent reputation. Someone whom he could trust when he asked, "How can I kill spiders as *immediately* as possible?"

A few minutes later, Francis was looking at Randy McDonnell's website.

# ... 8 ...

Trey paced and paced, counting the minutes until Alistaire woke up. He could not remember ever feeling this anxious before.

He wrung his hands as he looked at Sean, lying on the bed. His Irish friend was in such bad shape. The bite wounds on his shoulder and forearm were swollen purple-black, with angry red lines flaring around all of it. He shivered in his sleep (and Trey knew that calling it "sleep" was too hopeful a word for it). Sean's body temperature always ran high compared to a normal human, but Trey could feel the heat coming off him every time his pacing brought him close to the bed. He had put some Ziploc bags of ice under Sean's neck and in the crooks of his armpits, but the ice was almost melted; he would have to replace them soon, again.

Between checking on Sean and making a sloppy effort to clean up the vomit in the hallway, Trey had researched online what he could about dealing with spider bites, allergic reactions, and something called "anaphylaxis." But most suggestions he found were just dead ends. The Triumvirate did not keep any common medicinal stuff at home, because Sean's being a werewolf usually made it almost impossible for him to get sick! So Trey had no more access to Tylenol or Benadryl than he had to the local emergency room.

In the end, he was left with nothing else but to try to lower the high fever, to keep Sean from burning up until his body could fight off the venom.

The only bright side to this nightmare was that his hunger had not bothered him all day. Instead, he was left with a growing anger, a rage to find who or what was behind this whole weird mission and hurt them, hurt them bad! But he had to keep a lid on that so he didn't accidentally tip too far over into one of his stupid tantru—

A whispered voice from the hallway brought his pacing and his thoughts to a screeching halt: "*Barmherziger G-Gott.*"

Alistaire!

He *had* heard it, right? It wasn't wishful thinking, was it? No, it had to be Alistaire. He didn't know enough German to imagine something like "Barm-whatsit."

He heard Alistaire say something like "*Eine Spinne...*" (more German!) before he could even reach the door. His legs were always sluggish, but now they felt almost gooey with relief.

"Alistaire!" he called.

"*Yes, Trey,*" the vampire answered.

"Alistaire!" he cried, literally.

They met at the doorway, and he threw his arms around the vampire, pulling him into a super-tight hug of desperate need.

Eventually, he stopped the hug, but he kept his hands on Alistaire's arms, just because it made him feel better. "Alistaire," he said, his voice a little thicker than normal, "Sean ... Sean's hurt bad. He's ... sick."

Alistaire gently pulled himself free and pushed past him into the bedroom.

"*Trey, tell me what happened ...*"

Trey told him everything after Alistaire closed his

coffin that morning. It took some time, with Trey's halted speech (so frustrating!), but he described the vampire-spider-thing's attack and Sean's reaction to the two bites in as much detail as he could.

"... so I've ... tried to keep his fever down ... with ice," he finished, knowing how miserable he sounded.

"*You have done very well, my friend,*" Alistaire assured him. "*Under the circumstances, I can think of no better recourse. Even if you had risked all to seek medical attention for Sean, I question what they could have done for him. Much like my reasoning for absconding with Summer Levin's body, precious few physicians in this world would have the slightest experience with these matters—*"

Alistaire cut himself off a little when Sean's eyes fluttered open. The vampire leaned forward, probably a little hopeful, but Trey knew better by this point.

"*Sean ...?*" Alistaire spoke.

But Sean didn't respond to his name, and his eyes closed again a second later. Trey had watched him do that several times over the day.

Alistaire didn't comment on the letdown, but leaned further forward, inspecting the horrible wound on Sean's shoulder. Then he turned to look past Trey at the vampire-spider-thing's body, still lying in the hallway. (Trey had thought, several times, about moving it ... but where? Outside, where someone might see or at least smell it? No, that was one more thing he waited for Alistaire to decide.)

"*This goes beyond my expertise,*" Alistaire said. "*I am at a loss. And as Sean noted last night, this has been occurring far too often on this mission.*"

These words wrenched a soft gasp of disbelief from Trey.

He felt bad about it right away (it wasn't Alistaire's

fault if he didn't know everything about *every*thing), but still ... he had spent this whole, terrible day just waiting for Alistaire to awaken and solve the problem. And hearing Alistaire admit that he was also stumped was a really huge disappointment.

Alistaire placed a comforting hand on Trey's slumped shoulder and said, *"We must pray that Sean's own system can fight off whatever venom or other toxins this creature introduced."* He even offered the big man a reassuring smile (and Alistaire didn't smile very often). *"Sean is strong, even by werewolf standards. I have Faith that he will survive."*

Trey nodded.

Stepping back into the hallway, Alistaire squatted in front of the destroyed creature. *"I had known her body had been mutating into* something, *but I'm astonished by how extreme a change occurred in the hours I slept."* He cocked his head to one side, studying her. *"The extra limbs, coupled with the startling alterations to her skin and face, do indeed give her the look of a dead spider."*

Trey offered, "She's really ... gross-looking."

Alistaire agreed. *"I suppose I should repeat my thorough, mist-form examination of the body, inspect the culmination of the transformation I observed, but the notion repels me."*

"She was ... after you."

This caught Alistaire off guard. *"I beg your pardon?"*

"I think ... she was after *you*."

He rose to his feet. *"Please explain."*

"When she first ... woke up ... she was focused on us." Trey's brow furrowed, his gaze drifting as he thought hard. "Actually, she might've been ... *confused* by me. But ... she didn't like Sean at all. I think ... she went through the wall ... to get around me ... to get to him." His eyes returned to Alistaire. "But then she started ... almost ignoring Sean, too. I think he ... only got bit on the arm ... because he grabbed her ... tried to stop her ..."

Alistaire cocked his head again. "*From doing what?*"

Trey pointed. "That."

Alistaire looked to where he indicated, at the scratched, gouged, torn up hallway floor over his coffin's hiding place. "*Ah, yes. I immediately noticed this upon rising, but learning the specifics behind it is not at all encouraging.*"

"Do you have ... any idea *why* she ... wanted you so bad?"

Alistaire considered his reply before answering, "*I have a hypothesis, which is even less encouraging.*" He indicated the fallen creature. "*This 'meta-spider,' for want of a better term, began its metamorphosis as a vampire. You recall our description of the photographer's remains — wounds which make more sense now, seeing what attacked you and Sean — but you yourself saw that the vampire girl suffered nothing more than two abdominal wounds. Something, almost certainly another meta-spider, fed upon the photographer and initiated the mutation of the vampire. If these meta-spiders are capable of continually 'procreating' their own kind, and if said procreation requires more than a mere human, then she might have been attempting to transform* me *into a meta-spider like herself.*"

"And ... Sean and me?"

"*It would seem that neither a werewolf nor a zombie met her necessary criteria. Perhaps only vampires will do, perhaps not.*" Alistaire stopped for a second, thinking. "*You said that the meta-spider seemed 'confused' by you. What did you mean by that?*"

Trey shrugged. "Not sure, really. Just ... a feeling I

got. It was ... well, she *knew* she didn't ... like Sean at all. But ... she didn't seem to know ... what do with me."

Alistaire nodded slowly, considering this.

Then Trey stood straighter as he remembered something, maybe something important! "Earlier ... just before you finished studying ... the, uh, the meta-spider ... and later, after I ... put Sean to bed, I think ... I heard something."

*"From within the house?"*

Trey shook his head. "I don't think so. It ... it was more like I ... heard it in my *head*. But when you ... came out of your mist form ... I, uh, I forgot about it. And ... later, with Sean so sick ..."

*"What was it? A sound that you recognized?"*

Trey shook his head again. "No, no, it was ... a voice, a *man's* voice."

*"A man's voice. Interesting. What did this man say?"*

"I couldn't ... understand him. He wasn't talking ... in English." He thought back on what he had heard ...

*Obeyi, araknid ...*

"It was kind of ... like French. But ... I think it was maybe Creole."

Alistaire raised an eyebrow at that. *"Very interesting. Did your family speak Haitian Creole in your home? Neither you nor your sister had a discernable accent, but I believe your grandmother did."*

Trey shook his head. "No, we grew up ... speaking just English. But I ... heard it from my relatives. You know ... cousins and stuff. And Grandma and ... Grandpa, yeah." He thought a moment longer, then nodded. "Yeah ... the more I think about it ... I'm pretty sure it was ... Creole."

*"But you did not understand the words?"*

"No. Sorry."

Alistaire waved that off. *"No need to apologize, Trey.*

*I would recognize, say, Romansh if I heard it, but that does not mean I would understand what was actually being said."* Alistaire tapped a finger on his chin as he considered this new information. *"And you say you heard this man speaking Creole the first time shortly before sunrise?"*

"Yeah. Right before ... you finished looking over ... the maybe-vampire."

*"In other words, shortly before she rose and attacked you."*

Trey's eyes widened. "Yeah."

Alistaire looked to the meta-spider. *"And you say the sunlight did not affect her?"*

"Not that ... I could tell, no."

*"So, in theory, this man's voice may have 'activated' her by some means, knowing that the sun's rays were no longer a deterrent. But this still begs the question of how. What, exactly, are we dealing with here?"* He pondered this. "And the second time he spoke?"

"That one wasn't ... wasn't as clear. It's funny ... but it sounded more like ... the man was maybe ... talking to himself ... or something. And there's more ..."

*"Yes?"*

"Something about the woman ... and the man's voice, everything ... gave me, um ..." Trey's forehead scrunched up as he fought to remember the right word. Man, he hated it when he couldn't remember the right word! "Gave me that ... repeat feeling, that ... you've, um ..."

Alistaire offered, *"Deja vu?"*

"Yes! That! This whole thing ... the spider, the voice, it kind of, um ... tastes or smells ...?" This time Trey waved himself off, a big gesture with both arms. "Anyway, what I mean is ... right before the, uh ... the meta-spider woke up ... and I mean *right* before ... I thought I might've figure out ... what it reminded me of. *Voodoo*."

Alistaire's eyes widened. "*Voodoo. Yes. Yes, Trey. I believe you have found the missing element.*"

For a moment, in spite of how bad things were, Trey beamed with pride.

Alistaire continued, "*In retrospect, I feel I should have made the connection. The metamorphosis I observed occurring within the female vampire is consistent with other transmutations I have witnessed in centuries past, such as when a hex caused its victim to begin transforming into a snake. Not the exact same, to be sure, but similar enough.*" He shook his head. "*Very slipshod of me, but excellent work on your part, Trey.*

"*So, it would seem we are dealing with a voodoo priest, presumably a Bokor to be working such dark magic. Not unlike the Bokor who murdered you, then brought you back as a slave — may things work out as poorly for our new opponent.*"

Trey grunted in agreement.

"*This Bokor has 'infected' the vampire community somehow; though I have never heard of this particular methodology, I have already demonstrated my general ignorance of voodoo. Under other circumstances, I might applaud such an attack on vampires. But we have seen what these meta-spiders will do to humankind as well. Vampires are serving as raw material for a new breed of monster that does what all monsters do, prey upon those we have sworn to protect.*

"*Now, Trey, you briefly mentioned something about 'taste' and 'smell' before cutting yourself off. What were you going to say?*"

"Just that ... well, this whole thing ... has a kind of ... of *feel* to it, that reminds me ... of taste or smell. Kind of. It's ... hard to describe. Sorry."

*"Not at all. To sum it up, you can* sense *the presence of this voodoo priest — or at least his handiwork — like a form of extrasensory perception. Would that be correct?"*

"Yeah. Yeah, I ... guess I can." He glanced back in at Sean, poor sick Sean. If only his extra-thing had been enough to—

*"Do you think you could use this extrasensory perception to* track *this Bokor?"*

Trey looked at Alistaire in surprise ... and then a big grin spread across his face.

# NINE

Randy McDonnell collapsed into his office chair. He did not sit, he did not plop, he collapsed.

How much of it was from working a truly long day, and how much was side-effects from his Widow bite? The scales might be tipped a little toward the latter. His neck was still inflamed, the muscles on that side — from his ear down to the outer curve of his shoulder — kept cramping on him, and he alternated between feeling chilly and feverish.

Strictly speaking, Randy knew he probably should have gone to the emergency room; Lori sure pushed for that when she saw the inflamed, red area around the bite. But there wasn't a whole lot the ER could do for him except give him painkillers and antivenin, and — thanks to a quid-pro-quo from a client who was also a doctor — he already had access to both. He had taken an extra-hot shower last night and this morning, which helped. And in the end, it was also a matter of pride: He was an exterminator, damn it; he wasn't going to run crying to mama every time he got bitten by a spider.

Fatigue, muscle aches, mild on-again/off-again nausea, and feverish symptoms aside, he had discovered a silver lining to getting bitten: His itchies had abated, somewhat. He guessed once he got a taste of exactly what he had feared ...

Stretching his very sore, cramping muscles, he pushed aside his latest captive — yet another unknown spider species; seriously, where were these things coming from? — and pulled up his company website. Lori often pitched in to help with work-related messages, but she had been buried under a mountain of essays to grade this last week. On Randy's side of things, he had booked so many back-to-back appointments this morning, he had turned off his phone's auto-alert.

Today, four messages awaited his attention, and every single one of them had "spider" somewhere in the subject line.

"Gee," he muttered, "what a fucking surprise." Which itself was a surprise, because Randy was not normally given to talking to himself.

He skimmed through the first two, one of which had actually come in last night after he shut down his computer. Spiders in the garage were now spiders in my kitchen, spiders inside my car, please get here as soon as possible, et cetera, et cetera, he got the gist and would message them back before going home tonight.

The third message down, however, got his attention.

The sender, who only identified himself as "FRM," was not requesting an appointment:

Mr. McDonnell,

I need your professional advice on something. Been looking online and reading Amazon reviews and all of them conflict, so hoping you can please help me.

I'm looking for an easy to get pesticide that kills spiders fast. And I mean FAST! Not worried about killing eggs. Also not worried about residue, no children here. I need something that kills spiders the SECOND you spray it on them. Money not an issue, so if I have to pay $100 per can, I'll pay it. I just need you to tell me *what* to buy.

Or if *you* have something I can buy, something "professional grade" or whatever, works for me. Just let me know. Again, money no object here. Name your price.

Please email or text me your feedback at earliest convenience. Please do not call, hours are weird here right now.

Thank you so much.

— FRM

Randy sat back, stretching his neck as unconsciously as he had been scratching phantom itches the day before. He rubbed his eyes under his reading glasses, then looked over the message a second time.

It wasn't the weirdest message he had ever received, but it was up there.

Clearly, he was dealing with some rich dude; that much was obvious. FRM wouldn't be the first rich client he had dealt with, so he knew how demanding they could be. But this guy's message had enough "please" and "thank you" to detract from any overt pushiness.

The message came in hours ago, so as far as Randy knew, he might have already gotten what he needed from another exterminator. Still, what could it hurt? If FRM really meant "name your price" ... again, his kids' college debts were always looming over Randy's shoulder. Until they graduated and started making real money of their own...

Clicking the mouse, he began composing FRM's email. He knew he would be more likely to catch the guy if he sent a text, but he really wasn't in the mood to single-tap his phone's keyboard.

> Good evening, FRM,
>     It sounds like you have a real spider problem on your hands! I would be more than happy to visit your home or work place, wherever you're having the trouble, and take a look. Maybe it's something I can take care of for you.

Randy thought for a moment, then signed off "Randy McDonnell." He could suggest some off-the-shelf pesticides, of course — name brands that supposedly killed on contact — but from first-hand experience, he knew none of them would work as fast as his own chemicals. And they really were his own, sort of. He had taken to mixing a few different ones together over the years, especially in cases where toxic residue issues didn't apply, which was evidently the case here. Not to mention that he had starting tweaking it just a little bit stronger since this whole "spider craze" got rolling. All told, he would feel a lot better handling the job himself than passing along a bunch of toxic chemicals to some amateur. FRM could end up making himself sick, then blame Randy for selling it to him.

And the more he thought about it, the more FRM's need for the "fastest" pesticide rubbed him the wrong way. Why would he need to kill spiders in the blink of an eye? Sure, he could be experiencing his own spider explosion. Or maybe he wanted it for something else entirely? Hell, the guy might want to use it to poison his wife or something.

Randy responded to all the other messages in simpler

"here's my schedule" fashion and was seconds from logging off when a reply from FRM popped onto his screen.

*Damn*, he mused, *it's like he was just sitting there waiting for an answer.*

Clicking it open, he read:

Mr. McDonnell,

I appreciate the offer but I need to handle things myself. My situation here is complicated by an unwanted houseguest (not the spiders).

Since a simple "try this brand" would have been the easiest reply for you, I'm guessing you do have access to professional grade pesticides that work much faster than anything I could get on the market.

If so, I would be forever in your debt if you could arrange delivery to my home as soon as possible. Again, money no object. Tomorrow at exactly 10 a.m. would be best, as I am already expecting some deliveries at that same time.

Seriously, if you have stuff that will kill any spider, big or small, on contact, name your price.

— FRM

*Okay, this is getting really weird.*

Randy leaned back in his chair again. Maybe the guy *had* stumbled across a massive spider infestation in his rich-man's basement or attic. Maybe he was trying to eliminate the problem before his "unwanted houseguest" — social rival? judging boss? mother-in-law? — found out anything was wrong. Except that his first message said he didn't care about residue, which suggested he didn't care about any chemical smell. And *that* poked a hole in the hiding-the-spider-problem theory, because surely his guest would ask about it.

Over the next ten minutes, Randy decided three times to just drop the matter, that he had other things to worry about right now ... and all three times, he reconsidered. "Money not an issue," "money no object," and "name your price" kept gnawing at his resolve.

Keeping up the business, being the little guy surrounded by larger companies ... wouldn't he be stupid *not* to take advantage of this? He didn't want to completely gouge the guy. He could quote, say, double what it actually cost him; FRM didn't sound like he would care, and Randy could replenish his stock at half-price.

*Or why not stall for time?* he asked himself. *He wants it fast, sure, but if he's in too big a hurry to wait an extra day, he can just get it somewhere else. Get his address, tell him you can deliver it the day* after *tomorrow. Buy yourself an extra twenty-four hours to think about this.*

*And to maybe find out who the hell "FRM" really is.*

So that's what he did. He agreed to sell FRM his professional pesticide blend — provided FRM was willing to sign the same waiver Randy always had to sign — and quoted him the double-price. He felt a little guilty about that last part, but kept repeating to himself, "College debts, college debts, college debts ..."

He stressed that the earliest he could make delivery would be at Noon the day after tomorrow. He didn't state "take it or leave it" flat out, but he was firm.

Less than two minutes later, FRM replied. He agreed to everything, requesting only that Randy arrive as close to exactly Noon as possible; apparently, he was really big on timing multiple deliveries to arrive together.

*His "houseguest" must be a huge pain in the ass*, Randy thought with a smirk.

Okay. That was that. He would deal with all of this tomorrow; he even pushed aside the container holding his latest eight-legged mystery. He would see what he could find out about FRM in the morning, maybe even drive by the guy's posh house — which he *knew* was posh, based on the address. But not now. Now, he was tired, achy, his Widow bite was burning again, and he just wanted go home to Lori and—

As he placed one hand on the laptop lid and the other on the mouse to shut it down, another email *pinged* in.

*Just ignore it. You already made that decision. Wife now, work later.*

And he was going to do just that, right after checking to see who sent it. What if FRM wanted to ask one more—?

Nope. It was from Google Alerts.

Randy had set up a Google Alert yesterday, priming it to search for anything including the words "spiders," "Los Angeles," and "unusual" or "bizarre."

*Okay, fine. I'll look at this one last thing. Hell, maybe someone's come up with an explanation for what's going on. Then I could sleep that much easier.*

He expected the Alert to take him to either a news organization or an exterminator's website. He was not expecting something called *Watchdogs of the Weird & Unusual*.

*Oh, for God's sake* ... He rolled his eyes as *The X-Files* theme played. Sighing, he skimmed over to the blog entry in question.

And then, in spite of himself, he began to read in detail ...

# ... 10 ...

Alistaire was not happy. That always made Trey kind of nervous, but tonight it also left him a little bit hopeful.

Alistaire was not happy because he was having trouble making a decision. And so long as he was having trouble, that meant he hadn't decided against it yet.

Sean began shivering again. Trey, who sat next to him on the edge of the bed, reached over and covered him with more of the blanket. He then rested his hand lightly on the sick man's chest, feeling his heart beating a little too fast.

Alistaire paced from their little bedroom, out into the hallway to stare at the meta-spider's body, and back again, thinking really hard about their situation. He had been thinking about it for a while now. Trey understood why Alistaire was torn, but he also knew the choice he hoped Alistaire would make.

When Trey told Alistaire earlier that, yeah, he was pretty sure he could use his voodoo-sense trick to track down the voodoo priest, they were pumped and ready to go (well, *he* was pumped, Alistaire never really got "pumped"). But then they both realized:

Sean. They couldn't leave Sean alone while he was so sick.

And usually it would be Trey who would stay behind for something like this. Yeah, they had never had anything quite like *this*, but with Trey's slow brain and lumbering body and dead-looking appearance, it was usually Alistaire or Sean who scoped things out. It was sometimes frustrating (especially lately, with the hunger gnawing at him), but he understood ... most of the time.

But this was different, because it was *Trey* who could sense the voodoo magic, *Trey* who could maybe track the voodoo priest down, so he *had* to go. But Alistaire didn't want him to go out alone. But someone had to stay with Sean. But Trey was the only one of them who had not entered the medical examiner's office, so no witnesses could place him at the scene, and no one should be looking for him for any reason.

But, but, but ...

That was why they were stuck in this situation (Alistaire called it a "dilemma"). And though he wasn't ready to admit it to Alistaire, it kind of hurt Trey's feelings, too, because it meant that Alistaire didn't think he could be trusted out on his own.

*And is he wrong about that?* his hunger snickered.

*Shut up!*

As if he could sense Trey's mood (and knowing Alistaire, maybe he could?), Alistaire chose that moment to stop in front of Trey. His hands clasped behind his back, he still took a few more seconds to actually start talking.

*"I have a number of concerns about your undertaking this reconnaissance on your own,"* Alistaire finally said. *"Not the least of which is that you have only driven our auto on a handful of occasions, and always short distances."*

"Like to the ... gas station and back."

Alistaire nodded. *"Precisely. However, I am forced to admit that my foremost reluctance stems from your recent moods."*

*Uh-oh.* But Trey said nothing, just tilted his head in

question.

"*Last night, for example, your out-of-character reaction to being asked to stay in the car. Other small examples, each inconsequential offhand, but collectively concerning. In short, Trey, you have seemed a bit out of sorts of late. Under less pressing circumstances, I would think little of it, if anything at all — everyone is entitled to the occasional sour mood from time to time. Now, however...*"

He paused, maybe to let Trey speak up. When he didn't, Alistaire went on.

"*Could you perhaps explain your recent hints of petulance, Trey? Anything you might wish to share, before we finalize our decision on how to proceed?*"

This time Alistaire set his feet apart and settled in, his face patient but serious, clearly ready to stand there and wait until Trey offered up some kind of answer.

*Now,* Trey thought. *Now's the time to tell him about the hunger. I won't get a better chance than this. I just need to spit it out, get it over with, and then Alistaire will help me.*

*Don't be an idiot,* whispered the hunger. *Think about it, if you can get that stupid brain of yours to focus long enough.*

He wanted to tell that voice to *Shut Up!* again ... but something about it made him sit and listen. Alistaire was waiting, so he didn't have a lot of time to decide what he was going to say.

*What's going to happen if you tell him that you've been fighting the urge to eat* people*? Do you think there's the slightest chance he'll let you out of his sight? Or that he'll even trust you around Sean, while he's so weak and helpless? Hmm?*

Trey did everything he could to keep his face neutral

as he stared at the floor. He could feel Alistaire watching, waiting ...

*He won't trust you on your own, he won't trust you at home. So what do you think will be his solution, Trey?*

*I ... I don't know,* he thought. If he could still sweat, he would be drenched.

*You know. You're just afraid to admit it.*

Trey opened his mouth. He had to say something.

*The vampire who has spent hundreds of years destroying supernatural threats ... and you want to confess to* being *a supernatural threat? Find two working brains cells, rub them together, and figure out what comes next.*

Trey's heart stopped. Well, not for real, but that's what it felt like.

And he was out of time.

"Yeah, I guess I ... have been, uh ... 'out of sorts' lately. I've had this ... new feeling. I've been, uh ... I've been feeling, um ..."

Alistaire waited.

"I've been feeling ... restless. Because I ... I want to do more."

*Coward*, Trey spat at himself, inside. But outside he looked up and met Alistaire's blue eyes, and held on to that eye contact.

*"In what way?"*

"You and Sean ... I know your brains work ... better than mine ... most of the time. But it still ... sometimes feels like I could ... do more for our Triumvirate. But ... you won't let me. Like, you don't think ... that I *can* do more. Like ... you don't trust me ... or something."

Alistaire opened his mouth to speak, but Trey kept going.

"I want a chance ... to prove myself. I want to ... show you and Sean ... that I can handle myself ... like you two.

And for *you* to show ... that you do trust me."

*Oh, you ... you liar!* he swore at himself. *You dirty, stinking* liar!

*I didn't lie.*

*Maybe not. But you're still twisting stuff around! Alistaire and Sean have been so good to you, and this is how you repay them? With these ... these twisty words?*

Even as the inner tirade screamed through his mind, Trey somehow kept his face blank. As disgusting and selfish as his sneakiness was, he really *hadn't* lied, either. He really had felt all those things as the years had passed and his condition had improved.

But this was Alistaire Bachman he was dealing with here. Would Alistaire see through him?

*Of course he will! He's Alistaire! Any second now he's going to vamp out and he'll twist your neck around until your stupid, lying head pops right off your crappy dead body and the last thing you'll—*

"*Trey,*" Alistaire said, "*we owe you an apology.*"

Trey swelled with both floating elation and crippling guilt. But still he kept his face (mostly) still.

"*I had not realized that you felt this way; nor did Sean, I am certain. You are and have always been a valuable member of our Triumvirate.*" Alistaire fell silent for a moment, a thoughtful look on his face, but before Trey could ask, he continued, "*If you are to track this voodoo magic, how will you proceed?*"

*Wow*, Trey thought, his mind filled with wonder. *He's ... he's not only gonna let me go, he's letting me make the plan!* His elation grew higher still.

But his guilt deepened, too.

"I was thinking that ... I would start by driving ... back to the morgue area. See if ... I can pick up anything ... from around there."

Alistaire nodded. *"A reasonable place to start. But if you find anything, we would need—"*

"I can bring along ... one of those prepaid cell phones ... that Sean got for us."

*"Ah, yes. The mobile telephones,"* Alistaire mused, looking kind of self-conscious while he did it. Trey thought maybe he was thinking back to when he first encountered one of the disposable phones (it had been kind of funny to watch). *"I often flatter myself as being more adaptable than my undead brethren, but ... sometimes these modern things escape my recollection. So, you would be able to contact me immediately if you find anything?"*

"Yeah."

Alistaire glanced at Sean, who was still shivering under the blanket.

*"Very well. Please show me the simplest way to operate one of these mobile telephones, then you may take the car to do some reconnaissance while I remain here to watch over Sean."*

Trey couldn't hide his excited grin anymore as he stood and crossed to the bedroom closet. He grabbed the boxes from the top shelf, dropped them at the foot of the bed, and opened one to pull out the disposable phone.

*"I do wish to stress, Trey,"* Alistaire said as he worked, *"that I want you doing this for investigation only. Do not take any offensive actions on your own; we do not know what numbers you may face. Find the trail, learn what you can, then return home. When Sean has recovered, we will strike together. Do you understand?"*

"I do." That much was completely, 100% true. He loved the idea of going on a mission by himself, of proving himself to the others (and this much important stuff to focus on should shove his hunger all the way into the background!). But he sure didn't want to go up against any more of the meta-spider-things without help. Yeah, he beat the last one, but what if he ran into two? Or three? No, thank you, sir!

*"Excellent. All right, then ..."* Alistaire eyed the phone with suspicion. *"What do I need to know to operate this?"*

"First thing we'll need to do ... is to plug it in ... and get it charging. I will be able ... to charge mine in the car..."

*   *   *

Trey drove, very slowly, into Los Angeles proper, taking the regular streets instead of the freeway, to give his slower reflexes time to react if he had any problems. He was grateful that it was late and traffic wasn't bad.

He kept both hands on the steering wheel at all times, at 10 o'clock and 2 o'clock, just like he had been taught. Funny enough, when Sean tried to teach him how to drive soon after they moved out to California, they were both really surprised that Trey already knew how — the lessons Trey's grandmother had given him, and those Lucius Bekele had given to Travis, worked their way to the surface of Trey's brain.

Arriving from a different direction, Trey glanced over at the morgue place. They had extra police cars parked there tonight. No question that the missing body had been noticed! He turned the corner, heading down the same street as before.

When he got about as far down as they had been on their previous visit, able to barely see the morgue around the gentle curve of the road, Trey made an extra-super-careful U-turn, then an extra-super-careful parallel park, just one car-length back from where they parked last time.

He set the parking brake, shut off the engine, and sat back.

*Now what?*

He didn't have an easy answer for that. So much of it depended on this sense of his for the voodoo magic ...

Trey pulled out his sunglasses, but set them on the dash, in case anyone walked up to the car or started giving him funny looks. His skin might get overlooked at night, but his eyes never did; his eyes never failed to freak out regular people. He then rested his hands on his lap, relaxed back against the headrest, and tried to clear his mind.

*That never takes much work, does it, you big liar?*

*Be quiet,* he scolded himself. *I'm doing an important job now — I get to be the scout this time. This is* my *mission.*

Once his brain felt (mostly) relaxed, Trey tried reaching out. Where was that smell, that taste of voodoo? Was it here? Did it stick around and spread out this far, or would he have to get out and walk closer to the morgue? No one would have seen him last time, but he would rather not do that if he could get around it.

A hint, a whisper, a whiff ... he needed something to get him started. After that, he was pretty sure he could follow it. But he needed that first clue ...

Time passed. Trey wasn't sure how much. His eyelids had drooped a little as he focused on not-focusing (which was kind of confusing), but at least, as a zombie, he was in no danger of falling asleep.

He just sat and waited, for *some*thing.

And then it came.

The taste (this time it definitely reminded him of a taste, not a smell) swept past him, jolted through him in a flash, then it was gone. But it was the something he'd been waiting for! He slipped on his sunglasses and got out of the car, wanting nothing between himself and that taste, not even the windows.

Shuffling around the trunk to get out of traffic, Trey waited for a repeat. He was tempted to stick out his tongue, to see if that would help, but he soon realized that it couldn't because he wasn't *really* tasting it, not with his mouth but with his mind. And besides, he would look pretty silly just standing there with his tongue out.

Movement caught his eye, and he looked to his forward-right. It took him a second to recognize the same homeless guy from before, the one who had pushed his shopping cart into the alley. The cart was already in its spot, the movement came from the guy messing around with his dirty blanket as he sat on the ground against the far wall.

When he saw this homeless man last time, the hunger had tried to tempt Trey out of the car with the "smell" of his flesh. Now that Trey was actually standing outside, he could tell he had been right about that being stupid. He couldn't smell the guy from here, so there's no way he could have from inside the car. *So there!* he thought with some pride.

In fact, looking at the homeless man tonight wasn't tempting him at all, which also made him feel proud. He had known that if he was given an important mission, with really important things to focus on, that he would be able to push the hunger away until this was all over with. *Then* he would talk to Alistaire and Sean about it, so he had been right to ... well, to fib his way out of the house.

*Is that so?* the hunger's dark voice whispered. *Then why are you stalking the vagrant even now?*

Trey was shocked. Without realizing it, he had walked around the car onto the sidewalk and was halfway to the alley! He stopped immediately, feeling the guilt on his face, looking around to see if anyone was watching him ...

No one was. Of the small number of people walking instead of driving, not one of them was giving Trey a second look, but he couldn't just stand there in the middle of the sidewalk, either. Should he get back in the car and drive somewhere else? Where else could he go? The morgue place was their only real lead ... well, here and the photographer's apartment, but he guessed it wouldn't be a good idea to go poking around an honest-to-goodness crime scene—

"You all right, hon?"

Trey blinked in surprise, glancing around to find the lady who had spoken (and to see if she had actually spoken to *him*).

"Here, hon."

Trey looked and saw that she was definitely talking to him. It was the homeless guy, except he wasn't a "guy" at all! The lady was just so rough and worn-looking, Trey had assumed she was a "he."

The homeless guy— uh, lady gestured for him to join her in the alley. "Shit fire, you look *terrible*, hon. Maybe you should sit down a minute."

Trey was so bewildered by her opening expression (which, with her Midwestern accent, sounded to him like "shit far") that he took yet another step forward without thinking.

*This is the second time I've seen this homeless lady here,* he realized. *Maybe she knows something. If not about the voodoo stuff, then about how the police are reacting to the vampire lady's body going missing. If she's always around, she might've heard something from her homeless friends, right?*

*Besides ... I don't want to be rude.*

Riding a fresh sense of determination, Trey shuffled

forward into the alley between the buildings.

"My word, but you look like death warmed over, hon," she said (which almost made Trey smirk, but he stopped it just in time). "Are you too cold? Might have another blanket in my cart, if you don't mind it being so dirty—"

"Thank you, but I'm ... not cold."

The homeless lady's eyebrows shot up, adding even more wrinkles to her leathery forehead. "Well, if you say so, but hope it's not because you got a temperature. Why'n't you take a load off for a few minutes?"

She waved her hand toward the opposite wall, so Trey kind of nodded and sat down across from her.

"You just take a little bit to catch'r breath there, hon, 'n then I'll help you on over to the Mission shelter on Gle—"

"I'm fine."

The lady dismissed that with another wave of her hand as she started shifting around to climb to her feet. "That's nonsense, hon. Shit fire, anyone with working eyes in their head can see how sick—"

"I'm *fine*. Really."

The lady looked over at him, then puckered her thin, dry lips and settled back down. Trey could tell he had hurt her feelings when she said, "Whatever. Have it your way, hon. Was just tryin' to help out."

"I know. Thank you."

The lady grunted at that. "You got a name, or gotta call you 'hon' all night?"

He opened his mouth to answer "Trey," then gave that a second thought. The cops at the morgue place didn't know anything about him yet, but he should probably play it safe. After all, he was on a mission.

So instead, he told her, "My name is ... Lucius.

What's yours?"

"Used to go by 'Pam,' back when," she said with a chuckle (though Trey didn't really get why that would be funny). "These days my street family call me 'Missy P'."

"Nice to meet you ... Missy P."

"Same you, Lucius."

She smiled. It was probably a pretty smile before she lost a couple of teeth. Still, Trey thought it made her look less like a guy and more like a lady.

Trey opened his mouth to question Missy P about the police activity around the morgue place, but before he could, she asked, "So, Lucius, how long you been ...?"

But then her voice trailed off as she stared at something in Trey's lap.

He looked down, but didn't see anything weird or out of place. His hands were resting there, but all he was holding—

"Got car keys there." She said it like it was an accusation.

Trey glanced at the keys. Was that bad? He wasn't sure, so he just said, "Yeah."

Missy P glanced back at the street, to where Trey had been standing before his feet decided to walk toward the alley. "That your car, then?"

"Yeah."

Missy P looked irritated, which confused Trey. What had he done wrong?

Pulling her blanket tighter across her body, she said, "Got a car, why're you walkin' the streets in the middle of the damn night, sick as you clearly are?"

"I, uh ..."

But then Missy P shook her head, burped out a heavy sigh, and waved her hand again, this time at herself. "Ack. Forget it, Lucius. Not my place to judge. Saw you standin' there, lookin' like you do — no offense — just assumed you were on the street, too. 'Course, maybe you are. Wouldn't be the first time one of us got their hands on wheels, but they're usually one tire in the dump already, and yours looks okay, so ..."

Missy P ran out of steam. She looked lost for a moment, then laughed a little. Like her smile, it made her look more like a lady when she laughed.

"Forget it. Mind's not so sharp anymore. Know I shouldn't, you know, 'make an ass outta you 'n me.' You know how it goes."

Trey wasn't sure he did, but he nodded a little anyway.

Missy P sighed and looked him over. "So ... nice enough car. Peep past your bad color, see your jacket 'n trousers ain't so bad, either. And you're a big fellow, with shoulders about a mile wide." She nodded to herself. "Ain't homeless, are you, Lucius?"

"No, ma'am."

"Oh, don't start with the 'ma'am' now. Not just 'cause I tried to put you in my little box. 'Missy P' will do just fine."

"All right ... Missy P."

She looked him over again, this time ending up on his face. "What's with the sunglasses-at-night? Got glaucoma, or too cool for school?"

Sean had actually gone over this with Trey before, so he knew to agree with, "Glaucoma. Not bad, but ... bad enough."

"Hear ya there, hon." She shuffled her legs a bit. "Got arthritis in both knees. Not bad, but bad enough."

Trey stretched an idle smile across his lips as she settled back against her wall. She was a nice lady, but he felt a little frustrated that she was controlling the conversation, not giving him any openings to ask about the activity around the morgue place. Not without it feeling really forced, anyway. If Sean were here, he would just charm it out of her, but this wasn't so easy for Trey. What if he—?

Missy P suddenly yelped and jerked her left hand up, startling him in the process. She then slapped at it with her right and started looking all around herself while cussing under her breath (including a whole lot of "F" words, if Trey heard right).

"Are you all right ... Missy P?"

"Goddamn *spiders*!" she snapped, leaning forward so she could check the wall behind her. "Swear, third fuckin' bite this week. Don't know what's gotten into the little shits lately, but sure as hell am gettin' *tired* of it. Aren't they s'posed to, I don't know, hibernate when it's cold or somethin'? Thought I saw that in a movie once. Goddamn it ..." Not finding any more spiders sneaking around (though how sure could she be at night, streetlights or no streetlights?), she sat back, with hesitation, and inspected her bitten hand.

"Do you need ... a doctor or something?"

"No, no. It's fine." She scratched at it, then her leathered face scrunched up, and she shook her hand. "Saw the little shit, wasn't a Black Widow or anything, just a plain little eight-legged fucker. Itches, and burns kinda. I'll live." She continued to scratch, then flinch in discomfort, then scratch some more.

Once it was clear that Missy P wasn't in any danger, the situation nagged at Trey. Forgetting about the police at the morgue place, his main reason for being here, his primary mission, was to investigate voodoo magic that turned vampires into big meta-spider-things ... and now this nice homeless lady was talking about getting bitten by spiders a lot more than usual. Coincidence? Maybe, maybe not. He would need to call Alistaire and see what he thought.

"Shit fire ..." Missy P was muttering. "Was hopin' to get a couple hours of sleep before this place opens up." She did an odd gesture with her head, sort of back and to the right, and Trey got the idea she was talking about the business building she was leaning against. "Now the idea of crawlin' up in my sleepin' bag makes me all itchy. Great ..."

Without thinking, Trey offered, "Would you like me ... to check your sleeping bag ... for spiders for you ... before I go?"

Missy P glanced up in surprise. "Oh. Why, thank you, Lucius. That'd be so nice of you." She smiled her almost-pretty smile and pointed up at a blue sleeping bag on top of the pile of stuff in her shopping cart.

Working his way up against his cold-stiffened knees, Trey crossed the ally in two strides and lifted the sleeping bag from the cart. Pulling away the single, loose strap, he let the bag unfurl to the ground, up-ended it, shook it really hard several times, then stepped deeper into the ally and beat it a few times against the wall.

Turned out it was a good thing he did. At least one little critter tumbled out and scrambled away. There might have been more, he couldn't be sure. Just to be safe, he beat it against the wall a few more times.

"Where would you ... like me to lay it down?"

Missy P was still smiling up at him like she was a little bit in love. "Right there behind my cart is fine, thank you." A touch of concern returned to her eyes. "You *sure* you feel all right, Lucius? You seem awfully creaky."

"It's just the cold," he told her truthfully. "I get really ... stiff in the cold."

"Oh, I hear ya, hon."

Trey gave the sleeping bag one last harsh pop against unwanted guests, and laid it out behind her cart and along the wall.

Missy P, in the meantime, had pulled down a medium-sized towel, then rolled it into a tube, and tucked it under her arm. Trey guessed she used it as a pillow.

She raised one hand toward him. "Help me up, hon?"

Trey stepped around the sleeping bag and offered her his hand, gently helping Missy P to her feet. She kept holding his hand as she shuffled around the cart, then lowered herself down onto the middle of the bag. Only then did she let go so that she could unzip the bag a little further.

"Ahhh, better," she said as she rotated around and slipped her legs inside, then she looked up at Trey. He saw this was uncomfortable for her, because of his height, so he flexed his stiff knees into a crouch beside her. She waved both hands around herself, kind of at the sleeping bag but really taking in the whole alley. "Don't mean to run you off, Lucius. Just that I was gettin' sleepy and 'bout ready to hit the sack before I noticed you standin' out there on the sidewalk, lookin' sick and all."

"That's all right. I ... should get going ... anyway."

"Sure, sure." She smiled, then cocked her head at him. "What *were* you doin' out there this late, anyway?"

Trey thought that over for a second before answering. Was this the opening he'd been waiting for, to ask about the morgue place? But no, since her spider bite, that felt somehow less important. What he wanted now was to talk to Alistaire about *that*, about the spiders, about what that might mean and how it could be connected to the meta-spider-thing.

So he said, "I was trying to ... find something. But it's

... it's turned out to be a little ... harder than I hoped."

She offered a friendly chuckle. "Ain't that always the way?"

"It sure feels like it ... lately."

Missy P smiled up at him. "Well, sure do hope it works out for you."

Trey smiled back. "Thanks. For, uh ... for you, too."

Her eyes glistened at that. "Lucius, nice meeting you." She held out her hand for him to shake.

Trey took her small hand into his big one—

*Feed!*

The hunger's ferocious command hit him so hard, he literally rocked back a little, his crouching legs twitching under him. Only his grip on Missy P's hand kept him from falling over backward.

"Lucius?" she asked, her voice filled with concern. "Lucius, you all right?"

Trey felt crushed under the weight of it.

*FEED!*

Trey yanked Missy P forward ...

... and sank his teeth bone-deep into her forearm.

Missy P opened her mouth to scream. But the shock of it, and probably the pain, was too much for her, so all that came out was a terrible squawk and a gagging sound.

*It won't last*, the hunger hissed even as it overpowered him. *Don't let her draw that next breath!*

Missy P's eyes rolled too large in her sockets as her jaw widened. Her chest puffed up as she filled her lungs with air—

Pulling up from her arm, strings of muscle ripping away (Trey had not bothered to unlock his own jaws), he slammed his left fist straight into her face. Her nose shattered with a loud *pop!*, and her skull echoed the same as her head struck the wall behind her. She repeated the gagging sound from before, twice, then collapsed onto her sleeping bag in a pile of dirty clothes and spreading blood.

Mouth opening wide, Trey descended upon her—

*Not just yet,* the hunger warned, *not here! You'll be seen before you can finish ...*

Trey glanced out at the street, then shuffled to the foot of Missy P's sleeping bag and dragged her deeper into the alley. Once he reached the end, he continued around the building and into the furthest, darkest corner.

Trey crouched over Missy P, the nice homeless lady who made the mistake of asking if he was all right. He placed one hand over her mouth, in case she woke up before the end.

And then, for the first time since rising as a member of the undead, Trey Matthews truly began to feed.

# ELEVEN

A fire blazed through Sean's shoulder and forearm —
a fierce, piercing burn nearly as painful as getting
wounded by silver. The rest of his body was freezing like
a bloody ice cube.

This was his wake-up call. Not something he would
be recommending to anyone.

Struggling to open his eyes, Sean's nose and ears
informed him that Alistaire was nearby, likely right here
in the room with him; his senses also pegged this location
as the bedroom. Right this moment, he couldn't recall
exactly *why* he was laid out on his bed with his shoulder
and forearm trying to spontaneously combust, but one
thing at a time.

He turned his head a little, which caused the muscles
in his neck to scream in pain. The burning had distracted
him before, but dear God, his whole upper body felt like
one giant cramp.

As he lay still for a moment, allowing his muscles to
calm down, he picked up a new scent, thankfully not
strong because it was unpleasant. Sour, toxic ...

Forcing his eyelids far enough apart to see, he was
treated to a warping, blurring, wobbling image that spun
his inner ear like a top. He could make out that the room
was dark, the only light coming from the bathroom across
the hall, but beyond that, all details were lost.

He opened his mouth but failed to make a sound, his throat drier than he would have thought possible; clearing it was out of the question. He closed his eyes, squeezing them tight — the act of which informed him that he also had a terrible headache.

*Jesus Christ, I'm in a bad way. The only thing missin' from the checklist is a set of swollen plums, and I'm not temptin' bloody fate. And what the hell is that sour stink?*

After a few seconds, he reopened his eyes to give it another go.

His vision was ... well, it was still shite, but a touch better than before. He spotted Alistaire this time; his German friend stood in profile near the open doorway, which threw him into silhouette. He was messing around with something in his hands ...

*Wait. Wait, what am I ...?*

He would swear on his mother's soul that he was seeing Alistaire Bachman tinkering with ... with a smartphone?

*Ah, hell. I must be in worse shape than I thought. I'm hallucinatin'.*

And so he allowed himself to drift back to sleep ...

He didn't know how much time had passed when he opened his eyes again, but he got the feeling it wasn't terribly long.

Aside from his burning wounds — *bites*? hadn't something bitten him? — he had been freezing before, but now his body was drenched with sweat; he would've given his eyeteeth for a nice, cool bath.

*"Sean?"*

Alistaire's voice startled him, prompting a jerk of the head that set off a new round of cramps in his neck; he gritted his teeth and sucked in a pained breath.

*"How are you feeling? A loaded question, to be sure,*

*but ... how* are *you feeling?"*

His vampire friend emerged from the nondescript gloom of the room to kneel next to the bed. Sean was grateful Alistaire didn't sit on the side of the bed; he doubted the jostling of the mattress would have been fun.

Sean tried to speak, but had no more success than earlier. Instead he settled for mouthing the word, "Water."

Alistaire nodded and disappeared. Was he doing his vampire thing, or was Sean's sight missing frames? Could go either way ...

He jolted yet again — hence, more muscle cramps — when Alistaire reappeared with a cup in his hand, leaving Sean pretty sure he had fallen asleep with his eyes open this time. Alistaire turned the cup, revealing a bendy straw; Lord only knew where he had managed to find it in this house.

That first sip of tap water tasted so sweet as it doused the glowing ache in his throat, Sean almost drifted off to sleep yet again. But he rallied to keep his eyes open, poor vision or no, until he drained the cup dry.

"Thanks ..." he mumbled as Alistaire pulled the straw away. "M' brains a little knackered. Could ye remind me what the hell happened?"

Alistaire relayed events as Trey had described them; it helped that each step reminded Sean of what he already knew — short of his status after seizing up in the hallway.

At the end, Sean commented, "So that bitter, manky shite I'm smellin' must be comin' from the woman-spider. Is it still in the hallway, then?"

*"No,"* Alistaire replied, *"I have removed the meta-spider to the dining room, until such a time as we can more properly dispose of it. But I am afraid the current source of the malodor is yourself. Your perspiration has been noisome for the past few hours; I presume you are*

*sweating out the venom as your body breaks it down."*

"Wonderful. We'll need t' burn the sheets when this is over."

*"Perhaps. However, so long as your wounds remained free of excess odor, I chose not to question the gift H-He has already given us with your recovery."*

"True." He rotated his head from side to side, searching for relief from his stiff neck. "Sounds like Trey did the best he could, given the circumstances."

*"Indeed."*

"Where is the big guy? I'd like t' thank him ..."

*"Ah. That brings us to a new development, though perhaps a more positive one."*

"Mmm ...?" In spite of his best effort, Sean was almost asleep once more.

*"Trey has driven the car back up into Los Angeles."*

That tidbit snapped him back around. "What? He ... he what now?"

*"Trey is performing some reconnaissance,"* Alistaire explained. *"It appears that his voodoo origins give him some extrasensory sensitivity to the nature of these meta-spiders. He has returned to the area of the medical examiner's office, to see if he can perhaps 'smell out' the culprit behind these recent events."*

"He's out there alone?"

*"We could not leave you unattended in your condition, Sean."*

"Aye, I get that, but ... Trey's out there *alone*?"

*"I had reservations as well,"* Alistaire admitted. *"But I now believe we have been underestimating Trey for some time. You remember our observation of his recent mood swings — his 'tiff,' as you put it?"*

Sean nodded, as best his neck would allow. "Aye, he got bent out of shape when we made him stay in the car.

And lately, he ... well ..."

Alistaire nodded. *"Yes, he has not been himself. When the suggestion arose of Trey's undertaking this task on his own, he confessed to feeling what could be summarized as 'underappreciated,' and I took heed."*

"So he just, what, took the car keys and drove off to L.A.?"

*"You were the one who taught him how to drive,"* Alistaire retorted with something akin to humor.

"I know, but that was, ye know, 'just in case,' for emergencies. Not for Trey to go hobnobbin' around Los Angeles all by himself."

Alistaire's voice took up a somewhat stern tone. *"Trey is not 'hobnobbing,' Sean. He is on a reconnaissance mission."*

Sean opened his mouth to argue further ... then succumbed to his burning wounds, his again-freezing skin, his aching muscles, and his pounding headache. "Sorry. I'm too fucked up t' think straight. I just ..." He struggled to find the right words before finally settling for, "I feel like our boy's grown up and gone off t' university without us, ye know?"

*"I understand,"* Alistaire assured him. *"I, too, am feeling uneasy. Before leaving, Trey showed me, again, how to send and receive texts on our phones, yet I have been unable to reach him for the past hour. Perhaps I am doing something incorrectly."*

"It's possible," Sean said with a knowing, teasing smile — while he wasn't exactly a tech wizard himself, he was ahead of Alistaire on that particular curve. "I'll ... I'll give it a try ... if, uh ..."

Alistaire placed a calming hand on his unwounded shoulder. *"Sleep, Sean. You have some time left before I must retire for the day; we can try to reach Trey again before the sun rises — if he has not already returned by then. For now, I am confident in Trey's ability to handle himself solo for this particular mission."*

"I trust yer judgment," Sean mumbled as his mind slipped away. "I just hope Trey hasn't bitten off more than he can chew."

## ... 12 ...

Trey awoke for the first time in years, and he was completely disoriented.

While the act of waking was not something he would've thought of as needing practice, having gone so long without doing it left him in a storm of confusion: What was that noise? Where was he? And, most importantly, why couldn't he open his eyes?

The noise rang out again, prompting Trey to bolt upright ... which brought even more questions. Was he lying on the ground? Outside somewhere? And why couldn't he *open his eyes*?! It was like his eyelashes were glued together!

Scrubbing hard at his face, step by step, he was able to pry them open ... but the sights awaiting him did little to explain things.

He was indeed sitting on the ground, on pavement behind a building he did not recognize. Two buildings, really, though he was more centered behind the one with the red brick than the one with the white tiles. The noise was coming from off to his right, on the far side of the white building. It sounded like someone was throwing really heavy stuff into a metal dumpster.

*Must be the first employee arriving to work—*

Wait, what employee? Arriving to work where? Where *was* he?!

The sun was up, but not by far. He couldn't see it yet, just knew it was on its way because of the glowing sky.

*Aw, man. Alistaire is gonna be really worried about me—*

That's when the pieces finally fell into place. The meta-spider things, hearing the voodoo priest, coming to Los Angeles by himself ...

... and Missy P.

Trey gasped, his hands covering his mouth as his eyes widened in spite of the gummy, dried blood caking his eyelashes.

*Oh, God. Oh, my God!*

Trey looked down at himself, confirming what he already knew, that he was covered in blood. It was all over his clothes, all over his hands, and his probing fingertips told him that it was definitely all over his face. He tried not to think about the taste in his mouth, as it both repulsed and excited him.

Looking around, he found Missy P's remains behind him. There wasn't a whole lot left, flesh-wise. All of her bones (except for some of her fingers) and some of her guts were present and accounted for, so whatever inklings he might've had of "hiding the mess really quick" went flying right out the window.

*Oh God oh God* oh God, *what did I* do*?!*

He had to get out of here, right now!

*I ate her, I* ate *her!*

But he didn't have time to fall apart right now. He would ... he would deal with what this all *meant* later. Right now, he had to get away from here before someone caught him with what was left of— caught him with the body.

This went beyond just getting in trouble. If the police got their hands on him, if they even got good video of him as he fought them off, the question of *what* he was would spread like wildfire. Between the way that photographer Gamall had died and the vampire girl's body disappearing from the morgue ... well, Alistaire and Sean were always telling him that superstition wasn't buried as deeply as modern people liked to tell themselves.

Jumping to his feet, Trey peeked up the alley. There didn't seem to be a lot of traffic going by out on the street (in fact, there was less now than there had been in the middle of the night), but he couldn't go out there like this. And where were his sunglasses? He looked all around, finally finding them in the mess that remained of Missy P. He plucked them out and shoved them into his jacket pocket, then returned to searching the area behind the two buildings. Was there something he could use to cover himself? Maybe if he crept back up the alley, he could get his hands on Missy P's blanket, use that to—

On the far corner of the red building, he spotted a rusty water spigot sticking out over a dirty yellow mop bucket. Crouching as he ran (he didn't know if that helped, but he had to make *some* effort not to be seen!), Trey rushed to turn it on. He didn't have a water hose to direct it this time, so he had to settle for shoving the mop bucket aside, kneeling before the water stream, and splashing handful after handful onto his face, against his neck, over his hair. Next he washed off his sunglasses, and after a moment, he thought to take his jacket and shirt off, then wrung the latter under the stream, over and over. He knew he'd never get all of it out, but a wet, "dirty" shirt was going to be a lot better than one crusty with dried blood. And he had to hurry!

Trey was so focused on getting cleaned up and away from the scene of the crime (and trying *not* to think about the horror of what he had done) that it wasn't until he had finished washing up, redressing, and jogging over to the alley entrance that it dawned on him that he was moving around a lot easier, a lot quicker than normal.

He paused, for just a moment, to consider this: Here he was, awakening after sleeping (sleeping!) for several nighttime hours, outside, in autumn ... and yet his undead body was showing only a hint of rigidity. He had turned the water spigot on and off with hasty, precise hand movements, had gotten undressed and redressed in record time, and was running back and forth without that stiff-in-the-knees hitch that should have him hobbling like an old (living) man.

And what was more, he realized that even his *thoughts* were flowing smoother, less stilted. Even though his brain was almost always ahead of his mouth, more often than not, he still felt slack-minded when compared to how rapidly Alistaire or Sean could form an idea. But now ...

*It's because I ate her.*

*Yes*, whispered the hunger, and it sounded so smug that Trey wished it were another person so he could rip its throat out! *You finally did what you were always meant to do, Trey. You fed upon the flesh of the living. And now you're feeling better than you have in years.*

Trey shook his head, looking back at what was left of poor Missy P ...

*Go ahead. Try to deny it.*

Trey whimpered as he thought, *Now I understand how Sean feels about his old friend, Eamon. Poor Missy P. I will never, ever forgive myself for—*

His eyes widened and he clasped a hand over his mouth again as a new thought occurred to him.

*Oh, no ...*

This was the first time Trey had eaten the flesh of a

normal, non-supernatural human being, so he had never had to deal with the *other* possible consequences before.

*I ... I can't leave her like this. Not without ...*

Slowly, on feet that were sluggish in a way not at all related to the cold or his dead body, Trey returned to Missy P one more time.

He took a good, impartial (or as close as he could get to it) look at her. He was created by voodoo rather than bite-transmission, so he didn't actually know if his own condition was contagious ... but he tried to consider whether or not enough remained of Missy P for reanimation.

Inspecting her head (after closing his eyes for a few seconds against the expression of horror on what was left of her face), he saw that it was mostly intact. Her ears and nose had been chewed off, but her skull ... her *brain* ... appeared undamaged.

*It's probably fine,* he tried to assure himself. *It's been hours. If she were going to arise, she would have already ... wouldn't she?*

That was the problem. He didn't know.

So he couldn't take any chances.

Feeling nauseous all over again, even keening somewhat in the back of his throat, Trey stepped forward, placed a heavy shoe atop Missy P's forehead, closed his eyes ... and stomped all of his weight onto her head.

Her skull crumpled with a terrible *crack!*, and for a moment, he thought he was going to vomit up every bite of her (and *that* thought only made the impulse worse!).

"Yo, Billy!" called a male voice from the far side of the white building, where he'd heard the dumpster noises. "That you? You early, man!"

Rushing as quickly as he could without outright running, for fear of his clomping feet making too much noise, Trey returned to the alley entrance. Cars were still passing by on the street, but he neither saw nor heard any pedestrians.

"Yo, Bill! That you, man?"

Footsteps approached the corner of the white building.

Trey had run out of time.

Hustling up through the alley, Trey had a terrible moment when he thought he might not have the car keys on him anymore, but a second later he found them in his left jeans pocket rather than the right. When had he put them there? He was as clueless about that as he was about everything else this morning.

*I fell asleep for the first time in, like, ever. Maybe some of this is just a dream?*

But he knew better than that.

"Billy, my man. What're you—"

The man's voice cut off suddenly, and Trey was pretty sure he knew why. He could picture the man cocking his head to one side, maybe rubbing his eyes, as he stared at what was left of Missy P. Trying to convince himself that, surely, he must be imagining things, that he couldn't really be seeing what he *thought* he was seeing ...

Stepping out onto the sidewalk, Trey spotted a few pedestrians coming his way on this side of the street, but they were still more than a block away. Too far to get a good look at his face, or his license plate, so long as he got out of here right now.

He reached the car, had to wait a few frustrating seconds for traffic to pass, then hurried to the driver's side. He had fumbled the key into the lock and opened the door before he spotted something a little strange. In his current state of mind, it was a wonder he noticed it at all.

Several spiders, big brown-and-red ones, were

crawling along the upper rim of his windshield. One of them had even started a web stretching over to the radio antenna.

He thought about Missy P getting bitten, her comments about spiders, how she said that they were supposed to hibernate or something in cold weather, and that his car had only been parked here for—

The man behind the building erupted into a flurry of frantic curses, his voice nearly a scream.

Trey got the hell out of there.

# THIRTEEN

Randy sat in his work truck shortly before 10:00 AM. He had not slept well, nor was he a happy camper about bumping a non-spider-related appointment to arrange to be here. His Widow bite still hurt and his itchies were back, big time.

If only his damned curiosity hadn't gotten the better of him ...

He was parked across the street and slightly south of the driveway that led to FRM's very nice house; "FRM" whom he now knew, thanks to Google and IMDb, to be Frances Ronald Morse, the semi-famous, Oscar-winning documentary filmmaker. Morse's driveway was gated, but it wasn't the deepest yard, so when the gate did open, this angle would give Randy the best view of the front door.

Having said that, Randy was aware that neighborhood security could stop by at any moment, so he kept checking his watch as the minutes ticked closer to ten o'clock. He also knew it was possible that Morse himself might spot his truck, specifically Randy's name on the side. In fact, he had brought some of his super-strong pesticide with him just in case that very thing happened; if push came to shove, he could pretend his time had freed up unexpectedly, and here he was — special delivery!

So Randy sat, checking the time, scratching at nothing, and stretching his still-sore neck muscles. Gee, what a great way to spend his morning.

Sure, right after the email exchange, the thought had crossed his mind to drive by Morse's house, but he hadn't really meant it. But then he had spent too much time reading that cockamamie paranoia blog about enormous spider webs infesting the apartment of a dead photographer — hence, the horrendous return of his itchies — and his curiosity had gone into overdrive. Maybe Morse needed such strong, fast-acting poison, not because he was dealing with an outbreak of little spiders, but because he was dealing with some sort of freaky, giant spiders?

What was he expecting to learn here, really? What did Morse's problem have to do with the massive spider webs found at that crime scene? Nothing, probably; just apples and oranges.

And yet ...

Movement in his side mirror caught his attention, and he sat up straighter.

*Here we go ...*

FedEx had just rounded the bend behind him, coming this way. A few seconds later, a brown UPS truck showed up behind the white FedEx one.

Randy checked his watch: 9:59 AM. The timing was too perfect. He suspected that both drivers, either by coordination or coincidence, had been waiting just down the road, timing it so they arrived right on schedule. Randy recalled that Morse had mentioned coordinating deliveries, and with his whole "money is no object" attitude, he had probably paid extra for punctuality. The two trucks had not quite reached the house when the gate opened; someone inside, presumably Morse himself, had been waiting for them to show up. That, or it, too, was on a fixed schedule.

Randy wasn't sure what exactly to make of that, but it was interesting.

Each delivery person emerged from their respective vehicles, puttered around in the back for a minute, then approached the front door of the house — again, timing it so they walked up together. *That*, Randy would guess, came from their own desires, maybe because they had been here before and knew the routine ... or found the whole thing oddball enough to seek comfort in numbers, even if that number were only two.

The front door opened before they reached the porch. He leaned back a bit, seeking what cover he could get from the morning shadow within his truck, and lifted a pair of binoculars.

By the time Randy focused in, a haggard-looking man — Morse? If so, he sure didn't look much like his IMDb photo these days — was already standing in his doorway, signing for the first of several packages; whatever he was receiving apparently required more than the usual scratch-your-name-here, because after he signed the digital tablet, the FedEx driver passed him actual paperwork to go through.

As Randy studied the scene, he considered Morse's appearance. Man, the guy looked really bad. Dark circles under his red-rimmed eyes; cheeks sagging as though from sudden weight-loss; short, uneven hair that looked dirty even from here ...

But the first thing that really caught Randy's attention was a spider bite on the man's pale forearm. It probably wasn't a Black Widow bite, as he could attest from very recent experience, but it didn't look like it felt much better. Red and a little infected-looking, it was hard to say how old it was. Then Randy spotted more bites on other parts of his arms and neck, and as he tilted the binoculars downward, he saw that Morse's bare legs were especially covered with them, as well as a large number of scabs that had probably started life as even *more* spider bites.

Even as he scratched at his own leg with his other hand, Randy panned the binoculars back and forth. His field of view was limited by the property's wall, but in the handful of windows that were visible, he spotted several telltale webs in the corners — in *all* of the corners; not a single window in view was web-free. And the longer he looked, the more suspicious, wriggling black dots he spotted skittering along the outside walls of the house.

*I guess I can see why he's looking for strong pesticide. But why the hell would he* stay *in the house? And why handle it himself?*

Great. He'd come here with vague notions of settling his curiosity, but now the situation was weirder than before.

*Forget about it,* he chided himself. *It's none of your concern. Just sell the poor guy the pesticide, make some extra bucks while you're at it, and then mind your own business.*

Tossing the binoculars into the passenger seat, feeling somewhat disgusted with himself as he reached for the keys to start the engine, Randy very nearly screamed when a voice suddenly spoke through his open window.

" 'Scuse me ..."

His heart in his throat, he turned to face the speaker, a very tanned, casually-dressed, thirty-ish gentleman. The only things that gave the guy away as "belonging" in this nice neighborhood were the expensive, oversized diving watch on his wrist and an extremely intricate ankh tattoo at the base of his throat that would not have come cheap. The man stood beside the van with his hands resting lightly at the base of the open window, and Randy's stomach folded over when he realized just how close he had come to getting caught with the binoculars in-hand

and pointed at Morse's house.

"Yes?" Randy replied, inwardly flinching at the puberty-like crack in his voice.

"Mister ..." the guy leaned back to glance at the side of his truck, "... McDonnell, is it? That right, that you, man?" The man's accent was a bizarre mishmash of Ivy League and surfer dude.

Randy forced an affable smile. "That's me. What can I do for you?"

"Hope I'm not, like, interrupting you, but I, uh ... you know ..." The rich surfer stumbled over his words for a moment, his expression striving for casual while betraying embarrassment. "What ... what brings you to the neighborhood? Like, are you here on business, or ...?"

Randy's guile offered up nothing helpful, so all he could think to say was, "Yes, I was here for a ... a meeting with Francis Morse over there. Just about to leave." His eyes flicked over to the man himself; luckily, though Morse was finished with FedEx, he was still occupied with UPS. He repeated, "What can I do for you?"

"Morse, huh? Yeah, weird dude," the guy commented, as though Randy had suggested as much and he was just agreeing. He shuffled his feet a little, then stepped closer to the truck, folding his arms and leaning in as if to share a secret. "Listen, are you, like, totally booked up? 'Cause I could use your services and it's like, you know, totally kismet that I ran into you like this."

"I do have a full schedule right now, but ..." Randy couldn't help himself; he had to know. "Tell you what, Mister ...?"

The guy unfolded his arms to offer his hand. "David Rinear. You can call me Dave, everyone does."

Randy shook his hand, while keeping tabs on Morse in his peripheral vision — still signing with UPS. "Nice to meet you, Dave. Now, tell me your problem, and maybe we can work something out."

"Ah, man, that would be so awesome. Listen ..." Dave refolded his arms and leaned closer still, like he might sneak a kiss, except Randy wasn't getting that vibe at all. "We got this party coming up this weekend, you know? And there's, like, a lot of people who are going to be there who I really need to impress. Especially for my wife. Don't want her bitchin' at me afterward, you know what I mean?"

Randy actually had an excellent relationship with Lori, but he nodded anyway to keep things moving along; Morse appeared to be wrapping up with UPS.

"We're having the party in the backyard, and I was out there this morning just, you know, checkin' things out in advance ... and good God, do I have a spider problem — like, no shit, it's like something out of a movie. You ever see *Kingdom of the Spiders*?"

"No, I can't say that I have."

UPS was walking away now; Morse was carrying in the first armful of boxes.

"Cool movie and all, starred Captain Kirk and it's ... well, anyway, I don't have tarantulas, but there's a ton of these little brown guys that—"

"Sounds like Brown Widows, but I'll have to see for myself to be sure."

Dave nodded deeply, as though Randy had given him sage advice.

The UPS driver stopped and stomped his foot, then shook it as though it had fallen asleep; Randy had little doubt as to what he was trying to get off his shoe.

"Tell you what, Dave, why don't you hop in and we can head to your place right now and I'll take a look."

Dave's face lit up like Randy had just offered him a

new sports car. "For reals? Ah, man, that would be awesome. I'm right around the curve up there—"

"Great. Hop in, Dave, and let's go see what's what."

Randy made sure to get rid of the binoculars as Dave was trotting around to the other side. He started up the engine and was in motion before Dave even had his seatbelt on.

Thankfully, his hustle paid off, as he was on his way just as Morse returned to the front porch ...

\* \* \*

The truck's revving engine snagged Francis' attention, but by the time he glanced over, all he caught was a fleeting glimpse of white. There might have been writing on the side, but he couldn't be sure; he had gotten so little fucking sleep over the past weeks, he couldn't rely on his vision like he used to. For some reason, the exterminator, Randy McDonnell, came to mind. Unfortunately, the man wasn't due to arrive until tomorrow, so that was probably wishful thinking on Francis' part.

Francis grunted as he was forced to bat aside a crab spider that had already crawled up onto the second stack of boxes. Too bad McDonnell hadn't been able to make it today — they could have tested his poison right here and now. At least the man had replied to his message; Francis contacted four different exterminators yesterday — three independents, and then he'd caved and tried one of the bigger outfits, too – but he hadn't heard back from any of the others yet.

As he moved the remaining boxes around, he spotted one that was coming from Amazon rather than the more exotic sources. He made sure to maneuver that one into the middle of the pile; that one was for him. When it had been clear that he was going to get his pesticide, he had overnighted a pressure-sprayer in anticipation — a few pumps, and he would be able to shoot a fine mist for the little fuckers, or a tight stream right into the faces of those giant mutants Bondye had lingering in the master bedroom. Francis didn't know how strong the poison would be against something that size, but he was betting his life, literally, that a shot to those eight freaky eyes wouldn't feel too good.

Francis was grinning, for the first time in quite a while, at the mere thought of this, when he stepped into the house and found himself face-to-face with one of those very freaks. He nearly screamed and dropped the boxes, but somehow managed to avoid doing either. The giant spider, which stood on its hind legs as erect as a human being, stared at him, not making a sound.

"Wha—" he tried to ask, but had to clear his throat and try again. "Wh-what? What do you want?"

It just stood there, gaping at him with all those nightmarish eyes for several long seconds ... and then it shuffled forward one step. He started to draw back from it, and felt the now-familiar tickle on his ankles, telling him the regular spiders had moved to prevent his retreat. He could step over them or on them, but he had been down that fruitless road before.

The giant spider lifted its six other limbs, the bigger human-like arms and the four smaller arms underneath reaching for him—

*Oh God, oh God, this is it, Bondye must've figured out about the pesticide, please God, the damned thing is gonna kill me!*

Should he run? He hadn't closed the front door yet. He could throw the boxes at it, maybe confounding it for a second and make a run for it!

*And what fucking good will that do? Huh? The fucker would be on me before I got off the porch. It's a human-fucking-sized* spider, *for Christ's sake. Hell, I couldn't make it out of the backyard because of the* regular-*sized spiders.*

"Wh-what do y-you want ...?" he repeated, too forlorn to be embarrassed by how it came out as a whimper. His eyes filled with tears, his bladder ready to let go, his bowels—

*I need the powdered Jimsonweed now,* Bondye's voice spoke inside his head.

Startled, Francis looked up toward the master bedroom. Was this the first time the bastard had deigned to project to him in English? He thought it might be.

*Give the Jimsonweed to my* araknid, Bondye continued. *Then remove the rest from their cartons and bring them to me.*

The *"araknid"* moved another step closer and its arms lifted an inch higher, as if to say, "Come on, come on, buddy, hand 'em over ..." It didn't actually speak, of course; it merely stared through his soul with those hideous eyes ...

Francis quickly set the boxes down on the floor — dozens of spiders scrambling out of the way — and checked through them. The sender of the Jimsonweed hadn't bothered with a return address, just their website domain where that would normally go, and as soon as Francis got his hands on that box, he stood and shoved it forward.

"Here," he said, holding it by the very back, hoping to make no physical contact with the monster if he could help it. "Here, that's the Jimsonweed. Take it."

It continued to stare at him. Could it understand him?

Maybe not. Maybe they were too stupid to do anything but exactly what Bondye told them. But what else was he supposed to do here? He averted his eyes, no longer able to meet those black orbs.

"Just ... just take it," he pleaded in a low voice.

It closed the distance between them.

Francis squeezed his eyes shut.

As it took the box from him, its hands brushed against his; he felt its coarse skin and prickly hairs scrape across his fingers. Given how he was holding his end of the box, he had to assume it was deliberate. He bit the inside of his cheek to avoid giving any reaction.

Not so "stupid" after all, he guessed ... or just smart enough to be cruel.

Then it was gone. He opened his eyes, expecting to see it walking up the stairs. Instead, he was not quite shocked — not anymore, anyway — to see it crawling up the wall on its way to the second floor, the box held in two of its smaller limbs.

Francis relaxed, or as close as he ever got to it these days. The only upside to these little brushes with horror was that the adrenaline made him feel more awake — for a short while, anyway. And at least his heart hadn't clenched up on him this time.

Crouching, he began gathering up the pile he had been forced to drop in his hurry. He needed to get the whole kit and caboodle into the kitchen, so he could start cutting them open and—

A smell struck him. He sniffed a little deeper, trying to both locate and identify ...

The smell was coming from him. Looked like he pissed himself after all.

Gritting his teeth, he returned to collecting his stack. He felt humiliated, sure, but he also felt anger. And that anger, like his adrenaline rush, felt good.

*Just you wait, motherfuckers. You'll probably end up killing me, I'm aware of that, but if I can get my hands on that pesticide, you'll know you've been in a fight before I'm done.*

*I guaran-fucking-tee it.*

# ... 14 ...

"Where are you?!" Trey shouted as he slammed his fist against the car's steering wheel.

And as if Fate were giving him the middle finger, the only answer was a *ping!* from his phone.

Yet another incoming text that Trey didn't have the courage to read, which only served to further elevate his frustration at his failure to track down the source of the voodoo magic.

He had been driving all around L.A., searching for hours and hours, and trying really, really hard to stay focused on his mission.

He had stopped for gas not long after leaving the scene of his awful crime, but he had first parked around behind the building so he could change into one of Sean's backup shirts from the trunk (man, did that fit tight!). Then, after he was done filling up the tank (having used the Bachman Foundation credit card Alistaire gave him), he used their bathroom to deal with his stained jacket and pants; Sean's jeans were just too darn small, so he settled for scrubbing his own pants in the sink and putting them back on.

He had looked into the mirror for one final check, and froze.

His eyes were ... well, not *normal*-normal, not healthy-looking by any means, but ... he had not seen them this clear, this *almost*-normal, since before he died. And his skin looked better, too.

Trey had cringed and looked away, pangs of guilt rushing through him. He didn't like it, didn't like seeing himself looking better in the mirror, not after what he had done to poor Missy P.

Luckily, the hunger didn't taunt him this time.

Once back in the car, he just sat there at first, not sure what to do. He had several voicemails and a bunch of texts from Alistaire and Sean (at least it meant Sean was awake and aware again), but he didn't answer them. He knew they would be worried to death, but he had no idea what to say to them. His guilt would shine right through his voice, he had no doubts about that.

So instead, he had picked a direction and started driving. And not ten minutes in, he caught a whiff of the voodoo magic.

The sensation came and went just like before, passing over and/or through him along its way somewhere else. But this wave was definitely stronger than it had been back home or by the morgue, and left Trey with an improved sense of where it had come from ... or a better general direction, anyway.

Then desperate hope swelled within Trey's chest. Could *that* be the reason for what he did to Missy P? Was the voodoo priest, whoever he was, to blame for his loss of control? Maybe these waves of voodoo magic crashing around Los Angeles and southward had affected him, making him more ... more "zombie-like" than his usual self, even as he was trying to follow them back to their source?

Maybe he wasn't turning evil after all, wasn't being drawn toward it as much as being *pulled* toward it?

It was a very appealing thought, but deep inside, Trey

knew better. This had begun months ago, up in Alaska, when he had eaten that werewolf, way before the first hint of weird vampire-spiders or voodoo magic.

His hope melted away as quickly as it had formed. He couldn't blame the voodoo priest. This was on *him*, Trey, and no one else.

*Maybe I can't* blame *the voodoo priest for what I did,* he thought, a dark notion that had nothing to do with the hunger's voice, *but that doesn't mean I can't take my frustration out on him when I find his evil butt!*

And so began Trey's weaving, winding drive through Los Angeles. But what started as determination melted into potent vexation when it sank in that he was crisscrossing a lot of the same darn streets, over and over again, as the various "whiffs" led him in different, zigzagging directions.

"I'm wasting my time," he growled, gripping the wheel so tight the material squeaked. "These magic trails ... aren't leading me anywhere."

*Ping!* Another text.

"Shut up!" he raged. "Shut up! Shut up! *Shut - up!*"

Trey seized the phone, wanting to throw it out the window. But he calmed down, just enough, to instead turn it off before slamming it back down onto the passenger seat.

And then, without any warning, the man's voice returned, clear as a bell.

*Zonbi ...*

The word startled Trey so badly, he very nearly rear-ended an old station wagon pulling out of its driveway. In his rattled state of mind, he offered a clumsy "I'm sorry" gesture, drove just a little bit further, then pulled over to the curb to collect himself.

He waited for the man's voice to return. He didn't

have to wait very long.

*Zonbi, ou te okipe ...*

Trey didn't understand the words (except maybe for "zonbi," which wasn't too hard to figure out), but he got the feeling that the man was speaking directly to *him* this time ... and was taunting him.

"What do you want?" he said out loud, not knowing if the voodoo priest could hear him or not.

*Ou yo ap chanje, zonbi ...*

"I don't understand you."

*Apre sa, mwen renmen sa mwen wè ...*

"I don't understand you!"

*Byento, zonbi ... tankou araknid, byento ...*

Trey still wasn't getting it, of course, but like "zonbi" before, he picked up on "araknid" now, which sounded too close to "arachnid" to mean anything other than *spider*. Was he threatening Trey with one of his meta-spider things? If so, he must not know how Trey had dealt with the last one.

*Ou pral jwenn m', zonbi ...* the voice whispered, already sounding further away. *Lè sa a, mwen posede ou...*

Then it was gone, leaving behind only a thin but steady trace of the magic, a thread Trey thought that he might be able to follow.

And even though he was slower than Alistaire or Sean on his better days, the idea that this might be some sort of trap did occur to him.

"I should go back," he said out loud again, this time in a whisper to himself. "I should go home ... and tell Alistaire and Sean what I've done. And then they can come back here ... and deal with this."

It probably would be just them, too, because once they found out what he had done to Missy P, Trey was almost sure they would lock him up somehow. Or maybe even put him down. Either way, he would deserve it.

The problem was, they still would not be able to follow the trail like Trey could. Even though he had the strongest sense yet of which direction to go, he didn't know the final destination.

He had to keep going, for now. He had to complete his mission. He *had* to!

Trey pulled back onto the street. So what if it was a trap? Instead of forcing his partners ... his friends ... to punish him for what he had done, he could let the bad guy do that, right?

Slowly (though not as slowly as usual), a plan began to form in his mind: He could find the voodoo priest, figure out exactly where that was, call Alistaire and Sean to let them know (and tell them to get there as fast as they can, before the villain could make a getaway!) ... then he would march in there and do his darned best to take the guy out himself. And if he failed, if the guy's spiders took him out? That would be his proper punishment, and he would accept it.

*How exactly,* asked an inner voice that smacked of the hunger's sneering attitude, *are they going to get there "as fast as they can," when* you *have the car?*

Trey sighed, which trailed off into a bit of a frustrated groan. His brain might've gotten better since he started eating living flesh ... and gotten better yet after poor Missy P ... but he was still falling short.

"Okay, fine, whatever," he muttered. "I'll just ... I'll find the guy, and then ... decide what to do next."

Trey was so focused on this debate, while also trying to drive safely and keep track of the thread of voodoo magic, that he almost didn't notice the pang of hunger in his gut ... almost.

*No ...*

He felt like crying. It had been barely, what, twelve hours since he had ... had fed? He knew (remembered) that regular people usually ate three meals each day, but goshdarn it, *Alistaire* could go several nights without feeding if he had to! After what he had done, he thought he would have more time before going through this again.

And to make matters that much worse, this early hunger was already a little stronger than what he had been dealing with since Alaska.

*Maybe it is the voodoo magic, after all? Maybe?*

He wanted to believe that, but ...

He could keep driving, for now. Keep searching for the voodoo priest, for as long as he could focus. And when he couldn't handle it anymore, he would deal with it, somehow. Maybe get his hands on another cat or a dog, anything mammal, but he would be *damned* if he would feed on another human being!

*"Would be damned?" That's cute. You don't realize you're* already *damned, Trey my boy?*

Yeah. All he had to do was remember Missy P, and he already knew that he was.

But, as Sean would put it, he wasn't going down without a fight.

# FIFTEEN

"Trey's never come home," Sean said without preamble as Alistaire opened his eyes that evening. "I've been textin' and callin' him all day, he doesn't answer. Somethin's wrong."

Sean shifted to the side as Alistaire rose from his coffin to the hallway floor in one smooth movement. *"I fear you are correct."*

"Ye're damned right I'm correct," Sean snapped with unexpected rancor. "Ye never shoulda let him go out on his own."

*"I recognize that now, Sean. And I find it both distressing and disappointing, to be sure."*

" 'Disappointing'? I'd say this goes way beyond 'disappointing,' Alistaire!"

*"Disappointing in regards to my own judgment,"* he clarified. Stepping into the living room, with Sean close on his heels, he eyed their computer and the mobile telephones next to it. *"Do we have any means of tracking Trey's phone?"*

Sean exhaled heavily through his nose as he switched tracks from venting frustration to working the problem. "I don't know. I mean, I *think* there're things ye can do, apps along the lines of 'Where's My Phone?' an' the like, but I don't know how t' use such things." He rubbed absently around the bite on his forearm. *"Trey's* the one who might know how to do that."

Alistaire appraised Sean's appearance. While he was by no means fully recovered, the Irishman had definitely improved over the course of the day, the most notable advancement being the decrease in the pungent odor seeping from his pores. *"You look better, my friend, but how are you feeling?"*

" 'Better' is relative, but ... aye, I'm doin' better than I was. I'm sore and stiff, and the bites still hurt like hell, but they're no longer in the neighborhood of silver. No more nausea, headache's mostly gone, too."

*"Excellent. Now ... I am open to suggestions as to our next step. We know he planned to begin his quest in the area of the medical examiner's office. While I am not keen on returning to the scene of our own crime, if we were to do so, would you be able to track Trey's scent from there?"*

Sean shook his head. "Sorry, but I doubt it. Even if he had the car window down, the lack of contact with the street or sidewalk ... I gotta good nose, but I canna perform miracles."

*"I feared as much. My own olfactory is strong, but as you say, not miraculous. However, I am at a loss as to where else we could begin our search."*

"What about yer psychic sense? I'm not talkin' about yer dreams, I mean that 'sense' ye get for supernatural things, like when ye detect other vampires. Could ye use it to find Trey?"

*"Proximity is a factor, which brings us back to the last place we know he planned to go. I suggest we take our chances with the local authorities and make our way to it."*

"All right, no argument there. But ye're forgettin' one thing: *How* are we going to get there? Trey's got the car, and I doubt takin' the bus will get us up there fast enough, let alone gettin' us back in time to tuck ye safely into bed before dawn."

Alistaire waved that away. *"If we fail to return before sunrise, I will make do as I have in centuries past. If push comes to absolute shove, I could abscond into the sewer."*

Sean's nose wrinkled at the thought. "Nice."

*"It is not pleasant,"* Alistaire agreed, *"but preferable to the alternative."*

"But we still have to get up there in the first place. So ... what should we do? I'd hate to steal a car ..."

*"If it comes to that, we would, of course, return the vehicle as soon as possible."*

"Right, right. Or we could take care o' just the one-way by callin' a taxi — or, for that matter, I suppose I could even try to figure out Uber."

Alistaire repeated in confusion, *"I am sorry, 'figure out über'...?"*

"Uber is like a taxi service, so I understand, but it's just a local, ye know, 'civilian' makin' money by—"

Sean cut himself off when he saw Alistaire stiffen. The vampire's face might have been carved from alabaster as he rotated until he was facing the front of the house.

"What is it?" Sean whispered, the hackles on the back of his already hairier neck rising in anticipation; he had seen Alistaire shift into "battle mode" countless times, but never here at the house.

Then again, they had experienced a lot of firsts of late.

*"A warning from the foremost of my 'psychic senses',"* Alistaire replied in his own low voice. *"But what I do not understand is why—"*

A knock, very tentative, sounded from the front door.

The two shared a look of disbelief. Sean muttered, "Are ye serious? When has—? I mean, when have we—?

They don't just ..."

Alistaire acknowledged Sean's bafflement with a nod. *"I suggest answering the door may help resolve the mystery. But be prepared."*

Sean nodded as well; he was already in nearly full-wolfman form, the fur helping to camouflage his wounds.

Stepping forward, Alistaire's senses reached out beyond their conspicuous visitor, but he detected no accompaniment for the fellow in question. In his over five centuries as a vampire, he had never encountered this particular scenario.

Alistaire opened the door.

The slender, male vampire standing several feet away was very young, both in appearance and aura; in an instant, Alistaire classified him as having been undead for less than a decade. Dressed in what he probably viewed as "Goth" fashion, he stood with his arms held somewhat in front of him, his fists clenched, but the stance smelled less of aggression and more of *fear* — though he fought not to expose himself, the vampire reeked of dread.

And yet, here he was, almost literally knocking on Death's door, as far as the vampire community was concerned.

Again, Alistaire reached out with his senses, searching for any hint of additional vampires; he found none. This fledgling was, it seemed, quite alone.

Alistaire stepped out onto the front stoop. He halted there, waiting, mindful that this could still be a trap by some other means — a mesmerized, mortal sniper with blessed silver bullets, for instance. He prepared to shift into his mist form at the slightest provocation, but, for now, he locked his gaze with the young vampire's.

The vampire fidgeted under Alistaire's scrutiny, another betrayal of his relative youth. And then, as if simply knocking on his front door wasn't unprecedented enough, he did something else Alistaire would never have anticipated: He genuflected before his elder, remaining on one knee with his head bowed.

"Y-Your, uh ..." he fumbled his words, his vocal quality lacking the nearly-subconscious undertone of vampires; definitely new to this world, and almost certainly a thrall. Then he cleared his throat and tried again. "Your Eminence ... I, um, I come here before you, presenting my master's desire for a parley with Your ... um ... with Your Eminence."

"Ye've *got* to be shittin' me."

The vampire's head jerked up in surprise, though Alistaire did not react at all; he had known exactly where his partner was. Sean had exited through the kitchen door at the side of the house, probably to perform his own check for ambush, then had crept around to keep an eye on things. He emerged from around the corner of the fence and approached, his fur receding as he resumed a more human form.

It was a good thing that he did. A car drove past their house, and Alistaire noticed the driver doing a double-take at the male kneeling before him in their front yard. For that matter, as he eased his focus for trick or trap, he became aware that, with the sun having only recently set — which, he also noted, meant that this thrall had arisen very nearby — the neighborhood was still very much awake. Children were playing in a yard at the far end of the street, and someone was carrying on a phone conversation on their front porch a few houses down the opposite direction.

Best not to call attention, though there was no way he was going to invite this vampire into their home.

"*Rise,*" he commanded as he stepped forward off the stoop.

The vampire did as he was told, taking only a moment to brush stray grass from the knee of his black jeans.

"Did he really just call ye 'Yer Eminence'?" Sean asked as he came alongside his partner.

*"It would seem so."*

Sean shook his head and muttered, "Just when ye think ye've seen it all ..." He folded his arms and took a step back and to the right, letting Alistaire hold the reigns on this one. Alistaire also noticed, in his peripheral vision, that Sean was rolling his neck, trying to loosen the muscles; transforming to near-wolfman and back must have exacerbated his symptoms from the meta-spider's bites, their supernatural provenance plaguing his normally rapid healing.

*"What is your name?"* he asked the vampire.

"Blayze."

Sean laughed out loud, " 'Blaze'? Jesus Christ ..."

Blayze shot him a go-to-hell look, but said nothing.

*"How old are you, Blayze?"*

"I'll be twenty—"

*"How long have you been a vampire?"*

Oddly enough, Blayze actually twitched at the word, flicking his eyes in Sean's direction, then around the nearest houses before being drawn back to Alistaire's gaze. He was apparently not used to having his nature openly discussed.

Alistaire was not remotely surprised when Blayze answered, "I, uh, I was turned about a year-and-a-half ago, I guess."

Sean whispered, "Means he was reborn here. In this world, not ours."

Alistaire nodded.

"What's that 'spose to mean?" Blayze demanded with impotent force.

Ignoring that, Alistaire asked, *"Do you know who I am, Blayze?"*

Blayze swallowed hard, another mortal trait. "Yeah, you're, um ... you're Alistaire Bachman. The older vampires call you 'the Scourge' and a bunch of other creepy shit."

*"And do you know why that is?"*

Another hard swallow. "You ... you kill vampires. They say you've killed a *lot* of vampires."

*"I prefer the term 'destroy,' but so long as you understand your peril in being here. You* do *grasp your current situation, do you not?"*

Blayze's eyes dropped, and he nodded. "You, um ... you could kil— could destroy me anytime you want."

"Ye got that right," Sean chimed in, a smirk in his voice.

Blayze glared at Sean again, his expression suggesting he was looking at something filthy, but it was to Alistaire he asked, "Why do you let *it* interrupt us like that?"

Before the young vampire could react, Alistaire stood directly in front of him, the fingers of his right hand embedded a quarter-inch into the muscle of his left pectoral. Blayze yelped in shock, then gasped in pain and tried to pull away, but Alistaire's fingers curled inward enough to maintain his grip.

*"I can penetrate your rib cage just as easily,"* Alistaire stated in a casual tone.

Near panic, Blayze grabbed Alistaire's wrist with both hands and tried to pry his fingers away from — out of — his chest.

Alistaire's hold did not loosen.

*"If you show my werewolf friend even the slightest disrespect again,"* Alistaire continued, his demeanor still quite relaxed, displaying no effort at all even as Blayze

struggled, *"I will rip your heart from your body. I view such acts as falling somewhere between liberating a lost spirit and exterminating a parasite, so doing this would prove quite satisfying. Do you understand?"*

Blayze merely whimpered as he desperately tugged at Alistaire's wrist. His eyes bulged as it sank in that he wasn't getting out of this unless Alistaire *let* him out.

Alistaire raised his voice only slightly. *"I asked you a question: Do you understand? I will not ask again."*

"Yes, yes," Blayze cried, "I understand, I do, I swear, I *swear*!"

"Keep yer voice down," Sean commented.

Blayze looked over at the werewolf again, and to his credit, his face betrayed no sign of its former sneer. "Yes ... yes, sir." He even released his grip on Alistaire's wrist, dropping his hands and accepting his submissive position.

Content that he had made his point, Alistaire removed his fingers with a soft *shuck!* and snapped his hand to one side, flicking the young vampire's watery blood into the grass.

*"How did your master know where to find us?"* Alistaire asked, continuing as though their conversation had never been sidetracked. *"My colleagues and I are not in the habit of advertising our home address."*

Blayze's posture remained cowed, but his inflection returned dangerously close to insolence as he replied, "Well, um, do you really think you can be the, um, the *threat* that you are, and they wouldn't track you down? I mean, come on. The masters have known where you live for a while now, at least since before I became a, um, you know ..."

"If that's the case, if ye're tellin' the truth, then why haven't they attacked us?"

Blayze scoffed, "Man, they don't want *anything* to do

with you. You guys have got a reputation, you know? No one's tried to 'attack' you because the masters have learned to never, ever fuck with you, if they can avoid it."

"No shit?"

*"Interesting,"* Alistaire said. He glanced back at Sean and knew they were sharing a similar thought: Blayze might have been turned in this world, but for their reputation to be so well known, the "masters" almost certainly came from their home dimension. *"A lesson, centuries in the teaching, has finally been learned."*

"I heard a rumor," Blayze added, "that some big shot vampire wanted to blow up your house in the middle of the day. I mean with something wicked strong, that would take out the whole block, to make sure they got you. But the other masters, um ... well, I heard they decided to put him down before risking that it might fail, and you'd come looking for revenge."

*"Not exactly how we work,"* Alistaire pointed out, before admitting, *"though the results would be the same. But we digress. What, exactly, is it that your master is proposing? What are the terms of this so-called 'parley'?"*

Blayze cleared his throat and, back on the job, bowed his head. He began speaking a clearly memorized, well-rehearsed message, "My master, His Eminence Aaron Spencer—"

Sean snickered upon hearing another usage of "Eminence," but Alistaire and Blayze both ignored him.

"—extends his sincerest respects, and asks that you return with me to a neutral location, so that he may discuss with you a matter of grave importance to the entire vampire community. He pledges free passage to you, your werewolf, and your, um ... your zombie ..."

Blayze faltered for a moment, glancing up long enough to scan the front yard, as though someone else might have been standing there whom he had somehow missed. When he failed to locate said someone, he continued.

"You will not be assailed in any manner. You will be free to come and go without harm, and he asks only that you pledge not to cause harm in return. If you agree to these terms, he wishes to hold this exchange now, tonight."

Sean inched forward and commented in a low voice, " 'The entire vampire community,' huh?"

Alistaire met Sean's gaze and nodded his agreement. Vampires suddenly being attacked and transformed into meta-spiders ... and now some master vampire requests a parley, under armistice, with the Triumvirate? Not a coincidence.

Blayze stood waiting in silence, his head still bowed. Another car passed by, but a bent neck did not command attention on the level of a bended knee, and the driver ignored them. A pair of evening joggers were heading in this direction, and Alistaire deemed it prudent to wrap up this conversation, one way or another, before they were within earshot.

"We doin' this?" asked Sean.

Alistaire hesitated only a moment, then, *"Yes, I believe we are."*

Sean, trusting Alistaire's instincts, grunted a little under this breath, but otherwise did not react.

To Blayze, Alistaire stated, *"We accept Master Spencer's invitation for discussion. For the duration, we will initiate no hostilities, unless provoked. But if we are attacked in any manner — even by other, outside parties who may not be involved in this parley — we will destroy Master Spencer and every single one of his thralls, including you. Have I made myself clear?"*

Blayze answered, "Yeah, perfectly clear."

Alistaire nodded, then said to Sean, *"Secure the house."*

Sean stepped back inside.

"Your Eminence," Blayze asked Alistaire, "may I have your permission to call my master and let him know that you accept? And, um, your terms?"

Alistaire nodded. Blayze pulled a phone from his back pocket and started to turn away for privacy.

*"You may call, but stay where you are."*

Blayze shrugged as though he didn't care either way, and passed along the message, slipping in no code that Alistaire could detect, while the German exchanged a neighborly nod with one of the two joggers as they passed by.

When Sean emerged a very short time later — Alistaire and Blayze said nothing else to one another in the interim — he had changed his clothing, adding a jacket he normally shirked except for the coldest winter days; Alistaire suspected it was to further hide his injuries. Sean locked the front door, shoved the keys in his front jeans pocket, and rejoined Alistaire.

"All locked up," he said in a normal tone, then turned his head away and leaned into Alistaire, sub-vocalizing so low that even Blayze's vampire hearing would hopefully miss it, "I left a note for Trey to wait here until we return, just in case."

Alistaire responded with a slight nod, then said to Blayze, *"We are ready. I presume you have transportation?"*

"Yeah, sure, of course," Blayze said, half-distracted as he again scanned the yard and both sides of the house. When he failed to locate what he was searching for, he asked, "Where, um ... where's your zombie?"

Without missing a beat, Alistaire replied, *"Trey has been monitoring our conversation from our other residence. I take it your master did not bother to share with you the location of our secondary home?"*

Blayze blinked. "Um ... no."

Alistaire shook his head, just slightly. *"If Master Spencer has this address, I trust he has the other as well. No matter. Trey will follow us in our own vehicle, to keep tabs on the situation from an independent perspective. Merely a precaution, I assure you."*

The young vampire was terribly confused. "Um ... I'm sorry, he ... he's going to follow us? Like, um, *drive* a car after us?"

*"That is correct. Shall we go?"*

"But ... but he's a *zombie*. Um, how ...?"

Sean played along, "Trey's an apple who fell pretty far from the zombie tree. Don't ye worry, he'll have no trouble followin' us. Trust me, ye'll never even know he's there."

Blayze looked back and forth between them, as though trying to decide whether or not they were punking him. In the end, he dropped the matter and settled for pointing out his car as he led the way with, "I'm just over there, the BMW."

Alistaire and Sean looked to where he had indicated. Sure enough, a shiny, black, late-model BMW was parked curbside across the street and a couple of houses west. The windows were tinted, but not enough for protection against unfiltered sunlight; Alistaire again considered that Blayze had already been in their area at sundown, but he still detected no other vampires nearby.

Sean, for his part, was admiring the car with a light whistle. Then he smiled and said to Alistaire, "So much for Uber, eh?"

Alistaire replied only with a slight smile.

In a lower voice, Sean said, "Trap?"

"*Quite possibly.*"

"And we're goin' anyway?"

"*Absolutely.*"

Sean chuckled, shaking his head. "Well, no one can ever say our lives are boring."

Alistaire offered another wisp-like grin as the two of them followed after the fledgling.

*    *    *

Self-employed business owner or not, Randy was seriously considering turning off his phone at 5:01 PM from now on.

First, he'd had to play catch-up from that morning, both from his little "surveillance" of Francis Morse's house and his unexpected job at Dave Rinear's place — though the latter had paid well, courtesy of Dave's gratitude for Randy's saving his party. Then he'd come across not one, not two, but three new spiders with which he had no familiarity. The situation was still bugging the hell out of him, but he hadn't bothered capturing these newest fellows; he didn't have time to deal with that today.

At the end of his work day, Randy had gone straight home to be with Lori — he was feeling better from his Widow bite, and was hoping for conjugal therapy to help him kick it for good. And he had just walked through the door when his damn phone rang.

"You don't have to answer it, you know," Lori said as she walked in from the kitchen; Randy could smell something hot and appetizing on its way. "That's why you have voicemail. You can call them back tomorrow."

Randy had been thinking along the same lines until he checked the Caller ID. "Aw, hell," he groaned. "It's Dave Rinear."

"The appointment you squeezed in this morning?" Lori had always possessed an amazing memory.

"Yeah. I better take it, in case something went wrong. Don't want a bad Yelp review."

"Do rich people Yelp?" she asked, but Randy was already answering the phone.

"Randy McDonnell."

"*Randy!*" Dave cried so loud that Randy had to pull the phone away from his ear. "*Hey, it's Dave. From this morning?*"

"Yes, Dave. The Brown Widows in your backyard, right?"

"*That's right! I wanted to thank you so, so much. My wife was out there this afternoon, she didn't have a clue there'd ever been a problem. That stuff you used didn't leave any smell, and the only spider she saw was, like, already dead. All the tables are totally spider-free!*"

"That's great to hear, Dave. I appreciate the call, and your gratuity."

"*Not a problem, dude. You totally earned that tip. You did good by me, I wanted to do good by you.*"

"Thanks again. Listen, I—"

"*In fact, that's why I'm calling. Are you, like, available this evening?*"

"I don't generally work nights, Dave. If there's a problem with—"

"*Oh, no, there's no problem, like, at my place. But I have this lady friend who lives nearby—*"

"Dave, I—"

"*—and she's got this wine cellar. Well, I mean, it's not a wine cellar, not like down under the house, it's really* *more of, like, a guesthouse that she's turned* into *a wine cellar. Seems kind of silly to me, but she's got the big bucks, you know what I mean?"*

"I think I—"

*"Anyway, my lady friend, Sharla, she went out there to grab a bottle for dinner, and the way her girlfriend puts it, I'm surprised I didn't hear her scream all the way over at my place. She's got tarantulas, dude! Like,* inside *her wine cellar-guesthouse."*

"I'm sorry to hear that, Dave," Randy raised his voice a little, desperate to get a word in edgewise. "If you give her my number—"

*"She could call you tomorrow, yeah, I know, that's what I told her. You see, they called me over to see if I could do anything, but I took one look inside that little house, and let me tell you, the damned things are all over the place! I got my tanned ass right the fuck out of there!"*

"That's probably for the best—"

Lori poked her head back in, asking with gestures if Randy wanted her to do something to get him off the phone. He swallowed a sigh and shook his head.

*"Damn right! But listen, I understand you don't work nights, I really do. Hell, I never work nights! But my lady friend and her girlfriend? They're, like, never gonna get any sleep, knowing they got about a thousand eight-legged freaks right there on their property. And they were already upset, see, 'cause they couldn't find their Schnauzer before and ... holy shit! You don't think the* tarantulas *got their dog, do you? Dude, now* I'm *not gonna get any sleep!"*

Randy could see where this was going and decided, rather than let it drag out, he should just cut to the chase. "Listen, Dave, I suppose I could make a special run out to your lady friend's property, but she needs to understand that I'll have to charge double for the late—"

"*That's awesome, dude! But listen, just between you and me, you should probably charge her, like,* triple *for your inconvenience. Like I said, she's got the big bucks!*"

"Double will be fine, but I appreciate the suggestion. If you shoot me your friend's phone number, I'll call—"

"*Not a problem, my man. I'm calling from her driveway right now. I'll text you the address, then just pop back in there and tell her you're on your way. You got any idea, like, how long you might be?*"

"You said she lives close to you?"

"*A little ways, but not too far, yeah.*"

"Okay. I'll need to stop by my office first. I can make it in, say, half an hour? Forty-five minutes if I hit traffic."

"*I'll just tell her, like, 'less than an hour.' Sound good?*"

"Sounds good."

"*Thanks so much, dude. They're* really *gonna appreciate this!*"

"My pleasure. Thanks for thinking of me." He meant it, too. Mostly, anyway.

Hanging up the phone, Randy let out a long groan, rolled his still-stiff neck, and turned around to go give Lori the bad news—

—only to find her already standing right there, a large thermos in each hand.

"Hot coffee in the brown, hot soup in the yellow. Don't mix 'em up."

Randy smiled, accepting the thermoses with gratitude. "I love you."

"I love you, too." She stood up on her tiptoes to kiss him. "Go save the day."

And so, like a complete idiot, he had left that fine woman behind and headed out for a fun evening of dealing with tarantulas. Great ...

Now, loaded up from the office and finally on his way, Randy punched the address from Dave's text into his GPS and absently glanced toward the special pesticide mixture, still sitting in an extra-large container on the passenger-side floorboard. The whole Francis Morse situation still nagged the hell out of him, but he figured that, after tomorrow, it wouldn't really be his concern anymore. When they met at Noon, Randy would offer, one more time, to handle the spider problem for him; the place appeared to be crawling with them, so surely Morse's unwanted houseguest—

That brought Randy up short. He thought back to how Morse had looked that morning, all haggard and spider-bitten, grungy and unwashed, exhausted eyes ...

*Something's off*, he thought yet again. *No way in hell Morse is just hiding the spider problem from some guest staying under his roof, not looking like that. I get why he wants the pesticide so badly, after what I saw ... but why the hell does he want to handle it by himself? I deal with these things all damn day, and* I've *got the itchies over what I've been seeing lately.*

This prompted a fresh round of scratching, but at this point, he was almost beyond noticing his new habit.

Randy's mind cast back to that blog entry he had read the night before, the one about the freakish death of the photographer and the bizarre "super-webs" found at the crime scene. He had confirmed on Google that, yes, some sort of strange death had indeed occurred, a photographer named Mitchell Gamall, and that police were investigating the matter. He found no mention of the webs at the scene, so either the *Watchdogs of the Weird & Unusual* had fabricated that element, to give the story a creepy factor ... or the webs were being treated as "evidence" in some capacity, and the information withheld from the *Los Angeles Times,* et al.

Of course, he still had no real reason to connect the webs at the crime scene with the Francis Morse situation ... so why did he keep doing it? What did one have to do with the other?

Another tidbit he found while corroborating the blog was that some news outlets were starting to comment on the rise in spider activity — which he found strangely validating, on a personal level, but which also confirmed that spiders were going ape-shit all over L.A., not just his side of town.

So the presumed spider activity at the crime scene did not need to have a single, direct thread connecting it to Francis Morse.

*Just drop it, for God's sake,* he chastised himself. *They have nothing to do with one another, and you have no reason to think otherwise.*

Except his gut kept telling him that something—

*Apples and oranges, damn it! Apples and oranges. Let it go.*

In the end, his little conflict halted by default when he pulled into the open-gated driveway of one Sharla Macke and girlfriend. He was on the job again, so he needed to get his head right.

Leaving his equipment in the truck until he made a preliminary inspection, he barely reached their front walk before the door opened and two young-ish ladies flew out to greet him; they talked over each other so much, he had trouble following everything they said. He gathered they were terrified of the tarantulas ending up in the main house, they were worried sick about their dog, and Dave had apparently told them Randy was nothing short of a miracle worker.

They escorted him through the house — a very nice house, he noted, even by the standards of the neighborhood — but left him on his own at the back door. They huddled together, staring out through the fancy French doors as he strode along a gravel path, bordered by solar-powered stake lights, across their expansive backyard to the guesthouse-slash-wine cellar.

Clicking on his Maglite — either the ladies or Dave had left the one-bedroom guesthouse's porch light on, but he wanted something a little more directional — he pointed the bright beam into the darkest corners. He spotted one critter near the far end of the porch, a medium-sized Calisoga spider, a.k.a. the "False Tarantula," but that was it. Between the Calisoga and civilians' natural tendency to exaggerate spider encounters, Randy presumed this would be a fairly easy job.

Boy, was he wrong.

As he eased the front door open and shined the beam of his Maglite inside, Randy released a very unprofessional, undignified gasp.

The open, accessible interior was set up in a very cool manner, both figuratively and literally; a breath of chilled air greeted him as he stuck his face inside. In the dim, mood-lit space, he could make out bottle-laden racks running away from him in three neat rows, and the walls had been papered to show the stone of a classic, European basement.

What did *not* belong, what had prompted his embarrassing pant, were the multitudes of true tarantulas dominating the faux wine cellar.

While the tarantulas did not number in the thousands, as Dave had indicated, Randy guessed they did number in the hundreds. In all his years as an exterminator, he had never encountered anything like it; even the recent explosion of spider activity didn't prepare him for this. Dave had likened his Brown Widow problem to a horror film, but this was a hell of a lot closer to the mark; outside of Hollywood movies, he had never before seen so many tarantulas together in one place.

Randy felt movement against his work shoe and glanced down to find one of the hairy little buggers trying to sneak out the open doorway. He sort of push-kicked it back inside and closed the door, shining his flashlight all around as he retreated a few steps. He saw one Mexican Redknee Tarantula making its way through the grass, but that was all. From his perspective, they appeared to be confined to the guesthouse — for the moment — but it was dark out here, so he couldn't be sure.

He had brought a few traps along in the back of the truck, as well as his normal odorless spray and some Boric acid powder ... but that had all been on the assumption that Dave had been embellishing his story; clearly, that was not the case. Embarrassing as it was from a professional standpoint, he was ill-equipped to handle something like this.

Except ... he did have the special pesticide he had mixed for Francis Morse.

That notion made him a little sad, as using the strong stuff would not be his first choice. Paradoxical as it might seem to some, tarantulas had not been triggering his itchies; scary as most people found them, he took comfort in the fact that they were so big, they couldn't sneak up on him — hell, a moment ago, he'd felt the one runaway *through* his shoe, let alone one of them trying to crawl up his sleeve or down his collar or whatever.

Still, he didn't have a lot of options here. The alternative was to admit that the job was too big for him, and try to call in a favor from one or more of his colleagues — *if* he could convince any of them to come out at this time of the evening. That, or slink away with his tail between his legs, letting one of the bigger companies snatch up yet another client ...

No. Ashamed as he was to admit it, that last notion stuck in his craw. No way was he letting any of the big boys take this. He would handle this himself.

A little voice in the back of his head, a voice which sounded an awful lot like Lori, whispered, *Pride goeth before a fall ...*

*Shush,* he thought back. *I got this.* He looked at the guesthouse. *Sorry, my hairy friends, but as my sons would say, you are going down.*

Returning to the main house, Randy explained to the ladies that the situation in their guesthouse was, in his qualified estimation, "quite serious." Yes, he told them he had the means of dealing with it, but it would involve highly toxic chemicals, which would require that they ventilate and avoid their "wine cellar" for—

He never got to state his suggested time window.

"Mister McDonnell," Sharla informed him in a no-nonsense voice, "after what I saw this evening, I might *never* go back out there! You do whatever you need to do to keep those— those *things* out of our house!"

Sharla and her girlfriend, whose name turned out to be Darla — Randy had to fight very hard not to guffaw when he heard this — signed a safety waiver without blinking an eye, then hurried him back out to the driveway to collect whatever he needed.

Standing at the open back of his truck, Randy suited up: Full-body coveralls, from ankles to wrists — half against the pesticide, half against the tarantulas themselves; safety goggles against over-spray; water-proof, chemical-resistant work gloves; and a heavy-duty respirator mask with replaceable filter cartridges.

Carrying his spray canister in one hand and the container of his special mixture in the other, armored for arachnoid war, Randy felt pretty cool, actually, and had to resist a childish urge to walk in slow motion like something straight out of a Michael Bay flick. Hell, Sharla and Darla fairly gushed at the sight of him ... well, maybe "gushed" was overstating it, but he would not have been surprised if one or both had addressed him as "My hero!" as he marched back through their house and up the gravel path to the wine cellar.

His bravado held fast until he opened the guesthouse's front door, and even gave it the old college try as he stepped inside and closed the door behind him ... but after that, his mouth dried up, his heart climbed into his throat, and his bowels were threatening possible mayhem. So many tarantulas ...

As he looked around the room, over the wine racks, along the walls, up at the ceiling, Randy was struck by another oddity, beyond their sheer numbers: They were walking around like they did in the movies. In his personal experience, tarantulas tended to be very still most of the time, until they honed in on prey, at which point they launched themselves forward rather quickly.

The tarantulas here in the guesthouse behaved erratically, constantly on the move — like they were all males seeking mates. Whatever the cause, something sure had them stimulated ...

He again felt activity across his feet. Glancing down, he saw two of them sauntering along their merry way, but another one had decided it wanted to go exploring up his leg. He stomped his foot hard a few times, and the critter fell away, landing on its back and kicking its legs frantically until it managed to turn over.

Stalling wasn't going to help, so he set down his sprayer and opened it up, tucked his Maglite into his left armpit, and armed himself with the strong stuff even as more tarantulas stopped by to see what was what. The sooner he got the job done, the sooner he could open all the windows and start checking around the outside of the—

An odd sound caught his attention, making him pause as he finished prepping his sprayer. He turned his head to one side, trying to zero in on whatever it was. For a moment, it had sounded like ... sucking?

Huh. Nope, nothing now, just him and hundreds of tarantulas. Maybe it had been the collective sound of their moving spider-feet? No, that didn't make sense, either. But regardless, he had a job to do.

Randy set the empty pesticide container by the front door and readied himself for the spiders' reactions when the first spray hit them — he was confident the primary targets would drop almost immediately, but those who only got mist or droplets on them were not going to be happy campers. Holding the sprayer's canister in his left hand and the nozzle in his right, twisting so that his arm-pitted Maglite pointed into the front-left corner of the room, he took aim and—

There it was again, that weird sucking/suckling sound. What the hell *was* that?

He recalled that the ladies' dog — Edward, their Schnauzer — was missing. He had dismissed the notion that "the spiders might have gotten him" as typical civilian paranoia, but that had been before he saw how many tarantulas he was dealing with here. It still seemed more likely that the dog would feast on, rather than be feasted upon, but if that was the explanation, then why wasn't he hearing *chewing* noises?

The sound stopped again, but at this point it intrigued him. For several seconds, he teetered between dealing with the major task at hand or checking out the rest of the small guesthouse, until he settled on two birds, one stone.

With a final whispered apology, he sprayed the tarantulas as he eased his way toward the back. As anticipated, those struck head-on curled in on themselves in an instant; unfortunately, also as expected, those who only caught runoff or a light spritz went absolutely ape-shit, tearing off in one direction or another, in one case actually attacking a neighbor. Randy took no pleasure in it, though he was proud of his formula's proven efficiency; Francis Morse was going to be a happy customer.

Passing beyond the wine racks, he found only a short hallway, illuminated by more dim lighting, and two open, dark rooms. A quick glance to the left revealed a tarantula-infested bathroom — he wouldn't be taking a leak in there anytime soon! — leaving the right as the would-be single bedroom. Peeking inside that unlit room, he saw movement in the far corner, but couldn't make it out with only the weak bulb from the hallway.

Rotating his body like before, he aimed his Maglite from his armpit, directing the beam more precisely into the—

Randy's mind absolutely rejected what he was seeing, so at first, he saw nothing at all.

That wasn't entirely true, though. He could tell that a dog was involved, somehow. Except he thought that Schnauzers were usually grey, and this fellow was black. And bigger, like a Doberman. Huh. Must be someone else's dog, then. But why was it in here, in their wine cellar? And why was it just letting all those tarantulas stand all over it? A dog that size should be able to shrug them off, even after multiple bites. Of course, that was a huge bite on its belly there. And up by its neck, where the spider fangs were moving around, sucking, making that sucking noise, that sucking noise that he'd heard, that sucking noise as it fed on the Doberman, which it probably dragged through that open window and now this spider this fucking enormous spider was feeding on a large dog like most spiders fed on beetles and it was so big that he couldn't wrap his mind around it no no no this didn't make sense he could not he could *not be seeing* what he was seeing!

The impossible thing that he was not seeing, that he was absolutely *not* seeing, because it must be the fumes or something, something must be wrong with his mask that was all — that impossible thing lifted its head from the dog's throat and turned to stare into the light beam from his Maglite. A flicker of relief passed through Randy when he realized that it wasn't, *of course* it wasn't a giant spider, but a *person* — except why would a person be suckling on the bloody neck of a dog? — but it was only a flicker and it did not last. Because in spite of the size and shape of that human-looking head and neck, those were decidedly *in*human eyes staring into the bright light — two big ones, and six little ones. Eight, count 'em, *eight* ... fucking ... eyes.

Randy screamed. He screamed like a little boy discovering that the monster under his bed was real after all.

The scream did not faze this monster from Randy's worst nightmares, and the flashlight's beam only seemed to confuse it. But when he stumbled backwards into the doorjamb of the bathroom behind him, that got its attention.

The bloody fangs glistened as it hissed, its hideous mouth wide. It crouched a bit lower, then launched itself at Randy; had it not needed to clear the doorway first, he knew the monster could have reached him with that single leap. But it did need to clear the doorway, giving him one — *one* — extra second to do something, anything.

Randy's mind was blank, but his body had an idea. As the monster lurched into the hallway, six of its eight limbs grasping for him, he lifted the nozzle of his pesticide sprayer and squeezed the trigger.

The spray struck the monster squarely in what passed for its face. For a heart-stopping moment, Randy thought it was going to shrug it off ... and then it was the monster's turn to scream.

Staggering away while unleashing a high-pitched sibilance, the monster pawed at its face, clawing with freaky, long fingers at its eyes; Randy thought he could even see the black orbs actually smoldering, an extreme reaction even for his potent mixture. The monster was so aggressive it accidentally punctured its own large eye on its left side, which prompted even more spasms of pain.

Randy did not wait to see how it ended. He dropped his Maglite but held onto his sprayer as he ran for the front door, squashing tarantulas along the way. Those wonderfully *normal* spiders, the fellows that were his original reason for being here, were jumping and scampering and fighting amongst themselves, but only the smallest sliver of Randy's mind paid any attention.

Before reaching the door, his toes came down right on a pair of battling arachnids, the resulting gunk causing him to slip to the right and stagger into one of the wine racks.

It saved his life.

The monster — which had been chasing him after all by running along the fucking *ceiling* — dove and raked its forearms through the space where his head should have been. Instead, it also struck a wine rack on the other side of the aisle from Randy, shattering bottles there whereas Randy had only rattled his. It righted itself quickly, hissing in presumed anger as it lashed out, missing Randy by a good measure until it stumbled around in a full circle.

Randy could see that the monster's remaining eyes were cloudy and runny. It couldn't see him. It couldn't see him!

Biting his lower lip to avoid whimpering, with only partial success, he took a very careful step backwards ...

Not careful enough, unfortunately. The heel of his work shoe *tinked* against one of the wine bottles that had fallen loose, and the monster instantly zeroed in on it. Instead of lunging forward, this time it curled its torso, and pearly webbing squirted at Randy.

Randy tried to avoid the thick silk, and almost made it; most of it spurted across the canister of his pesticide sprayer, with just enough getting on his left arm and the wine rack to prevent his slipping away. It wasn't a strong hold and, especially in his adrenaline-filled state, he would be able to pull free ... if he had more time. But he didn't.

The monster approached him, actually crawling on its eight legs before rising to loom over him. He tried to bring his sprayer to bear, but the space between them was too confined.

*Lori was right. I shouldn't have answered the phone.*

The monster — the giant, humanlike spider — opened its mouth, fangs poised. Randy pressed the side of the nozzle against it, to shove it away, but he might as well have been pushing against hirsute stone.

*I'm so sorry, Lori. I love you.*

The monster hissed and jerked forward, aiming for his throat.

# ... 16 ...

Having taken the edge off his hunger again (a little bit, anyway), Trey planned to tiptoe out of the big backyard, where he had hidden to deal with it, and get back to the car. He was so, *so* close to the source of the voodoo magic, he could just *feel* it! That, plus he was seeing more and more spiders and spider webs and dead, webbed insects, and that was too much of a coincidence. But his hunger had gotten so bad again, he'd known that he first needed to—

A man's scream startled the heck out of him. The crazy thing was, it sounded like it was coming from right out here in the yard, instead of the big house up front.

Crawling out from behind the hedge, he first looked toward the big house, but more ruckus pulled his attention the other way. He spotted a cute little house he hadn't noticed before, since he had been ... distracted. The scuffle was coming from there, so loud because of an open window on this side.

A familiar hissing sent chills down his spine.

Moving as quickly as he could, he thought about trying to find a door, but it didn't sound like he had time. Skidding to a halt at the open window, he lifted his big right leg and stepped inside, thankful in this case for his height. He shifted his balance and ducked his head through, and he was in.

The room was dark and shadowy, but a dull light from the hallway gave him just enough to see by. Man, there were a lot of really big spiders in here! He thought they were bad outside, but this was—

A double-crash from somewhere else in the house snatched his attention back into place. He hustled into the hallway, looking into the bathroom across the hall before more movement, and someone's whimpering, drew him to the left.

He didn't have long to take it in: A man, dressed up like people did in the movies when they were entering a poisonous or disease-ridden place, just got webbed to a long shelf-unit by one of the meta-spider-things, and now it was closing in on him! Trey's first impulse was to run and tackle it before it could reach the poor man, but a bunch of bottles (some broken, some still in one piece) littered the floor around both of them, and he was worried he would slip or trip. So he moved as quickly as he could, just as the meta-spider opened its jaws and lurched for the man's throat!

Seeing no other choice, Trey lunged forward and thrust his right hand in the way, blocking the meta-spider's attack by taking the bite himself. Its huge spider-fangs snapped down on the fleshy part between his thumb and forefinger, one fang tearing a channel straight through and away while the other snagged on a tendon on its way out. Had he been alive, the pain would have been excruciating. Even as a zombie, it didn't exactly feel good.

Unleashing his own growl, Trey used that damaged-but-still-working hand to grab the meta-spider's face and shove it away with all his strength, slamming it against the already crooked shelf unit. The whole thing toppled away from them, making a horrendous racket of breaking glass and hissing-roaring giant spider.

"Thank you," the man whispered, tears streaming from his goggle-covered eyes, "thank you, thank you ..."

"You okay?" Trey asked him, but he kept his attention on the meta-spider. The thing was having trouble getting back onto its legs because of all the littered chaos under it, the cracked shelves and all those bottles ...

Bottles. That gave Trey an idea.

"I-I-I think so," the man answered, half-sobbing, " ju-just kind of stuck, a l-little. It w-webbed my arm." Then he pleaded, "Please, *please* ke-keep that monster away from me!"

"I'll do my best," Trey reassured him, even as he reached back with his good left hand and lifted a bottle off the closest shelf. He then adjusted his grip so he was holding it from the bottom, the circular base cupped in his large palm.

The meta-spider finally got itself fully upright. Hind legs bent and ready to jump, fangs spread as though to hiss again but staying quiet, it slowly twisted his head first one way, then another. Trey wondered what the heck it was doing until he saw that one of its big eyes was hurt, and the others were all frosted and yucky-runny. The man must've blinded it somehow, so it couldn't see Trey. Was it trying to hear him? Smell him? Feel for movement?

Thinking back to how the one acted in their house, Trey stomped one of his feet.

The meta-spider snapped its head straight at him.

Even when they couldn't see, they were drawn to movement. He would have to remember that, so he could—

The meta-spider leaped, which was fine by Trey.

As it slammed into him, Trey shoved the glass bottle forward, neck-first, right into its open mouth. The spider's own momentum forced the bottle in further still, its humanoid gullet bulging as the glass object stretched and tore its way past where the Adam's apple would've been, the fatter base wedging its mouth wide open.

The meta-spider held still for a moment, bewildered by what was happening to it, and Trey took that opportunity to punch its swollen throat.

The muffled sound of shattering glass made even the scared man cringe. The spider released a guttural, wet moan from deep inside, which sounded more human than the hissing these things usually made.

Trey showed no mercy. He placed his wounded hand on top of its head, then used his good hand to uppercut its jaw, breaking the bottom portion of the glass bottle inside its mouth. Still holding its head, he then punched it one more time, right between all of its runny eyes, caving its mutated eye sockets inward.

Trey let go, and the meta-spider fell over backward. It twitched and spasmed on top of the shelf unit, but showed no sign of trying to rise again.

A muffled woman's voice called from outside, "Mister McDonnell?! Are you all right in there?! What was all that noise?!"

Trey looked at the man ("Mister McDonnell," he guessed), then at the meta-spider and around the room. "You should probably answer ... unless you think the lady ... could handle this?" He made a vague gesture at the disaster surrounding them, including all the big regular spiders (wow, there were even more in here!) and the giant, impossible one he had just brought down.

"Mister McDonnell?" The speaker sounded closer to the little house now.

The man nodded, huffed a few breaths, pulled and tugged his webbed arm, the sleeve of his coverall stretching, until he was a little closer to the front door.

"Ye—" He cleared his throat. "Yeah, yes. Yes! I'm fine, I'm okay, I just, uh ..."

A different woman spoke up, her voice sounding less worried, more angry, a tone Sean had described before as "shrill." "Hey, Randy, what are you *doing* in there? Huh?!"

"I, uh ... I, uh ..." The man ("Randy") looked at Trey for help. Trey had no idea what he should say, so he instead stepped over, braced Randy with his less-messy hand, and ripped the webbing free.

Randy nodded thanks, then hurried to the front door. He put his hand on the doorknob, then hesitated as he looked around. Selecting an especially large spider (by normal standards), he plucked it off the wall and placed it on his own elbow, then opened the door and leaned outside, making sure the arm with the spider on it was visible. Trey caught the sound of a squeal and scuttling feet, and pictured two women backing up in a hurry, away from the little house.

"I'm sorry," Randy explained. Trey could tell he was still upset by his close call, but the mask-thing over his nose and mouth and the goggles might, hopefully, hide this from the ladies. "I, uh, I came across a ... oh, excuse me..." He casually lifted the big spider from his arm and dropped it back inside the little house. "I came across a nest in here, and it was bigger than I expected, and uh, the tarantulas started jumping and, I ... I'm afraid I knocked over one of the shelves, broke some bottles, and—"

"*What*?!" came the second voice, the harsh one. "You did *what*? Oh, hell no!" This was followed by the sound of feet clomping on gravel back toward them.

"Darla, *no*!" cried the first lady.

"I want to see!" snapped the second ("Darla"). "Look, I'll just take a quick peek inside, all right? See what kind of *damage* this 'gentleman' has done to our—"

"I wouldn't suggest that," Randy cut in, speaking quickly and pulling the door tighter until there was only enough space for his leaning body. "I'd be happy to pay for the damages, but your spider situation is a little worse than I first thought. The, uh, the nest wasn't just a regular tarantula nest, it belongs to Goliath Birdeaters."

The sound of approaching feet came to a screeching halt. "To ... to what?"

"Goliath Birdeaters," Randy repeated. Then he started sounding like one of Trey's old school teachers as he went on, "They're a member of the Tarantula family, indigenous to South Africa, but these fellows have been doing some traveling, I gather. They usually prefer more swampy—"

Darla interrupted, her voice even more shrill than before. "Did you say 'Birdeater'? Like, the goddamn things eat *birds*?!"

"Sometimes. But they're just as likely to eat lizards, rats, maybe snakes—"

The footsteps retreated again. "Okay, nope, no, fuck that, you do *whatever* you need to do, Randy. We can ... we can discuss payment and damages and whatever when they're all dead. Deal?"

"Deal," Randy replied, keeping it light and jovial. Trey thought the man was a darn good actor, especially since the meta-spider-thing was still spasming on the messy floor just a couple of yards away from him during all this.

"Do ..." the first lady spoke up again, and she sounded like she was crying a little, "... do you think these, these Birdeaters or whatever ... do you think they got our little Edward?"

Trey had no idea who "Edward" might be, but Randy didn't waver. "I still think it's unlikely, ma'am, but ... I'm afraid I can't say for sure."

A sad sniffle was his only answer, and then two pairs of footsteps trailed away. Randy leaned back inside, closed the door, and sagged against it until his hands were resting on his knees.

Trey let him take a moment, keeping an eye on the not-quite-dead meta-spider. Once he was sure it wasn't going to get back up, he would need to find something to wrap around his hand before Randy noticed ... the ...

Trey's eyes widened as he looked down at his wounded hand, his *bleeding* hand. Bleeding, as in real blood. Well, it was maybe a little too thick, too murky to be *real*-real, but it was red and it didn't give off a foul odor like the dark brown stuff that usually oozed out of him when his skin was broken deep.

He was again struck by the paradox (and struck yet again by how quickly, how easily that uncommon word, "paradox," leaped to mind): The more monstrous he behaved, the more "normal" his body became.

Wait, did that mean the meta-spider's venom would affect him, like it did Sean? No, no, he felt okay, didn't feel any symptoms like Sean showed so soon after getting bitten. So he guessed that meant he was still—

"I have a first aid kit in my truck."

Trey looked up. Randy had risen from his hunched-over position, but he remained with his back to the door, far away from the *still*-twitching gigantic spider-thing that had almost killed him.

"For your hand. And your mouth. You've got blood all over your mouth."

"Thank you," Trey replied, hastening to wipe a forearm firmly across the lower part of his face, hoping that Randy did not ask or wonder at what point Trey might have gotten bloodied there.

"Thank *you*. You saved my life from ... from whatever the hell that is, and I don't even know your name. I'm Randy." The words and demeanor matched the offering of a handshake, but Randy made no move to get any closer to the meta-spider.

"I'm Trey."

"Nice to meet you, Trey. I— excuse me."

Randy turned away from him and the meta-spider, pulled the mask and goggles off in a smooth, double-handed sweep up his face, and vomited. The tarantulas moved out of the way as though they'd been struck by an unexpected downpour ... which was sort of the case, if a gross one.

After emptying his stomach, followed by some dry heaves and lots of spitting, Randy fumbled his mask and goggles back on (not nearly as smooth this time, since his hands were shaking). "Whew. If I'd remembered how strong the fumes are, I guess I might've tried to hold that in a little longer."

"Probably not ... a good idea," Trey offered. Now that Randy said it, he noticed the strong chemical smell that permeated the place. Between that, Randy's coverall, and the exchange he'd just overheard, Trey guessed Randy was an exterminator, and had probably been out here dealing with the serious spider problem when the real danger struck.

"I guess not." Randy had been staring at the meta-spider again, but now he lifted his gaze to Trey, really looking at him for the first time. "Don't take this the wrong way, Trey, because I'm really, truly grateful to you for saving me, but ... who *are* you? Where did you come from? And what ..." He pointed at the meta-spider. "... the *fuck* ... is that thing?"

Thinking of how Sean might handle this, Trey replied,

"Long story short, I'm someone ... who deals with monsters." Even through the goggles, he saw Randy's eyes squint with skepticism, so he pointed at the meta-spider. "Monsters just like *that* one ... that tried to kill you. That would then ... have *eaten* you, if I hadn't been here."

All of (well, most of) the disbelief faded from Randy's eyes as he followed Trey's finger to look at the meta-spider once more.

Trey pressed on, "There are more of these things ... out there right now. A lot more, I think. I'm doing ... my best to find them and to stop them."

When he began, he had been merely trying to bluff his way out of too many questions, but then an opportunity occurred to him. After all, if he was right about the man's job ...

"May I please ask you ... a question?"

"Sure," Randy murmured, lost again in dark fascination as he watched the meta-spider twitch its eight legs and jerk its broken, human-shaped head back and forth.

"You're an exterminator ... right?"

"Yeah."

"Have you been seeing ... a lot of spiders lately?"

"God, yes."

"Okay, please really think about this: Is there any ... one place that you've seen more spiders ... than in other places? A lot more?"

Randy didn't answer right away, but then sort of shook himself and shifted his gaze to meet Trey's. "Recently, yeah, yeah. There's this place. I mean, just look around you."

Trey did, and nodded. There were more spiders here than he had ever seen before.

"This looks really bad, because tarantulas are so big,"

Randy went on. "Hell, even I freaked out a little when I first saw what was going on in here. But for sheer numbers ... I squeezed in a job this morning, new client, had a severe Brown Widow problem. Not as shocking to the naked eye, but I'd wager there were way, way more spiders in that backyard than we're seeing here. More spread out, not as easy to spot as tarantulas, but way more than there ever should've been. Brown Widows usually prefer nooks and crannies, tucking up underneath lawn furniture and garbage cans, but these things were everywhere, right out in the open, on top of the benches, on the porch, on the plants, the trees ... everywhere."

"Is that the worst?" Trey pressed. "Have you seen ... any place worse than that?"

"Hard to say. *All* spiders have been acting strange lately, exotic species popping up everywhere, but between Dave's backyard and here ..."

Trey, who had returned to keeping an eye on the meta-spider, looked up when Randy's words trailed off. The man had a focused look in his eye, like he was putting together pieces of a puzzle.

"No," he said. "No, this or Dave's might not be the worst, I just haven't gotten a really close look yet." He returned his attention to Trey. "There's another client — sort-of client. Guy wanted to buy pesticide off me, wanted something very strong and very fast, as fast-acting as possible. That's actually what this is." He gestured toward his sprayer, the canister of which was still partially webbed to the shelf where Trey had found him (and as he kept talking, Trey quickly stepped over and freed it for him). "He wanted the pesticide, but he didn't want my help, wanted to do it himself. I got curious and, uh, drove by his house — you know, just to see if there was anything ... Anyway, I drove by, and I saw the guy himself. He was in bad shape, all spider-bitten, and even from the outside, I saw tons of evidence that suggested a major, major spider infestation." He fell quiet for a moment, then asked, "Do you think that could have something to do with ... *that* thing?"

"Possibly. Where they go, where they're active ... spiders seem to go nuts. That's ... my theory, anyway."

"Good God ..." Randy whispered. He started fumbling around inside his coverall, eventually pulling out a phone. "We, we, uh ... we should call ..." Then he laughed at himself, a sad sound. "Yeah, right. Who the hell do we call for things like *that*?" His laughter stopped, and he looked to Trey, pleading for help with his eyes again. "Who *do* we call? What ... what can we even ...?"

Trey got the feeling he was about to lose Randy, so he asked, "Would you be able to ... take me to the really-bad house? With the guy who ... wanted your pesticide?"

"Yeah, yeah, sure, I guess."

"Right now?"

"Right *now*? But I still have to ..." He looked around at the tarantula-covered floor, walls, racks, then looked at the meta-spider that was *still* not giving up the ghost. "Christ, this is fucked up. We can't just leave, but ... how...?"

Trey thought a moment before saying, "What if you tell them ... that you need more equipment, or something? You said ... something earlier about 'Goliath Birdeaters'...?"

Randy nodded. "Yeah, it was all I could think of. The Goliath Birdeater is the biggest tarantula in the world, and I knew that the 'Birdeater' part would get their attention; it gets *everybody's* attention when I bring it up at parties."

"Tell them that you need something else ... to deal with it. And tell them *not* to come out here ... until you get back."

"I doubt that'll be a problem. But ..." He shook his head, a shuddering motion. "You understand that I *can't* really come back here, right? Not after seeing this. Hell, after tonight, I might have to get out of the business." He shook his head again, slower this time, more a sign of general disbelief. "Imagine a dog-trainer getting attacked by a gigantic, rabid Rottweiler straight from hell. Imagine a doctor finding a cancer tumor that was contagious. Imagine—"

"I understand," Trey interrupted before Randy's words could come any faster. "If we can just get out of here ... we can work out what comes next."

"Okay ... okay, that sounds good." He looked Trey up and down. "But how are we going to get *you* out of here? You're not exactly easy to hide ..." He blinked a few times. "And where the hell did you come from, anyway?"

"Through an open window."

"Ah." Another few blinks. "Were you ...? Why were you in their backyard? I mean, I'm guessing they don't know about you, am I right? I'm right, aren't I?"

Trey nodded.

"So why were you in their backyard?" he repeated.

"I was tracking it. And I try to avoid ... complications with civilians."

"Oh. Okay," Randy said, though he didn't sound like he fully believed it. If Sean were here, he would've charmed his way through, or Alistaire could have mesmerized the man into believing him. On his own, Trey just had to do his best.

"Let's do this," Trey suggested, trying not to sound like he was giving the guy a command. "I'll go back out the way I came in. You ... go through the house, tell them whatever you have to ... then meet me out on the street side."

"Okay. Um, which street?"

"Let me show you." Trey turned and took a few steps, then realized that Randy wasn't following. Before he could ask why, Randy pointed a shaking finger at the ever-stubborn meta-spider.

Nodding his understanding, Trey returned to its side, lifted his foot, and brought it down hard on the thing's head. It finally stopped twitching.

*Not too different from how you took care of Missy P—*
*Hush. Not now.*

Trey looked back up to find Randy's eyes so wide, they threatened to pop his goggles off his face. Trey didn't want to lose him again, so he raised his voice, "Follow me, Randy."

After a long moment, Randy did, though he opted to take the furthest aisle from the meta-spider that the shelves in here permitted (why were there so many wine bottles in this little house, anyway?).

Trey led him into the bedroom and over to the window. He held up a "Wait a second" finger, climbed through it, and once standing outside, he pointed. "Do you see that gap ... in the hedge? Behind the big tree?"

Randy leaned out with him, trying to find the spot. A tarantula dropped from the upper windowsill onto his shoulder, but after a brief flinch, he calmly brushed it off to the floor inside. "I'm sorry, I don't see— wait, a few feet past the little sculpture?"

Trey himself hadn't notice the small, stone decoration before. "Yes. I'll go through there ... and you can meet me next to—"

"Wait, hold on, hold on. Is that ...?" Randy leaned way out, then grunted and removed his goggles for another look. "Hold on a second ..."

He disappeared back into the house. Trey waited as patiently as he could, but the thought that he might have found a new lead made him edgy, ready to move on ...

Randy reappeared with a powerful flashlight in his hand. He shined it over to the gap Trey had indicated, except he aimed the beam at ground level.

"Oh, no," Randy said. "Oh, God. Is that a little grey dog? Right there by the hedge?"

*Uh-oh.*

"It is, isn't it? Ah, hell. It's their Schnauzer. Eddie? Edward." His shoulders sagged. "I was really hoping ... I mean, when I saw that thing eating a different dog, I ..." He glanced at Trey. "Did that thing do it? Eat their little dog?"

"Yes," Trey answered without hesitation. "Yes, it did. That's ... one of the, um, the clues ... that brought me here."

*Really, Trey?* whispered the smug voice. *You found the compelling clue after you were already crawling around in someone's backyard hedge? Think he's going to buy that?*

Luckily for Trey, he seemed to do just that. "Oh, that's too bad, too bad. One more thing we're going to have to figure out how to tell the ladies when ... when we figure out all the *rest* of this crazy shit." He clicked off his flashlight with a heavy sigh.

"Can you find your way around ... to that spot?"

"Yeah," Randy told him, "sure. I'll just hook a right at the end of the block. That's the direction we need to go anyway." He fell still, then snapped two sharp shakes of his head, as if trying to wake himself up. "Get going. I'll ... I'll come up with something and meet you there."

Randy withdrew into the little house, and Trey hustled over to the gap in the hedge ...

\* \* \*

Waiting for Randy to drive around the corner was difficult for Trey. He wanted to get going, to find the voodoo priest and wrap his hands around the evil monster's throat and do *some* good to maybe, in a very small way, make up for what he had done to Missy P. Yes, he was supposed to report back home, but that ship had long since sailed.

How much longer was this going to take? Fancy cars were driving by (a lot fancier than the Triumvirate's little car, which Trey hoped wasn't going to attract unwanted attention where it was parked not far away), and he doubted he'd done a good enough job cleaning his mouth. He couldn't even smile back at those who glanced his way, because he had no way of knowing how bloody his teeth might be.

*And fur. Don't forget, you could even have some grey dog fur stuck in there.*

Trey didn't say anything back to that side of himself this time, he merely growled at it ... and was only partially aware that he had done it aloud.

After what seemed like for-*ev*-er, a white truck rounded the corner and slowed as it pulled to the curb. Trey placed a hand on the passenger door handle, but Randy had already killed the engine and hopped out, heading around to the back. Trey huffed in impatience, but kept it quiet.

And he ended up feeling guilty, too, because it turned out the reason Randy wanted into the back of his truck was for Trey. As the latter joined him, Randy (who Trey saw was no longer wearing his mask or goggles, but still had on the coverall and gloves) lowered the tailgate and pulled out a small first aid kit.

Randy started to hand it to Trey, then hesitated. "Trey ... are you feeling all right?"

Trey was confused for only a second before realizing that, 1) thanks to the street lamp over them, this was the best, most brightly-lit look Randy had gotten at him so far, and 2) somewhere along the way, he had lost his sunglasses, and he had no idea where or when—

"You look kind of pale," Randy was saying, "and your eyes are a little ... are you sick or something?"

"Just tired," Trey said. "And my ... hand hurts. But I can take care of it, if ..." He looked at the kit in Randy's hand.

This last bit prompted Randy to pass it over, and Trey popped it open on the tailgate. Even as he hurried to pour alcohol onto the wound (just for show, of course; he even remembered to suck in his breath in "pain" as he did it), he felt Randy's eyes on him, studying him. If he were his old, pre-Alaska self, the exterminator would probably be running for the hills by now. Tonight, especially since Missy P ...

"Do you think ...?" Randy asked. "I mean, do you need to worry about *venom* from that thing?"

*Dang it.* "No, I don't think so. It ... didn't bite me the right way ... to inject any venom. Just ... went through the flesh." Then, not wanting to sound *too* confident about his immunity, he added an, "I hope."

"I suppose," was Randy's doubtful response. "Do you need help with that?"

Trey had finished with the alcohol and was wrapping gauze around his wound (while keeping it in the shadow cast by his body, because it did look really nasty!). "No, thanks. I'm ... pretty ambidextrous."

*There I go again. How long would I have had to search for the word "ambidextrous" before?*

"I can at least do the driving," Randy offered. "I know the way. Do you have a car nearby? Do you need to stop for anything?"

"No, I'm good." He taped the gauze several times around, then closed the first aid kit.

"Okay. I, uh ... I guess we should get going, then ..."

Once underway, Randy stuck his phone on a little mount on the underside of the dash, then his fingers kept hovering over it, like he wanted to touch it but couldn't.

"Do you need to ... make a call?" Trey asked.

"Yes. No. No, I probably shouldn't," he decided as he moved his wavering right hand to the steering wheel. "I want to call Lori — my wife — just to hear her voice. But I know better, I know *her*. Even if I try to act like everything's okay, she'll figure out something's wrong in a heartbeat. I've never been able to keep secrets from her. And if I actually try to tell her what *is* happening tonight?" He laughed, and though it sounded less sad than earlier, it was still a little too edgy. "Believe it or not, knowing her, she might actually believe me. But then she sure as hell wouldn't let me take you to Morse's house. Hell, *I'm* not really sure I want to be helping you. No offense."

"None taken," Trey offered, but Randy sailed right on over him.

"I just ... I'm still trying to wrap my brain around this, around that giant, mutant, were-spider or whatever the fuck it was ..."

*"Were-spider?"* Trey thought with a slight smile. *I'll have to share that with Sean.*

"... I mean, I'm man enough to admit that I just want to go home and hide under my bed, you know? But ... but if there are more of these things, and if you think they're somehow connected to Francis Morse's spider infestation..." He fell quiet for several seconds, then asked,

"What *are* you hoping to accomplish, Trey? You said before that you 'deal' with monsters like that, but do you think that Morse's house might be their, I don't know, their nest or something? Even if you burn the place to the ground ..."

"It's hard to say," Trey told him, and he meant it in more ways than one. How much should he be sharing with this man, this regular human? "I'll have to see ... what the situation is. There *might* be a way ... to stop them all, somehow. I'll just have to ... see what we're dealing with when I get there."

Randy responded to that with a vague nod.

They fell quiet after that, Randy only mumbling to himself under his breath from time to time as he navigated their way through the nice neighborhood (and kept scratching his arms and legs, like he had a rash or something). The silence felt awkward to Trey, yet he had no idea what more to say, or if he should say anything at all.

*You could always admit that* you *ate that grey dog. That should go over well.*

Trey ground his teeth. Concentrate. He needed to concentrate on what he would do when they reached the Morse house, where he *hoped* he might find the voodoo priest. The lingering trace of the bastard's magic definitely grew stronger as they drove along. He needed to be at his best for this—

*You* can *be at your best,* the hunger whispered, *easily. Wait until you're there, wait until this man has identified the exact house ... and then* feed *upon him.*

*Shut up. I don't need this right now.*

*He didn't call his wife, the women he was working for can't know where he's really going. It would be so easy ...*

*Shut. Up.*

*You might as well accept it, Trey. I'm here to stay.*
*SHUT UP! JUST SHUT THE HELL UP OR—*
"Here it is."

Trey blinked, startled but pleased that they had arrived so soon. Or had he drifted off again? Had he been half-dreaming his inner conversation? Hard to say, since the God-awful hunger was speaking up with more and more authority.

He looked to the house Randy was indicating. Like the others in this neighborhood, it was a lot more extravagant than where he lived with Alistaire and Sean. A small number of security lights lit the yard, but even though it wasn't very late yet, he didn't see any lights on inside the house from where they sat across the street.

Although ... when he looked closer, he noticed a muted flickering in one of the upstairs windows, barely visible through heavy curtains. Was that firelight?

"You can't see it now, because of the shadows and the closed gate," Randy told him, "but trust me, the place must be lousy with spiders."

"I'll take your word for it."

"So now what?"

"I'll try to find a way ... to sneak in. But I'm a little worried ... about his alarm system. In a house like that ... he's got to have an alarm system."

*If Alistaire were here,* he scolded himself, *that wouldn't be a problem, would it?*

"You may catch a break there," Randy said. "Spiders are hell on alarm systems. Security alarms, motion detectors, smoke detectors ..." He huffed a smile. "Most of the time when a house or, better yet, hotels get false fire alarms, it's because a spider waltzed across the mirror inside or tried to web some mechanism." He gestured toward the Morse house. "If his spider problem is even half as bad as I suspect, I'll bet he's had to turn the security systems off. That, or he's had to deal with a ton of false alarms, and I know for a fact that he doesn't want unexpected visitors, claims it's because of an 'unwanted houseguest.' I was curious before about *who* that might be, now I'm wondering *what* it might be."

"Okay," Trey digested it all, "so no alarms."

"Can't promise, of course, but I'd bet on it."

"That'll make things ... easier for me." Trey placed a hand on the doorhandle. "Thank you for bringing me here. You ... should go home now."

"Wait, wait, you ... you can't just *go*, Trey. I mean, you need to— I ..." Randy floundered, his breath quickening with everything he wanted to say but couldn't get the words together.

Trey sympathized with having trouble expressing thoughts. "It's all right, Randy. Go. Go home ... to Lori."

But Randy shook his head in large, shoulder-to-shoulder swings. "Huh-uh, huh-uh, *no*. You can't just send me off like this, not after what I saw earlier. I still don't know what to say to Sharla and Darla, I don't know how to explain the monster we left in their guesthouse, not to mention how to handle all the hundreds and hundreds of tarantulas still there with that ... that body." He held his breath for a moment, then continued in a rush, "Look, the point is, I, I, I hate cliffhangers, I don't like mysteries and monsters and spiders showing up from all over the goddamn world and acting crazy, and, and, and I'm never going to get any sleep if I don't get *some* kind of closure on all this!"

He gasped for more breath. Trey waited, hiding his impatience as best he could.

"Look," Randy continued, "Trey ... I don't, I don't even know you. If I hadn't seen that thing with my own eyes, I'd think you were a complete nutcase. But you saved my life, okay? And you seem to know *something* about what's going on. And I have *got* to understand this, somehow, got to process it. And if those things are loose in the city, if they're a danger to my wife, my kids—" He swallowed hard, then said, "Look me in the eye, Trey."

Trey did, half-expecting the usual *What's wrong with your eyes?* question.

Instead, Randy asked, "Do you *swear* to me, swear to me that you *do* understand what's going on here? And do you really, truly believe you can do something about it? There, in Morse's house?"

Maintaining the eye contact, Trey answered honestly, "I don't understand all of it ... but I do have some personal experience with it. And ... if this *is* the center of it all ... then yes, I really believe I can do ... something about it. I swear."

Randy nodded, slowly, the motion lasting several long seconds. Then he turned the truck's key, shutting off the engine. "Okay. I'm going with you."

Trey stiffened. "That's not a good idea."

"I know," Randy agreed as he collected his pesticide sprayer from the floorboard and his goggles and mask from the dash. "Trust me, I very much agree with you. But I don't ... I *have* to do this. I have to help make sure that I don't wake up tomorrow morning, that *Lori* and my kids don't wake up tomorrow morning, to find one of those monsters hanging from the ceiling over our beds. And I'm running on adrenaline here, so please don't try to talk me out of it."

Trey got out and stood there, torn, as the mortal man came around to his side of the truck, and slipped on his protective gear.

"Let's ..." Randy panted, "... let's get this over with,

okay?"

Still very conflicted about this (even the hunger seemed at a loss), Trey said, "Okay. But Randy ... if I tell you to run away, you need to *run away* ... as fast as you can. All right?"

Randy nodded. "Yeah, I got it. Trust me, I got it."

They spent a minute debating the best way to approach the house. They agreed that simply ringing the speaker at the gate was out, but unlike the ladies' house, with its thick hedge all the way around, Morse had an actual privacy wall. In the end, they opted to go around the north side, as the house next door showed no lights, not even maybe-firelight, in the windows.

Mindful of working security cameras or motion detectors on the neighbors' parts, they hugged the side of the wall as they made their way around to Morse's backyard. Then Randy waited while Trey did a chin-up to peek over the top.

"Big yard ..." Trey reported in a whisper, "...swimming pool, looks like it hasn't ... been used in a while."

"Any webs? Spiders? Egg sacs along the ridge of the wall?"

"Too dark to tell for sure ... but don't think so."

Randy grunted under his breath. "I'm guessing you would've already said something if you saw any of *those* things."

"Yeah."

"How do you want to go about this?"

Trey lowered himself back to ground level. "We can climb over—"

"Trey, I'm over fifty and not in the best shape."

"I'll help you."

Randy sighed. "Wonderful," he grumbled.

The process took longer than either of them cared for, but each held their complaints. First, Trey climbed over the wall (appreciating his new agility, then feeling guilty for doing so), then Randy passed over his equipment. He tried, and failed, to heft himself up, so Trey had to go back over, lift him up (Randy seemed surprised by his strength, but said nothing), then climb into Morse's yard again and help him down.

Once settled within, they looked around, waiting for any sort of reaction to their entry. Nothing big happened, but Randy did tap Trey's shoulder and point to the corner of the wall nearest the front of the house.

Trey wasn't an exterminator, but even he could tell the webs in that corner looked out of control.

Randy tapped him again, pointing around as he whispered, "There. And there."

"I see them," Trey whispered back. The backyard was a disaster zone of spider activity.

Randy scratched at his ribs with his gloved hand, then at his thigh. "Different webs, different breeds. Should be fighting for dominance, eating each other." He glanced at the pool. "You couldn't pay me enough to clean out those filters ..."

Despite their surroundings and the circumstances, Trey smiled. "I thought people *do* pay you ... to do that sort of thing."

"I'm rethinking my life choices." He gathered up his sprayer. "I am *so* glad Morse wanted something so strong. Oh, and before I start spraying, you're going to want this..." He fished something from a coverall pocket, producing a standard nose-and-mouth filter mask, the cheap kind Trey had seen people use when they were sick. "Sorry it's not a real one, like mine — I don't usually work with partners — but it'll be better than nothing. Just make sure to look away, so it doesn't get in your eyes."

Trey couldn't admit that the pesticide wouldn't hurt him, so he settled for pulling on the flimsy mask and saying, "Thanks."

"Okay, we're in the backyard. Now what?"

"You sure about the alarms ... probably being off?"

"After seeing this," he gestured around the yard, the bushes, the nice patio furniture, all showing signs of webbing and little creepy crawlers, "I'd take my bet from earlier and triple it."

"Then we find a door ... and sneak inside."

"It may not be alarmed, but I'd guess it'll be locked. You bring along a lock-pick kit?"

"No," Trey said, then started working his way around the house's rear security lights toward the back patio. After a few steps, he heard Randy following him. And although they needed to be as quiet as possible (until it was time to stop bothering), he heard Randy intoning, over and over, "What the fuck am I doing, what the fuck am I doing, what the fuck am I doing ...?" It sounded almost like a prayer, though he doubted that Alistaire would've approved of Randy's potty mouth.

The door on the patio was, unfortunately, well lit by the nearest security light. He knew there was a very good chance the voodoo priest suspected (or straight-out knew) that he was coming, but he hoped the villain might be less aware of his human companion. The same could not be said for any of the meta-spiders, since they seemed to feed on live flesh.

*Just like you,* the hunger giggled.

He ignored it this time.

Reaching up with his long right arm, Trey placed his hand over the security light, then wiggled his fingers around until his middle fingertip was squarely in the center, over the bulb itself. It felt pretty hot, and he got the idea that, if Randy did the same thing, it might burn him. He *also* felt something wriggling around his other fingers and thumb, but didn't bother saying anything.

He pressed forward with his middle finger, harder, harder ... until there was a single *clink!* as his fingertip penetrated the casing, then another *crick!* as he busted the light bulb.

Lowering his arm, he realized that he had used his injured hand, and wondered if Randy would say anything about it. But no, the man had his back to Trey, his sprayer held at ready, and he was still reciting his "What the fuck am I doing?" chant. He hadn't bothered watching how Trey shut off the light, so Trey was free to pull a sliver of glass from his finger and toss it aside.

Stepping over to the patio door itself, he peered inside. As the unlit windows had suggested, the kitchen was dark. He could see little glows here and there, stuff like the clocks on the stove and microwave and so on, but no lamps or overhead lights. As he was looking around, a yellow-and-red spider of some sort crawled right over the glass before him. It wasn't a tarantula, but it was pretty big. And now that he thought to look, he saw other suspicious shapes moving over the glass and framework.

"Randy," he said in a low voice.

"Yeah, yeah."

"You might want to have ... your sprayer ready."

Randy turned to face him, gripping the nozzle tight as he lifted it. "Is the door open?"

Good question. Time to find out.

The door had a deadbolt lock, but he couldn't tell from this side if it were engaged or not. If it was, he'd have to shoulder the door open. He could do it easily, but since they were trying to avoid noise as long as possible ...

Gripping the levered doorknob, he twisted downward. The knob's thumb-lock was definitely engaged, so he pushed harder until it gave with a sharp *snap!* that made Randy flinch. Trey waited a moment, then pushed the door. No deadbolt, it opened with only the slightest of squeaks.

Spiders immediately began crawling outward, over the doorway's ridge and toward their feet (only the lightest-colored ones were visible in the dim, so there might've been even more he wasn't seeing). A very brief, fairly quiet *psht* from Randy's sprayer not only stopped them in their tracks, it sent the following batch scattering in all directions as they retreated deeper into the house.

"Sorry," Randy whispered, so hushed Trey could barely hear him, "I think I might've gotten your shoes."

Trey said nothing, just stepped into Francis Morse's gloomy house.

The pair took nearly a minute just to make it out of the kitchen. Randy wasn't spraying his pesticide constantly, but he wasn't being too stingy with it, either. Spiders were everywhere, to the point where Trey couldn't help stepping on them as he walked. They were bold, too, scrambling forward until Randy's spray killed the first wave and sent the rest running.

Once they reached the hallway, the spiders thinned a little. Trey saw more of them to his right, toward a big winding staircase, but fewer of them to the left ... and that was where he spotted more light. It hadn't shown from the windows, because it appeared to be coming from a reading lamp that was set on the floor rather than a table. And ... was that a man leaned up against the wall? He thought so, but if he was right, the guy wasn't moving.

Heading that direction, Trey tiptoed into the room. There were surprisingly fewer spiders in here, though still more than anyone would be comfortable with, scattered about the walls, ceiling, and floor. In fact, as Trey approached the slumped man, he saw the guy reach forward and knock a little one off his shin. But it was a sluggish move, almost lazy, and Trey decided that, whoever he was (Francis Morse?), he was doing it in his sleep.

"Randy," he whispered as the exterminator (who had paused for more spraying in the hallway) caught up to him, "is that Morse?"

Randy looked, then knelt before the man. "Yeah, I think so. He's wearing the same ratty clothes, anyway. And really ..." He squashed a spider beneath an almost angry fist. "... who else could live in this place? I don't understand why *he* is."

Randy's voice had gotten louder as he'd spoken, and Morse stirred a bit.

Trey joined Randy in kneeling in front of him, then reached out and shook his spider-bitten arm as gently as he could. "Mister Morse ...?"

Morse stirred some more and mumbled something, but did not wake up.

"Francis?" Randy tried. "Wake up, buddy."

With a sudden jerk, Morse's head shot up so quickly he bumped the wall. He didn't seem to notice, though, as he was staring wide-eyed (not afraid so much as boggled) at the two of them.

"Are you ..." Trey asked, to make sure, "... Francis Morse?"

Morse continued gaping at them, and Trey wondered if maybe the filter-masks were at least partly to blame. He reached up and pulled his down until it hung below his chin. Randy did the same.

Morse did relax a little, though his eyes were still very

glassy. And though he hated to be the pot calling the kettle black, Trey thought his eyes also looked a little ... weird. He then realized that it was the man's pupils: Morse's pupils were tiny, way smaller than they should've been in the low light from the lamp. The man was clearly beyond exhausted, but hadn't he read online that people's eyes tend to *dilate* when super-tired? Maybe the man had been spider-bitten so many times—

"Is this a dream?" Morse asked in a croaky voice. "Am I dreaming? I need to wake up, or he might send the spiders after me again ..."

In spite of his professed need to wake up, Morse's head started sagging, so Trey shook him again.

"You're not dreaming, Francis," Randy assured him, then added, "Or should I call you 'FRM'?"

That brought a few blinks to Morse's glassy eyes as his forehead wrinkled in concentration. Then he looked over Randy's coveralls, his equipment. "Are you ... are you Randy McDonald?"

"McDonnell, but close enough."

"The exterminator?"

"Yeah."

"What ...?" He glanced at Trey, couldn't seem to decide what to make of him, so dismissed him to return his focus to Randy. "What are you doing here?"

"Delivering your pesticide." He hefted the sprayer. "I hope you don't mind that I'm a little early."

Francis stared at Randy for several long seconds, as though he were trying to decide whether or not that was a joke. Then he caught both his visitors off-guard when he threw himself forward, wrapped his arms around Randy, buried his face in the exterminator's chest, and began crying like a baby.

Randy looked to Trey, his expression clearly asking,

*What should I do?*

Trey shrugged. He had seen this sort of reaction before, when he and his partners freed people from vampire enslavement or other supernatural captivity. If they had time, they often let the victims cry themselves out. Trey actually liked giving that kind of comfort (though it was almost always Sean they turned to, since he was the most human-looking) ... again, if they had time. And though the spiders weren't exactly swarming at the moment ...

As he glanced to the hallway, he had to amend that assessment: The spiders weren't swarming in *here*, but the numbers in the hall had at least tripled, and they were all ambling this way.

"Stay with him," Trey told Randy. "Get him out ... if you can."

"What?" Randy gasped. "Why? Where are *you* going?"

"I can only help so much against ... regular spiders. I'll do the most good ... by going after the source."

"But—"

"I need to find the source," he repeated. "If you can, get Morse ... out of here."

"I didn't have much luck with that wall," Randy reminded him. "I can't imagine he'll do much better, in his condition."

"Then go out the front. But either way ... you're going to need your sprayer." He nodded toward the mass forming in the hallway.

"Fucking hell," Randy muttered as he gripped his sprayer's nozzle tighter.

"Here, Morse should have this." Trey pulled his mask off, offering it to Randy since Morse's face was still covered, and stood. "Get him ... to your truck. Get inside, lock it. Don't bother ... calling the police. They can't handle ... something like this. And if you see ... any of the *big* ones, leave right away. Don't wait for me."

"No argument here. I'm just worried one'll show up *before* I get him out." He half-reached for Trey, though he stopped himself short of actually grabbing his pant leg like a frightened child. "Do you *have* to go?"

Trey nodded. He couldn't explain his sensitivity to the voodoo priest's magic, so he settled for, "I have a feeling that ... I'll find the source upstairs."

"No!" Morse blurted suddenly. He turned his head and looked up at Trey, and then he *did* latch on to the leg of Trey's jeans. "No, you can't, you can't go up there ..." He blinked a few times, then went on, "... whoever you are. Trust me, don't go up there!"

Trey knelt again. "You said before that ... 'he' would send the spiders."

Morse nodded, a frantic gesture to match his wild expression.

"The man you're talking about, who would send ... the spiders. He's upstairs, isn't he?"

More nodding, which kept going as Morse said, "Yes. He's upstairs. In the master bedroom. But it's not just him. That would be bad enough, but it's *not - just - him*!"

Randy gently shushed him, and even stroked his shoulder like a caring parent. "You're talking about the spider monsters, right?"

Morse twisted around, separating from Randy enough so that he could look at the exterminator's face. "You— You've seen them?"

"Oh, yeah. Big as a person, right out of a nightmare. And Trey here killed it."

Morse looked back to Trey, his eyes widening ever further. "You *killed* one?"

"Yes."

"How—? What did—? That's not—" Morse shook his head, trying to frame his thoughts, but all he came up with was, "Who *are* you?"

"My name is Trey, and I hope to … put an end to *all* of this."

Morse said nothing to that, but Randy responded, "Go, Trey. I'll do what I can." He eyed the wriggling hallway floor, walls, and ceiling. "*Those* I can handle. I'm just glad I'm starting with a nearly full canister." He sounded more confident, but Trey noticed he was scratching himself again.

Trey nodded, rose, and stepped out into the hallway. He expected to have to stomp his way through a carpet of spiders, but most of them scurried out of his way (those that didn't? Squish!) as he headed toward the winding staircase.

"No … *no* …." he heard Morse whimpering behind him.

"It's okay, Francis," said Randy. "I got you." This was followed by the now-familiar *psht*-ing of his pesticide sprayer.

Hoping he wasn't leaving them to be spider food, Trey reached the bottom of the staircase. The amount of spiders here was insane … at least, that was the impression he got, since it was too dark to even attempt a real estimate. He looked up and all around, but saw no sign of the meta-spiders, the ones that would truly mean death to Randy and Morse.

He was painfully aware, of course, that they could be lurking outside the house, that they could enter the lamp-lit room through a window and kill both men before he could get back. Heck, if one appeared right here, in front of him, and made a run for them, Trey was too slow and too far away to make it there in time ...

*This is why we work as a team, ye daft fool,* he could almost hear Sean scolding him. *If those men die, it'll be partly yer fault for comin' here* alone. *What are ye thinkin'?*

*I'm thinking,* he answered his phantom partner, *that I don't have much time left, that I might not be* me *for much longer. If my hunger keeps growing ...*

*So yer solution is to run off 'n tackle a voodoo priest* by yerself, *leavin' two innocents to get gobbled up? That makes a lotta fuckin' sense.*

Trey grunted and literally, physically waved the conversation away. He already had his hunger speaking up inside his head whenever it felt like it, he didn't need a make-believe version of Sean doing the same thing. Part of him wondered why a make-believe Alistaire hadn't spoken up yet, but that led to thoughts of damnation that he didn't have time for right now.

Gripping the banister (and squashing another spider in doing so), Trey climbed the stairs.

The top floor was, overall, as dark as the rest of the house, if not darker. The windows at each end of the upper hallway were covered, and all doors were closed ... save one. And that one provided the only source of light to be found up here, the jumping, flickering glow of firelight.

That open doorway beckoned, so Trey gave it what it wanted.

Even before he stepped into the large bedroom, Trey realized he had found the mother lode of meta-spiders. He couldn't know how many the voodoo priest had made, but surely this was the bulk of them. They were lined up along the walls, a couple of them on the ceiling further in, thrown into silhouette because of the fire from a huge, bronze kettle. But in spite of the shadows, he could see their glossy, alien eyes ... and they were all on him.

What's more, when he actually set foot in the bedroom, he saw that the meta-spiders were forming a crude sort of honor line, their misshapen bodies creating sloppy rows leading to the fire, and the man hovering just beyond it.

"You've come alone, I see," the man said in a casual tone, a deep voice for someone so much smaller than Trey. It was hard to tell for sure, with his sitting criss-cross-applesauce on nothing but air, but he looked pretty unimpressive, physically ... which did not, Trey knew, reflect his actual threat.

Trey glanced to either side of the room. There had to be at least a dozen meta-spiders in here. Not counting what tricks the voodoo priest might have up his sleeve (well, maybe not up his *sleeve*, since he was buck naked), he doubted he could take them all on at once. He had proven himself against them, one-on-one, but these odds were too steep. Maybe if he stepped back into the hallway, forcing them to funnel through the door one at a time ... except he'd already seen one of them go straight through a wall, so that was out.

"I am pleased you left your *lougarou* and *vanpir*," the voodoo priest continued, spitting the v-word with a vehemence that Trey noticed right away, "so that we may *konvès* together."

" 'Konvès'?"

The man smiled, his teeth glistening in the firelight almost as intensely as his bright blue eyes, which really stood out in that dark face, darker than Trey's own. "Forgive me. So that we may converse, may *speak* together."

" 'Speak'," Trey said, keeping it neutral. "Since you can ... speak English after all, sure."

Still smiling, the man nodded. "Yes, I am bilingual — *tri*lingual, actually — but projection is always easiest in my native tongue. Now, please ..." He gestured, and one of the meta-spiders moved just enough to place a wooden chair on the opposite side of the fire. "Would you like to sit?"

*Wow,* Trey thought, *this is not the way I thought this would go.* He again considered his tactical options. If he accepted that he could not fight this many meta-spider at once and win, then maybe he should play the man's game. If nothing else, it would bring him within arm's reach of the kettle, and if he were to grab it and sling it around, the fire would spread quickly. Would fire kill these things? He was pretty sure it could.

Not wanting his pause to drag out too long, Trey strode across the room and lowered himself into the chair, his muscles remaining tense. He kept his eyes on the voodoo priest the entire way, watching for any hint of a sneak attack. Even if he was only "pretty sure" that fire could hurt the meta-spiders, he was pretty *darn* sure that it would hurt the man sitting/floating across from him.

If he accomplished nothing else, if he would be torn limb from limb and chewed apart by the things surrounding him, he would make sure to take the voodoo priest out with him.

"My name is Young Bondye," the man stated when Trey was settled. "And you are ...?"

"Trey."

"It is my pleasure to make your acquaintance, dear Trey. Would you like some tea?"

Trey frowned, wondering if Bondye was mocking him. "You, of all people, should know ... that zombies don't drink *tea*."

"Not necessarily true," Bondye corrected, as though

Trey were being a poor student (not a relationship he cared to have established). "*Zonbi* do not *usually* drink tea. But ..." He smiled again. "I have been watching you, my dear Trey. You are not like the *zonbi* I have known. Granted, *zonbi* are not my forte. I have other specialities." He gestured to the meta-spiders around him. "*Araknid* are more difficult, and I always like a challenge. But I digress ... I was noting your uniqueness within my experience, *and* your behavior over the past days."

Trey stiffened.

"Yes," Bondye chuckled, sounding very pleased with himself, "however you came to be the way you are, it appears that your behavior has been ... evolving?"

Trey still said nothing, but as his hands squeezed his thighs, he imagined they were crushing Bondye's skull.

"And this evolution has been changing you physically, hasn't it?" Bondye concluded. "You move easier, you think faster — '*even* faster', I should say, since you were already beyond the intellect, such as it is, of a vodun *zonbi*." His eyes dropped to the bandage on Trey's right hand. "And you even bleed now. Don't you?"

Trey glared at him.

"So, with all of that at the forefront of our minds ... are you sure you wouldn't like to try some tea?"

*God, I want to wipe that smug grin from his fucking face.* He didn't even chastise himself for the potty thoughts.

Instead, he asked, "Did you do this to me?"

Bondye shook his head. "No, I did not. Oh, I suppose my proximity might have exacerbated your situation, but as I said ..." He again gestured to the surrounding meta-spiders. "Yours is not my area of expertise. My focus, dear Trey, has nothing to do with you or your kind."

"So you just make ... big spiders out of vampires?"

Bondye said nothing to that, just kept smiling.

"And make all the regular spiders ... go whacko all over the city?"

He shrugged. "I was not aware that was occurring, but it does not surprise me. Again, proximity. I strive no more for the aggravated spiders than I do your lost control."

"Then what *do* you ... strive for?"

Bondye laughed, a deep boisterous laugh. "Is this the part where I share my evil plot with the grand hero? Hmm? That is how you view yourself, and your former abstinence, dear Trey? Heroic?" He calmed, and his smile transitioned into a sneer. "Might that have something to do with why you reside with that filthy *vanpir*? How old is it, anyway? Three centuries? Four?"

Trey sneered right back at him.

This, however, seemed only to amuse Bondye. "Fine. I should think my 'evil plot' would be obvious: I plan to transform as many *vanpir* as I can into *araknid*. Surely you have figured out that much?"

"I'd figured out the what ... I don't understand the *why*."

Bondye's scorn returned. "Because *vanpir* deserve no better. They are foul, pretentious, self-satisfied parasites, who are not fit to rule over their betters!"

*If you're one of their "betters,"* Trey wanted to ask, *then how can they rule over you?* But he chose not to interrupt.

Bondye's torso shifted side to side, as though he wanted to pace the room but refused to stop his showy little levitation trick. "Where I come from, the *vanpir* lord over the supernatural world. They rule from east to west, north to south. We also have *lougarou* and *zonbi*, *fantom* and *bansi* ... but it is always the obscene *vanpir* who lurk at the top."

Bondye continued on in that vein, but it was the "Where I come from" that Trey latched onto more than anything. Had Bondye come from *their* world, the place the Triumvirate originally called home? Or someplace else, where vampires were even more dominant? They had met others like themselves, like Bishop or that alpha werewolf up in Alaska and any of the older vampires, who had crossed over the same way they had. Some had used hypnosis as their channel, like Trey and his friends, while others manipulated LSD users or avid lucid dreamers on this end. But the longer the Triumvirate was here, the more they encountered supernatural beings *from* here (like the alpha werewolf's wolf pack). Since voodoo was already a religion in this world, and the supernatural was spreading further, sinking into the fabric of this reality, Trey had thought—

"But no more!" the voodoo priest suddenly shouted, bringing Trey's attention back to where he was. "I was forced to hide, to exist within their penumbra, lest they envy and fear my power. *No - more*! My shift in venue has opened doors I had not considered, and now that I possess these secrets, I will turn the tide on the *ondèd* vermin. When I have bled this breeding ground dry, I will find my way back and seize control—"

"'Your way back'?"

Trey hadn't meant to speak aloud, had simply been noting all the references to "shifting venues" and "opened doors" and so on, but even though he had spoken barely over a mutter, Bondye heard him.

"I have no particular interest in this *raz* world," he snapped. "Here the *munden* humans rule, and there is no challenge in that — I could rule here too easily. And the *vanpir* of my world?" He smiled, a dark expression made more sinister by the flickering firelight. "They have it coming ... and *I* shall be the one to deliver."

Trey thought furiously. Was this something he could use, something to deflect the danger away from the millions of innocents around them? If he could prevent the meta-spiders (or "*araknid*," as Bondye put it) from feeding on any more people, and *only* attack the vampires, which were the Triumvirate's enemies to begin with ...

How would Alistaire feel about turning evil against evil? How would that fit with his religious sensibilities? Saving as many people as possible would be worth it, right?

"So you need vampires ... to make your *araknid* things."

Bondye nodded, his eyes narrowing.

"My partners and I ... the werewolf and, yes, the vampire ... fight against other vampires. And stuff like them." He chose his words carefully, thankful that he could speak with fewer pauses these days. "If you could keep your spiders, your *araknid* ... from hurting anyone else—"

Bondye chuckled. "My dear Trey ... are you proposing an alliance?"

Trey couldn't tell if Bondye liked the idea or not (heck, he wasn't sure if *he* liked it). "Of a sort."

Bondye laughed this time. "How interesting. But as you can see around you, I am not in need of your assistance."

"I didn't mean that you ... need our help. I just thought—"

"If either of us 'needs help,' dear Trey, it is *you*."

*That doesn't sound good.* "I'm only asking—"

"In fact, dear Trey ..." He reached down into his lap, between his crossed legs. For one confusing second, Trey thought he was grabbing his penis! But when he lifted his hand, it was cupped, mostly closed, with just a hint of some sort of white powder leaking through his fingers. "... I believe that *I* can help *you*." He smiled another dark smile. "Let me help you. And you can thank me later."

Trey moved, standing so abruptly his wooden chair fell over backward. He kicked back without looking, even as he threw both fists outward. Never having seen the *araknid* that surged forward to grab him, he struck all three, the chair itself slamming into the one that came up behind him.

He knew he wasn't safe, not by a long shot, not with how fast these things could move. If he wanted to complete his backup plan, he had to act.

Reaching out, he latched on to the copper kettle. A sizzling sound told him his hands were burning, and he felt it, too, in an abstract way, the same unreal, disconnected way he always felt pain. Whatever other changes he might be undergoing, his resistance to pain remained unchanged, and for that he was very grateful.

Lifting the kettle, the flames licking up toward his face, he prepared to throw it at Bondye before the *araknid* could stop him ...

... but it was already too late. As swift as he had been, all Bondye had needed to do was lift his powder-filled hand up to his own mouth.

Bondye huffed all his air out in one big puff, just like the Big Bad Wolf, blowing the white powder directly into Trey's face.

# SEVENTEEN

"Over there!" Francis pointed. "The window, the window!"

"I got 'em," Randy assured him.

Francis Morse's "rescue" was not going very well. The spiders — only *regular* spiders, thank God — started swarming almost as soon as Trey disappeared up the stairs at the end of the dark hall. Rather than escaping, Randy had been forced to focus on keeping the bastards from getting in through the open door, while Francis watched the windows, the air vent, and any other points of entry.

And his supply of pesticide was not infinite. He had mixed it strong, but he couldn't keep spraying it like this before his tank ran dry.

If push came to shove, as it very much looked like it was going to, they would have to go "nuclear."

"Francis," he said as he finished spritzing the window and turned back to the doorway, which — once again — begged another spray of its own, "do you have any aerosol cans we can get to?"

"I ... I don't know." Francis was trembling and twitchy, but so far he was holding it together pretty well for a civilian. "Maybe. My ex sometimes slept in here if we got into a fight. She might have left some hairspray in the bathroom." He pointed toward the next open door in the hallway.

Randy stomped on a Black Widow that had dropped from the ceiling. "Got matches? A lighter?"

"Don't smoke. Used to, but quit. Why?" Then, before Randy could answer, he got it. "Homemade blowtorch?"

"Not if you don't have fire to go with the hairspray, but that was the idea." He twisted the nozzle of his sprayer to get a finer stream — his canister was feeling awfully light. "I'm guessing you wouldn't mind burning your house a little at this point."

"Burn the fucker right down to the ground," Francis responded with gusto. "I'd have done it myself weeks ago if it hadn't been for—" He cut himself off with a strangled gasp.

Randy looked up from his nozzle — about a dozen spiders were working their way into the room, maneuvering around the pesticide residue like soldiers through a minefield, but he was guessing that wasn't what provoked such a reaction from Francis. And he was right.

Down the hallway, looming over the hundreds of regular spiders, he could barely make out two human-sized, eight-limbed shapes; one walked on the floor on its hind legs, while the other crawled along the left-hand wall. Neither appeared to be in a big hurry, but they were moving this direction.

"No, no, no ..." Francis was mumbling, "no, I'm not going to die like this, I am *not* going to die like this ..."

Randy agreed with his sentiment, but he wasn't sure what to do about it. He knew from experience that his pesticide could blind those things — assuming he had enough left by the time they got here — but God only knew how many more of them were skulking around.

Without warning, Francis was standing beside him, grabbing his right arm, clawing at the sprayer.

"Give it, give it to me," Francis spat, suddenly more

enraged than afraid, "I'm gonna kill them all, fucking kill them, guaran-fucking-tee it, fucking *kill them* all—"

"Francis, stop it."

"—they're gonna know they've been in a fight, gonna kill them all, gonna kill *him*, gonna fucking kill Young-fucking-Bondye if it's the last thing I fucking—!"

Francis had a fairly large frame, and under normal circumstances, Randy would have been very reluctant to fight him — but circumstances were not normal. All it took was a well-placed elbow to his midsection, and Francis dropped to his knees.

"I'm sorry, Francis," Randy told him, and meant it. "We have to keep it together if we're getting out of this mess." He punctuated this with a short, controlled burst of pesticide at the spiders crawling along the top of the doorframe.

Francis began to cry again, but this time his release was interrupted as more spiders scrambled onto his hands; he fairly barked as he knocked them away, swatted them, squashed them.

Randy thought in desperation, *Where the hell is Trey?!*

He had been hoping that Trey would go upstairs, deal with the bad guy — a young "Boned-yee," whatever that meant — and all this madness would ... would just *stop*.

As he sprayed the approaching spiders once more, he saw another human-sized shape descending the staircase.

Fuck it. That was it, they were going out the goddamn window if that's what it—

Wait. The third shape was Trey!

Randy smiled with relief. Okay, so maybe there would be no magic wand to send them all back to the land of nightmares, but he had seen the big man handle one of these things, and he was pretty sure Trey could handle two of them.

But instead of attacking them, Trey shoved past the monster spiders, pushing toward their room, fast.

Fine, that was fine. Together, then. Together they would—

Trey stormed into the room. He did not pause to assess the situation, he did not ask why they hadn't left the house yet. He marched right in and kept coming, right up to Randy, giving the exterminator just enough time to think:

*What the hell is that white stuff on his face?*

At the last possible instant, Francis got between them. The bedraggled man seemed oblivious to whatever the hell was happening to Trey, was rambling again even as he moved, pointing at the spider monsters down the hallway, pointing upward toward the second floor, making little sense—

Trey seized the old filmmaker by the shoulders, lifted him off the ground ...

... and took a bite, a fucking *bite*, out of his neck.

Francis screamed. Randy screamed. Trey made animal noises. And, somewhere else in the house, Randy might have heard a man laughing.

Randy backed away until he hit the wall next to the window. Some regular spiders dropped onto his shoulders, but he could not have cared less.

*That's it I'm done TREY FUCKING BIT FRANCIS gotta go gotta get out of here out the window out the window and don't stop until I get back to Lori and forget this whole nightmare ever happened*

He turned and, using the nozzle of his sprayer, smashed the glass out of the window. It wasn't neat, there were lots of jagged bits and pieces, but he chose a handful of cuts over getting—

One of the monster spiders, hanging upside-down outside of the house, hissed at him through the craggy hole he had created. It was a statement on how his night was going that he barely hesitated before shoving his sprayer right into its eight-eyed face and firing. The thing fell backward with a thud that was audible even over Francis' screaming.

Randy had lifted one leg toward the windowsill when he half-heard, half-felt the movement behind him. He knew he had no chance of getting out in time, so he turned back to face the latest threat—

Trey loomed over him, as much red on his face now as there was white ... powder? All traces of the gentle giant were gone as he bared gore-stained teeth down at Randy in a nasty grin. Behind him, Francis still writhed on the floor, his hands clawing at his chest rather than the horrific wounds on his neck, but his movements were sluggish and blood was everywhere and the spiders were already closing in—

Hyperventilating inside his mask and running almost entirely on instinct, Randy swung the metal canister of his sprayer around, smashing it across Trey's face.

Trey's only reaction was a slight widening of his grin. That was all.

Switching tactics, Randy raised the nozzle, aiming for Trey's face, his eyes. If his pesticide could blind the mutant spiders from hell, surely it could—

Trey caught him on the way up, his large hand closing around Randy's own. The savior-turned-psychopath squeezed and twisted until Randy's bones were little more than loose gravel inside his skin; it was so painful, he couldn't even scream again, merely sucked in air until it felt as though his lungs would explode.

His last coherent thought was, *Lori ...*

Trey pulled him forward until they were chest-to-chest, ripped off Randy's mask, and sank his teeth into Randy's face.

# 18

*This?*
*This is what I've been resisting, been fighting against? This is what I've shunned? This?*
*I've been a fucking idiot.*

# Nineteen

Blayze drove them back into Los Angeles — Alistaire sitting in the front passenger seat; Sean in the back behind the young vampire. They caught the end of rush hour traffic, so the drive took much longer than any of them cared for, but it also gave Sean time to try texting Trey again, more than once ... to no avail.

When they finally got off the freeway, Sean asked, "So where's this 'neutral location' we're goin' to?"

"A construction site," Blayze told him, "for an unfinished hotel. Place was supposed to be a big, um, Hilton or Marriott, I think, but they must've run out of money, 'cause it's just been sitting there for a while."

"Why there?"

Blayze shrugged. "It's neutral, and, um, it's all open, and last night we put a *ton* of motion detectors all around the outside grounds, so nothing can sneak up on us. And between what it is and what it was going to be, it's, like, totally public. So, um, you know ... no invitations needed for any of our kind." He nodded his head sideways toward Alistaire.

Alistaire glanced over his shoulder to share a knowing look with his werewolf partner.

As Alistaire had once explained to Jimmy Edwards and the other young people from Neil Carpenter's production of *Deathtrap*, many erroneous legends regarding vampires were encouraged by the undead, to misinform mortals into a false sense of security — their supposed *bête noire* of running water and garlic, for example. Some of these myths, however, had taken on a life of their own — such as the threat of the wooden stake through the heart — to the point where even vampires no longer knew if they were fact or fiction, and were therefore forced to treat them as the potential threats they might very well pose.

The requirement of an invitation before entering a personal home was another example. Even Mikhail, the vampire who cursed Alistaire, believed in this obligation, whereas Alistaire himself had never found it necessary.

Apparently, Blayze's master — 'His Eminence' Aaron Spencer — fell more in line with Mikhail on this matter. Something good to note before meeting with the creature.

Even before they pulled into the large construction lot, Alistaire sensed the other vampires. They varied in power, with the majority ranking as low as their young chauffeur, but he was impressed by the number of them. Most masters kept a handful of thralls close to them, but either Spencer himself was quite old and powerful, or more masters would be in attendance for this "parley."

Blayze pulled the BMW to a rough halt on the gravel, and the three exited the vehicle. Blayze led the way toward the steel and concrete shell, while Alistaire and Sean followed at a slower pace.

Sean sniffed a few times. "Lotta company here."

"*Agreed.*"

Having drawn the same conclusion as Alistaire, he asked, "How many masters, ye think?"

"*I sense at least two. Possibly three, if the third stands weaker by comparison.*"

"Not the best sign, when masters start socializin'."

"*Agreed,*" Alistaire repeated, old memories of the Brigade of England — Sir Kenton, Sir Lloyd, and the tenacious Sir Bishop — coming to mind. The Brigade had been a rare cartel of master vampires working together toward a singular, long-term goal; in their case, Great Britain's complete domination over the entire world. Master vampires were typically too self-interested to work well with others of their kind; they inevitably double-crossed or openly turned on one another, usually sooner rather than later.

"Then again," Sean commented as Blayze disappeared into the broad, door-less entryway of the building's would-be lobby, "if they're desperate enough to reach out to *us* ..."

"*Very true.*" They were close to the entrance themselves, so he lowered his voice further. "*Are you up for this? Physically, I mean.*"

Sean rolled his neck and shoulders. "I'll be fine. Mind ye, I wish Trey were here."

Yet again, Alistaire said, "*Agreed.*"

And they entered the nascent hotel.

The structure was, indeed, very open. The outer walls were done, mostly, and the same went for the three-story ceiling — in both cases, Alistaire and Sean saw exception areas, presumably left unsealed for electrical work and the like. But there was no furniture, no concierge desk, a fountain stood waterless and incomplete, and the front desk was skeletal. An unpolished railing ran along the spacious mezzanine, which would allow eventual hotel guests to safely congregate and gaze upon the prospective beauty of the lobby. Numerous vampire thralls, all young, lingered in the shadows around the perimeter of the large room, watching and waiting.

Two male master vampires enjoyed heavy-handed symbolism by placing themselves on the mezzanine, so that they could look down on Alistaire and Sean as they entered the lobby. A small number of work lights had been left on here and there, and two lights on that higher level threw the masters into partial silhouette. They stood with several yards of space between them, both with rigid postures — but then, the latter was true of most elder vampires, including Alistaire much of the time.

"Only thing missin' is a fog machine," Sean mumbled under his breath as they came to a halt.

The master on their left spoke. Much like Alistaire's own, his voice carried a hint of many accents, which counterbalanced to suggest no particular accent at all.

"*Alistaire Bachman,*" he called out in grandiose fashion. "*Thank you for agreeing to meet with us.*"

Alistaire half-nodded, but otherwise did not reply.

"*I am Master Aaron Spencer,*" he continued, then gestured to the vampire standing to the side of him. "*This is Master Liam Tremblay.*"

The second master, Tremblay, inclined his head as Alistaire had done.

"*As I instructed Blayze to tell you,*" Spencer went on, "*we have sought an audience with you and your associates, to discuss a matter of grave importance. We trust you understand that we have not done so lightly.*"

"*Of course,*" Alistaire said.

Spencer opened his mouth to speak further, but Tremblay interrupted, "*Where eez your pet zombie, Bachman?*" Unlike Alistaire and Spencer, he spoke with a noticeable French-Canadian accent, and enough ego to fill the lobby.

Spencer was clearly annoyed with Tremblay, though it was to Blayze that he addressed, "*You only brought the two of them?"*

Blayze — who had faded into the background somewhere to Alistaire and Sean's left, his master's "side" of the entrance hall — stepped forward and dropped to one knee, his head bowed. "Th-they, um, they were the only ones at the house where, uh, where you sent me, Your Eminence. Their zombie was, um, was apparently at their *other* house, but they said he was going to follow us on his own, so ..."

Spencer glared at his thrall for a moment, then flicked a hand to one side. Even though Blayze could not possibly have seen it with his head down, he immediately withdrew once more.

*"Well, Bachman,"* Tremblay demanded, *"where eez 'e, then?"*

Running with the fabrication he had already laid before Blayze, Alistaire replied with a simple, *"Trey is near. That is all you need to know at this time."*

Tremblay sneered at this dismissal, but it was Spencer who spoke next, and he directed his rebuke at Tremblay. *"An understandable precaution, given the circumstances. Now, if we could continue with the important matter at hand ..."*

Alistaire was pleased to witness the tension between them. Clearly, their cooperation did not signify the birth of a new Brigade-style partnership; in spite of the threat that concerned them both, they could hardly stand to be in the same place together.

*"As you may or may not be aware,"* Spencer continued addressing Alistaire, *"a new — and rather unique — threat has emerged within the Los Angeles area..."*

As Spencer paused for effect, Alistaire interjected, *"I believe you speak of the 'meta-spiders'?"*

Tremblay grunted in annoyance, but Spencer nodded. *"A mutation of vampires into some form of arachnoid monstrosities, yes. You have encountered them yourselves, then."*

*"Yes. An unusual situation came to our attention, and shortly thereafter, we witnessed such a mutation firsthand. The resulting meta-spider was brought down by Sean and Trey, but I inspected the aberration before and after."*

Spencer may have raised an eyebrow on that note; it was difficult to be certain with their dramatic lighting in effect. *"Your associates are as formidable as we have heard. We presume they were forced to resort to sheer brute force trauma?"*

"Aye," Sean answered for himself. The shuffling of feet could be heard from the shadows around them, again betraying the general immaturity of most of these vampires. Tremblay offered a snobbish sniff, but Spencer again endured the words of his perceived "inferior" with grace. "She had no particular 'weakness' that we could figure — she wasn't even bothered by sunlight."

*"Indeed?"* Spencer asked with genuine interest.

"Near as we could tell. We didn't drag her outside or anythin', but it was well after dawn an' she dinna pay any mind to the windows. Even settin' aside her, ye know, new *spider*-look, by the end ye'd never have known she'd started as a vampire. Even her scent was drastically changed."

*"I see. You have said 'she' and 'her' a number of times."* He returned to speaking to Alistaire. *"Were you, by any means, responsible for removing this female, very recently, from the city coroner's office?"*

Alistaire nodded.

Spencer did as well. *"Ah. That would be Summer, then. She was one of my newly acquired serfs. A pity. I did not create her, but I was rather fond of her. She had unique characteristics — predatory cuspids like I had never before seen! And her rebirth had left her most uninhibited. Quite enjoyable company.*

*"But to the point: You have seen what these things, these 'meta-spiders' are, and you also understand how they are spawned. I presume, therefore, that you understand the necessity — or, yes, as I'm sure you and your associates would put it, the 'necessary evil' — of our coming together at this time of crisis. That we face a threat to our existence unlike any those of us here have ever encountered. Surely even you, Alistaire Bachman, whose hatred of his own kind is famous around the world, can see that we have no other alternatives available to us."*

As Alistaire paused to choose his words, Tremblay blurted, *"We are wasting our time, Spencer, as I told you."* He gestured toward Alistaire like a *maître d'* would toward a maggot in the chef's soup. *"This eez* the *Alistaire Bachman, the Scourge from Germany, worshipper of prey, defender of the weak, traitor to all 'is kind. You are a fool, Spencer, if you think—"*

*"Silence!"* Spencer snapped, revealing a high forehead and plump lips as he turned to face the Canadian vampire. *"You are here as my guest, Tremblay! You will abide by* my *wishes,* my *commands, if you want to leave my territory intact."*

*"We are losing a golden opportunity 'ere,"* Tremblay spat, also turning to face off against his would-be colleague; his own pale features were less dignified, more murine than Spencer's. *"We 'ave Bachman 'ere before us, we 'ave dozens of serfs at our mutual command, 'is zombie eez not to be found, 'is werewolf eez sick or injured in some way ..."*

"Uh-oh," Sean commented in a whisper. So much for hiding his wounds.

"*... we should* seize *this moment, Spencer! Seize the chance to end the greatest menace our kind 'as known for 'undreds of—*"

"*Exactly!*" Spencer shouted him down. "Exactly! *The greatest menace 'our kind has* known.*' That is my point, why I reached out to you, why we then reached out to* them. *Why else would I humble myself like this? Do you think I enjoy kissing his German ass?*" He glanced down briefly at Alistaire, mindful of his faux pas, but then continued berating Tremblay. "*But I repeat to you, even as I say to them, that it is this* unknown *threat that must concern us. We have endured Bachman for centuries, but he is one individual. His little Triumvirate has complicated matters further, but the werewolf is not immortal and the zombie may one day decay beyond functionality, and then Bachman will stand alone once more. But how many of these spider mutations have we detected thus far?*"

Tremblay tried to dismiss that. "*Bah! That eez* connerie *and you know it. We cannot sense those things as well as—*"

"*Exactly!*" Spencer barked again. "*We* think *we have detected several, but we cannot* know *because we cannot trust our senses against this unknown. Where did they first come from? What is their genesis? We - don't - know, do we?*"

Tremblay huffed and turned away, choosing to glower down at Alistaire instead. Alistaire returned his scowl without flinching, so Tremblay shifted his hostility to Sean, who offered up an amused — and hopefully infuriating — smile.

The silence hung for several long seconds. Alistaire heard more shuffling in the shadows, just as he had made note of Tremblay's statement of having "dozens" under their command. If Blayze were any indication, Alistaire was confident he could stand alone against all of those, but he could not dismiss the two masters, nor the fact that Sean was in less than optimal condition. He reached out again with his "vampire detector," as Sean called it, trying to discern the exact odds they faced—

At the extreme periphery, he encountered something uncomfortable, something vile yet familiar.

At almost the same time, someone's phone chimed. The glow of its active screen illuminated the vampire's location within the shadows underneath the mezzanine balcony. Moments after the undead woman checked it, she beckoned in near-mortal alarm, and Blayze circled the unfinished lobby to inspect the phone himself.

The noxious sensation Alistaire detected drew closer — and it was coming from all around them.

*"Now, Tremblay,"* Spencer stated through tight lips, *"if we may continue* without *further disruption, perhaps we—"*

Still gripping the other vampire's phone, Blayze rushed forward from under the balcony until he could see Spencer. "Your Eminence!"

Spencer shouted, *"Don't! Interrupt!"*

"But, Your Eminence—!"

Snapping his head around, Spencer pierced him with eyes that glowed solid, bright amber. *"Blayze, I am moments from severing your head from your body!"*

"Your Eminence!" Blayze persisted, a determination in the face of his master's wrath that finally sunk through even Spencer's anger.

*"Sean?"* Alistaire whispered.

"Aye?"

*"Prepare."*

"Aye."

"The motion sensors we set up!" Blayze was shouting. "Something's tripped them! *All* of them—!"

The boards covering a glass-less window to Alistaire and Sean's right exploded inward. One meta-spider crawled inside and immediately scaled the wall; another followed and latched onto the back of the nearest vampire, sinking its teeth into the side of the young undead's neck.

The thralls scrambled in every direction. Two more meta-spiders leaped in through the main lobby entryway behind Alistaire and Sean. Sean, already in wolfman form, spun around in time to deflect one's attack, but even as he batted it aside, it kept going past him after one of the vampires. After that, he and Alistaire moved back-to-back and began inching their way more toward the center of the lobby as more meta-spiders appeared from every direction.

"*Oh,* excellent *plan, Spencer,*" Tremblay stated with dripping sarcasm; with the growing din echoing around them, the only reason Alistaire and Sean heard it at all was due to their mutually enhanced hearing. "*You* imbécile, *bringing us all together like this appears to 'ave rung their* damné *dinner bell!*"

Spencer opted not to debate the issue, saying only, "*Shut up and fight before we lose all our thralls.*" He lifted one foot onto the balcony railing, leaped into the air, and shape-shifted into amber mist.

Tremblay growled, "*Damn you, Spencer ...*" and crawled onto the railing on all fours. Alistaire was distracted by a passing meta-spider, but not enough to miss seeing Tremblay shift into his large, rat-like form.

"What's the strategy here, Alistaire?" Sean slurred through his wolfen lips as he tossed aside his jacket and kicked his tennis shoes off, freeing his toe-claws. A brave female vampire tried to tackle a meta-spider a few yards from them; instead, its many limbs tied her up and wrestled her down, turning her from aggressor to victim in seconds. More and more vampires, most of which were too young to change form, were ending up webbed to the walls or floor, and many of those appeared to have been bitten in the abdomen, where Summer Levin's body had been punctured before her metamorphosis — not a good thing. "Fight? Run?"

*"Hold our ground for the moment, and stay back-to-back."*

"Next question, then; a tricky one: Help the vampires ... or help the spiders?"

Faced with the writhing, growling, struggling, hissing, biting, and increasingly gory chaos around them, Alistaire deliberated over those options for all of two seconds before answering, *"Fallen vampires now could mean more meta-spiders later. While I find it distasteful, we must help the vampires."*

"Aye. Any particular ideas on—? Down!"

They both ducked as a meta-spider sailed inches over them. Their first assumption was that it was attacking, but as it struck the floor and tumbled head-over-heel to crash into the far wall, they realized it had not leaped but had been thrown.

Spencer, the presumptive thrower, stormed by them in pursuit. As he passed, he kept his eyes on the rising meta-spider and carped, *"You're here, Bachman, so make yourself useful, damn it."*

"Hey," Sean called after him, "if ye'd prefer we leave, arsehole, just say the bloody word and—"

A meta-spider dropped onto them from above. It impacted them both, knocking each to the floor, but revealed its focus on Alistaire: Grabbing at him, its grip a mixture of sticky arachnoid feet and quasi-human hands, it sought to bury its massive fangs into his belly.

Twisting with grace that never failed to impress Sean, Alistaire seized one of its arms in his left hand while placing his right hand against its face, keeping its maw away from him and squashing one of its large eyes in the process. The creature hissed in pain and anger and strove to move forward, to pierce his abdomen, but all it accomplished was sliding both of them across the concrete floor.

"Alistaire!" Sean called as he jumped on its back, mindful of how his forearm had gotten bitten before as he attempted some measure of a half-nelson wrestling move. "Ye can't let it bite ye!"

"*I am attempting to avoid just that.*" Alistaire's voice betrayed some of his strain as they slid another foot across the floor. To top things off, spiders — normal spiders — began to crawl along his sides and onto his chest and arms; he regarded this only absently, as they were no real threat to him.

"Christ," Sean muttered as he glanced around; the hotel was suddenly crawling with the regular critters. Where the hell had they all come from? Even the work lights were beginning to cast odd shadows as the pests swarmed across their safety grills. He was thankful for the thick fur that covered his wolfman body.

All of which passed through his mind in a mere second, then he refocused on keeping the big freak from infecting his friend.

"Alistaire, go *mist*."

Alistaire took his advice and shape-shifted. The meta-spider face-planted into the floor as its own strength worked against it. Sean was happy to help as he dug his clawed hands into the thing's half-hair, half-whatever spiders had and lifted its head only to slam it down again.

Swirling about as his ivory mist, Alistaire "looked" around the tumultuous lobby. Things were not going well. While the vampires had initially outnumbered the meta-spiders about three to one, said numbers were dropping quickly as the young undead fell before the vicious beasts. Spencer and Tremblay were the only non-Triumvirate who were holding their own; Spencer shifted back and forth from mist to solid as he fought the same meta-spider he had thrown, while Tremblay tussled with another one in his rat-form along the balcony railing, each attempting to cause the other to fall, with the meta-spider's sticky, multi-limbed grip making up for its somewhat inferior strength.

A familiar bark-howl brought Alistaire's attention back around to find Sean in trouble. The meta-spider with whom he had been wrestling had turned the tide on him — Sean had his legs tucked in and against the meta-spider's belly, tearing at it with his hind claws even as it snapped its teeth closer and closer to his face, its four smaller limbs tugging him in. Were Sean at full strength, Alistaire believed he would win, but under the circumstances ...

Alistaire solidified standing over them, seized the meta-spider under its chin and at the back of its scalp, and twisted. The meta-spider's neck broke with a sharp *snap!*, but as was so often the case with supernatural beings, the attack was not as devastating as it should have been. The creature continued to flail, reached back in both self-defense and an apparent attempt to attack the vampire holding its head.

The distraction was enough for Sean to get a good, solid placement with his clawed feet. Snarling, he kicked downward, disemboweling the meta-spider. And still it hissed and twitched, until Alistaire pinned its angled head against his body and slammed a fist into its face, rupturing its remaining large eye and destroying what was left of its once-human nose.

Dropping the destroyed creature aside, Alistaire offered Sean a hand up, which the Irishman gladly accepted.

Sean muttered, "Not goin' well, is it?"

*"Working together like this,"* Alistaire replied, *"we should be able to eliminate them, one by one. But that will take time—"*

"Alistaire, look!"

Sean pointed up toward the balcony, where Tremblay continued to tussle with his dogged opponent. Alistaire opened his mouth to debate the merits of helping the Canadian master, but then realized that Sean had been pointing *past* Tremblay, along the balcony and further back, almost out of sight. One of the work lights that Spencer and Tremblay had arranged for their dramatic illumination had been knocked askew, and its spider-obstructed beam shined against the side wall of the mezzanine. Moving through the beam, enlarged by perspective into a giant that filled the unpainted surface, the shadow of a muscular man crept forward toward the meta-spider and Tremblay.

The shape consisted of nothing but darkness against light, a shadow puppet amidst the chaos, but Alistaire would know that contour anywhere, and he released a rare open smile, one of relief and pleasure.

Trey Matthews had arrived.

"Don't know where he came from," Sean said with his own bifurcated smile, "but don't care right now."

Alistaire could not dispute his sentiment.

But how to best unite with Trey on this battlefield? Alistaire presumed the zombie had followed the meta-spiders here, using his ability to detect the voodoo magic, so it was possible that he possessed some inside—

"Watch it!" Sean blurted.

A meta-spider scuttled on all limbs across the floor toward them, rearing up at the last moment to attack. Alistaire backhanded the creature, redirecting it in a stumbling stride off at a new angle, and much like when Sean struck one earlier, it opted to target another vampire rather than turn around for a second pass.

Sean resumed his stance with his back to Alistaire's. "How do ye want to go about joining up with Trey? The elevators probably won't be working—"

"—*and the meta-spiders have cross-webbed the staircase, yes. Suggestions?*"

"Ye could shift into yer mist and join him."

"*That would leave you alone.*"

"Aye ..."

Alistaire returned his attention to the balcony, attempting to relocate some trace of Trey. The zombie's shadow was long gone, but he did look up just in time to see Tremblay finally defeat his opponent, sinking his long, sharp, protruding rat-fangs into the top of the meta-spider's skull. The eight-limbed creature kept moving, so Tremblay shook it back and forth, worrying the spider like a cat might worry a mouse. He did this until the meta-spider's skull peeled and separated, the still-twitching body dropping to the ground floor as Tremblay spat the dome of bone, and the brain tissue lingering within, to one side. The vampire then shifted into humanoid form, hopped off the railing back onto the mezzanine floor, and spat some more, cringing at whatever vile aftertaste the meta-spider's bluish blood left in his mouth.

Tremblay looked around, then glanced over his shoulder and tensed, his hands fisting in preparation for a new fight. But then the Canadian relaxed, somewhat, and looked down to find and meet Alistaire's gaze.

*"About time, Bachman,"* he called, heavy with derision. *"Now, by all means, impress me with 'ow powerful your pet zombie eez. Because your wolf 'asn't—"*

Trey emerged from the shadows to stand directly behind him, threw his long arms out, and seized Tremblay from behind in a crushing bear hug — literally crushing, as the sound of the master vampire's ribs breaking was audible throughout the lobby. Tremblay's eyes widened in shock even as he cried out.

"Oh, bloody hell," Sean swore. "He doesn't know we have a truce goin' here."

Feeling torn between their strategic needs and satisfaction at seeing the zombie taking down a master vampire, Alistaire called, *"Trey!"*

Sean echoed, "Trey!"

Fighting to maintain his strong hold on Tremblay, who had shifted to his rat-form and back again in a failed attempt to free himself, Trey turned his head just enough to look down, finding them in an instant ... and then disregarded them as he refocused on crushing the vampire.

"What the fuck?" Sean muttered, then was forced to look away as another meta-spider snapped at them as it passed in pursuit of a thrall.

Alistaire, however, continued to stare up at Trey, trusting his werewolf partner to protect him for the moment. Something was off about Trey — beyond his odd dismissal of their call. When he had looked down at them, when he met Alistaire's gaze ... something about his eyes, and even how he was moving as he fought with—

*"Damn it, Bachman!"*

Spencer stormed toward them, striking aside an attacking meta-spider without breaking stride; the creature hissed in anger, but as they had seen several times, it redirected its ire at the next thrall who came near it.

Ignoring that, Spencer bore down upon them, zeroing in on Alistaire; claws ready, Sean prepared for an attack.

Spencer stopped before the German, pointing a long-nailed finger in his face. *"You pledged not to raise arms against us! You treacherous, honor-less—!"*

"Trey doesn't know about the truce!" Sean cut in.

*"I am speaking to your master, dog!"* Spencer shot back without taking his eyes off Alistaire.

When Alistaire spoke, his voice was cold even by vampire standards. *"Sean speaks the truth. Trey is not aware of our armistice."*

Spencer fumed, *"You assured us—!"*

But he was cut off by a pair of blaring bellows that resounded throughout the lobby. Even the meta-spiders and thralls, while they did not exactly cease their fighting, paused for a brief moment to regard the source.

One howl, which had burst from Tremblay, was born of shock and fear.

The other, still erupting from deep within Trey's chest, was a roar of exertion and triumph.

As they had struggled, Trey had dug his large, splayed fingers into both of Tremblay's shoulders and arms, burying each past the first knuckle. Now — under witness of thralls, meta-spiders, another master, and the rest of the Triumvirate — Trey pulled his own arms apart and spread them wide ... *without* releasing his hold on Tremblay. The master vampire attempted to twist, to turn, to outright squirm free, but to no avail, and all looked on as Trey's fingers tore trenches through hardened muscle tissue and bone, ripping Tremblay's upper body apart, one pulverized arm wrenching from its socket and tearing away, the other snapping loose even as the rib cage split along his already cracked sternum, bending and warping until his heart and lungs were exposed.

And then, before the astonished Tremblay could collapse, Trey released those destroyed arms — the separated one bounced onto the balcony railing before falling to the floor below — reached around the bloody mess he had created, and slammed both fists into the master vampire's bared heart.

The organ exploded in a splash of gory pulp.

Half of the vampire thralls gasped in shock, the others moaned in anguish, and then they were too occupied with the meta-spiders to indulge their emotions further as the fighting resurged.

"Holy shite, Alistaire ..." Sean murmured.

Alistaire nodded in agreement. Such raw power was beyond anything Trey had ever displayed before.

What was happening here?

Then Alistaire's contemplation collapsed as Spencer growled and struck him across the face hard enough to stagger him.

*"Damn you, Bachman!"* Spencer shouted as he vamped out, his face turning demonic. *"And damn your fucking zombie!"*

Alistaire stood ready for more, knowing he was the elder but never dismissing the threat of another aged vampire.

However, instead of pressing his attack on Alistaire, Spencer whirled about, shifted into mist, and rose to engage Trey on the mezzanine.

Alistaire stepped forward, intending to pursue Spencer, but then a spray of webbing shot right at his head. He twisted to one side, avoiding the gossamer trap, but this unfortunately allowed it to catch Sean across the arm he lifted in his own defense, pinning it to his chest. The Irishman pushed and pulled at it with vigor, but its viscous threads were firmly attached, made even worse by its adhering to the coarse fur exposed across his tattered shirt. And the meta-spider that shot the webbing emitted a sharp hiss as it climbed over one of its kin — which was biting into the abdomen of another victim — and leaped at Sean.

Alistaire moved to intervene, but Sean stepped forward with a kick that turned the creature aside to crash into the floor. With a growl of anger and pain, Sean ripped his arm free, taking his shirt and plenty of fur along with it, and as the meta-spider rose, he belted it across the face. Alistaire pitched in by shoving it right back, and this time Sean greeted it with claws at ready, sinking them deep into its throat and tearing outward. The meta-spider hissed, but in a different way as the air escaped through its open trachea. Alistaire gave his own kick to its back, breaking its spine and sending it again to the floor.

*"Sean, finish it off,"* he said as he turned around to face the mezzanine.

Trey stood at the edge of the balcony, his arms loose at his side. His eyes might have been closed, but it was difficult to tell for certain as, in addition to the spider-disrupted lighting, Trey was enshrouded by Spencer's amber mist. The master vampire swirled all about him, surging in eddies at various points, his density pulsing to and fro ... none of which appeared to affect Trey in any way.

Alistaire considered this with some gratification. Trey was no mortal for Spencer to suffocate. He supposed the vampire could attempt something more extreme, such as entering Trey's body and solidifying, to rupture Trey from the inside out. But while this would undoubtedly hurt Trey, his heavy, solid body might as easily damage Spencer. No, it was only a matter of time before—

Sure enough, Spencer was shifting back into normal form beside Trey, his long-nailed fingers reaching for the big zombie's eyes, which were indeed closed—

The instant Spencer grew dense enough to touch, Trey's arm shot out, catching the vampire in the gut; while vampires did not need to breathe as mortals, Alistaire knew from experience that a sufficient blow to the solar plexus bore a strong echo of how it felt while alive. Spencer was stunned, if only for a moment.

Trey placed his left hand on the master vampire's shoulder, again squeezing hard enough to fracture bone, as he drew his right hand as far back as he could ...

... and then his large fist came around with such force that Spencer's head detached from his body.

The thralls under Spencer's control — those few still capable of feeling their master's demise — wailed. The master vampire's head tumbled over the railing to join the carnage below.

"Good God," Sean whispered as he stepped away from his defeated opponent, "*that* was a haymaker for the record books. Alistaire, seriously, what's going on with Trey? How did he ...? I mean, since when ...?"

"*I don't know. We should—*"

The concrete floor cracked as Trey, who had hurtled the mezzanine railing, landed a few yards from them; a number of the regular spiders crawling everywhere were thrown off their eight little feet. His landing barely caused him to bend at the knees, and as he straightened to his full height, he seemed almost larger than normal, which was saying something for the muscular man who already stood well over six feet.

His face expressionless, Trey met Alistaire's gaze without any trace of his usual deference or diffidence, and Alistaire was again struck that something was different about his eyes ...

"Alistaire," Sean whispered, "look around."

With the exception of one that was still struggling in a far corner — Blayze, as it turned out — every vampire thrall had been defeated. Several appeared outright destroyed, but most of them were merely dormant, lying on the floor or caught up in oversized webs. Alistaire didn't know how many had been infected, but he doubted the answer would please him.

A few of the meta-spiders had been destroyed as well, but even if Trey were still on their side, which Alistaire was beginning to question, they were now the ones who were outnumbered.

As the remaining meta-spiders surrounded them and crept forward, they were ignoring Trey, their many eyes locked on Sean and himself — *especially* himself.

Sean, who hadn't made the leap yet, said to Trey, "Get over here, big guy. Ye've seen how these things act. We're gonna need to protect Alistaire as best we—"

"No," Trey stated.

Sean gaped at Trey. " 'No'?" he demanded. "The fuck ye mean, 'no'?"

The meta-spiders were inching closer, and by now even Sean could see they were incorporating Trey into their circle. But it was Trey alone who Alistaire studied — Trey, with smooth, barely-decayed skin and his dark, clear eyes.

And when Trey spoke again, his words flowed easily and without any trace of the deliberations or hesitations that usually littered his speech. "We weren't here for you. Young Bondye has been keeping loose tabs on you, thought you might be in this area, but I told him that the great Alistaire Bachman would never, ever associate with vampires. Clearly, I was wrong."

"Trey," Sean pleaded, his confusion and sense of betrayal bringing tears to his wolfen eyes, "what are ye doin'? What the hell is *wrong* with ye?!"

Trey ignored him.

By now, the meta-spiders had formed a tight ring, including Trey ... and there they halted, as though waiting for some signal or order.

Trey shook his head, suggesting sadness or regret, but neither reflected in his cold, clear eyes.

"Alistaire," he said, "you really shouldn't have come here."

"Trey ..." Sean whispered, that single word heavy with despair.

Trey stared at Alistaire a moment longer, then looked to the meta-spider on his right.

"Get them."

# 20

"Get them," Trey ordered. He had half-expected the *araknid* would only respond to commands spoken in Haitian Creole, but as Young Bondye pointed out, they had all begun as English-speaking vampires, so they were bilingual by default. Fine by him, since that saved him the headache of memorizing a bunch of foreign language directives.

Not that memorizing was such a challenge for him. Not anymore.

The *araknid* performed as instructed, turning away from the encircled Triumvirate (though he supposed they were now more of a "Duumvirate") and spreading out to collect the vampires they had infected for conversion. They had lost a few of their own, as anticipated, but judging by the webbed bodies, he imagined they would more than make up for those numbers.

As the *araknid* pivoted, Trey could not fail to notice how Sean, and even the usually unflappable Alistaire, tensed for an assault.

He commented, "You guys thought 'Get them' meant to attack you? You think I'm that far gone, after all we've been through together?" He shook his head and punctuated with a sarcastic, "Nice."

"Well, what the fuck are we *supposed* to think, Trey?" Sean growled. "What the hell's happened to ye, damn it?!

Ye look different, ye're talkin' different — and I can't say that I like yer new choice of accessories."

Trey glanced down, realizing that spiders were crawling all over his body, and shrugged.

"Alistaire told me ye came up to L.A.," Sean was babbling, "to track down the voodoo magic that created those freaks. And then ye show up here outta nowhere, take out *two* master vampires without breakin' a sweat, and ye're now in *charge* of these fuckin' meta-spider things?!"

Trey shrugged. "Still doesn't mean I'm going to kill the two of you." And then he allowed just a little more threat into his voice. "Unless you *force* me to, by interfering with what's going on here."

"*Trey,*" Alistaire asked, "*what* is *going on here?*"

"From your point of view? You can think of it as a little 'housecleaning'."

"And that means ...?" Sean demanded.

"The Triumvirate's most consistent challenge has been dealing with vampires, correct? More than werewolves, more than zombies, way more than odd or unexpected things like these ..." He gestured toward the *araknid*, which were helping one another web vampires to their backs even as they collected other victims up into their four stunted limbs. "... we deal with vampires, always vampires, the thinking monsters that can cover their tracks and live to bite another day. Am I wrong?"

Alistaire and Sean merely looked at him (Alistaire staring and Sean glaring; truthfully, Sean's glare was starting to get on Trey's nerves).

"After Young Bondye has his way, your little team won't have to worry about vampires for a while. Not around Los Angeles, at least. But since I know, Alistaire, that you're too determined to enjoy the time off, you can shift your focus south, toward San Diego. I'm sure plenty of bloodsuckers have set themselves up there."

"*I notice,*" Alistaire said, "*your reference to 'your' little team. No longer 'our' team then, Trey?*"

Trey shook his head. "I'm afraid I've got my own plans now, apart from the Triumvirate. Sorry."

Sean fumed, but Alistaire merely nodded. "*I see. And I presume that this 'Young Bondye' is the voodoo priest responsible for the meta-spiders?*"

"You presume correctly. And they're called '*araknid*,' by the way."

Sean sniffed and rolled his eyes. "Oh, 'arachnids.' That's bloody original."

"They're called '*araknid*'," Trey repeated, putting a stronger emphasis on the Haitian pronunciation as Bondye did, and allowing some of his irritation to slip through, "and there's no 's' on the plural."

"*All right,* 'araknid,' *then,*" Alistaire agreed. "*But that was hardly the point of my question.*"

Trey shrugged. "Yes, Young Bondye is the *mèt Bokor* behind the *araknid*. And he has no interest in harming humans. His beef is with vampires."

"*And what about the human photographer?*" Alistaire pressed (because when *didn't* Alistaire feel the need to press his points?). "*The one partially eaten by an* araknid *when Summer Levin was infected?*"

Trey waved that away. "I guess you could call that collateral damage ..." Sean snarled at this, but Trey pointedly ignored him. "...but I'm telling you that it won't continue. Once the *araknid* are gone, that will stop, obviously."

"*And where, exactly, are the* araknid *going?*"

Trey stared at the German vampire, at his smug face with his pompous voice, and wondered how he had put up with it for so long. Instead of answering yet another question, he addressed both of them with, "You know what, we're done here. The *araknid* are ready to go, and I'm getting a little tired of your probing and condescension. In the name of our partnership over the past several years, I'll give you this advice: Do yourselves a favor and stay out of Los Angeles for a while. The next few days, the next few weeks ... I don't know." He smirked at Alistaire. "You're Mister Sensitive, right? I'm sure you'll *feel* when it's safe again. Until then, stay home."

Alistaire and Sean both opened their mouths, but Trey turned away, addressing the nearest *araknid*, "Let's go."

As before, the *araknid* did not nod or otherwise acknowledge his order, but they moved with him as one toward the lobby entrance.

"*Trey—*"

"Goodbye, Alistaire, Sean," he said without looking back. "With luck, our paths won't cross again."

"Come on, Trey ..." Sean whined, practically begged. "This isn't *you*, Trey, and ye know it. This isn't—"

"Fuck off, Sean."

For a brief moment, Trey got some blessed silence out of them, until—

"*TREY MATTHEWS!*" Sean shouted, and it was enough of a growl-roar-howl that even the *araknid* slowed their departure.

Trey sighed, making a show of it, and turned back around to face them. "What?"

"Ye don't really think we're letting ye go, just like that, do ye now?"

Once again, Trey shrugged. "Sean, I don't care if you plan to 'let me go,' because you're in no position—"

Even with his years of fighting alongside Alistaire

Bachman, Trey was astonished by how fast the vampire moved. He registered a blur of motion, and then Alistaire was standing over him, his hands grasping either side of Trey's face, and Trey had no idea when or how he had been driven to his knees.

Sean, in a feat of velocity nearly as impressive, exploded out of his tattered clothes into full-wolf form and stood between them and the *araknid* with his teeth bared, pawing at the concrete floor in threat and challenge.

Trey tried to call out to the *araknid*, to order them to get this German asshole off him ... and found that he couldn't, couldn't form words, was even starting to have trouble thinking, because Alistaire was staring into his eyes, forcing his eyes to stay open, thrusting his will into Trey's mind with his fucking vampire version of the Vulcan mind meld—

*"Listen to me, Trey Matthews,"* Alistaire said, his voice steeped in the quasi-reverberation of the vampire's undertone, his eyes glowing an intense white. *"You are better than this, you are* stronger *than this. You have proven yourself time and again ..."*

Trey struggled to break free ... at least, he wanted to. His movements, such as they were, had taken on a sluggishness as though he were deep underwater ... no, deep within a tar pit. He wanted to shove Alistaire away, he wanted to stand up and step back and free himself from the vampire's grasp, but everything took so much effort, took so long to ... to ...

The *araknid* understood that something was amiss, but their minds were too simple to comprehend what it was.

*Like what's happening to* you *right now?* his hunger whispered. Funny, that part of himself had been utterly silent since he had fed on Randy and Francis ...

The *araknid* shuffled back toward them (though Trey could barely see it out of the corner of his eye; Alistaire wouldn't allow him to look away), but they were all loaded down with infected vampires, webbed to their back, to the fronts, in the arms, and they were confused and Trey doubted they would be able to help, not without going through Sean who was sounding more ferocious than ever and his own thoughts were getting so languid, so lethargic ... so ... so ...

*That's right*, the hunger seethed, *he's turning you back into an imbecile, into his little dullard, all over again...*

*No ...*

And through it all, Alistaire droned, *"Return to us, Trey Matthews. You are better than this. I believe in you, we believe in you. We can help you ..."*

*Yes*, the hunger retorted, *he "believes" in you so much that he's fucking raping your mind, trying to force you back to his side, trying to make you stupid again, so stupid, slow, pausing all the time when you speak, searching for the words. Is that what you want, Trey?*

No. It wasn't.

*"Please, Trey,"* Alistaire said, trying to sound like he really cared, like he was truly doing this to help Trey, instead of just dragging his big, dumb ass back into the training-wheel position of their stupid little Triumvirate. *"You can do this. We'll help you ..."*

*Yeah*, Trey thought, *help me Mister Christian Savior. Help poor, disabled Trey.*

If Alistaire wanted old, slow Trey back ... then that's what he would give him.

Acting on emotion, on need rather than thought (which sucked, because he enjoyed, so much, being *able* to think clearly again), Trey slowed his movements even further, and let his face go really slack.

"*That's it, Trey,*" said the asshat, totally falling for it. "*Come back to us, Trey. Come back to yourself ...*"

Trey could probably come up with some choice retorts for that "back to yourself" bullshit, but he kept his mind clear instead (which was frighteningly easy to do under the circumstances).

He blinked a few times, tried to give a little shake of his head, like he was waking up, but Alistaire's grip on either side of his face was too firm. Parting his lips, he found that he could speak again (probably because he was about to say what Alistaire wanted to hear).

"Aaah ... Aaah ... Alis ... staire ...?"

Was he overdoing it? Apparently not, because the overconfident, controlling vampire actually looked happy to hear it.

"*That's it. That's it, Trey. Come back to us ...*"

Trey lifted his hands, fumbling around until he "found" Alistaire's arms, touching and probing them like he wasn't quite sure what he was feeling.

"*Come back. Come back, Trey. I'm here for you ...*"

Trey's fingers walked their way up to Alistaire's shoulders, then slowly, carefully, up his neck until Trey was cradling Alistaire's head, much like the vampire was cupping his own face.

"*That's it, Trey. I'm here for you ...*"

And at the last moment, Trey could not resist saying, "And *I* am here for *you*."

Alistaire's eyes widened, but as fast as he could move when he was prepared for it, even The Great Alistaire Bachman faltered when caught off his guard.

Trey flexed his tremendous muscles, utilizing his old and newfound superhuman strength, and slammed his hands toward one another with everything he had.

The hideous *Crack!* that erupted from Alistaire's skull was truly disturbing. Alistaire gasped like a human, his eyes stopped glowing (though they stayed pure white) and his vice grip on Trey's face clinched, then relaxed and fell away.

In a proverbial heartbeat, Trey's thoughts began to clear. But before he could press any advantage, or even enjoy his victory, something impacted his side with enough force to knock him off his knees and send him sprawling onto the ground several feet away.

"What did ye *do*, Trey?!" Sean roared as he reverted to wolfman. He stood sentry between Trey and Alistaire, who had slumped to his own knees, holding his head. *"What did ye do*?!"

Before Trey could reply, he saw that Sean had made a tactical error. He lifted a hand and drew breath to call out a command, but between Alistaire's mind-rape and Sean's barreling him over, he was just too slow (the story of his afterlife) ...

Sean saw, heard, or just plain old sensed it coming, but he had been too focused on Trey, and so he, too, was too slow ...

The *araknid* that Trey had spoken to before had dropped the burden from its arms, and the small female vampire on its back wasn't enough to interfere as it shot forward, like a tarantula leaping onto an escaping cricket, and sank its spider-fangs into Alistaire's gut.

Trey shouted, "No!" But it was lost in the roar of Sean's rage as, already back in full-wolf form, he tore into the *araknid*, his large jaws clamping onto the creature's midsection. He jerked the creature side to side, ignoring the undersized arms that clawed at his snout and eyes, and ripped at his long ears.

Trey regained his feet and rushed forward. Sean heard

him coming and twisted his body around to place the trapped *araknid* between himself and the zombie, but he had misunderstood Trey's intentions, and this new position suited Trey just fine.

Kicking out with his long leg, Trey caught the *araknid* under the jaw, punting the creature so hard that it flipped end over end, a large portion of its abdomen shredding loose from Sean's teeth, which left a gory stream of entrails following after it until it collided with the lobby wall. It wasn't until the thing settled that it became clear that Trey's kick had also thoroughly broken its neck and left what remained of its chin resting on the far side of its face.

After pushing down the urge to follow it and continue stomping it out of existence, Trey snapped at the others, "Go get the vampire off its back, then start heading out! *Now!*"

The *araknid* were unmoved by his emotional outburst, but shuffled to obey his command.

Trey turned back to Sean, who, having reverted to wolfman once more, was rocking Alistaire in his arms. The vampire's eyes were still all-white, but only halfway open and giving the impression of not truly seeing anything. Thin vampire blood oozed from his ears, nose, and the corners of those sightless eyes, and Trey couldn't be sure if that was a reaction to the *araknid's* bite ... or the result of his own skull-fracturing attack.

"Sean ..." he began.

"Don't ye lay a finger on him, Trey Matthews!" Sean barked, though Trey had made no move to touch Alistaire in any way. "Ye did this to him. *You* did this!"

"I know, I ..." And Trey discovered that, even with his improved mind, he could not find the words.

An *araknid* appeared at Trey's side, looking up at him

with its eight repulsive eyes.

"What?" he demanded.

The creature stood still and silent for a few seconds, then pointed at Alistaire, a question tilting its head.

Sean growled, tensing for a fight, but Trey interceded by telling the *araknid*, "Stay the fuck away from this one. He's ... broken, so he won't make a good one of you. I told you to go, so *go*."

The *araknid* stared up at Trey long enough for him to wonder if it hadn't understood, or worse, if it saw through his feeble pretext. But then it finally turned away and followed after the others.

Trey looked down at Alistaire (the Great Alistaire Bachman, struck down by Trey Matthews), and was astonished to consider that, if Bondye were wrong and the *araknid* infection *did* work on older, master-level vampires ...would Alistaire, reduced to a spider-mutation, then be following *Trey's* orders as they scoured the city for more vampires?

A minute ago, that notion might have pleased him. Now, he found it less appealing, maybe even appalling.

*Stop it,* he chided himself. *You warned them, you gave them every chance to walk away.*

*Except they wouldn't leave ... because they wouldn't give up on me.*

He waited for the hunger to speak up, to refute that suggestion, to nip it in the bud with a wisely worded cynicism ...

... but the dark side of himself remained silent.

A wave of anger flowed through him, and he had no idea where to direct it, so he huffed and followed after the *araknid*.

"I'm still not lettin' ye leave here, Trey."

This time Trey did not rise to the verbal bait

(probably because he didn't want to have to look at Sean right now, didn't want to have to meet his eyes), but kept going while tossing over his shoulder, "Don't be stupid, Sean. Alistaire needs you."

"Get *back* here, Trey!"

But Trey grit his teeth against his unwanted second thoughts and kept walking.

# TWENTY-ONE

Though his traumas had struck him blind, Alistaire could hear all of this, but he was paralyzed, incapable of responding. He grieved to hear Trey's departure, more so that — once alone — Sean was moved to tears, speaking his name, but he remained helpless to acknowledge him.

A great deal of time had passed since Alistaire had experienced this much physical pain. He knew other kinds of pain, spiritual pain, on a daily basis, when he prayed to God and suffered through the repercussions thus inflicted upon his vampire state. Being a vampire allowed him to shrug off most physiological damage, with silver, fire, and especially sunlight being the most notable exceptions.

But having his skull cracked between Trey's large, strong hands ... that was enough to ring even his bell. And the meta-spider, the *"araknid,"* sinking its virulent fangs into his belly ... that, too, was sufficient to get his attention. He suspected his loss of sight was the result of his severe concussion, but it was that bite, that contamination, that led to his paralysis.

Even now, from within that searing point, a low-level burning was spreading throughout his body. Would he metamorphose, as Summer Levin and the others had? His primary hope lay in Trey's assault on Spencer and Tremblay. As Trey appeared to now side with the *araknid*, and as he arrived here tonight as part of some mass assimilation plan for the vampires ... why would he destroy two of the most powerful vampires on site? Alistaire *hoped* it was because their age made them unsuitable for transmutation.

This was, of course, just a theory.

A sense of motion suggested that Sean was carrying him — the spreading heat and decreasing connection to his body made it difficult to know for certain. He hoped his friend would not attempt to return to their home. They had no transportation, and Sean couldn't very well throw him over his shoulder and climb onto a public bus. He wished he could suggest holing up here, in this unfinished hotel; odds seemed good that it contained a basement level, and that would protect Alistaire from the dawn while he recuperated ... *if* he recuperated.

Alas, he still could not speak. He had to trust that Sean would draw such conclusions on his own.

Trust in Sean, and in God. And so he prayed.

*Our F-Father*, he began, *who art in H-Heaven, hallowed be thy N-Name, thy Kingdom come, thy will be done—*

The heat, which had spread throughout his every cell, ramped upward in degree, pulsing its way toward matching the fire around the *araknid's* bite.

*V-Vater unser, der du bist im H-Himmel,* he began again, taking comfort in his native German, *geheiligt werde dein N-Name; dein Reich komme—*

Again the heat pulsed, growing with such intensity, Alistaire felt as though he were literally *on* fire, something with which he was intimately familiar, but never from head to toe.

*I see,* he thought. *This is to be a contest of wills, is that it? My Faith against the voodoo magic spreading within me?*

The heat pulsed again, almost as if in response.

Were Alistaire capable of smiling at the moment, he would have done so.

*So be it,* he thought at the infection, at the magic, perhaps even at the *mèt Bokor* himself. *If you wish to test my Faith, if your success hinges upon my Belief flagging ... then you shall be greatly disappointed.*

The heat surged. And Alistaire prayed.

*V-Vater unser, der du bist im H-Himmel, geheiligt werde dein N-Name ...*

# 22

Trey drove the passenger van, with its tinted windows and its silent, eight-limbed charges, back to Bondye's house (it was more Bondye's house than ever before, now that Francis Morse was ... gone). He had no idea where, when, or how Bondye had gotten his hands on the outsized van; he assumed it was something Francis had arranged before he ...

*Go ahead, say it. Before he was eaten by a certain someone whose name rhymes with "Prey."*

*Not funny.* Except he wasn't sure who he was talking to now. Himself? His hunger?

His guilt?

He gripped the steering wheel tighter in frustration.

Trey had felt so good, so very *good*, when he finished with Randy and Francis. The *araknid* removed what was left of them, while Trey had used the downstairs shower to clean up. The bathroom had been lousy with spiders, sending them scrambling to clear out when the water started, but Trey had barely noticed. He had felt so light, so energetic, so *free*, free in ways he hadn't known since before he had fallen into that voodoo priest's trap back home, and then arisen from the dead as a zombie. He felt ... *alive*, in the most literal sense.

Bondye had needed to drip very few honeyed words into his ear to convince him to go out vampire hunting with the *araknid* in tow. After all, Bondye had freed him from his intellectual bondage, so he owed the bastard something. Even when Bondye suggested that Alistaire and Sean might be among the gathering of vampires, it had hardly bothered Trey. First: Seriously, what were the odds that Alistaire Bachman would be caught dead (no pun intended) at such a meeting? Second: Thinking of his time with Alistaire and Sean now bordered on embarrassing! How he had needed their pity, their benefaction for so many years ... he already thought of his old self as "Stupid Trey."

Had Stupid Trey gone along with their heroes' quest against the legion of evil throughout the world? Sure. Had he truly understood what they were doing? Well, yes, once he had time to absorb it, he supposed he had. But still, come on, he had been mentally handicapped, for Christ's sake, and Alistaire and Sean had taken advantage of that.

And the idea of going back to that life ... no, never. If he had known that all he had to do to fully regain his mind, that the only price was to feed on human flesh ...

In spite of what Alistaire or Sean might think (hell, in spite of what Bondye might think), Trey hadn't given in to "evil." He wasn't a villain now, he had no plans to run rampant through the streets, feeding on the living. Yes, he had slipped with poor Missy P, he admitted that. And yes, with Francis and especially Randy, he truly, sincerely wished they hadn't been in the wrong place at the wrong time.

But now he had his *mind* back. And, so similar to Alistaire and Sean, he could make his own choices. Was he going to feed on the living? Yes. But going forward he would be on top of his hunger, would have some breathing room to recognize the warning signs when it got stronger, when it was in danger of getting out of control, and he could *choose* his victims, the *right* victims.

For instance, he was good at computers (he could only imagine how deft his new self would be), so he could do a little hacking. Maybe break into the files of suspected sex offenders, find the worst ones (especially if they'd been caught before and were under suspicion for relapsing), and go visit them in the dark of night. Or maybe he could poke around Child Protective Services, see if he could find some cases where the authorities knew damn well that parents were abusing their children but couldn't prove it, then he could go visit *those* assholes whenever his need arose ...

*And if the children of those "assholes" walk in on you while you're feeding?*

He gripped the steering wheel tighter still. He knew *that* pestering voice in his head: Alistaire, breaking his silence at last.

*What happens then?* it persisted. *Would you be able to halt your frenzy before it was too late? And if you do, who will take care of the children then? And what if the "authorities" might* believe *the parents are abusing the children ... but they're wrong?*

"Goddamn it, Alistaire," Trey whispered aloud (though he needn't have bothered lowering his voice, since the *araknid* wouldn't care either way). "Leave me alone."

Alistaire, Alistaire, always about Alistaire Bachman and his damned morals.

He had felt so good about himself, so sure that he was done with Alistaire and Sean and being their pet idiot, their Stupid Trey ...

... but then, after Alistaire got hurt—

*Fuck that! After I hurt Alistaire! After I broke his head!*

*Only because he was doing that mind-rape thing!*

*That does not change your—!*

Fine! Fine! After *he* hurt Alistaire ... the sight of Alistaire, lying there in Sean's arms, and then especially after that goddamned *araknid* bit him, infected him ...

After he *let* Alistaire get infected ...

Gritting his teeth, he spat, "Fuck you, Alistaire. Fuck you and your guilt trip. Bondye doesn't think it'll work on someone your age anyway, so you'll be fine. You'll be fine, and we'll be gone, and that's it. That's *it*."

Bondye was still working on his plan to get them back, *physically* back, to their old world. He promised that, in exchange for Trey's help building his *araknid* army, he would take Trey with him. Back home, back to his sister Gayle and Grandma, back to his *old* life, before any of this madness started. Sure, there might be confusion over this new body, Travis Bekele's body, but they would work past that. They were his family.

*And when Grandma asks about Alistaire? When Gayle asks about Sean?*

It wouldn't matter, damn it. They - were - his - family.

Did he worry about the voodoo nightmare he was unleashing upon his old world, upon his home? No, not really. Because back home there were *way* more vampires, not to mention werewolves, other zombies, and a plethora of supernatural types to keep Young Bondye occupied. He figured that enough vampires would eventually team up (just like they appeared to be doing here, at that bare-bones hotel building) to take care of the problem.

And either way, with his experience dealing with the supernatural, with *being* supernatural, he knew enough to keep Gayle and Grandma safe, to avoid the wrong places and the wrong things, and ... once he'd worked out all the kinks of handling his own "affliction" ... he might actually get his Happily Ever After.

Would he ever get that with Alistaire and Sean? With Sean's sister issues and Alistaire's martyr complex? Hell no.

The GPS spoke up, Trey followed its directions, and shortly thereafter he was driving through the open gate to Mors— to Bondye's house.

Trey shut off the engine and got out. The *araknid* didn't need any commands at this point — they filed out the side door (he bet the ones in the back would've preferred to climb out the windows, but not with those comatose *araknid*-née-vampires webbed to them) and marched into the large house.

He shouldered one out of the way as he entered and headed for the staircase. The *araknid* were spreading out, presumably to deposit their payloads in different places. As he well knew, they wouldn't have to hide them from sunlight anymore, not in their new state. He imagined that might've been a boon for the vampires, if it weren't for the unfortunate tradeoff.

Upstairs, Trey made his way to Bondye's room. The voodoo-meister had retained a single *araknid* while Trey had been out running his errand, and that creature took a step to block the door to the bedroom. Trey could have commanded it to move aside, but its audacity irritated him, so he placed a hand on its prickly-haired chest and shoved it against the wall hard enough to mar the drywall. It remained there, stunned, as Trey let himself into the room.

Bondye hovered before the bronze kettle, as usual. Trey wondered if he ever moved from that spot, not knowing that his thoughts echoed those of the late Francis Morse.

"That wasn't necessary," the Bokor stated without taking his eyes from the flames, though he didn't sound especially put out about it.

"You want me to act as your lieutenant, or whatever," Trey returned, "then teach those things to stay out of my way."

This seemed to amuse Bondye, but he made no comment. Instead, he said, "*Rapò.*"

Given the context and tone, Trey could figure out that he wanted to know how the mission had gone. "Things went well, all considered. Lost a few *araknid*, infected enough vampires to more than make up for it. There were two masters, both over a hundred years old, maybe two hundred. I dealt with them."

Bondye nodded absently as he tossed what looked like black ash into the kettle, causing the fire to crackle green for a moment. When Trey looked closer, he realized a metal thermos was in there, too, hovering by means no more visible than Bondye's own levitation.

"And your 'friends'?" he asked. "Your *lougarou* and your *vanpir*?" As usual, he made "*vanpir*" sound like a curse word.

Trey hesitated only a moment, then admitted, "You were right. They were there."

"Ah," Bondye responded with a nod, that little sound doing more than any "I told you so."

Knowing the information would be dragged out of him eventually, Trey continued, "They tried to interfere, so I dealt with them, too."

"You 'dealt' with them."

"Yes. Alistaire tried to, uh ... tried to mesmerize me. It didn't work."

"I see." Bondye nodded some more. "And they just allowed you to walk away after that?"

Grinding his teeth, Trey answered, "No. I ... hurt Alistaire. And, uh, one of your *araknid* even bit him in the belly. So I guess you'll find out if you *can* transform an age-old vampire after all."

More nodding. "Good, good. And did you applaud the *araknid* responsible?"

Side-stepping the issue, Trey replied, "They don't understand that sort of thing. Not coming from me, anyway."

More nodding (Trey wondered if the man's head was loose on his neck). "And did you bring your infected *vanpir* friend back with you?"

Again, Trey hesitated (and cursed himself for doing so!) before saying, "No."

At last, Bondye shifted his gaze from the flames to the zombie, his bright eyes piercing Trey. "And why not?"

"Sean is recovering from his own bites, yes, but he's *still* a werewolf of considerable power, and he went berserk after Alistaire was bitten, destroying the *araknid* that did it. The other *araknid* were loaded up and ready to go, weighted down with infected vampires, and so ... I decided it wasn't, uh, tactically sound to attempt to take Alistaire from Sean." He tried to shrug it off. "Like I said, Alistaire's bitten. Even if he *doesn't* transform under your magic, I imagine he'll be in bad shape, right? That makes two of them." He thumbed his own chest. "*I* am the only member of the Triumvirate still on his feet, and I'm stronger than ever. And I want to go home, so for now, you've got me. And *that* means you don't have to worry about Alistaire or Sean, not anymore. Satisfied?"

Trey hoped that all the truth in his little speech would gloss over the fibs and fudges, but if it didn't ...

Bondye stared at him for a long time, staring into him in a not un-vampire way. Trey met his gaze without flinching, and was grateful that he didn't need to blink like a living person (especially a nervous one).

At last, Bondye returned to looking into the fire. "I would have preferred to have the *vanpir* here ... but perhaps you are right. Young *vanpir*, my *majik* can overcome; less so, the masters. You were right to destroy the other two; they are not worth the risk. *If* this 'Alistaire' returns as one of my own, then I shall reconsider my stratagem. If not, I'll proceed as planned." Then he looked to Trey once more. "And if you should encounter the wolf again, destroy him. Or you may forget returning home with us. Is that understood?"

Trey really, really wanted to fire back at him, to tell him to fuck off ... but instead he bit the inside of his cheek and said, "Sure, I understand. The next time I see Sean, he's done."

"Good. Now go."

Trey went.

# TWENTY-THREE

Sean was sick. He was sick with fever, sick with worry, sick with betrayal.

It had taken him no time at all to realize he would never get Alistaire back to the house. The German was dead weight — hell, he might've even been outright dead. How could Sean tell? He wasn't breathing, his heart wasn't beating ... but he was *never* breathing, his heart *never* beating. All Sean had was the hope that, somehow, Alistaire would pull through this, that he would conquer whatever the *araknid* venom had done to Summer and the other vampires.

Speaking of the devil that was the *araknid* venom, Sean wasn't doing well himself. Shape-shifting back and forth in rapid succession during the fight had aggravated his condition, and his muscles were cramping and his fever was back. But he had pushed that aside long enough to figure out where the hotel's basement was and carry Alistaire downstairs.

So here he sat, shivering and miserable, next to his infected friend, who lay upon the employee locker room bench. The place was *still* crawling with spiders, so Sean maintained a quarter-wolf form to keep a layer of protection for his skin. There was a single window, high up near the ceiling, but it was on the opposite side of the room, past a line of empty lockers. Sean didn't mind the gloom, as looking at the odd, angled shape of Alistaire's broken skull was disquieting, but he would know when dawn arrived, and he hoped it wouldn't bother Alistaire too much.

Assuming Alistaire survived long enough to *be* bothered.

This thought brought another wave of betrayal and anger toward Trey.

How the fuck could this have happened? Both Alistaire and he had noticed that Trey had been a little "off" lately; they'd even discussed it, briefly, right before they stole Summer's body from the morgue. That was part of the reason Sean had been surprised when Alistaire let Trey go off on his own ...

But it was a far cry from Trey's acting a little weird to his turning to the Dark Side. And even a critical switch of allegiances didn't explain how he had suddenly looked so much more *alive*, had spoken so smoothly and with such confidence, his mind clearly running on all cylinders — which it shouldn't have been, since Trey was a fucking zombie, for God's sake. And *powerful*; Sean had never seen Trey so powerful in combat.

So what had happened? Sean hoped, *really* hoped, that the voodoo magic was to blame, that whoever was out there pulling the *araknid's* strings — this young "Bondye" snake — was controlling Trey in some way, twisting him, clouding his perceptions.

The problem was, Trey hadn't behaved like someone being controlled; ironically, his *normal* self would seem more like that. This Trey was sharp, not clouded, which just made Sean feel worse.

*What if this really is, truly, Trey's choice?*

That thought both brought tears to Sean's eyes and prompted him to clench his hands into fists so tight, his long fingernails dug into his palms ...

... which actually gave him an idea.

Alistaire consumed human blood — he had to, since feeding on animal blood drained his vitality over time — but he had a fierce code against taking it straight from a person. Alistaire would rather go thirsty, would rather feed on his own fluids, than sup from a human being.

But then, Alistaire wasn't in any position to argue, was he?

Would feeding blood to Alistaire help him? He had no idea, but at least it gave him *some*thing to try.

*Like how Trey cared for me when the* araknid's *venom had me down — just ... one day ago? Two? What the hell happened to* that *Trey, to* our *Trey?*

Moving around to kneel next to his supine friend, Sean nudged the vampire's chin downward. A quick inspection revealed Alistaire's teeth to be in their standard "human" mode, leaving his fangs barely sharper than most people's; Sean wouldn't be able to just prick his skin on those. And besides, though he was about to break Alistaire's no-sucking rule, he wasn't crazy about the possibility of the German vampire's latching onto him out of pure instinct; he could probably free himself, sure, but not without doing some damage to either or both of them.

Willing his right hand further toward wolfman form, which pushed his fingernails even closer to claws, Sean dragged his index finger along the underside of his left forearm until he had a fairly deep cut about an inch long.

Holding his arm in position, the blood dripped into Alistaire's mouth. He couldn't be sure, but he thought the vampire's tongue might have moved around a bit, reacting to the vital fluid. At least Sean didn't have to worry about his drowning if he failed to swallow; he was already dead.

The blood's trickle slowed as Sean's body gradually

healed itself. If he saw any indication that it *was* helping his friend, he could always cut himself again. Only time would tell, he supposed.

So he stayed where he was, watching for signs of improvement ... or of anything worse. Alistaire didn't appear to be changing, but neither had Summer Levin, at first.

Time passed, and before he knew it, the murk of the locker room began to brighten.

*That's it for now, then,* he thought. *Dawn. Alistaire won't be waking up, not until sunset. Not unless the venom starts changing—*

Alistaire opened his eyes.

# 24

A low rumbling noise prompted Trey to look up from Morse's laptop. Was that the front gate opening? He wasn't sure, but when it was followed by the sound of a large truck approaching, he stood up in anticipation.

The doorbell wasn't a traditional chime; he got the feeling that Francis had chosen some popular movie theme, but he didn't recognize it offhand. A few seconds after the tune finished its announcement, he heard a voice in his head (and for once, it wasn't one of his own nagging at him):

*Repons. Ak rekipere.*

Trey grunted. He could figure out what the message probably was: "Open the door." But it annoyed him that Bondye was already snubbing English again, whatever he might claim about his native language being easier for him to project. It was like he didn't want to bother, didn't want to help Trey out ... like he thought Trey was already an owned man.

*Think that if you want, asshole,* Trey rumbled. *I didn't turn my back on the Triumvirate just to become your fucking peon.*

And yet ... he closed the laptop and went to answer the door.

Trey opened it (noticing that the regular spiders cleared out, for the most part, and the *araknid* had made themselves completely scarce) to find a delivery driver bent over several boxes on the front porch, scanning them into his standard device even as he thumbed through some actual paperwork. Trey glanced over at the gate, which indeed stood open. He couldn't imagine Bondye (or an *araknid*) messing around with a remote for it, so maybe it was on a timer? Sensor? If the latter, it didn't make for good security.

"Got another one of these for you, Mister Morse," the young man said as he rose back to his feet; he was nearly as tall and well-built as Trey himself. "You know the— Oh, 'scuse me." He blinked several times in surprise, as if Trey's presence was somehow totally unexpected. "I'm sorry, I just assumed ... um, is Francis Morse at home?"

"I'm afraid not," Trey returned with ease. "He had some errands to run, so I'm all alone here today."

"Really? Wow." The driver ("Darius," by his name tag) chuckled. "I was starting to think Mister Morse *never* left the house, you know?"

Trey smiled back at him. "Sure seems that way sometimes." He found it surreal for Darius to *not* be gawking at him, not asking him if he were sick because of his skin, or avoiding looking at his eyes. Trey had checked himself in the mirror since feeding on Randy and Francis, so he knew he wasn't *completely* normal-looking, that medical people might peg his health as being "suspect" ... but if this was his litmus test, it confirmed that he would be able to go out in public again without feeling like a freak.

"Look," Darius was saying, "I kind of need Mister Morse to sign these for me. I mean, the man paid extra to have me stop here at straight-up Noon, so ..." He trailed off with a shrug. "Don't suppose you know when he'll be back?"

Trey shook his head. "It could be a while. Days, maybe."

"Shoot, that's not good." He glanced past Trey's shoulder, then leaned a little closer and lowered his voice. "He's not in the hospital, is he? He hasn't been looking too good lately, you know?"

"I do know. To be honest, if he *were* going into the hospital, I'm not sure he would tell me. He just left me in charge of the house, and I didn't ask too many questions."

"I hear that. Thing is ..." He indicated his paperwork. "We normally just get an electronic signature these days, but the stuff Mister Morse's been receiving lately? I have to get all kinds of signatures — real, on paper. When you say he 'left you in charge,' you think that might mean ...?"

Trey nodded. "Yes, I should be able to sign those for you."

But Darius sought further comfort. "Because I don't want to get in trouble later, you know? Mister Morse had to set up a contract with us and everything, so that we would agree to ship Hazardous Materials here to his house." He lowered his voice again. "Between you and me, I think he might've greased a few palms, too. Because he's been getting a *lot* of hazmats lately."

"I can sign for it," Trey assured him. "That's one of my jobs, signing stuff." Then Trey lowered his own voice. "If you want, I'll even sign his name to it. I'll make it so illegible, no one'll notice the difference—"

Darius held up his hand. "No, no, we can't do that, I don't want to do that. I'm okay to fudge the rules a little, but I'm not comfortable with forgery."

Trey nodded, a serious look on his face. "I understand completely. Just trying to help you out of this little mess."

"Just print and sign your name a few times for me. We'll make do with that." He handed over his clipboard.

"Yo, man, what happened to your hand?"

Trey glanced down at the large bandage, which covered the bite he'd received saving Randy from the *araknid*.

*Fat lot of good that did Randy in the long run.*

*Shush.* "This? Just a nasty run-in with garden sheers."

"Ouch."

"Very. Trust me, you don't want the details."

"I'll take your word for it."

Waggling the clipboard, Trey asked, "Where do I sign?"

"Down at the bottom of each, the two yellow forms and the short red one." Darius turned his attention back to his regular device. "What's your name, sir?"

Trey said the first thing that came to mind. "Lucius. Lucius Bachman."

"Nice to meet you, Lucius."

The last time someone called him "Lucius," it had been a sweet, unassuming homeless lady named Missy P ... and Trey had murdered her, *eaten* her.

Trey wasn't at all comfortable with how that made him feel — the guilt he had been experiencing more and more since leaving Alistaire in such a state last night — so he dodged his own self-reflection by asking Darius, "What is this stuff, anyway? You said it was Hazardous Material? Any idea what's in there?"

" 'Fraid I couldn't tell you that, Lucius. Not for sure, anyway. You could ask Mister Morse when he gets back..."

Trey shook his head as he finished signing the forms and handed the clipboard back. " 'Fraid *I* couldn't do that without making the boss mad. He doesn't like too many questions."

Darius nodded as he checked Trey's signatures. "I can

see that. He's polite enough, don't get me wrong. I have to deal with some really rude people sometimes, but Mister Morse is okay. Just not too chatty." He chuckled. "But I guess you know that even better than me, huh?"

"Yup." Trey looked down at the boxes, poking them with the toe of his shoe to play up his misgiving (in reality, he was just curious what Young Bondye was getting here). "I'm not going to need, like, special gloves or anything, am I?"

"God I hope not, because I haven't been using any." Finished up with the details, Darius lowered his device to his side, glanced past Trey into the house once more, then up and around the porch (after a moment, Trey guessed he might've been looking for security cameras). "Okay, just between you and me, got it?"

Trey gave him a conspiratorial smile and a thumbs up.

Darius inclined his head toward the stack of three, plain-wrapped boxes; all three sported different Warning stickers on all sides that Trey could see. "I have no idea what's in those top two, but that bottom one? You see that sticker right there?" He nudged the spot in question with his foot.

"Yeah ..."

"I been seein' that sticker, and ones a lot like it, on most of these packages your boss has been getting for the past few days. Asked a buddy of mine at the warehouse who's into a bunch a crazy stuff. Dude knows something about *every*thing, I swear — I keep telling him he should get on *Jeopardy*. Anyway ... that little sticker right there? That's for *hemlock*."

" 'Hemlock'? What's hemlock?" Trey asked, putting a confused look on his face, though it actually rang a bell.

"I didn't know, either, but my buddy did. Hemlock is a poisonous plant. Seriously poisonous, like kill-you-dead poisonous."

"Really?"

"Really. I mean, I guess they can make medicine out of it, too, but still ..." He looked at Trey. "Any idea what your boss might want with this stuff?"

"Not a clue. When it comes to Mister Morse, I usually don't know, and don't ask."

"I hear that." He looked around the porch again, but this time he was mainly eyeing the cracks and corners. "I've been noticing that Mister Morse has a pretty bad spider problem ..."

Trey nodded, making sure he looked concerned. "You're right about that. You should see his backyard."

"Think maybe he wants the hemlock for that? I mean, there's gotta be easier ways to go about it, like just ordering Raid from Amazon, you know?"

"True." He extended his hand. "Thanks for the heads-up. It was nice meeting you, Darius."

Darius shook with him. "You, too, Lucius. You have a nice day, all right?"

"Will do."

Darius saluted, then retreated to his oversized truck. A minute later, he was waving and turning out onto the street. A moment after that, the gate closed without Trey lifting a finger.

He looked down at the three boxes. He could guess, of course, what all of this was for, including the hemlock: Bondye's work, the nonstop "cooking" he was always doing upstairs over that bronze kettle.

Between the voodoo and poison plants, it did not give Trey a warm-and-fuzzy feeling.

As if in response to this, words echoed through his mind.

*Rekipere, Trey Matthews.* Then, in English, he added,

*Bring them to me.*

Trey's lip curled into a disgusted smirk. *Guess he isn't above using English after all, when he really wants something.*

Thinking less than happy thoughts, Trey collected the boxes, *all* of which were probably dangerous, and took them into the house.

# TWENTY-FIVE

Father Crow was the only living soul moving about in Saint Christopher's as dusk approached. For most churches in any major metropolitan area, Episcopal or otherwise, this would be unheard of; even between services, someone was always about, either Good Samaritans working on a volunteer basis, staff members cleaning up the nave, junior clergymen rehearsing their next sermon under their breath at the pulpit, or members of the congregation or visitors stopping by for a quick prayer.

But no longer. Saint Christopher's was in its death throes as a church for the people of Los Angeles. Over the past two decades, its congregation had either moved on to the larger, more popular Episcopal churches — Saint James, Saint Paul, Saint John's, the list went on — or had shuffled off their mortal coil and returned to the Lord in Heaven. First, the clergy were whittled down until Father Crow had become the only permanent minister in residence ... then his support staff had been reduced to a single volunteer ... and finally, the announcement came from the diocese that Saint Christopher's would be shutting its doors for good at the end of the year. Anyone in Los Angeles seeking "Saint Christopher's" would find only the hospice off Hollywood Boulevard.

And so, Father Crow found himself the only member

of God's flock in residence this evening, sweeping up around the front pews and preparing to lock the doors for the night. He was getting a little old to be bending and twisting his back around to reach all the nooks and crannies, but he just couldn't bring himself to wave it off; that would be disrespectful.

But he would be finished soon, and he would shut off the lights, close the doors, and make his way home on foot — a rarity in a town where everyone was supposed to have a car — where he would spend another quiet night, alone with only his thoughts and prayers.

*I will not be bitter,* he ordered himself, not for the first time. *I served the Lord here for thirty-seven years, and I will be grateful for my time tending His flock.*

His eyes wandered to the western-facing, stained-glass window behind the pulpit. He would remain until the sunlight was no longer visible, he promised himself; arthritis be damned, he would do his job.

A very familiar squeak sounded from the vestibule. Father Crow sighed under his breath — he knew that sound well; it came from the lowest hinge of the church's front door. It meant that he might have to stick around a little bit longer, which did not please his back ... but it also meant that he might get to do his *real* job, which was to offer spiritual guidance to His flock, and that brought a smile to his face.

For the moment, he continued his sweeping. It was possible the visitor might simply light a prayer candle, or dip their fingers into the stoup of holy water — a sort of "self-help" comfort for many. In either case, he would shortly hear the squeaky hinge again as the visitor left. In the meantime, he kept an ear tuned for the sound of approaching footsteps ...

A minute passed, then two, and Father Crow realized

that he had heard neither. It was entirely possible, of course, that His reticent guest was simply in prayer, but why would he or she be praying out in the vestibule? Even if seeking privacy, most would have slipped into the backmost pew, except that he would have heard them enter the nave. Perhaps he should step out and check, just to—

Father Crow jerked in a very unprofessional manner when he turned to find that the backmost pew was, indeed, occupied after all. How had he not heard the gentleman come in here? He knew well how footsteps echoed off the tiles to the high ceiling when the nave was empty. Unless this individual was barefoot? From what little he could see of His caller, the man was dressed a little too well to suggest his being shoeless. Still ...

Slipping on a slight, paternal smile, Father Crow gathered his broom and dustpan and worked his way out of the front pew and toward the back.

The gentleman was sitting rather than kneeling, but his head was bowed and his clasped hands were resting upon the back of the pew in front of him. As Father Crow drew nearer, he reevaluated the man's attire — he was well-dressed, ostensibly, but his nice clothing had seen better days; it was sprinkled with grey dust, and sported small tears in a few places. Perhaps the man was barefoot after all?

The gentleman looked up, and Father Crow noted an intense quality about his eyes; a rich blue, they carried an impressive weight and depth. But they were also glistening, as though with an unhealthy heat, suggesting either a fever or pain, or both. He also noted the man's pale skin, which was looking a little discolored, almost mottled around the hairline and along the sides of his throat.

"Good evening, my son," he offered in a welcoming tone.

The man nodded. *"Good evening. Father ...?"* The man's voice carried an interesting, subtle element as well, but it was also a touch raspy.

"Crow, my son, Father Crow. And you are ...?"

*"Alistaire."*

" 'Alistaire'," Father Crow repeated as he sat in the pew before the younger man. He set the broom and pan down next to him, then turned sideways so he could continue to maintain eye contact with the fellow. "That's a solid, traditional name that I have not heard in a while. Scottish?"

*"German,"* Alistaire corrected with a slight grin, *"though a good friend of mine has tried to convince me of its Scottish origins on more than one occasion."*

"Ah. Well, if memory serves, 'Alistaire' originally came from the Greek 'Alexandros' — meaning 'man's defender,' if I recall correctly — so you may both be right."

Alistaire's eyebrows rose slightly. *"I ... did not know that. About its coming from Greek, I mean."* His gaze shifted away, and then he chuckled. *"No matter how old and experienced we are, it's refreshing to know we can always learn new things."*

"Very true," Father Crow agreed, though he inwardly observed that Alistaire did not appear nearly "old" enough to be making such a statement. Still, he saw no reason not to humor the man.

As Alistaire continued to stare into the middle-distance, he looked the gentleman over again. Upon closer inspection, he spotted little flexes on his fingers against one another, minute twitches in the muscles of his jaw, and his shoulders. He suspected Alistaire was indeed in a great deal of pain; between that, his eyes, his slight sweat, his raspy voice ...

"My son," he asked, deciding to delve into the matter straightaway, "are you ill?"

Alistaire considered the question, with a little more deliberation than seemed strictly necessary, before answering, *"Yes and no. I recently contracted an infection that is ... lingering. And I am afraid that I ... that parts of me ... are not welcome in His house."*

Father Crow balked at that. "We are *all* welcome in His house, my son. Our Almighty Father is open to all sinners, if they are seeking redemption."

This made Alistaire smile. *"It's not that, Father Crow. Not exactly, anyway. Our Faith carries me through, allows me access where others like myself cannot go ... but at a cost."*

"I see," Father Crow said, though he didn't. "I'm pleased to hear of your faith, my son. Episcopalian?"

*"I was raised Catholic, but left notions of strict denomination behind long ago. I simply consider myself a C-Christian."*

Father Crow nodded, even as he noted the hitch in Alistaire's voice. An interesting fellow, this Alistaire; an engaging challenge the Lord had brought to his proverbial doorstep.

"Tell me about this infection of yours, Alistaire. You say it's 'lingering.' Have you sought medical treatment?"

A half-smile sneaked onto Alistaire's lips for a moment, then he answered in a serious tone, *"I have chosen to deal with the matter on Faith."*

"A laudable goal, to be sure, my son. But the Lord has given us access to modern medicine for a reason ..."

*"I'm afraid this particular infection is beyond the means of medical science."*

*Ah,* Father Crow thought, taking in his untidy appearance once more, suggesting a fall from reasonable wealth to something less. *Drug use leading to AIDS, perhaps? Or maybe Hepatitis C?*

"*I must admit,*" Alistaire was saying, "*that I have enjoyed some unexpected* blessings *as a result of this infection.*" Father Crow expected him to comment on spiritual support from his community, but instead he said, "*I had not seen true daylight — not without great discomfort, anyway — in an unspeakably long time. And yet, very early this morning and very late this afternoon, while the sun was low on each horizon ... I was able to step outdoors and gaze upon a blue sky. A* blue *sky ...*" He stared past the minister and shook his head in evident marvel; Father Crow followed his eye line, and he appeared to be looking at the still-glowing stained glass. "*Whatever may come next, that was ... wondrous.*"

Father Crow could not make heads or tails of this particular proclamation — not seeing daylight without "great discomfort"? — so he opted for a touch of humor. "Don't get out much, I take it?"

Alistaire did appear amused by his attempt at levity, but he said nothing in return, merely shrugged, still gazing at the light of the stained glass.

"If I may ask ..." Father Crow asked, trying another tact, "... is it the weight of your infection that brings you to God's house this evening, my son? If your symptoms are overwhelming you, you could still seek medical support — pain management, and the like — without hospitalization over at ..."

But Alistaire was shaking his head, all traces of good humor replaced by sorrow, and a notable touch of anger.

"*No, no. That is not what brought me here this evening, Father Crow. Very sadly, a good deal of my physical hardship shall pass when I am done here, when I leave His house."* He shook his head once more. *"No, I came here tonight, Father, because I am grappling with a terrible betrayal, and thoughts of what I must do, what actions I must take, as a result."*

"I see. If you would prefer to pray in solitude ..." He shifted his weight, preparing to rise.

*"No ... no, if you had asked me when I first set foot inside, I might have answered otherwise. But now I believe I would enjoy your devout counsel."*

"Very well, my son. Tell me about this betrayal. Does it involve infidelity? Money?" In his experience, those were the top two issues that left people addled and torn, and sometimes even homeless, as he thought Alistaire might be.

*"Nothing so pedestrian, I'm afraid. I speak of something more fundamental, a treason of core ideology."* He sighed. *"I initially believed that Trey was under an outside influence. I pray that this might still be the case. But if it isn't ..."*

"Tell me ... what will happen if this person — 'Trey'? — if Trey has indeed betrayed your creed? Are we speaking of something illegal, or unethical?"

*"It goes beyond either label, I'm afraid. It crosses over into the immoral."*

"I see. Perhaps if you were to persuade your friend to come to church ...?"

*"No. Though I have often tried ..."* He shook his head. *"My belief in C-Christ is my fount of strength, but I'm afraid I have not been able to convert either Sean or Trey. Sean has followed our mutual path in his own search for redemption. Trey ..."* He shook his head again. *"Trey always just seemed to be an unshakably good person, a* strong *person. Perhaps we took both apparent qualities for*

*granted.*"

Father Crow nodded in understanding. "That is a failing we are all guilty of at one time or another. Mine was ..." He looked around him, at the church that would soon be gone, then chose not to make this about himself. "But if I may ask again: What will happen if Trey has denounced your ideology of his own free will? If this really is *his* decision, and his alone?"

"*If we find that to be the incontrovertible truth ... then we will be forced to destroy him.*"

Father Crow tensed. "I hope, my son, that you speak metaphorically?"

"*No. I am afraid I speak quite literally.*"

Father Crow swallowed, thinking fast, or trying to. In his decades as a man of the cloth, he had never before faced premeditated violence.

Alistaire was still speaking, more to himself than to Father Crow. "*And it must be tonight. Neither Sean nor I are in top form, but we cannot allow this to continue. The enemy has doubled — at least — his recruited numbers, and they will soon rise in their new forms. We must take the fight to this Bokor, this 'Bondye,' and we must do it now.*"

Father Crow opened his mouth to speak, to denounce this course of action, but there were just enough confusing, and rather melodramatic, terms to give him pause.

"*When I suggested before,*" Alistaire continued, "*that being allowed to see a blue sky was the only favorable quality to this infection, I misspoke. It has left me another advantage: Like Trey before me, I believe I can now track this dark magic to its source ... and do what must be done.*"

"All right, that's *enough*," Father Crow chastised him. "This is the house of God, my son. When you come in here, talking about 'destroying' someone — about *murdering* someone, if I understand you correctly — you disrespect Him. You claim to have faith, yet you forget His commandment, 'Thou shalt not kill'? You forget Christ's instruction to love thy neighbor?"

Alistaire offered no defense, but nor did he appear contrite, so Father Crow could not tell if he was getting through. Probably not, he suspected, but he had to try.

"What has this Trey done to deserve being 'destroyed,' Alistaire? What sin has he committed that you would consider—?"

*"Cannibalism."*

Father Crow gaped at him, his jaw moving as he tried to continue speaking, but only a few half-formed words issued forth. He had thought Alistaire would make accusations of rape or perhaps even murder, but ... cannibalism? Truly? He floundered in a limbo somewhere between shock and incredulity.

*"Trey was very different last night. Over and above his switched allegiance — which, I might add, involves collusion with dark voodoo — Trey's mannerisms, his speech, his physical improvements ... I fear this could only have been accomplished by his partaking of living, human flesh."*

First cannibalism, now 'dark voodoo' of all things? The explanation to all of this was very clear: Alistaire must be mentally unstable. And given that he had already admitted to contemplating acts of violence, Father Crow wished that he were not the only person in attendance here this evening. The church's only working phone was at the back, in what passed for his rectory when he couldn't make it home on any given night. Making a run for it was out of the question, because he knew the much younger Alistaire would catch up with him in no time.

He would have to do what he had always done; he would have to use his words.

"If what you say is true, Alistaire," he began, "if Trey has partaken in acts of cannibalism, if he has joined the practice of black magic ... then I can understand why you might feel that you *may* be forced to, um, to destroy him." He held up a finger. "*But* ... would this not be the most critical time to place your trust in the Lord? When things seem darkest, is it not the most essential time to embrace His holy light, to trust in Him that all things will play out as He intended?"

Again, Alistaire looked at him without speaking, his eyes shining brighter than before, the blue seeming somehow paler by comparison. No wonder that mental patients were often described as having "feverish minds."

"By taking Trey's life," he persisted, "you eliminate any possibility of his seeing the error of his ways, of Trey's turning away from these terrible sins and seeking redemption in the love of our Savior, Jesus Christ."

"*I see,*" Alistaire said with a slight nod. "*And I understand, even agree with, your position ... given your world-view. But what if I told you that doing nothing would lead to the death of innocent people? Remember —* if *what I fear is true — Trey may not be merely consuming human flesh, he may be actually feeding upon living beings.*"

Father Crow pretended to consider this. "Yes, I can see how this raises the stakes. *But* ... I notice your return to saying that '*if* ' it is true, he '*may*' be doing these things."

Alistaire nodded. "*True. We do not know for certain, yet. I am proceeding on an educated theory.*"

"Then might I suggest spending time, a great deal of time, in prayer until the matter is made clear beyond any shadow—"

But Alistaire shook his head. *"While I very much appreciate contemplation through prayer, we simply do not have that luxury. People are already in danger, may be dying even as we speak. We would have already taken action, but in spite of the infection's lending me a temporary* —hopefully *temporary, given the alternative— resistance to sunlight, we decided it would be best to move at night, when both of us will be at our strongest."*

Fearing he foresaw where this was going, Father Crow nevertheless pressed on. "And why, may I ask, would you both be 'strongest' at night?"

"For Sean, the presence of the moon — although the full moon is not until next week, each passing night gives him incrementally more power. For myself, the mere absence of sunlight."

Father Crow sighed under his breath before he could stop himself, but he did manage to avoid pinching the bridge of his nose to forestall a headache. "I see. So ... if I remember my folklore, that would make your friend Sean a werewolf?"

*"That is correct."*

"And you would be a vampire?"

*"Again, correct."*

"I see. And since you mentioned cannibalism, should I presume that Trey is ...?"

*"A zombie."*

"A zombie. Of course."

Father Crow shifted his weight, as though considering all of this new information, when in reality he was preparing to stand. The next time Alistaire shared something "significant," he would rise and pace into the aisle, clasping his hands behind his back. After that, he could find some excuse, any excuse, to head for his rectory and the telephone therein.

"So, tell me, Alistaire ... being a vampire, how is it that you are able to come into His church?"

*"As I mentioned, my C-Christian Faith has granted me the ability to go where other vampires cannot. Physically, I will admit that it is causing a good deal of pain to be in here ... but I chose to* embrace *that particular suffering, as it offers me even more spiritual solace."*

"I see. Suffering as Christ Himself did?"

*"Something like that, yes."*

"I see, I see ..." That was his cue, so Father Crow rose and commenced his reverential/professorial pacing, pursing his lips as though lost in thought.

Alistaire awaited his next question.

Glancing down as though in casual surprise that it had slipped his mind, Father Crow reached back into the pew and collected his broom, disregarding the dust pan. His next question might provoke a response, so he wanted some semblance of a defense, be what it may. If Alistaire remained calm, as he had so far, he would politely excuse himself and head for the rectory; if not ... he was ready, as best he could be.

"Tell me, Alistaire ... if you are, in fact, a vampire — even one who somehow still has enough Christian faith to enter the house of God — why would you risk confessing this to me, an Episcopal clergyman? And your friends being werewolves, zombies ... shouldn't that be kept a secret from a man of the cloth? Why would you tell me any of this?"

Alistaire answered with another slight smile before saying, *"Because you have given me some healthy food for thought, reminding me of messages which I already know, but never tire of hearing ... for which I am grateful. Regardless of whether or not I am able to, ultimately, take your advice, it is greatly appreciated. And so I felt you deserved the truth."*

"I see, I see. Thank you, then, for your honesty—"

But Alistaire cut him off, rising to his feet, though he made no move to step out of the pews. *"That, plus now that night has fallen, it is time for me to take my leave ..."*

Father Crow glanced over his shoulder to find the stained glass had indeed gone dark.

*"... and you will not remember any of this."*

He turned his head back around to face Alistaire ... and gasped.

Alistaire's eyes were no longer blue or pale blue, they were completely white, as though they had rolled back in his head, yet he could *feel* that Alistaire was still looking at him, was still *seeing* him.

*"You will not remember any of this,"* Alistaire repeated, his voice sounding deeper than before, *"but I will leave one bit of advice intact, something that will resonate within you on a subconscious level ..."*

"God in Heaven," Father Crow whispered as he took a single, stumbling step backward, "Christ our Savior, please help me. Please help ..."

In one graceful, sideways motion, Alistaire was standing in the aisle with him. And ...

*Dear Holy God, please save me!*

... his white eyes were *glowing.*

*"Remain a good man of G-God,"* the man, the vampire, said. *"Always embrace H-His light, but always harbor a healthy fear of the darkness. Monsters, Father Crow, are* real, *and sometimes we must take steps, make sacrifices for the greater good of G-God's children, to protect them in H-His name. I value the words you have shared with me tonight ... but I* will *do what I must."*

Father Crow whimpered at that, terrified of what might come next.

Alistaire somehow loomed over him without drawing any closer, and the glow of his eyes intensified.

*"But you will forget that I was here, Father Crow. I detest doing this, but we will both rest easier. You will remember your cleaning, you will remember that someone entered, and then left. You will sit now, and rest, and sleep, and awaken in a few minutes feeling that you merely dozed off ..."*

What should he do? What should he *do?* He had never been so frightened in all his life. Dear God, if vampires were *real* ...?

Alistaire frowned, looking confused. *"You will sit, Father Crow, and rest, and sleep ..."*

Amidst his terror, Father Crow shared some of that confusion. Was he being ordered to sit? Alistaire sounded as though he were making a prediction, not issuing a command. Should he play along? Was that what the man, the *creature*, wanted? Were they acting something out here?

Alistaire shook his head a little, and the white glow of his eyes faded a bit. When he next spoke, he sounded like he was speaking to himself, rather than to Father Crow. *"I don't understand. Perhaps the infection is interfering ..."*

*Dear God, what should I do here? Please help Your humble servant, please give me a sign!*

At long last, Father Crow remembered — or, perhaps, was reminded of — something that might help him out of this terrible situation, but he feared he had already taken too long, that he would move too slowly to make a difference. Reaching up, he fumbled at the chain around his neck.

Alistaire wasn't even looking at him any longer, he was staring toward the pulpit, toward the stained glass window ... and the old-but-true cross that hung beneath it.

*"Yes,"* he whispered, so low Father Crow barely heard him. *"Of course. I stand within the house of G-God, by H-His blessing and compassion ... but I may not use my dark talents here."* He nodded with a deep bow of his head. *"Of course, of course. I humbly apologize, L-Lord, for failing to see ..."*

Father Crow finally finished his clumsy pawing and pulled the chain free of his collar — the chain, and what hung at its length. Dropping the broom, he grasped the silver cross with both hands and wielded it before the vampire.

"Back, monster!" he demanded, but his voice sounded far weaker than he wished. "Get back, by the will of God!"

Alistaire flinched, his face tensing further in undeniable pain, but he did not "get back" as Father Crow had hoped.

"I ... I cast you out!" he tried again, thrusting the cross forward as he spoke. "I cast you out of the house of God!"

Alistaire leaned away, his eyes closed, one defensive hand raising to about chest height, but he still did not give ground.

"I cast you out!" He sounded desperate, and he knew it.

Relaxing, if only slightly, Alistaire lowered his hand and opened his eyes; they were no longer white, but their original deep blue. His face continued to reflect pain, but it seemed that some increased wave — a wave Father Crow had believed brought on by His holy symbol — had passed.

*"Father Crow,"* he said, his tone placating and reasonable, *"how can you cast me out, when G-God H-Himself has allowed me in?"*

Father Crow floundered. He had seen those glowing eyes, he knew this man was not human; had, in fact, proclaimed himself to be a vampire!

Yet ... he *was* standing here, here within the nave of Saint Christopher's, wasn't he? If he were some evil force of any sort, would God allow that?

*"I beg your forgiveness, Father Crow,"* Alistaire said as he lowered himself back into the pew with a very human-looking slump of fatigue. *"I honestly believed that, after speaking so freely, I would be able to erase my presence from your memory, which requires me to ... exert myself to a minimal degree, as you have seen. It did not occur to me that I would not be able to do so while within a church, but it* should *have occurred to me. I do not know what I was thinking. I can only blame the infection and my distress for my misstep."* He met Father Crow's eyes. *"I am truly sorry to have burdened you with this knowledge ... and yet, I do stand by the message I had intended to leave as a 'post-hypnotic' suggestion: Monsters are real, literal rather than metaphorical. Always have a care, especially after nightfall."*

Father Crow did not sit down, nor did he lower the cross. He did, however, allow himself to lean against the side of the nearest pew. "Then everything you said before, about your being a vampire, and your friends being werewolves and zombies, about voodoo magic ... that was all true?"

*"Yes."*

"And the zombie, Trey. He's really feeding on the living, just like ... just like in those horror movies?"

*"Yes."*

"I ... I don't know if I'll ever sleep again."

Alistaire half-smiled at that. *"I sympathize."*

A long, quiet moment passed. Then, "What happens now?"

*"Now ..."* Alistaire sighed as he rose to his feet once

more; his movements were slow and measured, but Father Crow straightened and retreated another step, "... *I must take my leave. I must meet with Sean, I must pay a visit to the local Bach— to a local blood bank, I must do my best to follow the trail of the voodoo magic, and then ... then, as we have discussed, I face the possibility of having to destroy my friend.*"

He closed his eyes for a moment, his lips moving without sound, and Father Crow was amazed to realize that he was praying — and was then stunned when Alistaire whispered an audible *"Amen"* and crossed himself!

"I don't claim to be an expert," he stated when Alistaire's eyes were open once more, "since I never believed you existed until just a minute ago. But ... I've never read or heard anything about a vampire like you."

*"Sadly, to the best of my knowledge, there are no other vampires like me. I wish it were otherwise."* He bowed his head, this time in farewell. *"Goodbye, Father Crow. Thank you for hearing my troubles, and I apologize once more for leaving you with such a burden."*

"I'm a man of God, a man of the cloth. I suppose, if these things are real, it's best that I know. I'd try to warn my fellow clergymen, except I know they'd never believe me."

Alistaire nodded in understanding, but offered, *"They might, but choose carefully."*

Father Crow decided he would have to think about that. "I do stand by what I said before, Alistaire. Give your ... your zombie friend a chance. If he can be Saved, help Save him. If not, if you find he *cannot* be Saved, if innocent people are threatened by his actions ... then do what you have to. I ... I believe you would be doing God's Will either way."

Alistaire nodded very slowly at this. Then he bowed his head in farewell once more as he stepped back out into the aisle. *"Goodnight, Father Crow,"* he said before walking away.

A heartbeat later, Father Crow surprised himself by calling, "Wait!"

Alistaire halted, looking back in question.

"You … you mentioned needing to stop at a blood bank, and before that you said ..." He swallowed. "Were you about to say 'the local Bachman Foundation'?"

Alistaire sighed as he shook his head in frustration. *"Yes. Another slip on my part, I'm afraid. I must need the blood even more than I realized."*

"We've done some work with the Bachman Foundation. They help a member of my congregation who suffers from hemophilia."

Alistaire said nothing to that, merely waited.

Very cautiously, ready to snap it back up in an instant, Father Crow lowered the cross. "If you require blood to do this thing, this thing that will save lives, that would be God's work ..."

Alistaire waited.

Drawing a deep breath, Father Crow suggested, "What about the Eucharist, receiving Holy Communion? Would ... would transubstantiation serve your special needs?"

Another long moment passed … and then Alistaire's eyes widened in sheer wonder, and a beatific smile spread across his pale face. *"I do not know, Father Crow … but I would love, very much, to find out."*

# 26

Trey awoke hungry.

The hunger took about a minute to speak up, to make itself known as he blinked away the cobwebs. Sleeping was already becoming a bittersweet change to him: He loved the *idea* of being able to sleep again, like a living human being ... but after spending so many years going 24/7, running all day and all night without feeling any sort of drag or depletion of what had passed for his mind, the sudden *need* for slumber was not particularly pleasant.

He sat up from the couch, in the room where Morse had kept his massive TV, and rubbed at his face. Night had fallen while he was down, another unnerving twist to this shift in his status quo — time slipping by without his knowledge. He definitely did not like that. How had he done it his whole life before? How had he accepted such a loss as ... normal?

Then his stomach rolled over, and it sank in how hungry he was.

He couldn't believe it. So soon? Yes, he had felt the occasional rumble earlier in the day (it was the same day, right?), but he had assumed (hoped) that was just what passed for "digestion" in a zombie. Preying, *gorging* upon Randy and Francis had been the biggest single repast of his undead existence ... so how, having eaten so much such a short time ago, could the hunger be returning already?

*Maybe this is going to be a bigger problem than I feared ...*

He half-expected the hunger to whisper something snide through his mind, but it remained silent. Perhaps it felt that his growing need to feed again said enough on its behalf.

He didn't know if the new *araknid* would have risen yet. It had taken Summer Levin longer than that, but that was when she had been in the Triumvirate's custody. As far as he knew, mutating here, within Bondye's direct sphere of influence, might accelerate matters.

But he had to do something about his hunger, maybe sooner rather than later. When the *araknid* hunted once more, Bondye would expect Trey to fulfill his end of their little bargain — "chaperoning" in exchange for passage back home, to Gayle and his grandmother. If he were distracted by the hunger, that might prove difficult. Maybe he could slip out of the house, find a neighborhood pet ...?

No, that wouldn't work. He didn't live here, he didn't know the place, the neighbors, the general lay of the land. Even Stupid Trey had known to watch and wait before acting so close to home base.

Okay ... what about his thoughts of feeding on criminals? He already had access to Francis' laptop. Maybe he could do some research on the local jails. He wouldn't have time for his idealized plan of feeding on the worst of the worst, but if he picked a jail, at least he would know he was getting his hands on someone of baser quality, right? What day was it? Was it the weekend? He couldn't remember, but if it happened to be Friday or Saturday, he could get his hands on a drunk driver or something ...

*And how're ye goin' to do that?* Sean's voice piped up in his head. *Just walk up to the constables and say,*

*"Ay! Can I please have one o' yer—"*

"Shut up," he snapped aloud. He was getting really sick of the voices in his head, had thought that one more advantage of getting his mind back would be an end to that noise.

And then, as if on cue: *Vini non mwen, zonbi mwen.*

Anger flushed through Trey. "If you need something," he grumbled, "how about you speak fucking English?"

No reply, of course. What frustrated Trey the most was knowing that he was probably being summoned yet again ... and because he couldn't understand the language, he would have to go upstairs to find out what Bondye wanted ... so, in the end, Bondye got what he wanted either way. It was almost like all he'd done was replace Francis, giving Bondye a suped-up version of his non-spider-ized servant.

*Like ye're already an owned man?*

*Fuck off,* Trey thought, but this time his reply wasn't a snap, it was just ... tired. Tired of always somehow ending up on the short end of the stick.

*No, not always,* said the voice of Alistaire — fucking Alistaire Bachman. *Not always, Trey. Because you should have been a mindless zombie, but you weren't. You should have been a slave to your hunger, but you weren't. Your problems, your "short end of the stick," did not begin until you fed on that werewolf in Alaska ... and then, little by little, you fell into this trap.*

And again showing impeccable timing: *Vini non mwen, zonbi mwen. Mwen pa pral rele ankò.*

Trey clenched his jaw, and his fists. Years ago, he had shrugged off the reigns upon him, to save his sister by destroying the voodoo priest who created him ... and now here he was, answering to another fucking voodoo priest.

How was Gayle going to feel about that?

His hunger rumbled once more ...

He uttered an angst-filled, "Fuck." And then he rose and headed for the stairs.

When he entered the master bedroom, Bondye made no comment on Trey's slow response time. Instead, his eyes gleamed with excitement as he said, "Your *vanpir* friend is coming."

Trey froze, his anger and frustration replaced in an instant by confusion and anxiety. "So ... it worked? You, uh ... I mean, Alistaire changed into one of your—"

"No," Bondye stated, and he didn't sound especially disappointed by it. "No, as I suspected, his great age appears to have left him too grounded in form for my *araknid's* venom." He smiled. "Which is *not* to say that he is beyond my *pouvwa*."

Trey said nothing, striving to keep his face neutral of both his turbulent feelings and his nagging hunger.

"When he arrives, and presuming he has your other 'friend' in tow, you will help my *araknid* to dispatch the *lougarou*, as we discussed — I have no need of him ..."

*Dispatch Sean. Goddamn it, why didn't they stay away like I told them?*

"... but I want you to bring the *vanpir* to me."

Trey blinked. "What?"

"Circumstances have changed, as I had hoped they might. I want this *vanpir*. You will disable him and bring him before me."

"But why—?"

"Am I being, in any way, unclear?"

Trey side-stepped that, saying, "Alistaire is a mist-vampire, not bat- or rat-, so if he decides to, you know, make a tactical retreat, there won't be anything I or your *araknid* can do about it."

"I do not believe your *vanpir* friend is coming to my

center of operations with any 'tactical retreat' in mind. He has witnessed — firsthand, and in more ways than one — what I am capable of, if left unopposed. From what you have told me, do you doubt he will do whatever it takes to eradicate me?"

Trey sighed and shook his head. Bondye was right. Alistaire was not above pulling back when the circumstances demanded it, but once he locked eyes firmly on a target ...

*You know why they're coming, don't you?*

Oh, yeah. He knew. Alistaire and Sean weren't coming for Young Bondye ... well, not *only* for Bondye, anyway.

One way or another, they were coming for *him*.

# TWENTY-SEVEN

Alistaire and Sean observed the house in question from a rooftop a few doors down; it was a nice residence, but then, this was a nice neighborhood, a well-to-do community reasonably cut off from the noise and general hubbub of the surrounding city. They could not detect, visually, anything untoward about the place, but between Sean's nose and both Alistaire's vampire senses and his diluted connection to the voodoo magic, neither had any doubts they had found the correct spot.

Sean, crouching in wolfman form on the apex of the roof, batted away another spider that had crawled onto his right hand-paw. He remained grateful for his thick fur, and made a mental note to stay in at least quarter-wolf form until he could climb into a strong shower, or maybe submerge himself in someone's swimming pool.

Alistaire, who knelt next to him, ignored the occasional spider that crawled on him with typical stoicism.

Taking another sniff of the downwind breeze, Sean huffed. "What do ye think? How many *araknid* can we expect?"

Alistaire shook his head. *"Difficult to say. At least as many as we saw last night, perhaps a few more. With G-God's blessing, the ones that were infected during our last conflict will still be transforming."*

Sean glanced over at him, noting that Alistaire looked better than he had an hour ago, and a far cry better than when he opened his eyes and started moving around that morning — *after* dawn — the memory of which still freaked him out a little. "How're ye feelin', with yer own infection?"

"*Fine, my friend,*" he said truthfully. "*In fact, I am glad we arrived here when we did. The infection is almost defeated past the point of my being able to use it to our advantage.*"

The visit to Saint Christopher's — as physically arduous as such things always were, and as disastrous as this particular visit had almost ended — had been exactly what he needed. No, he still did not know how things might conclude with Trey, but his exchange with Father Crow had strengthened his resolve to reach out to Trey one more time, to give him one final chance to make the right choice and turn his back on this path he trod.

And not only did he believe that his time spent in the House of the Lord had further flushed the blight from his body, but his partaking of the Holy Communion for the first time in *centuries* had fortified his spirit beyond expectation. To have tasted, not blood, but *wine* again ... only his peripheral experiences through Neil Carpenter's mortal body could correlate, and even those paled by comparison. And if he needed proof that it went beyond pure psychology, he had only to consider that his vampire body had *not* rejected the Eucharist, that symbolic wine and wafer.

Alistaire could not question the intensity of the battle to come, but through the body and blood of Christ, he felt ready for anything.

"Aye, then. What's our approach? Snake our way in? Kick down the front door?"

Alistaire pointed. *"Can you see the flickering light peeking its way through that upper window?"*

Sean squinted. "Aye, barely, 'round those heavy curtains. Is that firelight?"

*"I believe it is. And, now that I see it before me, I believe that was something I glimpsed in my dream, the one I experienced just as this all began. A man ... hovering before a fire ..."*

Sean smirked. "So, ye think this Bondye fellow is just relaxin' before the fireplace?"

Alistaire allowed a brief chuckle. *"We should be so lucky. But if our limited history with voodoo is any basis, he uses this fire to prepare, to ponder, to conjure ..."*

"So ... is that our first target?"

*"No, I think not. We should dispose of Bondye's* araknid *first, before bringing the fight to him. I do not wish to have them at our backs when we face that particular confrontation."*

"Aye, then." And then his features darkened, heightened by his wolfen visage. "And if Trey's in there?"

*"Then we shall attempt to reach him once more. But if we fail, we do what we must."*

"Aye, then." A long moment passed as they continued to stare at the house, then Sean repeated, "Soooo ... what's our approach? Snake in, or the front door?"

*"Perhaps not the* front *door, but follow my lead."*

"Lead on."

Alistaire launched forward, flitting across the rooftops in that weightless way that he had, almost as though he were in mist-form yet simultaneously holding a solid shape. Sean followed in his own manner; although he ran on all fours, he had found his wolfman better than his wolf for this sort of thing. He kept to the peaks of each house, distributing his weight as evenly as he could, trying to make as little noise as possible. Even so, he heard several reactions — including one distinct, "What the hell was that?" — from below; it was well after dark, but still too early for most adults to be sleeping.

Alistaire alighted just over the target house's wall, crouching on the side lawn without movement, listening. A few seconds later, Sean joined him, staying almost as quiet as they waited together. No reaction from the house, but all it took was a glance downward at the spiders — dozens of them — already skittering through the grass and onto their feet to know their intrusion had been noticed on some level.

They exchanged a look of agreement. If subtlety was pointless ...

Sean shouldered the side door open, heedless of the noise it made when the door jam split. A cloud of ivory mist swirled around him as he stepped inside, flicking on the lights to brighten the room, because why not?

He found himself in what most people would probably call a "den" or maybe the "telly room." A long couch and a few recliner-type chairs faced an extra-large-screen television, and the walls were decorated with posters of various movies or documentaries Sean had never seen before. A ceiling fan slowly began to rotate in response to the switch being thrown.

The fan also served to draw Sean's attention upward, which was just as well, since two *araknid* hung from high above, staring down at him.

"Hello, boys!" Sean called in a friendly manner. "What's the craic?"

The *araknid* — which were looking even more spider-like than before, their four smaller limbs bigger now, longer and thicker; not to mention the further "spiderizing" of their faces and heads — hissed at him, their thick fangs fairly vibrating with the intensity. As one, they tensed and leaped at him.

While they were still in the air, the mist that had enshrouded Sean surged forward, thickening as Alistaire resumed human form. The vampire caught each of the *araknid* by the back of their necks, and dropped to one knee as he slammed their heads into the floor so hard he cracked both the woodwork and their skulls.

And so the fight commenced ...

\* \* \*

Lori paced the kitchen until she thought she might wear a hole through the linoleum. Randy had been missing for a whole day, the police hadn't been any damn help because, according to them, not *enough* time had passed yet, she had been avoiding telling the kids about it but she got the feeling they knew something was up, and why oh why had she let him take that late call last night?

She drew a deep breath, as she had done any number of times since she woke that morning to realize Randy had never come home, and tried to calm herself ... well, that was bullshit, she wasn't going to get anywhere near "calm" anytime soon, but she at least tried to ratchet herself down a few notches.

She picked up her phone, put it down again, then picked it back up. She was aware that this was just further torture, that she would've heard if a text or call had come in, because she hadn't gotten more than five feet from the damn thing since this had begun. If Randy could respond to her seven voicemails and twenty-two texts, he would have. That was the thing, that's what the police didn't get: Randy was a good man, a *responsible* man, and a loyal and devoted husband, and he wouldn't do this to her. She could practically hear the officer she had spoken to thinking, "Ah, another wayward husband who's going to get an earful when he comes home, *if* he comes home ..."

But that. Wasn't. Randy.

Something was wrong!

She put the phone down, and in doing so caught movement from the corner of her eye. Looking over, she saw that a spider — a big one — was crawling across the top of the stove, its wiry black legs standing out against the white of the appliance.

Funny thing, being the wife of an exterminator: On the one hand, if she were too freaked out by creepy crawlers, she probably never would have gotten together with a man who spent his days dealing with the things, who came home on a too-regular basis suffering from bites and stings and what have you. On the other hand, Randy kept their home so rigidly protected and maintenanced, she actually didn't see common household spiders nearly as often as the average person, didn't have as many opportunities to inure herself against the sight of any pests.

And for a "common household spider," this was a doozy: Big and weird-looking, and it wasn't just sauntering across the stove, it was making a mad dash in her direction.

"Like I fucking need this right now ..." she muttered as she glanced around the kitchen for a magazine or newspaper or whatever might serve as an impromptu swatter.

What she found was another spider crawling toward her phone, and she knew this species: Black Widow, the same type that bit Randy on the neck in his office just a few days ago.

Her heart lurched with just a dash of fear, but her annoyance also flared into anger.

"I don't fucking *need* this right now!" she yelled at it. She snatched up her phone and — knowing she would regret it in about two seconds — slammed it down on top of the Widow. It wasn't a magazine or newspaper, but she heard a satisfying *smack!* as it made the spider go splat ... and probably jarred loose some delicate electronic inside.

As predicted, she immediately felt like an idiot. "Oh, hell ..." She turned the phone over. "Oh, *gross* ..."

She was carrying the yuck-smeared phone over to the paper towels when she remembered the first spider, the weird one, on the stove. She pivoted on her heel, figuring she already had to clean the phone, she might as well use it again, just maybe not as—

She stopped when she saw not one spider on the stove, but three.

"Okay," she murmured, and for the first time since that morning, Randy's absence was not foremost on her mind. "What exactly—?"

And that was when another spider dropped from the ceiling onto her head.

\* \* \*

When Father Crow entered his apartment and closed the door, he just stood there for a long time, the keys dangling from his hand, the lights still off as he stared into the darkness of his little single studio.

*What happened tonight?* he wondered. *What did I do? What did I experience?*

Oh, it wasn't that he had literally forgotten, not like what Alistaire had apparently attempted to bring about. He remembered every moment, in fact, in surprising detail. It was merely a case of his not being able to *believe* it had really happened.

Had he truly performed the Eucharist, given Holy Communion ... to a *vampire*?

There were so many things wrong with that notion, he didn't know where to begin.

He had been tempted to stay at the church, maybe stay all night, but there was also a certain appeal to following his routine, to grabbing onto something that was *normal*. So he had walked home as he always did, and along his way, he had experienced what he could only assume was a classic panic attack. Whether it stemmed from his hypothetical brush with death or his inability to process all the incredible truths he had learned in such a short time, he could not say.

*But were they really "truths"?* he thought as he stood there in the dark. *I am a man of God, but I'm also a thinking man, or so I like to believe. Is it possible I'm suffering some sort of psychotic break? Has stress from losing the church gotten to me?*

Except that, while he had been feeling very melancholy about it, he hadn't been exactly stressed, per se — not like he imagined would be necessary to prompt him to lose his mind.

All right, so he was still sane ... but if so, that would mean that vampires were real. Not only that, but they didn't follow the "rules" as he understood them. For instance, a vampire who could enter a church — without an invitation, to boot. A vampire who shied from the cross, but not overtly. A vampire who could have, should have killed him when he failed to wipe his memory, yet had clearly been willing to leave without doing so.

And, bringing things full circle, a vampire who had received the Eucharist, the emblematic body and blood of *Christ*. And who not only received this, but had seemed quite bolstered by it.

He was going to have to think upon this ... no, *pray* upon this ... a great deal.

Something tickled the back of his neck, and he slapped at the sensation with his free hand. Whatever it was squished under his fingers, a trace of wetness emerging a moment later. Was that a mosquito? In Los Angeles, at this time of year?

Another tickle prompted him to flick his other hand to the side, his keys rattling on their ring. What in ...?

Alistaire's words came to him then: *Always embrace H-His light ... but always harbor a healthy fear of the darkness. Monsters, Father Crow, are* real.

Father Crow suddenly did not care for standing there in the dark. He did not care for it at all.

Reaching out, he flipped the light switch on ...

... and saw that his apartment was swarming with spiders.

\* \* \*

James Eisenberg sat ramrod straight at his desk in the lobby of the medical examiner's office; no book, no crossword puzzles, just strict attention to anything even remotely out of the ordinary. He had arrived early for his graveyard shift, but this was nothing new of late.

He had really been going the extra mile since the girl's body was stolen.

What a nightmare that had been! First, after an uneventful night and just minutes before his shift had ended, all hell had broken loose when one of the two victims from some weird slaughter — or was it an animal attack? — had gone poof. Then, to make matters much worse, when he assured his bosses that no one had come through the lobby that night, they got all red-faced and accused him of lying, even going so far as to ask whether or not he was in on the body-snatching!

But the real kicker, the one that had been really haunting him, was when he saw the video of that night's shift. He could have sworn that he had just sat at his desk all night, reading a book and making easy money ... but there he was on the monitor, standing up and talking to some ugly guy in a T-shirt. The two chatted for less than a minute, then James watched himself let them in without getting their signatures or IDs—

And there it was again, right there, another little tidbit that was bugging the hell out of him. He kept thinking things like, *Why did I let "them" in like that?* or *Why didn't I look at "their" IDs or get "their" signatures?* For God knows what reason, he kept thinking in the *plural*. Why? He didn't even remember talking to Ugly Guy, let alone anyone else. So why did his stupid brain keep going there? Why did he keep wondering about *two* of them? And besides, the camera would have seen if anyone else had been present.

None of which mattered as far as the bosses were concerned — and that even included his lieutenant at his regular position as a policeman. The only reason he hadn't already been fired and blackballed right out of law enforcement was that none of the other employees who bumped into Ugly Guy remembered him, either. According to all the hallway cameras, after the guy had gotten past James, he wandered around for a while, spoke briefly to some other employees here and there, disappeared into one of the storage rooms for several long minutes, then walked out — *empty-handed*, let alone carrying a dead body. And *no one* remembered him.

Lucky for James, this was weird enough for the bosses to accept that something way out of the ordinary was going on, and maybe — *maybe* — James and the others weren't at fault.

So James was toeing the hell out of the line, performing his duties above and beyond the requirements — or, to be honest, the *needs* — of his front desk. It was more than the extra money, which had always been nothing but financial breathing room; it was about what the long-term effects on his law enforcement career would be. The last thing he wanted was—

James glanced at the security monitor, something he had been doing a lot more frequently since his Twilight Zone experience. This time it caught his attention, as there was something wavering along the bottom of it.

He leaned closer as his pulse quickened. Back when he had been shown the Ugly Guy video by his supervisors, James had noticed something no one else had really cared about: An odd distortion off to the side of the visitor, almost like mild waves of heat coming off pavement in the desert. He had no idea what it meant, but since he was grasping at any and all straws to help explain all of this ...

But what he was seeing now wasn't the same. These were brown lines passing through the image so rapidly that the motion blur had made them seem like something else. Probably just a spider crawling along the dome over the camera.

Yup. There it went, a small brown fellow. And there, another one. Guess they were having a little party—

A tiny *plop!* and the faintest trace of pressure pulled his eyes over to his uniform sleeve. He jumped and shook his arm until the spider fell away. Man, two on the camera and one dropping on him? What was up with that?

And then another one dropped onto the desk in front of him.

*What the hell?*

James looked up, and yelped. He had never been one to freak out over spiders, but it didn't take an arachnophobe to freak out over seeing dozens of spiders crawling along the ceiling right above his head.

On instinct, he reached for the silent alarm, then hesitated. Yes, he had been ready to sound the alert at the slightest suggestion of more oddities afoot ... but what did a bizarre spider outbreak have to do with a missing body? Nothing, so he should—

He cried out and jerked his hand away from the alarm button. The huge, evil-looking, red-and-gold spider that had bitten him clung to his finger, and bit him again.

\*     \*     \*

"I'm telling you, Sharla, he's screwing us somehow," Darla groused.

Sharla continued staring at the floor in front of the sofa for a moment, then blinked a few times and looked up at her girlfriend. "What?"

Darla paced back and forth, her footsteps heavy with anger, and each time she reached the picture window overlooking the backyard, she glanced out toward the wine cellar. "I said he's screwing us over," she repeated, and not for the first time. "How long are we going to wait before we go out there and see what the hell that ... that 'exterminator' Randy did to our wine collection?"

Sharla released a tired sigh, also not for the first time. "Darla, can we please not do this again?" She leaned against the arm of the sofa as though she might lay down her head and go to sleep right there. She missed Edward so much. Where could he have run off to?

Darla waved a frustrated hand at her and grumbled as she paced, "Leaves us here, makes a few excuses —

bullshit excuses, in my opinion — doesn't answer his phone, doesn't return our calls. Whole goddamn day goes by without a word, without a *word*, and *you* won't let me call another exterminator."

"Dave said he was very good," Sharla retorted, though her heart really wasn't in it.

"Yeah, *Dave* said. Wonder if he was high or something when Randy serviced his place. Bet Randy didn't break who knows how many expensive bottles of—"

Darla stopped walking and talking so abruptly, it broke through Sharla's haze. "What?" Sharla asked. "What's wrong?"

Darla said nothing, only pointed. Sharla turned, and gasped.

A tarantula was climbing up the outside of the picture window. No, two of them ... wait, make that three.

Sharla's eyes bugged out, and she had trouble breathing. She had to look away.

"Jesus, they're huge," Darla whispered, all thoughts of inspecting the wine cellar fleeing her mind. "But you don't think ...? I mean, they can't really eat *birds*—"

Sharla screamed, Darla whirled, and the tarantula that had been crawling up the back of Darla's pant leg almost lost its grip ... almost. And before Darla could slap it away, it sank its fangs straight through to the soft tissue of her lower thigh.

Sharla wanted to run to her lover, to help get the beast off her, but the sight of the other tarantulas crawling toward them from the dark kitchen paralyzed her.

\*   \*   \*

An obese couple gleefully took up the entire bench at

the bus stop, sitting with their arms out wide to take up what little space wasn't already occupied by their derrieres.

As such, they received minimal sympathy when they both cried out as the spiders crawled out from under the bench and started biting them. One young man in particular, who was leaning against the bus stop sign, giggled as he captured their wiggles and shimmies on his phone. That is, until a spider bit *him*.

\*     \*     \*

A tired mother had just tucked her little girl into bed when the three-year-old started screaming. The mother sighed and clamped down on the urge to cry out, "What now?!"

The urge vanished entirely when she realized the girl's bed was filled with spiders. It was replaced by an equally strong compulsion to scream, and this one she indulged.

\*     \*     \*

A police officer struggled to keep his cool as he handcuffed the suspect, who lay on his belly on the ground. The suspect had run from a convenience store just as the officer was entering, and the owner swore the young man had just robbed the place.

Having run the guy down, he had tackled him. There was a struggle, the officer won, the young man yelled and mouthed off, and the officer reminded himself that the last thing the police department needed was the shooting of yet another unarmed suspect, and the young man was indeed lacking in the obvious weapons department.

Then the suspect's yelling turned to screams of distress.

"Oh, shut up," the officer grumbled as he prepared to hoist the young man to his feet. Where the hell was his partner, anyway? "I'm not hurting you."

"Ow! Ow!" the suspect screamed. "Please! They're biting me! They're *biting* me! Ow! *Ahhh!*"

The police officer turned him over, and cried out in shock when he saw the massive spider hanging from the young man's cheek by its fangs. He knocked the damn thing away — which might not have been the best thing to do, as its fangs tore the suspect's skin — and pulled the young man to his feet.

"Wha—? What the hell?" He looked the young man up and down, batting away the thankfully-smaller spiders as he found them.

All up and down the street, people were beginning to react to spiders gone rampant, and the officer had not the slightest clue what he should do next.

\*   \*   \*

The first fledgling *araknid* that came at Sean was Blayze — who, if anything, looked a little undercooked, a touch less arachnoid than his new brethren.

The problem was, if Blayze was up and at 'em, that meant the young ones were waking up faster, and he and Alistaire could be swarmed at any moment.

The fighting had gone all right, so far. Sean suffered another bite, but it had been shallow and he had ripped out the *araknid's* throat almost immediately. His neck muscles were threatening to cramp again, but he took that pain and used it like adrenaline.

"Hey, Blayze!" he called as the spider-vampire

crawled along the wall toward him. "Tell me, lad: Ye think this Bondye shite will make ye call him 'Yer Eminence'?"

If his words meant anything, if Blayze recognized him at all, Sean saw no particular reaction. Then again, with a face like that ...

Blayze hissed, his enlarged spider-fangs flaring, and leaped at Sean. Sean jumped straight up into the air, and as Blayze passed beneath him, he shifted into full wolf and came back down, forepaws planted at the small of Blayze's back.

If Blayze had been as fully developed as some of these other *araknid*, he might have been able to catch himself on all eight limbs and bear the collision easily. As it stood, with his four new limbs thin and undersized, he ended up pinned to the floor beneath the werewolf. He kicked and flailed about, trying to get free as Sean reverted back to wolfman and dug his clawed hands straight in, just above Blayze's ass, until he grasped the bottom of his spine.

A sharp twist to the right, and the young *araknid's* humanoid legs stopped moving. Yet Blayze kept hissing and reaching back, trying but failing to grab Sean.

Sean turned about and tore into the back of Blayze's neck. Another twist, and the fight went out of him.

*"Sean, down!"*

Sean heeded Alistaire's warning and flattened right on top of Blayze. Webbing shot over him, coming so close that a few strands tugged at his fur. He whipped around, ready to counterattack, but Alistaire already had the thing's bleeding head in his hands while the body thrashed around on the floor. Alistaire dropped the head and shifted back to mist just as another one bit into the space where his belly had been the moment before.

The bottom floor of this nice house was bloody trashed, most of the furniture and bits and pieces of the structure itself in shambles. It was a big place — not like the hotel lobby, but spacious for a private home — yet it still felt cramped when allowing for the giant spiders that kept jumping them from every which way. Was Bondye even here? If so, why had he not put in an appearance, even if by proxy via his magic?

And where was Trey? Hopefully somewhere else, so they could deplete the *araknid* army without having to deal with one of their own.

Just this moment, Sean was under no immediate threat. Not a surprise, given how the *araknid* were drawn to Alistaire like sharks to blood. The German kept shifting from mist to solid and back again, attacking without leaving himself too vulnerable. That was starting to worry Sean — Alistaire was greatly recovered after visiting that church, but how long could he keep this up? Sean didn't know exactly how much of a strain it was for him to change form, but he had seen his vampire friend worn down before, after extended time as an incorporeal cloud.

Sean tensed, watching for an opening to help Alistaire, and was almost taken down himself by another *araknid* that had approached him along the ceiling. Sean half-felt, half-smelled it at the last moment, and twisted around just in time to catch it as it descended upon him. The two hit the floor with such force, they slid along the tile until they bumped into the bottom of the house's fancy, winding staircase. Their skirmish deteriorated into a mad scramble for control, four limbs versus eight, rough spider feet, sharp wolfman claws, fangs snapping and tearing, webbing spurting and getting as much on the *araknid* as it did on the werewolf.

Finally, Sean managed to break off one of its big

fangs; unfortunately, as it spasmed in pain, it gouged a deep cut over his left brow — the bleeding might have blinded him, but his fur managed to divert most of the flow. He drew in his legs and shoved the *araknid* against the railing of the staircase, emitting a *crack!* of bone and wood on impact. Before it could recover, he tore into its gut.

But as it gushed webbing upon its death, Sean's luck ran out. It coated much of his arms, body, legs — he quickly stood and tried to keep his extremities out and away from each other as it congealed, but it was still a viscous mess. To make matters worse, the *araknid* curled in on itself, as he had seen Summer Levin and other dead *araknid* do, and so he ended up stuck to it as much as himself.

"Bloody hell ..." he muttered as he struggled to extricate himself before another spider jumped him.

Too late, he realized it wasn't the spiders he had to worry about.

Trey slammed into him from the stairs above, then punched him in the kidney, leaving him breathless. Sean started to fall over, but this reminder of Trey's betrayal stoked his rage enough to keep him on his padded feet. Still tied up with the dead *araknid*, he lashed out as best he could, claws ready to rend the dead man to pieces—

But the new, faster Trey was too powerful. He blocked Sean's first, second, and third swipes, then backhanded him so hard his head snapped back and bounced off the railing as he slumped to the floor. He was still conscious, but only just.

Trey knelt before him, grabbing him by the thick hair on his head and twisting his face around. "You need to stay down, Sean."

Sean spat blood from his mouth. "Fuck off, Trey."

Trey bent closer still and snarled, "Stay. *Down*."

He tried to snarl back. "An' I said ... fuck—"

Trey's uppercut tagged him squarely on the chin, clacking his teeth together with a sound like a small firecracker.

He was out for a moment, losing himself in the darkness behind his eyes, then roused as Trey dragged him — *araknid* stuck to him and all — into the far corner behind and underneath the staircase. The zombie tossed him into the shadows, the dead spider-vampire landing on top of him, and now the back of his head connected with the baseboard. The regular spiders crawled over him within seconds.

When he passed out this time, the darkness prevailed.

# 28

After dealing with Sean, all Trey had to do to find Alistaire was follow the noise. That, and the trail of dismembered *araknid* — Bondye's little spider army was getting pretty damned diminished, not that Trey gave a shit.

Alistaire had ended up in the house's oversized kitchen, dealing with four *araknid* simultaneously. It was impressive, really. Trey had no idea why the vampire wasn't calling out to Sean for help (not that it would've done him any good), but it was a toss-up as to whether or not he actually needed any assistance. He would punch or slash, shift to mist, then go solid again to punch or slash some more. Trey had never seen Alistaire shift so often in such a short period, but it didn't look like his batteries were going to run dry anytime soon.

Time to end this.

Trey stepped into the kitchen and shouted, "Stop!"

The *araknid's* attack screeched to a halt ... well, almost. The short one at the back made one last attempt at webbing Alistaire before following its order — Trey was going to have to keep an eye on that one.

After a few seconds passed, Alistaire solidified. He scrutinized each of the *araknid* before turning his attention to Trey, his eyes slipping from glowing white back to their normal blue. *"I presume,"* he said, *"that it would be overly optimistic to believe the battle has ended?*"

"You could say that," Trey replied as he strode forward, approaching Alistaire one slow step at a time.

"*Trey,*" Alistaire began, and just from his tone of voice, Trey could predict the histrionic lecture coming; it was both endearing and aggravating as hell. "*It is not too late. You do not have to do this. You owe this Bondye nothing.*"

"Oh, you're wrong there, Alistaire," he replied. "I definitely owe him something."

Alistaire opened his mouth, no doubt to petition Trey's turning away from his evil path ...

... and Trey threw a handful of glitter right in his face.

It wasn't glitter, really; at least, not the kind used for harmless celebrations. But that's what it had looked like when Bondye poured it into his hand, and that's the mental label that stuck. He had almost lost hold of it when he fought Sean by the staircase, but only a tiny bit had slipped through his fingers.

And now the glitter was in Alistaire's eyes, his mouth, all over his face and hair.

While the German sputtered for a moment, blinking and spitting, Trey cocked his head, smiled, and said, "That's a good look for you. Very *Twilight*-esque. You should stick with that."

Alistaire scowled, his eyes flashing back to white again; with the glitter floating through them, it was even more dazzling than usual. But despite the anger evident on his glittery face, his voice was imploring. "*Please, Trey. Please. Don't make me—*"

Trey punched him, a solid right-cross to the cheek.

Alistaire staggered back, but did not go down. His eyes glowed brighter, his scowl deepened, and Trey half-expected him to say something like "So be it" or whatever.

Trey didn't wait for it.

"Take him down," he stated as he casually folded his arms, and the *araknid* surged forward.

Shooting Trey one last, stern glare, Alistaire shifted into mist ... that is, he *tried* to shift into mist. The look on his face was almost comical when he realized what had happened, the limitation that the "glitter" had placed upon him, but then he was all business, all Alistaire, and even with the four-to-one odds, two of the *araknid* were destroyed and one of them had lost a budding limb before reinforcements arrived. Once the odds grew to seven-to-one (though the newcomers were all fledglings, barely changed from their original, vampire forms), the ending was inevitable.

As Trey watched, Alistaire's arms were braced wide, his torso arched back, and he received two more bites to the belly.

It wasn't even all that hard to watch. Trey no longer had any doubts about what he needed to do, and Alistaire's getting bitten again? That was just how it had to be.

"*Trey* ..." Alistaire called, barely loud enough to be heard.

"Bring him," Trey said, and turned to leave the kitchen.

"*Where is Sean ...?*" Alistaire wheezed.

Trey ignored him.

Marching through the house (wow, what a mess), Trey led the *araknid* and their cargo to the staircase and up to the next floor. More heat and smoke poured from the master bedroom's open doorway than ever before; Trey could only guess it was a result of Young Bondye's ramping up his voodoo, but he didn't really care.

Leading the *araknid* inside, he announced, "Alistaire Bachman. As ordered."

Bondye was barely visible past the high flames, but Trey noticed that he was slowly rotating around the huge kettle, his levitation drifting in a counter-clockwise motion.

Bondye had been muttering under his breath, but he didn't seem to mind Trey's interruption. "And the *lougarou*?" he asked, still gazing into his fire.

"Taken care of."

"*Egzanplè*, Trey Matthews. You are an excellent *sèvitè*."

Trey said nothing to that. He heard Alistaire struggling behind him; the venom should have paralyzed him, but clearly hadn't. Still, he didn't believe the vampire posed any danger at this point.

Young Bondye halted his circular drifting on their side of the fire, then rotated in place until he faced them, his bright eyes shining with pleasure as he looked down upon Alistaire. He then lowered his legs, standing under his own power.

*Oh, my, he's actually walking on his own two feet like a lowly, normal person,* Trey grumbled inside, but he kept his face neutral.

"I have awaited an opportunity like this," Bondye said to the vampire, "for a very long time. My *zonbi* tells me that you have battled your own kind for centuries. Perhaps you will take some comfort in knowing that you will continue to serve toward this end."

Trey glanced back. Alistaire, his eyes still white but no longer glowing, stared daggers at Bondye, but said nothing. The tendons of his neck stood out and his fists trembled as he fought against the many *araknid* holding him in place.

"I have never personally encountered a *vanpir* as old as you," Bondye continued. "And even if I had, I would not have been in a position to take advantage of such a meeting ... until now. I have devoted much study to you, *vanpir*, in the days since you stole one of my *araknid*." He pointed at Alistaire and smiled. *"You* will provide me with the key. You will give me the means — over and above my *araknid* — to deal with your kind once and for all time to come. Then we shall see who thrives in our old world."

Bondye made a circular gesture. Trey nodded and retrieved the large thermos; the asshole had gone so far as to make Trey rehearse what happened next ... not that Trey had truly minded, under the circumstances. He removed the thermos lid and dropped it aside.

"By drinking the blood of such an aged vampire," Bondye shared with a grin that bordered on giddy, "already infected with *araknid* venom therein, and laced with potions of my own design ... I shall not only break you under my will, *vanpir*, but I will tap power within myself that none of my people — or yours — have ever before seen."

Alistaire released a strained, cynical chuckle. *"Power, power ... it's always about power with your type, isn't it? Will you 'conquer the world' next? And what then?"*

Bondye also chuckled, though his was far more buoyant. "We shall debate that very matter, when you answer to me. As Trey here does before you." He looked at Trey. *"Fè li."*

Trey nodded again, and from his back pocket drew a crude but nasty-looking knife. If he had approached just about anyone else on the planet while brandishing it, he would have expected an expression of fear, but Alistaire betrayed nothing of the sort.

*"Last chance, Trey,"* Alistaire said as an *araknid* forced him to extend his right arm, his words finally getting sluggish from the venom.

"I'm doing this," Trey told the vampire, his keeper, his partner, his friend, "because I'm tired of this place and want to go home."

With that, Trey dragged the blade across the underside of Alistaire's wrist, then poised the thermos to catch the thin blood that flowed from the gash, adding to the mixture of powders and noxious fluids already contained therein.

"*May G-God have mercy on your soul, Trey Matthews,*" Alistaire said; his face was already contorted with the pain of his *araknid* bites, so it was hard to say whether his sliced wrist added to it or not.

Trey met his white eyes without flinching. "We'll see."

Turning about with ceremony that clearly sickened Alistaire but pleased Bondye, Trey dropped the knife, stepped forward, bowed his head, and held out the blood-filled thermos.

*Whatever it takes,* he reminded himself. *Whatever it takes to make this happen.*

Bondye accepted the thermos with a smug smile and a dismissive-sounding, "*Deplase, zonbi.*"

Trey stepped aside, melting back into the shadows as best he could; not too difficult, with Bondye's kettle fire being the only light source in the room.

Bondye passed one hand over the thermos and sprinkled a last bit of blue powder into the laced vampire blood. The contents flashed and sizzled for a moment, then he held the thermos out to Alistaire in a very "Bottom's up!" gesture and lifted it to his lips, guzzling the contents in one breath. He grimaced at the end, clearly not as fond of the taste of blood as any of those around him.

He then smiled a bloody-toothed grin and tossed the thermos aside. "Now ..." he said as he stepped closer to

Alistaire. "Let us see. How long will this take, do you think, *vanpir*? How long before you feel my will tugging at your mind? Before you feel your power seeping out, and into me?" He mused, as though pondering an interesting philosophical question, "Will you fight me? Will you be able to? Will you even *want* to? I wonder ..."

Alistaire said nothing. Trey wondered if he could even speak at this point, or if the venom had stolen his voice.

Bondye made an amused noise in the back of his throat, then turned his head aside and spat on the floor. "I will say this, *vanpir:* Your blood tastes like shit — though I'm sure my particular seasonings did not help. Shall we begin?"

Wiping his shining brow, he gestured to the *araknid* to force Alistaire down onto his knees. The vampire struggled a bit, but it was a token effort at this point.

Bondye knelt on one knee before him. He spat again, this time in Alistaire's direction. "Come, *vanpir*. Give me your eyes, let them glow bright. Try your will upon me, and then I will try my will upon you. Let us see who is the strongest, the *pwisan*."

Alistaire stared at him, and his eyes did begin to glow, though not nearly as bright as Trey had seen them even just a few minutes ago in the kitchen.

Bondye laughed. It had a thick, rattling quality, and he cleared his throat before saying, "Is that the best you have to offer, *vanpir*? Trey told me you were strong! That vampires 'round the world cowered at the sound of your name, *the* Alistaire Bachman. I ..." He cleared his throat again, another wet-sounding affair. "I would have ..."

Swollen though he was with pride, blinded though he was by his believed triumph, Bondye finally began to realize that something was amiss.

Blinking sweat from his eyes, he attempted to stand, but lost his balance and stumbled back to the floor. First he glared at Alistaire, to decipher if the vampire were trying something new, something with which he was not familiar. After all, this *was* the oldest vampire he had ever met ...

Then he dry-heaved once, twice, and finally vomited on the floor. And when he looked up, he was no longer staring at Alistaire.

He was gaping in disbelief at Trey Matthews.

"What—?" He coughed, hard. "What have you—?"

"You shouldn't have insisted on those pointless, demeaning rehearsals," Trey commented. "Or considered it so beneath you to bother watching me after that first time. I mean, seriously, you let me spend an awful lot of private time with that thermos."

Bondye's eyes widened, then sought the thermos where it lay on the floor near the kettle fire. "What did—?" he coughed again, dark phlegm coming up. When he finally spoke, his words rattled in his throat. "Wh-what did you—?"

"Hemlock, mainly," Trey told him. "I believe there's no antidote for that one. And a few other things, including something called Chlordane."

"No ..." Bondye whispered. Then, stronger, he barked, "No!" Pushing up, he successfully rose to his feet this time. "And just because your Western medicine has no antidote, you believe that means—" He coughed some more, spitting the results aside. "... believe that means that *I* have no antidote, that my *majik* cannot fix this *trayizon*?"

Trey shrugged. "I only wanted to weaken you, throw you off your voodoo game. I plan to kill you myself." He glanced around the dark, smoky, spider-filled bedroom. "Like I told Alistaire, I'm tired of this place and want to go home."

Alistaire may have smiled at that, but Trey kept his eyes on the *mèt Bokor*.

"You will never see your sister again!" Bondye roared, which prompted more coughing.

"Gayle would understand." And with that, he advanced upon Bondye.

Bondye looked to his *araknid*.

"Go ahead," Trey said, "if you think you can risk their letting go of Alistaire. Is he completely paralyzed yet? Maybe, but who knows?"

Bondye made a gesture and muttered a word, even as a cramp tore through his guts. Regular spiders swarmed onto Trey, climbing his legs and dropping onto his head from the ceiling.

Trey snickered at that. "Spiders? Really? You think a zombie gives two shits about spiders?"

Grunting in pain and anger, Bondye dove for Francis' dresser, where he kept the odds and ends of his work. As Trey reached for him, he spun around, opened his shaking hand, and blew the familiar white powder into the zombie's face.

"Back, *zonbi*!" he ordered. "*Obeyi!*"

Trey froze for a few seconds, rocking on his stiffened legs. Then he looked around the room — at the fire, at the *araknid* and the intense Alistaire Bachman ... and finally back to Young Bondye. He shook his head once, then again, harder.

"*Obeyi, modi ou!*" Bondye screamed, which prompted another hacking cough.

Trey shook his head one more time, harder still ... then his eyes came into focus, and he scowled down at the little voodoo shithead.

"You caught me off guard last time, Bondye," he

growled, his voice rougher than usual. "Lowered my inhibitions. Sent my hunger through the roof. Turned me loose on two innocent men. And after that, you dangled my new 'freedom' with little strings attached, didn't you?" He stepped closer, towering over the *mèt Bokor*. "Take me home? Recruit more *araknid*. See my sister again? Kill my friends. Constantly tugging, pulling, trying to keep me down, keep me under your thumb ... and all while hoping I would forget about your white powder, forget *that's* how you bent me to your will in the first place, that it was all a fucking magic trick."

"*Obeyi, modi ou!*" Bondye tried again, but it was weaker — on many levels — and was followed by a shivering, rattling cough. "I gave you ... your *mind* back! You ... *owe* me! You ... will ... *obey*!"

Trey bared his teeth. "The first trick *I* learned as a zombie was to break free from voodoo magic. And you're right, I do owe you, Bondye — I owe you big time. As for my hunger? Oh, yeah, it's back, gnawing at me right now, making me so famished I can barely think ... and who's the only living human being in sight right now?" He bent over the trembling, sweating, shocked, and hollow-eyed Young Bondye. "*You.*"

Bondye licked his blood-flecked lips and whispered, "No ..."

Behind him, Trey heard Alistaire say, "*Trey, don't ...*"

He ignored them both.

Opening his jaws wide, Trey sank his teeth into Young Bondye's throat.

The *araknid* had no idea what to do. They were not mentally equipped for something like this. They had their orders, orders which had not been countermanded ... and yet, the one who gave the orders was under attack ... by the one whose orders they were also supposed to follow? They couldn't cope. One of them swayed back and forth on its hind legs as though it might collapse; another backed into a corner, its huge fangs flaring in rage or terror.

Eventually, one particular *araknid* did take action — the short one that had been slow to follow Trey's order in the kitchen. It hissed, released its grip on Alistaire's left arm, and leaped at Trey ...

"*Trey!*" Alistaire warned.

Trey dropped Bondye, who crumpled to the floor, grabbing at his mutilated throat even as the light faded from his bright blue eyes. Trey backhanded the *araknid* hard enough to kill its forward momentum, and as it stumbled about, its eight limbs thrashing for balance and direction, he grabbed its shoulder with one hand, then put his fist straight through its chest to emerge out its back. Shifting his shoulder grip, he then ripped his trapped arm out sideways, very nearly tearing the *araknid* in two.

As the creature toppled into a nasty pile on the floor, Trey turned back to Bondye.

"*Trey,*" Alistaire tried again, "*that's enough.*" Alistaire struggled against the remaining *araknid*, but in spite of facing one fewer captors, he couldn't break free.

Trey ignored him as before ... well, *maybe* hesitated for a microsecond ... then descended upon Bondye once more, teeth tearing and rending and chewing.

\*   \*   \*

Time passed as Trey fed. He couldn't know how long, lost as he was in his gory repast. All he knew was that, as he consumed the last of Bondye's throat, neck, and shoulders, a low ruckus demanded his attention. Satisfied, for now, he let go of the voodoo priest's remains and stood.

At some point, Sean had recovered and come upstairs, and that was all the advantage Alistaire had needed. As he watched, the two finished off the final *araknid*; Alistaire held it by two of its arms, while Sean, in full wolf form, took its skull in his jaws and twisted until the ugly head came off, adding to the many arachnoid corpses strewn about the bedroom floor.

The room settled, then. Sean shifted back to wolfman form, and the three stood looking at one another, the crackling of the fire the only sound. The regular spiders, previously going berserk and clambering over all three of them, settled and began to retreat; Trey suspected the same would be occurring all over Los Angeles. Sean shook himself like a dog to fling them away faster, something that might have brought a smile to Trey's face under different circumstances.

What now? Trey had no idea. Sean was looking at him with enough of a knowing grin on his wolfish face to suggest that he had figured out what happened (hard to miss his feeding on Bondye's corpse, he supposed). But Alistaire was studying him as though he were under a microscope.

"Trey, lad," Sean said at last, "are there any more of these *araknid* things around?"

"Not that I know of. We'll need to check all the rooms, though, to make sure there aren't any more fledglings waiting to wake up."

Sean nodded. Alistaire continued scrutinizing him; it was starting to make him uncomfortable, and a little pissed off.

Sean picked up on the growing tension. "All right, then, let's check the house and get outta here. We can all talk about, um ... about things when we get back—"

"*Trey,*" Alistaire interrupted, "*was it his influence?*

*Or your own lapse? Which came first?*" Sean shook his head in confusion and started to interject, but Alistaire fairly snapped, "*He knows exactly what I am asking.*"

Trey drew a deep breath, conscious of the gore all over his mouth, his face, once again. "My lapse, mine came first. I kept meaning to talk to you ... to both of you ... about it, but—"

"*When?*"

"Alaska. After I bit into that werewolf when they stormed the cabin, when they tried to drag you out into the sunlight." He swallowed, the aftertaste of Bondye's flesh no longer so enticing. "It wasn't the first time I'd tasted blood in a fight, but ... this time I liked it. Really liked it. And I fed on another wolf, later, when we were all separated throughout the town. I ... I've been sneaking out, feeding on animals ever since."

"What? When?" Sean demanded, bewildered.

Alistaire waved that off. "*What matters is when he first fed upon a human being.*" He pointed at Bondye's remains. "*This was not your first.*" It wasn't a question.

Trey's head sagged. "... no, it wasn't."

"*And did you partake of living, human flesh before or after Bondye attempted to subvert you with his voodoo?*"

He looked at the floor.

"*Before or after, Trey?*"

He sighed. "Before. A homeless woman named Missy P. I mean ... it's possible that Bondye's magic influenced it, but ... it was before he hit me with that voodoo powder." He forced himself to look up. "So ... yeah."

The disappointment in Alistaire's face was matched only by his disapproval.

Sean just looked sad. "Oh, Trey ..." He shook his head, then perked up, just a little. "But yer turnin' against us, swearin' us off ... *that* was Bondye's doin', wasn't it?"

"It was, for the most part."

Sean raised a furry eyebrow, an odd look on his wolfen face. "'For the most part'? Not the reassurance I'd hoped for, lad."

Trey spread his hands in a helpless gesture. "Bondye played me, sure, manipulated me. But ... I have to admit that, all on my own, I was riding high from getting my brain in working order. By that point, I'd, uh ..." He flicked a look toward Alistaire, then shied away from that condemnation and refocused on Sean. "I'd fed twice more, and my mind was clearer than it's been since I died. That ... ironically ... clouded my judgment."

"But ye're back now, with us ... right?"

Trey tilted his head to the side, indicating what was left of Young Bondye.

Sean looked relieved, though he was mindful of Alistaire's silence on the matter. "Okay, then. We can help ye deal with yer hunger, now that we know it's awake, after all this time. So, please, let's all just check out the house and then get the hell—"

"*No more, Trey,*" Alistaire stated, deflating Sean's hope for a quiet exit. "*There must be no more feeding on human flesh.*"

Trey stiffened, panic of returning to Stupid Trey swirling around in his mind.

Alistaire saw it. "*No more, Trey. Never again. Do you believe you can do that?*"

Trey imagined himself saying, "Sure, Alistaire, I can do that" ... and then he imagined how the words would come out in how many days? Weeks? How long before it came out as, "Sure ... Alistaire. I ... can do ... that," each and every word a chore, his mind slow as molasses.

"*Never again, Trey,*" Alistaire repeated, his voice stern. "*Can you do that? Can you promise that?*"

Trey looked at Alistaire, then to Sean, then back to Alistaire. Then he squared his shoulders and stated, "No, I can't. I won't."

Alistaire closed his eyes, but Sean reassured him, "I know it feels that way, lad, like the urge will overwhelm ye. The closer we get to the full moon, and especially if we have to fight the night before, I feel—"

"I won't go back, Sean," Trey said, though he was still looking at Alistaire, waiting to see what would come next. "I *can't* go back to being an idiot! Alistaire drinks human blood. We'll have to think of some alternative for me."

"The raw beef—"

"Dead animal flesh hasn't been enough for months, Sean. And now, after Missy P and ... I don't think even living animals will be enough. Not anymore."

Alistaire's lips were moving, and his forehead creased and his closed eyes tightened in pain. Trey knew he was praying.

"C'mon, work with me, lad," Sean was pleading. "Securin' blood is one thing, but short of lurking around hospitals, waitin' for a failed surgery or whatever—"

"I've had some ideas," Trey tried to explain, still watching Alistaire, waiting. "The Triumvirate has never been above killing, so long as the targets are corrupt, right? So what if we—?"

Eyes still clenched shut, Alistaire said, "*You are proposing an excuse to* continue *feeding on the living?*"

Trey bristled at that. "I am not making an 'excuse,' Alistaire. I am proposing—"

Alistaire's eyes opened, and they were glowing white. "*Proposing a way to continue indulging your hunger, to stay in our fight without abstaining from that very quality that* defines *what we fight. Without turning your back on the darkness within.*"

Trey's jaw flexed. "I won't go back to being an idiot, Alistaire."

Alistaire nodded. "*Then I am sorry, Trey. I will pray for you.*"

Alistaire's face grew demonic, and his fingernails extended into talons.

Trey's hands clenched into fists, and he bared his teeth.

And then Sean was standing between them, a hand held out against each but his face turned to Alistaire. "Alistaire, stop this! Right now!"

Alistaire remained where he was, but if anything, his features contorted further. "*This cannot continue, Sean. Trey is* embracing *what you and I have always chosen to resist. I do not take human victims to slake my thirst; you lock yourself away every full moon. If Trey will not make the same choice, the same sacrifice, then we cannot allow him to continue. We must destroy him.*"

"Alistaire!" Sean blurted, aghast. "What's wrong with ye, man?!"

"He's not wrong, Sean," Trey admitted, after a fashion. "I would rather *be* destroyed than go back to the way I was. So long as you understand that I won't go down without a fight, either."

"*Sean, I will understand if you cannot join me in this task. But I need you to step aside.*"

"No."

"*I said to step aside, Sean!*"

"And I said, *NO!*"

The last word was closer to a bark than actual speech, but it got the point across, and both Alistaire and Trey looked away from one another to regard the werewolf.

"Alistaire Bachman, ye need to stop and think about

what ye're doin'. This is *Trey* we're talkin' 'bout here! How many times has he saved our lives — *both* of our lives? How many more monsters would still be walkin' this world, or especially our home world, if it weren't for him? Now ... has he done Wrong-with-a-capital-W? Aye, he has. And we're gonna have to deal with that, somehow. But this High and Mighty, all or nothing shite ye're trying to pull is not gonna fly — not this time!"

Alistaire opened his mouth to speak, but Sean sailed right over him.

"So Trey's no different from the monsters now, that's what ye're tryin' to say? Uh-huh, uh-huh ... and in yer years fightin' the Good Lord's fight, how many people have ye killed? 'Corrupt' or not, how many human lives have ye ended? For the right reasons or not, *you* – are – a – *killer*. So am I and so is Trey, and all long before this *araknid*-voodoo hell went down."

Alistaire, who had tried to interrupt twice more, closed his mouth.

"And if ye want to bring this 'round to what makes a monster? Well, only *you* have been so strong, so 'pure,' to have never given in to yer demons. Me? I killed one o' my best friends when I first turned. And what about what happened with my sister, Theresa? Ye *know* what happened between us, and what I had to do in the end. All of that ... and ye still forgave me. Remember?"

When it became clear that Sean wanted an actual, stated answer, Alistaire said, *"Yes, I remember."*

"If ye can forgive me, forgive me *all* that, then ye can forgive Trey, goddamn it. That, or ye can kill *me*, too. Right now, right alongside him."

Trey was so touched he could barely grasp it. Earlier, when he had assaulted Sean down by the staircase, Sean had looked ready to rip him to pieces ... and now the

Irishman was literally risking his own life to save him. "Sean, I ..."

Sean spun around, pointing a finger in his face. "But that's no excuse for ye to go *wild*, Trey Matthews. We're gonna discuss these 'ideas' of yers, for dealin' with yer hunger ... but if they don't cut it, then I'll be switchin' sides on this topic. Do I make myself clear?"

Trey nodded.

Sean turned back to the vampire. "So ... what's it gonna be, Alistaire? Can yer great Holy mission allow for imperfection after all? Or do we have to end our Triumvirate here and now?"

Alistaire fumed, "*I would hardly call* cannibalism *a mere 'imperfection,' Sean.*"

"Ye know exactly what I mean, ye stubborn mule. Don't go splittin' hairs."

"*I had been prepared to ... overlook, for the time being ... Trey's actions to this point, allowing for the circumstances surrounding what occurred in Alaska and whatever influence Bondye's voodoo might have had recently. But you heard him, Sean. He refuses to reject his hunger.*"

"Except that he has some 'ideas' for dealin' with the issue that ye refused to hear, let alone consider. Didn't ye?"

Alistaire blinked, something he rarely did, and which suggested that Sean was finally getting through.

"So ... what's it goin' to be? Will ye promise to hear him out *before* ye get on yer high horse and attack our good friend?"

Alistaire stood in silence for a moment. Then he nodded.

Sean's shoulders relaxed, a bit, as he turned to Trey once more. "All right, Trey. The ball's been kicked back to yer side of the field. I say we check the house, take care of whatever we might find, then knock this kettle over and burn the whole place to the ground. *But* ... the choice comes back to *you.* Will ye come home with us with the *understanding* that yer hunger must be dealt with, one way or the other? And will ye accept whatever that might mean? Or ..." He lifted his hands wide, then dropped them to this sides. "... does our Triumvirate end right here after all? Yer choice, lad. What's it gonna be?"

Many feelings shot through Trey, so conflicting he could barely sort them. Did he want to be destroyed? No, of course not. Did he want to break up the Triumvirate? No. Did he want to go back to being Stupid Trey? Hell no!

But what if he *couldn't* get a handle on this? Did he want any more victims on his conscience? Bondye he could live with, but did he want any more like Randy or Francis, or poor Missy P?

No. No, he did not.

"What's it gonna be, lad?" Sean asked again, as he and Alistaire waited for the answer.

And Trey made his decision.

# TWENTY-NINE

"Thinkin' pizza," David said out of nowhere.

"Mmm?" Vance didn't look up from his phone.

"Pizza, dude," David repeated. "I'm gettin' hungry."

"Mmm," was Vance's non-comment.

David rolled his eyes, stretched out his arm, and snapped his fingers. "Yo! Dude!"

Vance finally tore his gaze from the screen. "What?"

"I'm hungry. You want pizza or not?"

Vance shrugged. "Whatever." He went back to his phone, but added, "His Eminence doesn't like us leaving when we're on shift."

"Wouldn't leave, idiot. I'd call Pizza Hut or whatever."

"We're not supposed to call attention to the house, either."

"Duuude," David drawled in very put-upon exasperation. "Been doin' this job for weeks! What've we seen? Black dude sometimes takes a walk in the afternoons, white dude with the sideburns does the shopping, and white dude with the stick up his ass hardly ever shows his face ..."

"You need to expand your vocabulary," Vance muttered under his breath.

"... and that's, like, *it*. Seriously, the most excitement we've seen was a few days ago when Blayze showed up!

And even when he went 'n talked to the two white dudes, all they did was stand around the yard, then he gave 'em a ride and that's it. They get a ride in Blayze's sweet new Beamer, and we get to sit 'n stare at a fucking empty house."

Shrugging him off, Vance leaned over to peek through the blinds, to down and across the street. As usual, there wasn't anything interesting to see — just the same small house, all the windows draped, the car sitting in the driveway; they had driven it more than usual for a few days there, but now it was back to mainly collecting dust.

They fell silent again for about a minute. David squirmed and groused under his breath, watching the laptop with its four security camera views. Vance stuck to his phone — when it was his turn to take over the laptop, he would, but for now it gave him an excuse not to talk to David any more than he had to. He had never really understood the phrase "Silence is golden" until he got stuck on stakeout duty with David.

Sure enough, David finally said, "Fuck it. I'm orderin' pizza."

Vance shrugged. "Whatever. We get caught breaking the rules, it's your ass. I'm not risking my shot at immortality for cheap cheese and pepperoni."

"I'm *hungry*, dude!"

"So freakin' order already. But do it fast, because it'll be dark soon. Once their vampire is up, that'll give them two more eyes to maybe spot us."

"Dude. Seriously. They don't even know we're here." Several seconds went by, and then he added, "Borrow your phone a sec?"

Annoyed, Vance demanded, "What for?"

"To order the pizza!"

Vance stared at him as though he were an idiot. "You have a freakin' laptop *right there*."

"Don't wanna leave the security screen, dude."

"Oh, so *now* you're worried about doing our job right." He enjoyed the dig, reminding David that, when one of their targets had driven off by himself the other night, David had failed to spot which one was driving. Vance — who had been taking a crap at the time — tried to scan back through the footage to see who it was, only to find that David hadn't cleared the previous, uneventful video files from the partition, and so the drive was full and hadn't recorded it. They had reasoned — well, *he* had reasoned; David just kept squalling about its not being his fault — that the vampire never drove, and the zombie obviously couldn't drive, so it had to be the werewolf, right? But then they'd seen Blayze talking to both white dudes the next evening, so ... well, best they hadn't mentioned their blunder to Blayze; His Eminence might not care which of them was to blame.

"Dude! Seriously!"

Vance rolled his eyes, huffed a loud sigh, and threw his phone at David, all in one move. He stood and headed to the other window, not because he wanted to check out their target house from a different angle, but just to put a little more space between them.

David was right about one thing, though: This job was boring as hell. When His Eminence first called for volunteers to spy on these Triumvirate people, Vance had leaped at the opportunity to suck up a little. He figured it had to be worth some points, right? Doing a job that even Blayze, and the others that His Eminence had already turned, couldn't do?

Now he was wondering if maybe they were just getting him out of the way for some reason. Like David said, nothing ever seemed to happen—

A knock on the door made him jump. He looked back at David. "That can't be the pizza already, right?"

David, eyes wide, shook his head, Vance's phone still in his hands. "Dude, I'm still pickin' my toppings."

Vance swallowed, his throat suddenly dry. With the exception of Blayze, they'd never had any visitors. Could it be one of the other teams showing up early? No, that had never happened before, either. Had His Eminence sent another envoy, like Blayze? But they had been told in advance to expect Blayze, and no one had contacted them this time.

Come to think of it, they hadn't been contacted at all in a while; a couple of days, at least, since Blayze left. He hadn't really thought much of it, but now he—

"Gonna answer it, dude?" David asked.

Vance's irritation flared. "Why don't you freakin' answer it?"

David rolled his eyes. "Fine. Whatever." He dropped Vance's phone next to the laptop. "Still usin' that."

*It's my freakin' phone!* Vance wanted to yell, but he bit his tongue.

David left the room, Vance trailing him several steps back. When David reached the front door, he squinted through the peephole.

"Who is it?" Vance whispered.

David suddenly gasped, his shoulders hunching up to his ears. "Shit! Shi—!"

The whole door burst inward, the wood around the lock splintering and shooting off in every direction. The door struck David right in the face, knocking him back into Vance, who struggled not to fall down.

Not that it mattered. One of their targets was already stepping into the house.

"Afternoon, lads. What's the craic?"

Vance turned to run.

He made it one step.

# Sixteen Days Later

Jerry Lowe had been watching the brunette for over an hour. Not the easiest thing to just sit and do, not while managing a squirming puppy on his lap — the cough medicine he had fed the little Shih Tzu helped, but he didn't want the pup *too* groggy; otherwise, it wouldn't serve its purpose, couldn't play its role in the game.

The sun had set, and the little brown-haired girl had shown no indication of going home, or anywhere else. All the other parents had come and gone, and now the girl sat alone upon the rock under the park lights, lazily tossing tiny bits of bread to the ducks in the pond. The library, to which this small park was connected, had closed its doors early to host an A.A. meeting; and besides, the main doors were on the other side of the building.

If Jerry was going to make his move, it should be now. Otherwise she might have to leave, to keep up appearances, and they would both be so disappointed ...

The conditions of his parole were quite strict. He knew good and well that he could get arrested even talking to the girl, let alone what he hoped would come next. But he figured, what the hell? It was worth the risk! Jerking off to pictures online wasn't enough anymore. They had *never* been enough, never been the same as feeling that supple young flesh in his hands ...

*Ease up there, Jerry boy! If you're tent-poling your*

*trousers, any stragglers wandering by might notice. Hell, you might even scare* her *away.*

But he doubted it. Deep down inside, she wanted it. They all wanted it. They were all little cumsluts, and she was probably just as happy as he was that there was no one else around.

Drawing a shaky, excited breath, Jerry scooped the puppy up into one arm and approached the girl.

He meandered at first, as though he were just taking an evening stroll alongside the pond and didn't even know she was there. He could feel her watching him, yearning for him to approach her, to take her somewhere private ... but the ritual had to be followed, the game had to play out.

Finally, carefully, casually, he sat down on the other end of the big rock. When she didn't say anything or even look at him, he pinched the puppy; when it squealed, he gently shushed it and petted it lovingly.

When he checked this time, she was looking, all right. She pretended she was looking at the puppy, but he knew it was his groin she really wanted.

"Hi, there," he said, smiling a friendly smile — the ritual must be followed, the game played out. "Do you like puppies? Would you like to pet him?"

She looked at him, then back down at the puppy. Her hand started to reach out — hesitantly, just in case anyone was watching them; she had to play her part, too.

Jerry was so hard now, it hurt. He hoped he wasn't going to—

All of a sudden, someone else was there, a well-dressed man standing between the rock and the pond. Where the hell had—?

*"Good evening, Mister Lowe,"* the man said, and fuck if he didn't have a weird voice. In fact, it took Jerry a moment to register that the man had said his name! *"I had to wake up early to be here on time — never easy for me,*

*but I did not want to miss you. I wanted to 'see you in action' for myself.*"

Jerry forced himself to smile again. The girl hadn't been scared off yet — she was just staring up at the man, as baffled as he was — and he thought he might be able to salvage this.

"Listen, fella," he said in his best aw-shucks voice, "I think there might be some misunderstanding here. Who'd you say you were looking for?"

"Ye're the one we're lookin' for, Jerry."

Jerry spun around so fast he almost dropped the dog.

Another man was standing right behind him, this one with an Irish accent? Who *were* these people? Not cops, that much he was sure of, but—

"Here," the Irish guy said, "let me take 'im for ye."

He bent down and lifted the Shih Tzu right out of his arms. Jerry wanted to stop him, to at least protest, but his head was spinning and he was trying desperately to catch up with this weird turn of events.

The Irish guy took a couple of steps to the side and offered the puppy to the girl. "Here ye go, sweetheart. What Jerry here was gettin' ready to ask ye was, do ye like dogs?"

The girl, her eyes as big as saucers, nodded.

"Why don't ye take this little fella on home? Do ye think yer parents would let ye keep him?"

The girl reached out with tentative, timid hands and accepted the puppy. "I don't ... I mean, my parents aren't around anymore. I live with my aunt." She started petting the Shih Tzu, an unconscious reflex. "She likes dogs, but our place is kinda small ..."

"Now, wait a minute—" Jerry tried to say.

The Irish guy talked right over him. "Aye, I think I've seen ye around our neighborhood." His smile was so disarming, Jerry was envious of its potential. "Go on and take him with ye. Just promise me that, if yer aunt says no, ye'll find him a good home. Jerry here can't look after him anymore."

"Okay, now, listen here—!"

A hand closed on Jerry's shoulder. He looked up to find that the first guy had approached without his noticing, that he was staring at Jerry with the bluest eyes he had ever seen, that he ... he ...

Sean kept the girl's attention on himself. "Do ye promise to find him a home if ye can't keep him?"

She nodded.

"Run along then, lass. We've got some things to discuss with Jerry here."

The girl stood and walked away; she looked back once, but most of her attention was focused on the new puppy that had, almost literally, dropped into her lap.

Jerry caught some of that, but mostly he was lost in those blue eyes ... or ... or were they *white* now? He wasn't sure. He wasn't sure of anything.

The two men guided Jerry ... somewhere. He had no idea where. He spotted the library at one point, but then his feet were wet. Why were his feet wet? And it got a lot darker. What happened to the park lights? Were they underneath a bridge now? His mind was in such a fog ...

Then he blinked and *another* person had joined them, a hulking black man, standing right in front of him, looking down at him as though the big guy were a cat — a *hungry* cat — and Jerry a mouse. He had the sense that he should be afraid, that he should try to run, but ... but he just couldn't ...

*"Tell me, Mister Lowe,"* he heard the strange voice ask, *"what were your intentions for that young girl?"*

"I ... I just wanted to ..."

*"Speak the truth, Jerry Lowe."*

"I ... I want ... I want to *fuck* her, I want to shove my

cock down her throat until she gags, I want to fuck her ass—"

"*Stop,*" the voice snapped.

Jerry stopped.

"*And you have done these very things before, have you not? To other children?*"

"Yes. Ohhh, yes." Jerry was hard again.

"*And you refuse to see the* sin *of your ways? That you insult the L-Lord our G-God with this behavior?*"

Jerry almost laughed even as his lip curled into a condescending sneer. "What the fuck does that even mean?"

The big man never took his eyes off Jerry as he said, "Well, Alistaire? Are you satisfied with my research?"

And though he could barely see the big man's face in the dark, Jerry could hear something lurking behind his words — even through the fog engulfing his mind, he could not miss that sense of *need*, of a deep craving for something base and forbidden.

The man with the strange voice sighed. Jerry could not understand what followed, but his tone was the opposite of the big man's, steeped not in depraved appetite, but in heartfelt regret.

"*Vergib mir, o G-Gott, die Sünde, die ich gleich begehen werde ...*"

And when the man spoke next, the anguish was gone, replaced by loathing and disgust.

"*I am not happy about* any *of this, Trey ... but yes, I am satisfied. Do what you must.*"

The big man nodded, placed his hands on either side of Jerry's head, then opened his mouth wide.

Jerry wanted to scream, but as the big man's jaws sank deep into his windpipe, he could not.

## ABOUT THE AUTHOR

CHRISTOPHER ANDREWS lives in California with his wife, Yvonne Isaak-Andrews, their wonderful daughter, Arianna, and their Pug, PJ. In addition to his duties as stay-at-home Dad, he is always working on his next novels, and continues to work as an actor and screenwriter.

Excerpts from all of Christopher's novels can be found at www.ChristopherAndrews.com.

RISING STAR VISIONARY PRESS

continues the fine RISING STAR tradition of bringing you only the best and brightest undiscovered authors!

Explore the works of RSVP's featured author
CHRISTOPHER ANDREWS!

PANDORA'S GAME (ISBN #978-0977453528) – $11.95
Games involving hypnosis and the supernatural unleash the unexpected.

DREAM PARLOR (ISBN #978-0977453535) – $12.49
The novelization of the independent science-fiction film in the tradition of *1984* and *Total Recall*.

PARANORMALS (ISBN #978-0977453566) – $13.95
A tale of superhuman wonder in the tradition of the *X-Men* and the *Wild Card* anthologies.

HAMLET: PRINCE OF DENMARK (ISBN #978-0977453559) – $11.95
The novelization of Shakespeare's classic. Excellent for students or any fan of The Bard.

THE DARKNESS WITHIN (ISBN #978-0977453542) – $6.95
A collection of disturbing short-stories. Includes "Connexion," the bridge between the *Triumvirate* novels PANDORA'S GAME and OF WOLF AND MAN.

OF WOLF AND MAN (ISBN #978-0982488201) – $14.95
The **IPPY award-winning** sequel to PANDORA'S GAME.

NIGHT OF THE LIVING DEAD (ISBN #978-0982488218) – $13.95
The novelization of the public domain horror classic.

PARANORMALS: WE ARE NOT ALONE (ISBN #978-0982488256) – $16.95
The exciting second entry in Andrews' *Paranormals* saga.

MACBETH (ISBN #978-0982488270) – $9.95
The novelization of another Shakespearean classic. Excellent for students or any fan of The Bard.

Available everywhere books are sold. Visit the author's website:
www.ChristopherAndrews.com.